Finch's Fortune

Mazo de la Roche

Finch's Fortune

XYZ
Publishing

BIBLIOTHÈQUE ET ARCHIVES NATIONALES DU QUÉBEC AND
LIBRARY AND ARCHIVES CANADA CATALOGUING IN PUBLICATION

De la Roche, Mazo, 1879-1961

Finch's fortune

New ed.

Reprint. Originally published: Toronto : Macmillan, 1931.

ISBN 978-1-894852-27-2

I. Title.

PS8507.E43F56 2007   C813'.52   C2007-941255-6
PS9507.E43F56 2007

Legal Deposit: Third quarter 2007
Library and Archives Canada
Bibliothèque et Archives nationales du Québec

XYZ Publishing acknowledges the financial support our publishing program receives from the Canada Council for the Arts, the Book Publishing Industry Development Program (BPIDP) of the Department of Canadian Heritage, the ministère de la Culture et des Communications du Québec, and the Société de développement des entreprises culturelles.

Layout: Édiscript enr.
Cover design: Zirval Design
Cover painting: Magali Lefrançois, *Finch's Fortune*

 Set in Aldus 12 on 16.
Printed and bound in Canada by Marquis, in August 2007.

XYZ Publishing
1781 Saint-Hubert Street
Montreal, Quebec H2L 3Z1
Tel: 514-525-2170
Fax: 514-525-7537
E-mail: info@xyzedit.qc.ca
Web site: www.xyzedit.qc.ca

Distributed by:
University of Toronto Press Distribution
5201 Dufferin Street
Toronto, ON, M3H 5T8
Tel: 416-667-7791; Toll-free: 800-565-9523
Fax: 416-667-7832; Toll-free: 800-221-9985
E-mail: utpbooks@utpress.utoronto.ca
Web site: utpress.utoronto.ca

For

ELLERY SEDGWICK

WHITEOAKS OF JALNA

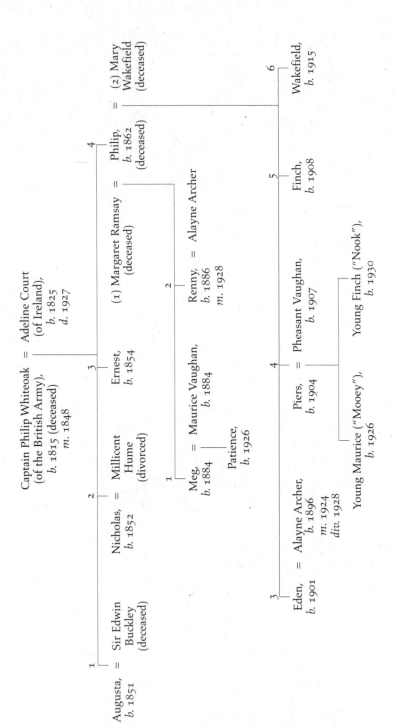

CONTENTS

I

Coming of Age

NICHOLAS AND ERNEST WHITEOAK were having tea together in Ernest's room. He thought he felt one of his colds coming on and he feared to expose himself to the draughts of passage and hall in such weather. He had had tea brought up to him therefore, and had asked Nick to join him. They sat before the open fire with the tea table between them. Ernest's cat, with paws curled under her breast and eyes narrowed against the blaze, lay close to her master's feet, and Nicholas's Yorkshire terrier, flat on his side, twitching in a dream. The brothers divided their attention between their tea and their pets.

"He's a bit off colour," observed Nicholas, his eyes on Nip. "He hasn't begged."

Ernest regarded the little dog critically. "He doesn't get enough exercise. Why, he scarcely leaves your side. He's getting tubby. That's the worst of terriers. They always get tubby. How old is he?"

"Seven. Just in his prime. I can't see that he's tubby." Nicholas spoke testily. "It's the way he's lying. He may have a little wind on his stomach."

"It's lack of exercise," persisted Ernest. "Now look at Sasha. She's fourteen. She's as elegant as ever, but then she goes off by the hour, even since this last snowfall. Only this morning she brought a mouse from the stables. Tossed it up and played with it too." He dropped his hand, and his white fingers rested for a moment on the cat's tawny head.

Nicholas responded without enthusiasm. "Yes. That's the cold-blooded thing about cats. They'd slink off to catch mice or have a disgusting love affair if their master were dying."

"Sasha doesn't have disgusting love affairs," answered his brother with heat.

"What about that last kitten of hers?"

"There was nothing disgusting about that."

"There wasn't! She had it on your eiderdown."

Ernest felt himself getting angry and that was bad for his digestion. The recalling of that morning when Sasha, with a cry of triumph, had deposited her young on his bed (and he in it!) upset his nerves. He forced himself to say coldly—

"I don't see what Sasha's kitten has to do with Nip's getting tubby."

Nicholas had broken his last bit of scone in his tea. Now he carried it in his spoon to his mouth and almost immediately swallowed it. Why did he do that, Ernest wondered. How often their ancient mother had irritated them by this very habit! And now Nicholas was taking it unto himself! He was looking self-conscious, too. His mouth, under his drooping grey moustache, had a half-humorous, half-shame-faced twist. Ernest had frequently observed this tendency in Nick to imitate their mother since her death a year and a half ago, and it never failed to irritate him. It had been one thing to see an old, old woman—over a hundred, in fact, though you never would have thought it—eat sops. Quite another to see a heavily built man, with at least a dozen of his own teeth still in his head, commit the same breach of niceness. If only Nicholas would imitate Mamma's fine qualities, of which there were so many—but no, it was always what he himself had deplored in her lifetime that he reproduced. And there was just enough resemblance—the shaggy brows, the long Court nose—to give Ernest a queer sinking sensation.

He regarded his elder with austerity to hide what was almost pain. "Don't you know," he said, "that that is very bad for you?"

Nicholas rumbled— "Must do it—teeth are getting wobbly."

"Nonsense." Ernest's tone was sharp. "I saw you eat quite tough venison yesterday without any trouble."

"Bolted it."

"Only this morning I heard you crunching a piece of horehound."

"They do better on hard stuff. Something they can get a grip on." He took a drink of tea, staring truculently over the cup into Ernest's eyes. He knew what Ernest was driving at.

They were well past seventy and the shadow of their fierce old mother still dominated them. Snowflakes flattened themselves against the windowpane, clung there. Other snowflakes fell on these and clung. They were shutting the world out, wreathing themselves like a white muffler about the house. A quantity of drifted snow slid from the roof and was deposited on the windowsill, with a soft thud. The shadow of the old mother was shut in the room with them.

A live coal rolled from the fire, across the hearth and on to the rug. Ernest kicked at it, then snatched up the tongs and captured it. The little dog sprang out of the way in terror, then walked with an insulted air to Ernest's bed and leaped stiffly to the counterpane. Sasha, however, with only a side-long glance at the coal, rose and stood with her forepaws against Ernest's chair. She thrust her claws into the velour and withdrew them with a tearing sound. Ernest replaced the tongs and tickled the back of her neck.

"A lot she cares for you," said Nicholas. "She only tolerates you because you're her slave. She'd just as lief I'd scratch her head."

Ernest murmured—"Sasha, Sasha," and felt familiarly for the most sensitive nerves in her neck.

"You'll get fur on your fingers. Have this piece of plum cake?"

"She's not shedding her coat." He rubbed his fingertips together. "Not a hair. No, no, have the plum cake yourself, I'm better without it." But he glanced longingly at the cake.

While Nicholas had inherited some physical resemblance to their mother, something of her rugged resolve and tenacity, Ernest had inherited only her love of food, without the grand digestion that had accompanied it. His digestion was weak, but his eyes lingered on the last piece of cake.

There had been five pieces of cake on the tea tray, two small pieces of Swiss roll, two small currant cakes, and one largish slice of the plum cake. Why just one piece of that, Ernest wondered. It was a strange thing for Wragge to have done. It was almost as if he had hoped to cast a shadow, be it ever so slight, on their tea hour. There was something very mischievous, even sinister, about Wragge… One piece of plum cake for two elderly men… very strange indeed.

"I don't want it," Nicholas answered, wiping his moustache, and returning his cup to the tray. "Bad for gout. You eat it. It's supposed to be very nourishing."

"Rather odd"—Ernest tried to keep the strain out of his voice—"that he should have brought only that one piece."

Nicholas glowered at the plum cake. "Ask him what he meant by it. Anyhow, I don't want it."

"Will you eat half of it?"

"Yes, I'll take half. Perhaps Wragge thought half was enough for each of us. We're not getting much exercise."

"In that case he should have cut it into two pieces. It might easily have been cut into two."

Nicholas chuckled. "You're a funny old bird, Ernie."

Ernest smiled, not ill-pleased, and cut the cake in two portions. He crumbled his bit into morsels, but Nicholas poked the greater part of his into his mouth. Through it he mumbled:

"That cat's going to tear your chair to ribbons. Only listen to her clawing it."

Ernest put an admonishing finger under her chin.

"Naughty, naughty," he said, and her eyes glowed up at him above her three-cornered grin.

"Silly, flibbertigibbet creature," growled Nicholas.

Ernest could scarcely believe his ears. Had Nick really uttered the word or had he dreamed that he heard it from Nick's lips? Were they both dreaming? That word—their mother's, above all words—flibbertigibbet! Was Nick getting *queer*? Or did he delight in hurting him by conjuring up that loved presence (so recently swept away) by feeble imitations of her habits and her words? And not her nicest habits or her prettiest words either... Well, it was in very bad taste, that was the least he could say for it.

Nicholas was looking down his long nose while he scraped the sugar from the bottom of his teacup that had all the pattern of gilt scrolls and red roses inside and was just plain white outside. He tried to look unselfconscious, but he did not quite succeed. There was an odd quirk to his grey moustache. Ernest made up his mind to ignore the word, to go on as though nothing had happened. He knew that was the best thing to do with young children when they had picked up a stray oath, just to pay no heed to the unseemly word and the child would, in all probability, soon forget it. It would punish Nick, too, for he always liked what he did to be noticed, commented upon. Instead of rebuking him, he would treat him as a naughty child. With sudden misgiving he wondered whether Nicholas might truly be getting childish—his second childhood—but he quickly put that idea away from him. One glance into those deep, sardonic eyes was enough to dispel it. No, Nick was sound enough except for his gout. The thing to do was to ignore the word entirely. He said testily:

"I wish you would order Nip off my bed. He's right on my new eiderdown. He may have fleas."

"He'll not have a puppy on it, at any rate."

Ernest raised his voice. "I don't like it. Please speak to him."

Nip's master rumbled—"Catch a spider, Nip!"

The terrier raised his head and peered sceptically through his fringe of hair, but he did not budge.

"No use," said Nicholas.

"Try him with cats."

"Cats!" shouted Nicholas. "*Stable cats!*"

Nip endured Sasha, but stable cats he would not endure. Galvanised into a hairy fury, he hurled himself from the bed to the window seat. He cocked his head, trying to see through the snow mounded against the pane. He saw, or thought he saw, an inky form slink with lowered belly across the white expanse of the yard. He raged against the window glass. Barks failed him. He made strangling sounds. He hurled himself from the window seat and raged against the door. He uttered ear-splitting screams. Nicholas heaved himself out of his chair and limped hurriedly across the room. Nip held his breath while the door was being opened, then, as its edge approached him, he caught it in his teeth and bit it savagely. He gnawed it, trying to worry it off its hinges, punishing it for hindering him. Then, spitting a splinter from his mouth, he flew along the passage and tumbled down the stairs.

The brothers heard the front door bang. Somebody had let him out. They listened attentively, wondering whether it had been someone just passing through the hall or someone coming in from outside. On these long mid-winter afternoons, when it grew dark so early, the comings and goings of the younger members of the family were of intense interest.

They heard strong steps mounting the stairs, then Nicholas, standing in the doorway, regarded with approval the advancing figure. It was the eldest of their five nephews—Renny Whiteoak—and he arrived in an envelope of air so icy that Ernest, with a gesture of self-preservation, put up his hand.

"Do you mind, Renny, not coming too close to me. One of my colds threatening."

"Well, well, that's too bad." He crossed the room, leaving two heel prints of snow on the rug, and stood on the opposite side of the fireplace. He looked down at his uncle with sympathy. "How do you think you got it?"

"I didn't say I'd got it," Ernest spoke irritably. "I said it was threatening."

"Oh! What you need then is a good dose of rum and hot water."

"That's what I tell him," agreed Nicholas, letting himself down into his chair which creaked under him, "but he always fusses more about his digestion than he does about his health."

"My digestion *is* my health," retorted his brother. "But let us talk of something else. It was you who let Nip out, was it?"

"Yes. You should have seen him tear through a snow-drift—after one of the stable cats, screaming like a maniac too."

Nicholas smiled complacently. "Yes. And Ernest was just saying that he's getting tubby."

Ernest asked: "Have you had your tea, Renny?"

He nodded. "In my office. There was a new foal coming and I didn't want to leave."

"I remember. Cora was going to have one. How did she get along?"

"Splendidly. She has never done so well before. She's frightfully proud of herself. When I went to her the last time she tried to tell me all about it. She stopped nuzzling the foal and rolled her eyes at me and went—'ho-ho-ho-ho-ho,' like that." Renny gave a not unsuccessful imitation of a loved mare's greeting to her master after a triumphant delivery.

The uncles gazed up at him, across the thirty-five years that separated them from him, with the tolerant amusement, the puzzled admiration, he always inspired in them. He was so different from what they had been at his age. They had been lovers of fine horseflesh, but not horsey. They had been living in England at that time and had never missed the races; Nicholas had kept a quite "dashing" pair of carriage-horses, had been a bold hand with the reins, had kept a hand-some Dalmatian to run beside the glittering enamel of the carriage wheels, but to have spent a winter's afternoon in a stable for the consolation of a mare in her labour would have been abhorrent to them. They saw him wiry, in rough tweeds, snow melting on his heavy boots, his knuckles looking chapped, as he spread his hands to the fire, his red hair in a defiant crest above his thin highly coloured face. They saw that face, wary, passionate, kindled by the vitality within, as the flames played over it, intensifying and sharpening it.

"Well, well," rumbled Nicholas, "that's good news."

"Are you sure you won't have some tea?" asked Ernest.

"No, thanks. Rags brought a plate of buttered toast and a pot of tea strong enough to raise your hair, to my office."

Ernest thought of the office, in a corner of the stables, its yellow oak desk, where were preserved the pedigrees of horses, overdue bills from the veterinary, newspaper cuttings concerning horse races and shows, and carefully kept accounts of sales. He thought of the bright lithographs of famous horses on the walls, the hard chairs, the bareness, the chill, the unyielding discomfort. He shivered. Yet he knew that Renny had consumed his clammy toast and bitter tea there with the satisfaction with which a plumber might devour his lunch in a flooded kitchen. A queer fellow, but a fine fellow too. Hot-tempered, wilful. "A perfect Court," as his grandmother had used to say, who herself had been a perfect Court. They had been a family who had glorified their faults under blazing banners of tradition.

Renny sat down and lighted a cigarette. Nicholas took out his pipe. The sound of a piano came hesitatingly from below. Renny turned his head, as though to listen, then he said, with a note of embarrassment in his voice:

"He's got a birthday coming. Young Finch, I mean." And he added, looking straight into the fire—"He'll be twenty-one."

Nicholas pressed the tobacco into the bowl of his pipe with his finger. He made little sucking noises, though it was not yet lighted. Ernest said eagerly:

"Yes, yes—by George, I'd forgotten! How the time goes! Of course, he'll be twenty-one. Hmph… yes… It seems only the other day when he was a little boy. Not so very long ago since he was born."

"Born with a caul," mumbled his brother. "Lucky young devil!"

"That's only a preventative against drowning," said Ernest nervously.

"Not a bit of it. It's luck all round. Good Lord, he's had luck, hasn't he?"

Nicholas made no effort to keep the heaviness out of his voice, no pretence of raising his head above the long wave of disappointment that, ever since the reading of his mother's will, had submerged him at intervals. He had no need to be reminded of the date of Finch's coming of age. It stood out as the day of sunny fulfilment for the boy, through the darkness of his own eclipse. "He'll be coming into his money, eh?"

Ernest thought—"It's up to me to be cheerful about this birthday. We must not seem bitter or grudging. But Nick's so selfish. He acts just as though he had been perfectly sure of the money when really Mamma was more likely to leave it to me. Or even Renny. I was quite prepared to hear that it would be Renny's."

He said—"There must certainly be some sort of celebration. A party—or treat of some kind for Finch." He still thought of Finch as a schoolboy.

"I should say," said Nicholas, "that the hundred thousand itself is treat enough."

Renny broke in, ignoring the last remark. "Yes. That's what I've been thinking, Uncle Ernie. We ought to give him a dinner—just the family, and one or two friends of his. You know—" he knotted his reddish brows in the effort to express the subtle convictions of his mind.

"I know," interrupted Nicholas, "that Piers had no party when he came of age."

"He was up North on a canoeing trip at the time."

"Nor Eden!"

"He'd just been suspended for six weeks from 'Varsity. Likely I'd give him a party! There were great doings when Meggie and I were twenty-one."

"Meggie was the only daughter, and you were the eldest son and heir to Jalna."

"Uncle Nick, do you seriously mean that you don't want any notice taken of the boy's birthday?"

"N—no. But—why pretend to rejoice over his coming into what all three of us had hopes of inheriting—more or less?"

"Then, I suppose, if I had got Gran's money, you'd have—"

"No, I shouldn't. I'd have been comparatively satisfied— if either you or Ernest..."

Ernest spoke, with a tremor of excitement in his voice. "Now, I'm quite with Renny in this. I think we should do something really nice for Finch. We were, all of us, pretty hard on him when we heard that he'd got everything."

Renny jerked out—"I wasn't!"

Nicholas muttered—"I don't remember your congratulating him."

"I could scarcely do that with the rest of the family on its hindlegs tearing its hair!"

After the impact of his voice—metallic when raised—there was a space of silence through which came hesitatingly from below the sound of the piano. The three were mentally reconstructing the hour when the family on "hindlegs" had created a memorable scene with the poor piano player as its centre.

Darkness had fallen outside. The invisible activities of the snowstorm were still further transforming the landscape, obliterating, softening; producing hive-shaped mounds where shrubs had been; pinnacles where had been posts; decorating with ingenious grotesqueness every projection of the house. So wasteful was the storm of its energy, its material, that, after changing the aspect of a tree by the delicate depositing of flake upon flake on each minute twig, or clinging cone, it would fling the entire erection into glittering particles with one contemptuous blast, then begin again to express the unhampered fantasy of its pattern.

Wragge, a white-faced, small-nosed Cockney, with a jutting chin and impudent mouth, came in carrying a lighted lamp. The lamplight fell on the shiny sleeves and shoulders of the black coat he always wore after his morning's work was done. "Rags," as he was called by Renny and his brothers, half affectionately, half in derision, had been brought to Canada with Renny after the War, and had married, almost on the day of arrival, another Londoner, a cook of no mean powers but with a taste for spirits and heated controversy. The pair were so firmly established at Jalna as cook and house-parlourman that the disapproval of the uncles and the genuine dislike of Renny's wife had no power to undermine their position. Wragge had been Renny's batman when he had been an officer in the Buffs, and a bond, seldom made manifest except in furtive, almost conspiratory glances between them, existed. Renny liked Mrs. Wragge's cooking, he liked her red aggressive face and stout body presiding in the brick-floored basement kitchen. He liked Wragge. And Wragge had the cocksure attitude of the unscrupulous servant who knows that his situation is secure.

He placed the lamp on the table and drew the curtains. He drew them as though he were scarcely less than the Almighty drawing the curtains of evening against the closing day. His nerves, sensitive to the moods of the family, were conscious of a feeling of dissension. He enjoyed dissension among the members of the family. Even when he felt it, rather than heard it expressed in resonant tones, it was exhilarating to him. Mrs. Wragge could always tell by the jauntiness of his descent into the basement that there were "doings upstairs." She would raise her face from peering into a saucepan and demand—"Well, and wot's up now?"

He lingered, arranging the folds of the curtains, hoping they would let themselves go a little. He noted the sombre look of Nicholas, the worried pucker on Ernest's brow, the half grin that denoted temper in the master of Jalna. But silence prevailed.

"Shall I mend the fire a bit, sir?" he asked, looking at Renny. He spoke in a hushed tone, and the fact that the question he asked of Renny concerned Ernest's own fire was intensely irritating to Ernest. He answered sharply:

"No, don't touch it."

Rags continued to gaze, almost beseechingly, into Renny's face. "It's getting very low, sir."

It was indeed. A chill was creeping across the room.

Renny said—"It wouldn't be a bad idea to put more coals on, but, of course, if you don't want them, Uncle Ernest—"

Ernest answered only by looking down his nose and making the gentle line of his mouth firmer. Wragge turned away and picked up the tea tray. He did not close the door behind him, but made way for two people who were just coming into the room. These were Piers and his little son Maurice, who rode on his shoulder. Mooey, as they called him, shouted, as he reached the fireside group:

"I've got a norse to wide! I've got a nish 'orsie!"

"Good boy," said Nicholas, taking a little dangling foot in his hand.

Ernest remarked: "He does not speak as nicely as Wakefield did at his age. Wakefield always spoke beautifully."

"Because he's always been such a conceited little devil," said Piers, setting his small son on the arm of Nicholas's chair, from where he scrambled on to his great-uncle's big relaxed body, repeating—"I've got a norsie to wide!"

"Now, now," admonished Piers, "less noise." Piers, like Renny, showed the vigour of an outdoor life, but his skin had the fresh fairness of a boy's, and his full lips had a boyish curve, half sweet, half stubborn, that could harden into a line of cruel contempt without changing the expression of his bold blue eyes.

"I wish," said Ernest, "that you would shut the door, Piers. Between the noise of the piano and the noise of the child, and the draught from the stairway and the fire being almost out, I feel my cold getting worse."

Cornering him, Renny observed—"I thought you said the cold was only threatening."

Ernest flushed slightly. "It was only threatening. Now it's here." He took out a large white silk handkerchief and blew his nose with an aggressive toot.

The piano below broke into a tempestuous Hungarian dance.

"I'll shut the door," cried Mooey, and he scrambled down, ran across the room and pushed the door so that it closed with a bang.

Ernest was fond of his nephew, he was fond of his little grand-nephew, but he wished they had not chosen this particular evening for congregating in his room. He thought rather resentfully of the number of afternoons when he sat alone, unless he went down to the drawing-room. When even Nicholas did not come to keep him company. Now, just when he was feeling rather off colour, they were crowding in. If one came others were always sure to follow. Then there was this troubling question of Finch's birthday party. He did not see any sense in it. He, like Nicholas, thought that a fortune of one hundred thousand dollars was treat enough in itself. Considering, of course, the way the lad had come by it. Mamma's leaving it to him had been such a surprise, such a shock, that to make Finch's coming of age a moment for festivity seemed too cruel. Yet, there was another way of looking at it. Might not the excitement of a party help to drown the bitterness of the moment for Finch's elders, as the clamour of a wake smothers the sorrow of the bereaved? Might they not well join their hands and sing—"For he's a jolly good fellow—," even while in their hearts they mourned—"Oh, sorrow, sorrow the day"? He grasped the nettle, as was his wont when driven to it, and, raising his eyes to Piers's face, said calmly:

"We've just been discussing some sort of celebration for Finch's coming of age. What would you suggest?"

Renny, with concentrated gaze, began to poke the fire. Nicholas turned his massive head and regarded his brother sardonically. So that was the way old Ernest was going to save his face! Well, let them see what Piers would say about it. Piers was a tough-fibred fellow, no damned sentiment about him.

Piers stood stock-still, his hands pushed into his pockets, considering the full import of the question. His mind moved slowly round it, as a horse might move round a suspicious object suddenly placed in his paddock. He knew by the way Renny beat the smouldering lump of coal in the grate, by the hunch of Uncle Nicholas's shoulders, by the nervously defiant expression of Ernest, that the discussion had not been one of purely affectionate interest in the event. How could it be? He himself, though he had never said so, had had keen hopes of inheriting Gran's fortune. She had said to him time and again—"You're the only one of the lot who looks like my Philip. You've got his eyes, and his mouth, and his back, and his legs. I'd like to see you get on in the world!" God, that had been something to go on, hadn't it? He had lain awake of nights thinking how much he looked like his grandfather. He had stood below the oil-painting of him, in the uniform of a British captain, that hung in the dining room, trying to look more like him. He had stood under the portrait pursing his lips, denting his brow, at the same time making his eyes more prominent, till his face felt rigid and he half expected the old boy to wink at him as though they had a secret in common. But it had not worked, it had not worked. Finch, with his lanky form, his hollow cheeks, and the limp lock hanging on his forehead, had, somehow or other, wormed his way into Gran's affections, had got the money. How he had got it was a question now dead, and why dally with the corpse? The living fact was Finch's birthday, Finch's fortune dropping like ripe fruit on that birthday, into the midst of the family.

He said, in his voice that had a ring of heartiness which made the labourers of the farm he rented from Renny put up with a good deal of arrogance from him:

"I think it's a very good idea. As for the sort of thing, anything at all will please Finch. Just the idea of goodwill, and all that—"

Renny was glad of this unexpected support from Uncle Ernest and Piers. He would have given the dinner party in any case, but he preferred that the guests should not be unwilling. (Even Nicholas gave a grunt that might be taken for acquiescence.) He thought—"We're closer together than anyone knows, far closer than anyone could know."

Piers swayed a little, hands in pockets, and went on— "We gave Finch rather a nasty time after the will was read. We were pretty rough on him. He went out and tried to drown himself, didn't he?"

"No need to drag that up," said Renny.

Ernest clenched his hand and examined the whiteness of his knuckles. Nicholas pressed Mooey to him. Suddenly flames sprang from the fire, filling the room with warm colour, turning Sasha, curled on the hearthrug, into a glowing golden ball.

"Well, there's just this need," returned Piers, "it reminds us that it's up to us to make him feel that that sort of thing's all done with. Make him feel that he's forgiven—"

Renny interrupted— "There isn't anything to forgive."

"Perhaps not. But you know what I mean. I know that all this year and a half—or whatever the time is—he's felt like a sneak—"

"And wasn't he a sneak?" demanded Nicholas.

"Yes. Probably he was. But he's got the money. And he's as weak as water. If his family don't stand by him, there'll be lots of other people who'll make up to him. Mark my words, he'll go through Gran's money in no time. And do no good to anyone—not even himself."

"A Daniel come to judgment," murmured Nicholas.

Piers smiled imperturbably. "You may be as sarcastic as you like, Uncle Nick, but you know I'm talking sound sense. Finch is bound to be a dud when it comes to handling money."

He broke off rather suddenly, halted by the expressions of the three others who could see the door to which he had his back. The door had been hesitatingly opened and Finch's long face had looked around it.

"Hello, Unca Finch!" cried Mooey. "I'm here!"

"Come in, come in, and shut the door!" said Ernest almost too heartily.

"We were just talking about you," said Piers cheerfully.

Finch stood with his hand on the doorknob, a sheepish grin making his face less attractive than usual. "I—I guess I won't come in then."

"Shall I tell him what we were saying?" Piers asked of Renny.

Renny shook his head. "Time enough for that." He moved along the settee to make room for Finch.

Finch dropped beside him, drew up one bony knee and clasped it in his long shapely hands. "Well," he said, "it's been an awful day, hasn't it? Lucky for me it's Saturday, so I haven't to go into 'Varsity. How is your cold, Uncle Ernest?"

"Getting steadily worse." Again he tooted his nose into his silk handkerchief.

"It has threatened, arrived, and grown steadily worse, all in the space of an hour," said Nicholas, in a soft voice.

"I've got one too," said Finch, and he coughed without restraint.

"You shouldn't have been hanging about the stables this afternoon," said Renny.

"I got fed up with the house. Been in all day. Swotting."

He was devoured by curiosity to know what they had been saying about him. He was sure they often talked of him. He had an uneasy and morbid sense of importance. He wished they would begin again. And yet he shrank, definitely, and quiveringly, from being the centre of discussion. He was like a convert to Catholicism who dreads the confessional yet yearns for it all too frequently.

Renny was conscious of Finch's unease. Through their bodies, in contact on the settee, there passed a communion instinctive as the passage of a bird by night. As though to give the boy confidence, his elder pressed closer against him, then, lest that should seem like a caress, he turned to chaffing.

"You should have seen this fellow's face!" he exclaimed. "He appeared in the door of Cora's stall just as she was dropping her foal. He was absolutely goggle-eyed. You'd have thought he'd been born only yesterday himself, he looked so shocked."

"Look here," cried Finch hotly, "you know, I always keep away from those things. I didn't know what was going on till I got there. I—it's just that I don't care about seeing—"

"Of course, you don't," comforted Renny. "And you sha'n't! We'll not let you be frightened again."

"Oh, hell, I wasn't frightened! It was only so beastly—coming on it all so suddenly."

Piers observed—"You see, he had thought all along that colts were brought into the world like babies. He believed that the vet brought them in his Ford, with their manes all crimped and their tails tied up with ribbon, and a little celluloid bit in their mouths in place of a comforter!"

Finch joined, in spite of himself, in the burst of laughter at his expense.

Mooey sat up and looked from one strongly marked laughing face to another. He declared, solemnly—

"Oh, hell, I'm not f'ightened!"

His father stared at him. "What's that you said?"

"I said—" he put his hands across his eyes and peeped between his fingers.

"Well, don't say it again!

"He should not be sworn before," remarked Ernest.

"Whose boy are you?" asked Nicholas, bouncing him.

"*Yours!*" shouted Mooey, reaching for Sasha's tail.

"Ah, ah, ah," admonished Ernest. "If you hurt the kitty, out you go!"

Renny had been reflecting joyously on Cora's safe delivery, on her marvellous intelligence. He said, raising his voice to drown out the others:

"I wish you could have heard her trying to tell me all about it. It was all over, and I'd been to the office for some tea. I thought I'd look in to see how she was getting on before I came to the house. The vet and Wright were with her. Everything was nice and tidy. She'd got clean straw and she was nuzzling the foal. But the moment she heard my step she lifted her head. She gave me a look. Well—you can talk about the looks in women's eyes, but I've never seen a look like that in the eyes of any woman I've ever known. They simply beamed. And she pricked her ears and whinnied to me—'Ho-ho-ho-ho-ho-ho'—like that!" Softly and with scrupulous understanding he imitated the maternal whinny.

Every eye was on him. A warm receptivity drew them close to him. The hour became beautiful to him. He looked at Uncle Nicholas sucking at his pipe, the deep lines of his face relaxed into tenderness as he cherished the weight of Mooey's soft body, his years numbering only five less than eighty. At Uncle Ernest smiling in the firelight, his fingertips against the pulsing of Sasha's throat. At Piers, with his fresh ruddiness, still standing, for he seemed, like one of his own horses, either to stand or lie down. At Finch, nursing his thin knee, reflecting his own grin of triumph. At Mooey in his blue jersey suit, his white bare legs, his waving brown hair and blue eyes. Here they were collected, six males, in the generous accord of kinship, of common interest. He said to Piers:

"Tell him, if you like."

"Tell him what?"

"About his birthday."

If a bomb had been thrown at Finch he might have been less staggered. To be told about his birthday! That day which was advancing on him like a juggernaut. That day when he would come into possession of that to which he could never feel that he had the right. When he must, under the eyes of his uncles and brothers, take, as it were, the food out of their mouths. Though, in truth, none of them had seen the colour of old Adeline's money for thirty years before she had died. All that time she had been hoarding it and living on Renny—and Renny's father before him.

"My birthday," he stammered. "What about it?"

Piers had been watching Finch's face. He had read his thoughts there as one might observe the shadows of frightened birds. He answered tolerantly:

"Only that we're going to celebrate it. Give you a party of sorts. Isn't that the idea, Renny?"

Renny nodded, and Ernest said—"Yes, we were talking about it before you came in. We thought a nice little dinner—some of your own friends—and Nicholas and I, if you don't think we're too old."

"Champagne," put in Nicholas heavily. "I propose to buy the champagne. And drink some too, though it will play the devil with my gout." Something in Finch's face had touched him. He gave him a smile that was not grudging.

They were not pulling his leg. They were not trying to make a fool of him. They were in dead earnest about the birthday party. His throat contracted so that he could not speak for a moment. Then he got out:

"Why—I say—it's frightfully good of you! I'd like it, of course. But, look here, if it's going to be much trouble or expense—please don't bother! But I'd like it all right!"

But, even as he stammered the words, doubt assailed him. Could he really stand the strain of a party on that birthday? Wouldn't it be better if he were to sneak away so that the brazen glare of its sun might not beat on him as the central object of its rising?

"Look here!" he cried. "I don't think you'd better do it! I really don't think you'd better do it!"

"Why?" Four vigorous voices boomed the question at him.

"Because," he almost whispered, "I—I really think—I'd just like to spend the day quietly."

He was not, at any rate, allowed to spend the next few minutes quietly. Laughter engulfed him, closed over him, submerged him. And when, at last, there was comparative silence again, he heard himself mumbling, with scarlet face:

"Oh, well, if you really *want* to give a birthday party for me, you can do it! I don't give a darn."

II

The Two Wives

WHILE the men of the family were gathered in the lamplight in Ernest's room, the two women of the family and the youngest brother, Wakefield, a boy of thirteen, were sitting in the twilight of the drawing-room below. The windows of this room faced southwest, so that a reluctant daylight still made the occupants visible to each other. Finch had been playing the piano to them before he had been drawn upstairs by the magnet which a group of the Whiteoaks in talk together invariably became to one of their number outside the circle.

"I don't see why he should have gone," remarked Pheasant. "It was so nice having him play to us in the twilight." She had drawn her chair as close as possible to the window to catch the last light on the diminutive jersey she was knitting for Mooey. She felt rather than saw the way with the needles now, her cropped brown head drooping on her slender neck above them.

"It's the same old thing," said Alayne quietly. "They can't keep away from each other. It's that amazing fascination they have for each other." Then, remembering that

Wakefield was curled up in a wing chair in a dim corner of the room, she added, with a constrained lightness in her tone—"I've never known a family so attached."

Wakefield asked, in the clear, probing voice of the precocious child:

"Have you known many families, Alayne? You are an only child, and almost all the friends you ever talk about are only children. I don't see how you can know what other large families are like."

"Don't be so cheeky, Wake," said Pheasant.

"No, but truly," he persisted, raising his face, a small white disc, in the shadow of the chair, "I don't see how Alayne knows really *anything* about large family life."

"I know all that I need to know," returned Alayne, with a little asperity.

"All you need to know for what, Alayne?"

"Why, for understanding this particular family. Its peculiarities and its moods."

He was sitting cross-legged, his hands clasped before him, and he began to rock gently on his buttocks, as boredom gave place to enjoyment. "But I don't think, Alayne, that understanding a family's peculiarities is all you need to understand when you've got to live with them like you've got to live with us, Alayne, do you?"

"Wakefield, you should not say the name of a person you are talking to so often!"

"You mean that I should not say your name because I talk to you so often?"

"No, I mean that you should not say my name so often when you talk to me!"

"Then, why don't you say what you mean, Alayne?"

"*Wakefield!*"

"Now you're saying my name every minute! In fact, you're saying nothing else. Isn't that rather unreasonable?"

Pheasant was making suffocating sounds. Alayne controlled her desire to quarrel with her small brother-in-law. She said:

"Well, perhaps it is. What is it that you think I should understand since I must live with you all?"

Continuing to rock himself, he answered—"It's why we're so fond of each other and why we can't keep away from each other. That's what you ought to understand."

"Perhaps you'll be good enough to explain it to me."

He unclasped his hands and spread the fingers. "I couldn't possibly explain. I feel it, but I can't explain it. Doesn't your woman's *infruition* tell you?"

Alayne forgave him his precocity, his impudence, for that exquisite mistake. She laughed delightedly. But Pheasant, not far from childhood herself, saw nothing amusing in the word. She said:

"I think it's a very good word. It sounds like a very good psychological kind of expression."

"I am wondering," said Alayne, for she was rather tired of the little boy's presence in the room, "why you don't go up to join the others. How can you be happy away from them?"

"I'm not happy," he answered sadly. "I'm just killing time. I'd join the other men like a shot, only that I'm not on speaking terms with any of them."

"But why? What has happened?"

"Oh, just one thing and another. I hate talking about old quarrels and bygone feuds. I feel myself getting friendly towards them even now. I think I will go upstairs." But he lingered, for he loved the society of women. In his own rather aloof way he loved his two sisters-in-law. He respected Alayne, but it was his delight to draw her into a quarrel. He patronised Pheasant, whom he called "my good girl" or even "my good woman." His delicacy kept him indoors in rough weather such as this. So he passed his time threading his way in and out of the various relationships of the family, his sensitive nerves alive to all that went on. He was happy, yet he was lonely. He was reaching the age when he began to be afraid that he was not understood.

The twilight was turning to dusk, and Pheasant rose to light the squat lamp that stood on the centre table.

"Light the candles instead," pleaded Alayne. "Let us have something different for this evening."

"Yes, do!" cried Wakefield. "It may cheer us up."

A shout of laughter came down to them from Uncle Ernest's room.

"Just think of the good time they're having," said Wakefield ruefully.

Alayne had risen too. She went to him and stroked his head. "Are you sure you're not yet friendly enough to join in?" she asked.

"Not yet. Besides, I like the candlelight."

The candlelight, she thought, liked him. It played across the clear pallor of his face and in the brown depths of his eyes as though in a conscious caress. It had a mind to Pheasant too, as she sat down under the branching silver arms, shining with a kind of tremulous serenity on her thin young hands as they moved above the scarlet of the little jersey.

Alayne began to walk restlessly about the room looking intently at objects, the minutest details of which she already knew by heart, picking up a small china figure and holding it in her two hands, as though to absorb something of its cool smoothness. She saw her reflection in the mirror over the mantelpiece and furtively examined it, wondering whether or not her looks had failed her in the past year. Sometimes she thought they had. And, if they had, or were failing her, small wonder, she thought. She had been through enough to fray the velvet edge of any woman's bloom. Her first marriage—that disastrous marriage with Eden. His infidelity. The torture of her thwarted love for Renny. Her separation from Eden. Her return to New York and the exactions of her work there. Her second visit to Jalna to nurse Eden through his illness. His affair with Minny Ware. Their divorce. Her marriage to Renny last spring. All this in four years and a half!

Small wonder if she had changed! Yet—had she changed? That was what she was trying to make out in the glass. But one could never really tell in candlelight. It was so flattering. Wakefield, for instance, who often looked sallow in the daytime, had a white flower-petal skin in this light, and there was the lovely pointed shadow of Pheasant's eyelashes on her cheek.

She drew a step closer to the glass, pretending to be interested in Pheasant's work, but her eyes returned to the scrutiny, almost sombre, of her own reflection. She saw the glint of the candlelight on the brightness of her hair, how it touched her cheekbones and the explicit curves of her mouth. No, she was not going off in her looks, but she had become quite definitely a woman. There was no girlishness in that face, the contours of which had come to her from the Dutch ancestry of her mother. She fancied that the salient expression of her face was one of stolidity. It showed, too, endurance, but not patience. Intellectuality subservient to passion. That capability for passion that might submerge all else seemed to her to have been grafted on to her original personality, her original conception of herself, at any rate, as a new species of tree capable of bearing extravagant flowers and fruit, might have been grafted on one of conventional species.

She had been married to Renny almost ten months, and she understood no better than before she had married him what his conception of life and love truly was. What did he think? Or was he guided only by instinct? What did he really think of her, now that he had got her? He had no taste for self-analysis. To dig into the depths of his desires, his beliefs, and produce the ore of his egoism for her inspection, would have been abhorrent to him. And apparently he had no curiosity about her beyond the most primitive. His absorption in his own life was immense. Did he expect her, she wondered, now that she was harnessed to his side, to gallop through her life without question, sniffing the bright air, grazing in the comfortable pasture, and returning at night to the dark privacy of their mutual passion? He had none of her relentless desire to see things clearly. His conception of their relationship was so simple that it was almost repellent to her finical mind.

She turned hurriedly from the glass, for she saw Wakefield's eyes on her. She began once more to pace up and down the room, her hands clasped behind her back, as she had often seen her father pace in his study. She smiled ironically, wondering if all these stirrings in her mind might possibly be reduced to the old feminine questions—"Does he still love me?" "Does he love me as much as ever?"

She heard him coming down the stairs noisily (as he always did) as though there were not a moment to spare. He seemed to her like the winter wind, sharp, full of cold energy, rushing by her. He must not pass the door of the drawing-room, perhaps go out again, without speaking to her! She went swiftly to the door, but, just as she reached it, he opened it wide. He stood, startled and smiling to find her so close to him.

"I was coming to find you," he said.

She returned, with childish reproach in her voice:

"I have been here all the afternoon. I heard you going upstairs ever so long ago."

"Yes? I heard the piano as I passed, so I supposed Finch was playing to you. You know I can't sit down and listen to music in the middle of the afternoon." He put his arm around her. His eyebrows shot up as he saw the lighted candelabrum. "Well, you are a ghostly looking trio! What's the matter with the lamp?"

Pheasant answered—"We like the candlelight. It's so mysterious."

His eyes rested appraisingly on the slender curve of her neck. "It's becoming, at any rate. I didn't know you'd such a pretty little neck, Pheasant."

"I was just thinking," said Wakefield, "that she looks like Anne Boleyn. What a nice little neck for the headsman!" He uncurled himself and came over to the two, pushing his dark hair from his forehead, smiling up at Renny.

Pheasant dropped her knitting and clasped her neck with her fingers. "Oh, don't, Wake! You make me shiver!"

That was just what he liked. "You may well shiver, my girl," he said. "You're just the sort who would have lost her head in those days!"

Renny drew the boy to his side and kissed him. "How have you been today, youngster?" he asked, with a solicitude that had once been touching to Alayne, but of late had more often irritated. He felt nothing of her irritation, but Wakefield did. He pressed against his brother, putting his arms under his coat, and looked sideways at Alayne, as though to say—"I can get nearer to him than you can." He murmured—"Not very well, thanks, Renny."

Renny sighed. "Too bad." He bent and kissed him again. "Now, I'll tell you something to cheer you. Cora has had a fine little foal this afternoon, and they're both as well as possible." He turned to Alayne. "You know, out of four foals she's lost two, and the others were weakly—but this! Why, it's a regular rip!"

"How splendid," said Alayne, trying to feel excited. Her voice was drowned in the enthusiasm of Pheasant and Wakefield.

Was it a filly? Was it like the dam or the sire? A filly. The very image of Cora. Up on its legs. A very grenadier of a foal. They talked all at once, their eyes shining. Mooey's jersey dropped to the floor.

Renny disengaged himself from Alayne and Wakefield and stood in the middle of the room making quick gestures as he talked, his highly coloured face alight. He repeated to them the story of Cora's sagacity, of her greeting to him after her labour, imitated that whinny so fraught with meaning.

Alayne watched him, scarcely hearing what he said, preoccupied by her love for him, by the fascination his presence had for her. She waited impatiently for him to finish his recital, eager to draw him away upstairs, where she might have him to herself, away from these others who seemed always coming between them. She held a pinch of his tweed coat in her fingers and, when the opportunity came, she drew him towards the door. "Come upstairs," she said, "I have something in my room I want to show you."

"Can't we see it later?" he asked. "Won't it be cold up there for you?"

"That doesn't matter."

"I'll come, too!" Wakefield clasped Renny's arm.

"No," said Alayne sharply. "It's much too cold for you up there."

But he walked doggedly behind them into the hall and followed them up the stairs. Renny hesitated at the door of his room. "Is it in here you want me to go?" He spoke like an obedient but slightly unwilling child.

"No; in my room."

She stood with her hand on the doorknob letting him go past her into the room, but, as Wakefield attempted to pass, she gave him a look so forbidding that he drew back and leaned across the banister pretending to gaze at something in the hall below to hide his chagrin.

She closed the door behind her and looked at Renny with a sudden feeling of wry amusement. She was like a gaoler, she thought.

This room had been his sister's before her marriage. It now bore little evidence of the padded, curtained, frilled comfort that had been Meg's delight. It was almost austere, the cretonne of mauve and cream, the few pictures in a small group together. In the summer, when she had furnished it with furniture that had been her mother's and stood a single porcelain vase on the mantelpiece with a spray of delphinium in it, the effect had been charming. The window had been open and the drawn-back curtains had discovered the warm beauty of the garden. But now, in the chill of winter, with the February snow furring the pane, the room looked aloof and colourless, even to her. To Renny, it struck a chill to the heart. She realised that she should not have brought him here, at this hour, in this temperature.

"Well," he asked, looking restively about, "what is it you want to show me?"

"This." She indicated an embroidered mauve bedspread she had been making and had that afternoon laid in its graceful simplicity on the bed.

He frowned, looking at it. "It looks like a stage bed. The whole room has a stagey effect to me. It's unreal. It's not comfortable. There's nothing inviting about it. Of course, I know it's in frightfully good taste and all that, but—" he gave the grin that was so like his grandmother's—"it's lucky I usually come in here in the dark or I might get depressed!"

Her eyes met his with a commanding look, saying—"Go no farther," but her lower lip quivered, saying—"Go as far as you like."

He sat down on the side of the bed and drew her on to his knee. He hid his face against her neck. She would have relaxed in his arms, but she remembered the new embroidered bedspread and sprang up. She took him by the lapels of his coat and gave him a little tug.

"You must not sit there!" she exclaimed. "You are crushing it dreadfully."

He got to his feet and looked on ruefully while she stroked the heavy silk. He always admired the grace of her wrists when she performed any quick and capable act with her hands. She had good hands on the rein too. That was one of the things that had attracted him to her.

She straightened herself and looked at him with a half-tender, half-reproving wrinkling of the nose. "Darling, I'm sorry! But I really *can't* let you sit there... And, don't you think you had better change your things? You smell… quite, quite a little of the stable."

He gave a noisy sniff at himself. "Do I? But I always do. It's a part of me. Do you mind so much?"

"This time there's a smell of disinfectant mixed with it."

"I scrubbed my hands in the office."

"Oh, my dear! Why will you do that? Icy water and a coarse towel! No wonder your hands look scraped!" She took one in hers and examined it. "And such shapely hands, too!"

"Well," he spoke with resignation, "if I must, I must! Come along with me while I do it."

As they went toward his room she remembered their first day at home after the return from their honeymoon. They had gone over the house, linked together, seeing it in the new light of their union. Each room they had entered had thrust forward its crowd of old memories to greet them. "Here we are!" memories had cried in the drawing-room; and there was Grandmother at her game of backgammon, her purple velvet tea gown rich in the firelight, her rings flashing on her strong old hands. There were family gatherings, family bickerings, and last, Grandmother, nobly extended in her coffin, with Uncle Ernest weeping at her feet. "Here we are!" memories had cried in the sitting-room; and there was Eden, pale and subdued, lying on the sofa, as he had looked when they had brought him home ill from New York. And again, there was the scene of the reading of the will, one not to be dwelt on. She had not been present at that scene, but she had heard about it and she knew it would be long before the room would surrender the memory of it. Memories had shouted—"Here we are"—in the dining room. Never, never could she change the dining room. She felt as impotent before it, its massive furniture, its heavy curtains, its family portraits, as a querulous mouse might feel nibbling at the base of a colossal cheese. There, was and always would be, the stronghold of the Whiteoak tradition. There, was and always would be, the shade of old Adeline vexed by any delay of the dinner, most forward of all in the sending back of her plate for renewals of food, her fiery brown eyes under their rust-red brows gleaming with satisfaction. There, were the unconquerable memories of heavy meals, eaten with all the more gusto because of dissension. And in old Adeline's bedroom across the hall, where her parrot Boney still perched on the headboard of her painted bed, feeding on his memories of her, Renny had said, hesitatingly—"I have sometimes thought I should like to sleep here. She left me the bed in her will, you know. God, what extraordinary dreams one might have!"

Upstairs, from every bedroom, memories had crowded out to them. They had begun their new life hampered by far too many memories. They had passed the room that had been hers and Eden's, with averted eyes, and had gone with relief to the open door of Renny's room. Looking about she had wondered how she would ever make herself at home in it, what could be done to ameliorate the uncompromising masculinity of it. Luckily it was large and airy. Two new walnut beds with straight lines there must be to take the place of the ugly light oak bed that sagged in the middle from his weight. Those hideous curtains that must surely have been his sister's choice, and that he usually kept tied in knots that they might not obscure the air and light, must give place to soft-toned casement-cloth, of mauve perhaps—no, not of mauve. Mauve would fade from the very atmosphere there before the sun had touched it. Mulberry would be better, or green… And the wallpaper… And the pictures on the wall-paper…

He had broken in on her thoughts by saying in a some-what constrained voice:

"I wonder if you would mind very much taking Meggie's room for yourself. It's next door, and it would leave me free to look after Wake. He has always slept with me, you know."

She had been startled, even angered by the request. Yet withal a subtle sense of relief had entered into her feelings after the first moment. The idea of a retreat of her own, a har-bour for her tastes and her reserves, had not been unpleasant. But to give up the shelter, the provocation of his presence… even more, to think that he was suggesting, almost laconi-cally suggesting, the giving up of her presence in his room. After what they had been to each other for three months! After all he had confessed to her of his fevered longings for her when she had been in that house as Eden's wife! Had his longings developed into no desire for sweet companionship?

"Well?" he had asked, with a sidelong look at her.

Something stubborn in her made her say:

"I think Wakefield would be much better sleeping alone. You must often disturb him coming in late. And your habit of smoking while you undress."

"I don't disturb him nearly as often as he disturbs me."

"All children—especially delicate ones—are better sleep-ing alone."

"Not Wake. Not with his nerves and heart!"

"It's quite all right, Renny, but—why do you only tell me now?" She had felt both irritation and mortification, unhappy feelings that he always had had, and always would have, the power to rouse in her, by a tone in his voice, by his silence.

"I didn't want to." He had spoken like a wayward child, and yet with a taciturnity that put him out of her reach.

That was all over now, but the recollection of it often returned to her, for it had seemed to show her quite definitely that her coming could change nothing of Jalna, that Renny had taken possession of her life, but that she could never do more than enter into his as a fresh stream into the salt sea.

Now, as they went together to his room, they passed Wakefield, still leaning against the banister in an attitude of dejection. He kept his eyes averted from them, and Renny did not glance at him. Alayne was conscious of the child's jealousy of her and she suspected that Renny also was conscious of it. She had a feeling that Wakefield grudged her the freedom of Renny's room, that he would have liked to give her such a forbidding look as she had given him, even reduce her to the condition of lolling disconsolately against the banister.

She closed the door with decision. Renny sat down and began to unlace his boots, the metal tips of the laces making small hurried sounds and, at last, the heavy soles two distinct thuds on the floor. She liked to watch him doing things, however commonplace. He was a delight to her and she wanted him all for her own, in tenderness, and in completeness. She said:

"Why can't we see more of each other, alone? I was for two hours this afternoon in the drawing-room! I hoped you would come."

Eagerly he began to explain, but she stopped him. "Oh, I know about the colt. It was beautiful having it come along so well. But there were others there. Surely you didn't have to stay with her all the time."

He looked about, with a troubled expression, for his shoes, as though, once in them, he would be impervious to her onslaught. She continued, love and peevishness making her voice tremble:

"You may not believe it, but I'm lonely sometimes. When I think of our honeymoon in England—travelling about—the voyage home—it all seems so lovely! And now you're so absorbed by things!" She sat down on the side of the bed with a disconsolate look. "And it isn't as though you were like many American husbands, absorbed by big enterprises that demand concentration—"

She was stopped by the outraged expression of his face. Egotism, hurt pride flamed there. She had thought his lean face could be no more red, but it was more red. And, deep in his eyes, was a look of sorrow.

"But—but—" he expostulated, "can't you understand?"

"No, I can't," she answered relentlessly. "Why, I really believe that if I were going to have a baby you wouldn't make a bit more fuss!"

"You're jealous!" he exclaimed. "Jealous of a mare! I never heard of such a thing."

Her womanhood was submerged by a desire to be petted. She said, with the whining intonation of a five-year-old—"I don't care. It's perfectly true! If I were having a baby this minute you couldn't do anything more for me than you did for her!"

"Yes, I could! I'd take to the woods, blizzard and all, and never come out again until it was all over!"

He came to her and sat down beside her on the bed.

"Do you know," he said, drawing her against him, "that for a sensible woman, an intellectual, almost high-brow woman, you can be sillier than any woman I've ever known."

She knew that what he said was true. She knew that he was both surprised and amused by her silliness, but she had worked herself up into this state and she did not care. She pressed closer to him pushing her shoulder under his arm. The room was grey and cold. He disengaged one hand and extracted a cigarette from his case. He lighted it, throwing the match on the floor. The smoke curled about their heads, fragrant in their nostrils. They held each other close, rocking together gently in the twilight. He said:

"Isn't it nice that there's one floor we can throw matches on, and one bedspread we can rumple?"

Downstairs in the drawing-room Pheasant waited for Piers to bring young Maurice to her. It was time the child was put to bed, but she was in no hurry to leave the pleasant warmth of the fire. She sat very upright on a beaded ottoman before it, thinking of Alayne and Renny. Were they happy? Was their marriage going to be a success? Speculation on the relations between men and women was the frequent subject of her thoughts. She had known too much of the suspense, the cruelty of these relations in her short life. There had been no mother to throw a protective shadow between her and her father. The two had been alone together—he unhappy, thwarted, his affection for her, when it was not negligible, half a sneer. Hers, for him, half deprecating, half defiant. He had let her run wild... and she had run wild—straight into her marriage with Piers. They too had had their own troubles. And when she had time to spare from their affairs, she had watched the complications hinging on the diverse personalities about her. She felt herself old in the wisdom of life. She felt maternal towards Alayne, who was ten years her senior, even though Alayne had been married and divorced, and was married again. And to

Whiteoaks each time! Ah, there lay the trouble! The Whiteoaks! Alayne never would—never could understand them. She was an alien, not so much in country as in soul. Pheasant had been brought up next door to the family at Jalna. She had been familiar with Renny since she could toddle. She wondered sagaciously if she might not come to the point one day of giving some good advice to Alayne. She laid her knitting in her lap, and her eyes became large as she pictured herself giving it. But still she could not imagine what the advice would be.

Piers and Mooey were descending the stairs, not with a rush as Renny had done, but slowly and carefully, to suit the legs of the little boy. All the way down Mooey was talking, reiterating the fact that he was not afraid, that he was not going to fall.

"Don't keep repeating that," Pheasant heard Piers say. "It's babyish."

"I'm not a baby," said Mooey stoutly; and after a moment of deep thought, he added—"Oh, hell, I'm not f'ightened!"

"What's that I hear my baby saying?" said Pheasant.

"He has nothing," said Piers, in the doorway, "between babbling like a babe in arms and cursing like a trooper."

"Oh, he hears too much, the poor darling!" and Pheasant held out her arms to him.

He flew into them, burying his face in her lap. The fire-light brought out a ruddy tinge in his brown hair.

"Look!" exclaimed Pheasant, touching it. "I believe he's going to have a tinge of the Court red in his hair."

"I hope not. One of them in the family is quite enough. What's that you're knitting?"

"A new jersey for baby. See, doesn't the colour become him?" She held it under his bright face.

"Where are the others?" asked Piers, sitting down, facing her across the fire.

"Renny and Alayne went upstairs. Wake went tagging after them. Really, Piers, I think she gets awfully fed up sometimes—never having him to herself."

"Does she? What does she want him to herself for?"

"Well, after all, they're practically newly married. And days go by when she scarcely sees him alone unless she tramps through the snow to the stable and corners him there. And she told me herself that when she does he's quite likely to ignore her and to stand gazing at some old horse as though he'd never seen it before. For my part, I have great sympathy with her."

Piers listened to all this with a broadening grin. He threw himself back in his chair, thrust his hands deep in his pockets, and said:

"Now what do you suppose the latest is? A birthday party for young Finch! With the family, ancients and babes, dancing around a birthday cake, with a cheque for a hundred thousand tucked away in the middle of it!"

III

THE TWO FRIENDS

FINCH felt that he must see George Fennel that night. He had not seen him for more than a fortnight, and ever so often the desire to open his bosom to this particular friend came upon him. It was not that George was sensitively receptive or understanding. In truth he often stared at Finch from under his tumbled dark hair with an expression in which humorous contempt mingled with bewilderment at Finch's rhapsodies or despairs.

There was nothing rhapsodical or despairing about George Fennel. Like Finch, he loved music better than anything else, but his pleasure in it was calm. If a piano were not at hand he would play on a banjo. If the banjo were out of order his brother's mandolin would do. If all else failed, well, there was the mouth-organ in his pocket! From these diverse instruments he drew much the same sensation—one of quiet comfort, of cheerful oblivion against the world. Finch's ecstasies, like Finch's despairs, were inexplicable to him; but he was fond of Finch, and he had a suspicion that this hungry-eyed friend possessed some strange inner quality that might either bring him fame or "land him in the soup."

What Finch found in George was the never-failing comfort of a friend who is always the same. George always met him with the same degree of warmth. Discussed by the hour, with stolid cheerfulness, the things that interested him. The only subject that caused George's serenity to flame into excitement was the subject of spending money like water. Then his eyes would beam and his quick sentences explode in reckless gaiety at the very thought of such felicity. All their lives the pockets of the two youths had been almost empty. It was George's invincible idleness that made the thought of a superfluity of money so captivating. Money without working for it. That was what Finch was going to have, and its advancing brightness already was touching Finch's lanky figure.

That figure, as George opened the rectory door, stood silhouetted against the moonlit snow with an air almost mysterious, the face in darkness, for the dim light in the hall marked no features but his eyes.

"Oh, hello, Finch!" said George, in a laconic welcome.

"Hello, Jarge!" boomed Finch, feeling suddenly hilarious. He entered, stamping the snow from his boots and flinging his cap and coat on the rack. "What's your latest crime?"

"Murdering Mozart," said George. "I've been playing him on the mandolin." He banged the door and kicked the snow that Finch had brought in off the rug into the corner. "Awfully cold, isn't it?"

Finch struck his hands together trying to bring feeling into them. "Cold, yes, but glorious coming across the fields! You'd think it was the first snow that had ever fallen, it's so white. And the shadows! Every smallest twig—as though it were done in blue-black ink. And my own shadow—I wish you could have seen it! It simply leaped and danced along beside me like a wild thing!"

"Now I wonder what made it do that," said George, looking at him round-eyed.

"Don't be so beastly prosaic, Jarge! If you had been there you'd have danced too."

"I don't see myself out on a night like this unless there is a girl or a party at the other end. I wish it hadn't stopped snowing though, because if it had kept on all night at the rate it was falling I shouldn't have been able to get into business on Monday."

Although George was a year younger than Finch, his course at the University had already come to an end and he had gone into a broker's office. He had chosen the career of broker's clerk because it seemed to him an easy life and one in which money was talked about largely even though not seen. He led the way upstairs to his own small room. It was as uncomfortable as a room could well be, its only warmth rising through an uncovered stovepipe hole from the kitchen below, but a kind of soft glow that emanated from George's compact person and the memory of hilarious times they had had there gave it a peculiar charm for Finch. He sank down on the sagging sofa and took out a pipe. George had never seen him smoke anything but a cigarette, and he looked on with astonishment while Finch filled it from an old pouch that had once belonged to Nicholas. Finch was a little embarrassed. He had had the pipe with him on his last visit to the Rectory, but had lacked the courage to produce it. He fancied that he looked more of a man when it hung from the corner of his mouth, though he could never hope to look so thoroughly at ease with it as Piers with his.

"What's the idea?" asked George, lighting a cigarette. "Trying to look like a Famous Author, an American Ambassador or a British Prime Minister?"

From a cloud of smoke Finch answered—"I don't know what you are driving at. I've been smoking a pipe for some time—off and on. It's less trouble and more economical."

George chuckled. "You're choosing an original time for economy. Just when you're twenty-one and more money in the offing than you'll know how to spend."

"Well, I suppose it's simply that I've come to the age for smoking a pipe," said Finch, with dignity. "Besides, it's good for me. You know, my nerves are pretty rocky. You've no idea how odd I feel sometimes. Absolutely up in the air for next to nothing."

"I'd feel odd, too, if I was about to fall heir to a fortune."

"I wish," observed Finch, rather nettled, "that you wouldn't talk as though I were a millionaire. What is a hundred thousand dollars!"

"I've no idea. I can't imagine such a sum."

"You say that, and you a broker!"

George, a junior clerk in a broker's office, liked the appellation. He became serious. "Oh, well, one's business is so impersonal."

"Yes, but look here. A hundred thousand isn't so very much in these days. My two uncles each went through that much and have scarcely a penny left."

"And yet they grudge you your chance!"

Finch flushed deeply.

"Sorry," said George. "But I couldn't help hearing things. They didn't take many pains to hide their feelings about it."

"I don't blame them!" cried Finch, twisting his long fingers together. "I don't blame them a bit... for anything they said."

"Perhaps, but it makes it hard for you."

"Oh, yes, awfully hard." He had to compress his sensitive upper lip on the pipe to keep it from quivering. He was lost in unhappy thoughts for a moment, then his eyes sought George's with a look of almost triumph in them. "But they are quite different about it now. They're awfully decent to me. I went into my Uncle Ernest's room this afternoon. He and Uncle Nick and Renny and Piers were there. I could see when I went in that they had been talking about me. I felt uncomfortable for a bit. Then I found out that what they'd been talking about was a *dinner* for me—on my *birthday*." No amount of compression would keep the lip still now. He clenched his teeth on the stem of the pipe.

George was impressed. "A dinner, eh? That's very decent of them. I wonder who thought of it first."

"I don't know, but it was Piers who first spoke of it. It's to be just a small dinner party; but we scarcely ever have people in, you know, and I think on the whole it will be less of a strain for us if we've a few guests to look after. Don't you agree?"

George reflected, trying to put himself in the place of these high-spirited, skittish Whiteoaks. The dinner party then was to be a bridge between the day before Finch's birthday and the day after. Across this bridge the family might march in gala procession. He said—"I like the idea. It should certainly help you out."

"I wish it were all over," said Finch, with almost a groan. "There's another thing I'm dreading. That is telling Renny that I'm not going back to 'Varsity. I simply can't do it."

George regarded him without surprise. "I think you're very sensible. I had to give it up. Too much of a strain. I suppose you'll go in for music?"

"Lord, I don't know! That is, if you mean my making a career of it; I don't believe I have it in me."

"What rot! You've got more talent than any chap I know. Everyone who hears you play thinks you're wasting your time doing anything else."

"I know I am. Yet I don't believe I'll ever be good at concert work. When I played at that recital last month I played my very worst. My teacher was awfully disappointed. He'd slaved over me. He expected something really good from me. And I'd practised like hell. But—you know how it was—I nearly broke down twice."

"You'll get over all that nervousness," said George comfortingly.

"No, I shan't. If I had felt nervous I'd be more hopeful about myself. But I didn't. I just felt half-dead. I didn't care about anything. Nothing looked real to me. The piano didn't look real. And when I nearly broke down it wasn't because I was nervous, or forgot. It was just that I felt too bored to go on. It was as though something inside the piano said to me— 'You blasted fool, do you think you can bring me out whenever you want, and show me off? I'll show you off for what you are–just a hopeless idiot.'"

George looked solemn at this. "I think the trouble with you, Finch, is that you take yourself too seriously. All your family are inclined to take themselves too seriously. It's in the blood. All that talk about the Court nose! And the Court temper! I tell you, it isn't done nowadays. It isn't worthwhile feeling yourself different from other people. As to there being something inside the piano that jeers at you and tells you things, when what you are is just frightened, that's letting your imagination get the upper hand of you. When I was a kid I used to imagine things, so I know all about it. That big stuffed owl that stands in the niche of the stairway was one of the things I got nervous about. I knew quite well that he was only a queer specimen my grandfather had shot in the North somewhere. I knew he was moth-eaten. But I got it into my silly young head that there was something queer about him... that he didn't like me."

"Did you really?" Finch leant forward, his eyes full of intense curiosity. He had never heard George talk like this before, and it brought them very near each other.

"Yes. And I'd never go up the stairs without wondering if it wasn't in his mind to nip me on the left leg as I was passing. I could have sworn that he moved on his perch."

Finch saw before him George—not the sober-eyed youth who faced him—but a little boy creeping up the stairs, his frightened gaze held by the owl's dark stare, his soft hair rising into a halo.

George gave a chuckle. "Well, one night, on my way to bed, I was so sure that he was going to nip me that I went up the stairs in about three leaps. My heart was pounding so I could hardly breathe. I stood at the top, hanging on to the banister and glaring down at my left leg to make sure it was all right. Just then Father came out of his study and looked up at me. 'What's the matter?' he asked, and I whined that I was afraid the owl was going to nip my leg. Well, he ran up the stairs and picked me up and carried me back to the niche where the owl was. He said—'Now put your leg right under his beak, and, if he bites you, I'll throttle him.' So I did, and of course nothing happened. Even after that I was a bit nervous. But the next night I got my courage up and I stopped on the step that was on a level with his niche. I stuck my leg in and I squeaked—'Bite me, old owl, if you dare!' And when he didn't, I gave him a good swift kick and ran on upstairs... Ever since then I am done with imaginings." His eyes beamed into Finch's. "Of course, I'm not comparing the fancies of a silly kid to the fancies of a grown man, but their root is in the same place, and the place is fear. I think if you had had someone like my father to take you in hand you mightn't be so full of fancies today. He did more for me that night than he ever knew of."

Finch nodded. "If one of my brothers had found out that I was afraid of a stuffed owl, he'd have told me things about its habits that would have curdled my blood."

"Look here, old fellow, take my advice. Get yourself in hand and make up your mind that you'll not let anything frighten you out of doing what you want to. You do want to be a great pianist, don't you?"

Finch mumbled—"I don't know what I want, George, and that's a fact, except that I don't want to go on with my University course. I could howl when I think of all the money Renny's wasted on me. He's got to let me pay it back. If I could just have a few months to myself—to think—to get used to myself. There's no use in talking—you can't imagine what it's like to be such a duffer as I am!"

They smoked in silence for a space, George regarding Finch's bowed head affectionately, Finch's mind playing, in spite of himself, about the white owl. George said suddenly:

"Well, you have your own life. Your own work, whatever it's going to be; and if you don't want to work at all you are your own man, no one can force you. Do you realise that?"

Finch started. "What's that? Oh, yes, my own man! Of course... I can do what I like."

"Yes," went on George, solidly. "You can do what you like just when you like. Now I think the first thing you should do is to take a trip. Travel round a bit and see things. You'd get a different slant on your life. You'd get used to yourself. You'd get away from the family."

Finch began to laugh. "Funny you'd suggest that. It's just what I have been planning—with one big difference. I'm thinking of taking my uncles with me."

"You're not in earnest!"

"Yes, I am! They've been wanting for years to visit the Old Country again. Their sister lives in England, you know. They are getting old. Haven't much time to waste. I know what it would mean to them. And if it came through me, you understand, well... it would make a kinder feeling."

George rumpled his hair in deep puzzlement. "It's your idea, then, to start out to see the world, and do this thinking you talk about, with an ancient uncle on either side of you," he said musingly. "And your sightseeing would be to visit an ancient aunt. Well, all I can say is, you are the world's champion philanthropist!"

"Rot! I'll go off on my own whenever I like. And I'm awfully fond of my aunt. I've been wanting to visit her all my life... My position is so peculiar, George. I can't quite explain, but it amounts to this. I can't really enjoy my money, and all the possibilities it opens up to me, until I've done something—not necessarily a big thing—but something quite decent for each of the others. It's as though there were a spell on me that I must work through." His eyes were fixed, with an expression George thought hallucinated, on the smoke from his pipe that hung in a level blue plane before him.

"Of course, of course," he agreed, yet thought—"What a queer egg! But one must take him as he is." Like the piano, the banjo, the mandolin, Finch was accepted by George for the peculiar qualities that gave companionship in season.

"What have you thought of doing for Piers?" he asked; and he remembered, a little grimly, times when Piers had bullied Finch.

"I don't know. Something he'll like for his work, or per-haps something for Pheasant. I'm not going to be in a hurry about it. They'd say at once that I was showing off. No, it's got to come slowly, beginning with the uncles." His gaze that had been remote, now moved, with speculative interest, to the stovepipe hole in the floor. A low murmur of voices came from the kitchen below.

"Yes," said George, "they're still at it—Lizzie and her steady—and they get no forrarder, as far as I can see." He moved to the extreme edge of his chair and peered through the opening as though into a cage at the Zoo. Finch also moved nearer, crouching beside him, their heads touching.

They could see one end of a clean kitchen table on which stood a dish of red apples. They could see a pair of man's hands, middle-aged and horny, paring an apple with a thick-handled pocket knife. The apple was being pared meticulously so that the paring should not be broken, but removed whole from stem to blossom. The two above watched, fascinated, seeing the fine rosy skin of the fruit drop from it, leaving the fruit itself, white as a woman's breast, in the coarse fingers. The paring was pushed across the table to an unseen person; the apple was halved. Then a slice was cut from it, impaled on the knife and put into the mouth of the peeler himself. They glimpsed his grizzled forelock as his head advanced to it. Another slice was impaled and presented to the mouth across the table, and so, a slice at a time, the apple was demolished. The clumsy hands gathered up seeds and core, disposed of them somewhere, picked up another apple and began to pare it. There was an indistinct mumbling of talk.

Finch returned to his seat with a sigh. "How long has this been going on?" he asked.

"About five years."

"God, isn't life wonderful?"

"Love is certainly a queer thing. Especially when it takes them like that."

"I expect it's queer no matter how it takes you."

"Been seeing much of girls lately?"

"No. Too busy."

"You liked Ada Leigh, didn't you?"

"H'm—h'm. She's been in France with her mother."

"I don't believe you've a great opinion of that sex, Finch."

"Oh... I don't know," he sighed deeply. "I haven't had much experience of them."

George folded his arms and spoke rather ponderously. "A really dazzling one comes into our office sometimes, about investments, you know. A rich widow. She always seems to want my advice about things. I can't see why, because I'm only a junior. She always seems to want to know just what I think about everything. Some women are odd, aren't they?"

"How old is she?"

"I couldn't possibly tell. Once they're past twenty I'm all at sea."

"But you've a way with you, Jarge," said Finch affectionately.

George unfolded his arms and unknit his brow. "How about a little music?" he asked.

On the way down the stairs, Finch had stopped to look at the stuffed white owl. He had thrust his hands under its great folded wings and felt the deep downiness there. He had put his face close to the black beak, the glittering eyes. A sensuous pleasure had run over his body at the feel of the owl's downiness. He thought of the pure whiteness where his hands were hid...

All the way home he exulted in thoughts of it. The face
of the earth seemed to him like the owl's breast; the stars had
the cold glitter of the owl's eyes; the bitter wind was its
hoot... It had left its perch and swept through the open door
of the Rectory with him, and had become one with the night,
the beating of its wings the rhythm of the universe.

He left the road and took his customary shortcut through
the fields, though the path had long been obliterated. The
snow lay in great drifts, light as mounds of fallen feathers.
He dashed through them, bounding, with each leap, as high
as he could. All his instinct revolted against being grown up.
He wished only to be a wild, half-mad boy, that the passage
of time might not touch him... He pulled off his cap and ran
bare-headed, dancing with his shadow, trying to wrest his
spirit from his body, and toss it, a glistening essence, into the
frosty air. He fancied how the great owl would pounce on it,
a tender morsel for its starry-eyed young, and sweep
Poleward with it, uttering a whoo-hoo that would shake the
universe.

He left the fields and ran through the pinewood. He left
the pinewood and ran through the birchwood, where the silvery trees bathed themselves in the moonlight as in a sea,
laying their round boles in it, keeping nothing of themselves
from it, shivering in their naked whiteness as they drowned
themselves in it.

He ran through the apple orchard, where the gnarled
black shapes of the trees were like old men dancing. There
was an icy pathway there from which the wind had blown
the snow, and he slid along it, cap in hand, in long graceful
glides.

He ran through the young cherry orchard, where the
trees stood in straight rows like timid, half-grown girls, and,

as he emerged into the garden, he saw the lights of the house welcoming him.

As soon as he saw them the shadow of the owl grew smaller, but still, he thought, it followed him, swooping, lower and lower, towards his legs. A sensation of terror took hold of him. He ran panting, his consciousness trickling from his brain to his nether parts. Would it catch him before he reached the door?

It was level with him, its eyes afire. He plunged across the lawn, and flung himself against the door. It flew open, and, at the same instant, he felt a cruel nip on the left leg!

"My dear boy," said Uncle Ernest, "what a draught you're letting in. Shut the door quickly! And you may as well bolt it for the night."

IV

The Birthday

It came on the first day of March. He had narrowly escaped being born on the twenty-ninth of February, which, in addition to having been born with a caul, would have singled him out with a directness almost ominous. As it was, he was quite satisfied to have first seen the light with the arrival of spring; and, on this particular birthday, the season did not, as was its wont, appear crouching under the cloak of winter. On the contrary, it was a day of remarkable mildness for the time of year. Rain had fallen steadily all the preceding day and night, and by the time the sun had emerged from the rain clouds there were already patches of bare ground on the lawn. By noon that part of it which was not in shadow lay revealed to the warmth of the sun. Last year's grass had retained something of its colour, and even seemed to have grown, as the hair of a dead person is said to flourish morbidly for long after burial.

The withered forms of last year's asters and calendula lay sodden on the soaking soil of the flower border; under the hedge last year's leaves lay in a discoloured ridge. Yet all was enlivened by a boundless hope. The abnormally large drops of rain and melted snow that were strung on every twig and blade and ledge were glancing with radiant brightness. The sky was swept clean of all that came between its sun and the earth. No return of cold and snow could efface the promise of this day.

The door into the hall stood wide open letting in the sun. It was on such a day as this that old Adeline would take her first walk of the year. Wrapped in innumerable cloaks, scarves, and petticoats, so that she looked a very battleship of a woman, she would come into view, supported by her sons, and present herself foursquare to the reviving world. "I'm out again!" she would exclaim. "Ha! I like the smell of the fresh air!"

Finch thought a good deal about her today, recalling their strange delayed intimacy that had drawn them so mysteriously together, wondering if it were possible to him to live in a way that would have won her approbation. Still, she had known him for what he was, had loved him, had accepted him as one of "the whelps" her son Philip had got by his second wife.

He stood in the porch sunning himself, and watched Rags furbishing up the hall. How shabby both hall and servant looked in the noonday brightness! The slender walnut banister and carved newel-post were elegant enough, but the wallpaper along the stairway showed dingy where small hands had been pressed against it. Certainly it had never been repapered in his time. The carpet on the stairs was threadbare. The Turkish rug on the floor had lost all its fringe. The fringe had reappeared miraculously on the cuff of Rags's coat. This cuff was being violently agitated as he polished the mirror in the hat-rack above which the carved head of a fox sneered down at him.

"Well," he said, seeing Finch, "many happy returns of the d'y to you, sir!"

"Thanks, Rags."

"We couldn't 'ave a finer d'y for the occasion, not if it 'ad been hordered! It's a fine thing to be twenty-one, sir, and to 'ave all the money in the family." He looked over his shoulder at Finch with an air of innocent envy.

Finch felt like taking the fellow by the scruff of his grizzled neck and shaking him. He said—"You don't know what you're talking about, Rags."

The little Cockney proceeded imperturbably:

"It's a 'appy d'y for us all, I'm sure, sir. Mrs. Wragge was saying to me just a bit ago that she'd prayed for a fine d'y. I don't go in for prayer much myself, but, as the saying is, strawrs tell which way the wind blows. Not that she is much like a strawr, sir. More like a strawr*stack*, I'd say. I 'ardly dare to go into the kitchen this morning, she and Bessie are that worked up with excitement. And the thought of those caterers coming out from town with all their paraffinaliar!" He came to the door and shook out his cloth. He then produced a small, foreign-looking leather pocketbook from somewhere about his clothes. He proffered this to Finch with a bow.

"Will you accept this from me, Mr. Finch, as a little offering? I brought it 'ome with me from the War. It belonged to a German officer. And I've always thought that if the d'y come when I 'ad a pot of money, I'd use it myself. But the d'y 'asn't come, and it looks as though it never *would* come—not in *this* country, and at *this* job—so, if you'll accept it, I'll give it to you with my best wishes, and may it always be full!"

Finch took it, embarrassed. It was a handsome pocketbook, and there was something touching in Rags's expression as he offered it; but Finch always had the uncomfortable feeling that Rags was laughing in his sleeve at him.

"Thanks, very much," he mumbled. "It's an awfully good one." He opened it, looked in it, shut it, Rags regarding him with an expression of mingled sadness and pride. He gave his duster another shake and re-entered the hall.

Mooey was descending the stairs on his little seat, a step at a time. Finch watched him, feeling suddenly very happy. Everyone was amazingly nice to him. Renny had given him a wristwatch. Piers and Pheasant, gold cufflinks. Uncle Nicholas a paperweight, and Uncle Ernest a watercolour from the wall of his own room. Alayne had given him a crocodile-skin travelling-bag, and Wakefield a large clothes brush which, he explained, would "come in handy to whack his kids with when he had any." Meggie's present was yet to arrive.

"Bump!" sang out Mooey. "I'm toming! Bump! Bump! Bump! I'm not f'ightened!"

Finch went to the foot of the stairs and snatched him up. He put him on his shoulder, and, out of the shadows of the past came a picture of himself, caught up thus by Renny. A queer thing life... One tall strong body, one little weak body after another... Some day Mooey would stand at the foot of the stairs and shoulder some tiny boy just as today he was doing... And Mooey would be twenty-one, and whose would be the tiny boy? Some little Whiteoak, out of a Whiteoak body...

Mooey clasped Finch's head, and pressed his round flower-like face to Finch's thin one. "I want to go out on the nish geen gash," he said.

"The grass may be green, but it's not nice. It's nasty and soggy."

"I l-like nawsty soggy fings."

"Very well, I'll carry you out and stand you on your head on it." He ran out the door and down the steps.

"There's a nish soggy spot," said Mooey, pointing out a puddle.

"I'll tell you what I'll do," cried Finch. "I'll take you to the stables to see Uncle Renny." He had got an idea. He would find Renny and approach the subject of quitting the University this very hour. Renny was always more or less absent minded and good humoured when he was among his horses. The presence of Mooey would be a help too, for Renny had a way of staring at him speculatively and only half-listening to what was being said.

They found the master of Jalna in the paddock, mounted on a bright bay mare which he was training as a high-jumper. Two grooms stood by a hurdle, the top bar of which they raised and lowered in accordance with the shouted directions of the rider.

Finch, carrying Mooey wrapped in a man's jersey, stood by the enclosure unnoticed save by a casual glance. The mounting strength of the sun was poured down on this sheltered spot, giving the impression of a day in late April rather than one in early March. The intrinsic quality of all on which the sunrays fell was made evident in smell or colour. The earth, newly thawed, trampled by the feet of horses and men, gave forth a pungent and profoundly vital odour. There had been pressed and soaked and baked and frozen into it—ever since Captain Philip Whiteoak, almost eighty years before, had chosen this particular place for this purpose—rotted straw and manure, and the impalpable essence absorbed by the earth from the sanguine activities of men and beasts. Every hair in the young mare's mane and tail seemed charged with energy. Her hide glistened as though varnished, her eyes flashed back the light. Renny's strong-muscled, mud-spattered legs, his weather-beaten, sweating face, his bare head against which the hair was plastered, the red healthy faces of Wright and Dawlish, their capable hands that took up and replaced the fallen bar, the skin of their hands dry from the grooming of horses and stained with harness oil, all these were discovered in the spring sunlight.

Between the two men, the mare, and her rider there existed a sympathy not needing the expression of words. When she felt panic and sheered off from the jump or valiantly essayed it and failed, a like shadow seemed to fall across all four. She blew out her breath in what seemed a great sigh. The grooms dubiously replaced the bar; and Renny, wheeling her about, drew his brows together in a rueful frown. But, when she swung clear of the hurdle, and hung like a bird for a space against the sky, before she alighted triumphant and cantered down the course, a brightness of aspect descended as the sun's rays on men and mare. A group of cows that had collected as spectators by the fence of an adjoining enclosure looked on the scene with complete lack of sympathy. At the critical moment one might stop chewing the cud, as though the better to concentrate on what was going on, but, be the leap never so birdlike or the failure never so forlorn, the cud-chewing was resumed with an aloof serenity.

Finch thought—"She has done well; I believe it's a good time to speak."

Renny had dismounted and given the bridle to Wright and was strolling toward him, scrubbing the palms of his hands with a crumpled handkerchief.

"Wasn't she splendid?" asked Finch, scrutinising his elder's face. "I think she's going to be a wonderful jumper."

"I hope so. She's a sweet thing. I intend to ride her in New York this fall, if possible." He turned to Mooey. "Hello, what's the matter with your nose?" He gave the small feature a decisive wipe with the handkerchief.

"I suppose," said Finch, "he should have something on his head."

Mooey, his nose quite pink, observed:

"I'm going to jump a nish 'orsey and not be f'ightened neider."

"He talks too much about not being frightened," said Renny. "It sounds as though he were trying to reassure himself. I hope he's not going to be a duffer at riding, like you."

"I hope not," returned Finch dolefully. It took so little to cast him down.

There was silence for a moment while Renny struck at the flakes of mud on his legs with his riding-crop, then Finch set the little boy on his feet, and, turning to his brother, broke out with the energy of despair.

"Look here, Renny, it's impossible for me to go back to 'Varsity! I simply can't do it!"

Renny continued to strike at his leg with his riding-crop, but he did not speak. His face hardened.

Finch continued—"You can't know how it is with me. You're always doing the most congenial work. 'Varsity isn't congenial to me. It isn't anything to me but a grind and a flatness and an unreality. I don't see any sense in sticking it out."

The fiery brown eyes, before which he quailed, were raised to his. "What the hell is congenial to you? I wish you'd tell me. I thought music was, and I've let you take lessons and spend hours practising when you ought to have been studying. Then, when you play at a recital, you play your worst, and you tell me that audiences aren't congenial—"

"I didn't!" cried Finch. "I didn't say that! I said that I was afraid of audiences—"

"Afraid! By God—afraid—that's the trouble! You're always afraid! No wonder the kid there whines about not being frightened! You've put it in his head!"

Finch had turned white. He had begun to shake.

"Renny! Look here! Listen! I—I—you don't understand—"

"Of course I don't! Nobody understands. You're not like anyone else, are you? You're a student, and you can't study! You're an actor, and you can't act! You're a pianist, and you can't play! You're twenty-one, and you act like a girl in her teens!"

Finch flung out his hand. The sun touched the face of the wristwatch Renny had given him that morning. He cursed himself for a fool. Why, oh why, had he chosen this day of all days for his declaration! He dropped his arm. He was cut to the heart.

Renny went on—"I suppose you think that because you're of age today and are coming into some money—"

"No! No, I don't! I only thought I'd like to tell you—at least, ought to tell you—"

"Why didn't you tell me long ago? Why did you let me go on planning for your education—"

In spite of the unhappy turmoil of his emotions, Finch could not help wondering what effort of the brain Renny had spent on him beyond the tardy digging up of his tuition fees, and the determination that he should not evade one lecture or examination.

He got out, hoarsely—"You shall have it all back!"

"Not a cent! I won't have a cent of it back!"

"But why? There's no reason why you shouldn't!" cried Finch distractedly.

"There's every reason. I won't take a cent of it."

"But why?"

"Because if I took it back I should not have reared you and educated you, as it was my duty to do."

"But there's no reason in that! I know how hard it is for you to get money. All along I've said to myself—'I'll make it up to Renny!' The thought of that bucked me up to tell you this today. Renny, you must take it back!"

"Not a penny. Well, I can't force you to go on, but I can feel that I've done my best, and, if you're a mess, it's not my fault!" He had worked himself into a temper. He showed his teeth, Finch thought, as though he would like to bite him. Things were blurred before Finch's eyes. The sunlit scene before him began to revolve. He put his hands on the palings and held himself together with an effort.

Mooey looked from one uncle to the other, his lip quivering. "I'm not f'ightened!" he said.

Renny made as if to strike him with his riding-crop. "Say that again and I'll thrash you!" Nothing on earth would have induced him to touch Mooey with the riding-crop, but he felt and looked as though he could. Mooey raised his voice in a howl of anguish.

At this moment Piers drove up to them in the car. He had been to the village and had brought the post. He got out with the letters in his hand. His son moved toward him screaming, in a kind of dance.

Renny said—"That's a nice young milksop you've got! He's frightened of his own shadow! He takes after his Uncle Finch!"

Piers's fatherliness was roused. He picked up his child and comforted him. "What's it all about? What's he been doing? It seems to me that you look fierce enough to frighten anyone."

"Oh, it's nothing," said Renny. "Only Finch has just been telling me that he's not going to 'Varsity any more. It's uncongenial to him."

Piers's prominent blue eyes took in the situation. He did not speak for a moment while he turned the matter over in his mind. Then he said in his deep voice:

"Well, it's no surprise to me. I always knew he didn't like college. I didn't like it myself. I don't see any sense in his taking a course in Arts—going in for a profession—unless he wants. If I were in his place I'd do just as he is doing."

Without another word Renny turned and strode toward the stable. Piers looked after the tall retreating figure with composure. "You've got his back up," he said. "He'll not get over this today."

"I don't know what I'm to do," said Finch bitterly. "I couldn't go on with it. And I thought I could make it up to him... but he won't let me. He simply got in a rage..."

"Gran will never be dead while he lives! You may have her gold, but he has her temper."

Finch broke out—"I wish he had them both." His jaw shook so that he had to clench his teeth to control it.

"Keep your shirt on," said Piers soothingly. "You won't be twenty-one for long. My advice is to make the most of it. Go away for a while and he'll forgive you and want you back." He looked over the letters. "Here is one for you from England. A birthday greeting from Aunt Augusta, I guess."

Finch took the letter and glanced at the spidery handwriting. He turned, with an ache in his throat, in the

direction of the house. "Thanks," he muttered; and added—
"And thanks for standing up for me."

"That was nothing. I don't usually see eye to eye with
you, but I do in this. You'd be a fool to waste your time in
doing what you hate when you have all the world before
you... Do you like the cufflinks?" Piers was one of those
who find it difficult to express thanks for a gift themselves,
but who take a sincere pleasure in the reiterated thanks of
others.

Finch brightened. "Oh, yes. I like them awfully."

"They're quite good ones, you know."

"I can see that. But you and Pheasant shouldn't have
done it. It was too much."

"Well, I've never given you a present before... and, if
you like them..."

"I like them tremendously."

"We went into town together to pick them out. The day
the car broke down and she got that chill."

Finch's gratitude deepened. "I remember. It was too bad
her getting a chill on my account."

"She didn't mind... There goes the stable clock. I'll be
late for lunch. I don't suppose it will amount to much today,
with the dinner coming on... I'll take the kid with me."

On the way to the house Finch opened his Aunt's letter. He had a deep affection for her. She had shown him
many kindnesses on her visits to Jalna, had worried considerably over his thinness, and tried unsuccessfully to fat-
ten him. It was like her to have remembered his birthday,
and to have posted her letter in time to reach him on the
very day. He read, his lips twisting into a wry smile at the
last paragraph:

LYMING HALL,
NYMET CREWS, DEVON,
18th February.

MY DEAR NEPHEW,

When you receive this letter you will, I trust, be well and happy, and at the *proud* moment of attaining your majority. You are arriving at manhood surrounded by the most *auspicious* circumstances. I only wish I might be with you to give you my good wishes in person. But I very much doubt whether I shall ever visit Canada again. The mere undertaking of the journey at my age is *terrific*. The sea voyage with its attendant *nausea*, the exhausting journey by rail in the discomfort and heat of your *trains*, and, added to this, the sad knowledge that my dear mother no longer awaits with extended arms for my coming. Neither do my brothers invariably show me that consideration which they should. Particularly I mention *Nicholas*. Mentioning him, of course, in the strictest confidence.

I should like very much to have you visit me this summer during your holidays. Even a short stay in England at this period of your life would help to broaden you.

I wish I could offer you lively society, as I might have done once; but those days are past. They are gone like the days when my parents entertained so lavishly at Jalna.

But I can offer you young company in the shape of Sarah Court, your cousin once removed. She and the aunt (by marriage) with whom she lives are coming from Ireland to spend part of the summer with me. Mrs. Court's husband was the brother of Sarah's father. They were the sons of Thomas Court, my mother's youngest brother. Mrs. Court is an Englishwoman, though still living in Ireland, and you would never think that Sarah herself was Irish. She is twenty-five, a quite superior girl intellectually, musical like yourself. I have always esteemed the aunt, though she is a very peculiar woman and places too much importance (in my opinion) on her high *blood pressure*. I am sure you and Sarah would get on together.

If you would like to visit me, I shall write to Renny and tell him that it is my desire to have you. It was such a delight to me that he and Alayne were married from my house and spent their honeymoon *nearby*. Give my fondest love to my other dear nephews and nieces, my brothers (I so often long to see them), and my baby grand-nephew.

I hope you will be very happy, my dear Finch, and I think you may rest assured that not one of us harbours any feeling of *malevolence* towards you in the matter of your inheritance.

Your affectionate Aunt,

AUGUSTA BUCKLEY.

P.S.—Quite recently I had a letter from Eden. He approached me for *money*. He did not mention *that woman*.—A. B.

Finch carried the letter to Alayne where she was arranging carnations on the birthday table.

"Look, Finch," she cried, "aren't they beauties? They arrived perfectly fresh. I arranged them at first with tulle banked about them, but it didn't suit the room at all. You can't do what you like with this room; it's got too much character."

Finch sniffed the carnations and eyed the expanse of damask and silver with some concern. He had never been the object of an occasion before, and the pleasure it gave him was overweighed by apprehension, even though the guests were only relations and the nearest neighbours. He said nervously:

"You don't suppose they'll drink my health, do you? Want me to make a speech or anything? I'd be in a blue funk if I thought that was hanging over me."

"Of course they'll drink your health. All you've got to do is to get up and make a little bow and say a few words of thanks."

Finch groaned.

"Don't be silly! How can you possibly be afraid of saying a few words at your own table when you played so splendidly before a hall full of people?"

"If you think you cheer me by bringing up that recital, you're mistaken. I hate the thought of it!"

"I don't! I look back on it with pride." But she dared not look at him for fear her eyes should betray her knowledge that he had not played his best.

He drew a long sigh. "Well, the table's awfully pretty. Where are we going to have lunch?"

"In the sitting-room. It's ready now."

"I've just had a letter from Aunt Augusta. Have you time to read it now?"

"Yes, I'd love to." She sat down on the arm of a chair near a window, in an attitude that suggested both repose and capability of purpose. Finch's eyes rested on the gold of her hair, the blue of her dress. Seeing her so he felt, as he often felt about her, that she never had and never could become one of them, even to the fitting of her person into the surrounding objects of the house. She looked as though she had just walked in from a different world, bringing with her an atmosphere of clarity and questioning, and would walk out again, her clarity perhaps disturbed, but her questioning unanswered. Yet she was easily agitated. Sometimes he felt a wildness of spirit in her, as though she would by her will force her way into the fibre of their life, take possession as she was possessed.

She looked up and found his eyes on her and smiled.

"What a characteristic letter!" she exclaimed. "I think her underlining is delicious. And her adjectives… Oh, my dear, what could be more perfect than *malevolence?*" She turned the page and read the postscript, but she made no comment on it, except by a scornful movement of the lips.

"What do you think," asked Finch, "of my going over to visit Aunt Augusta? I'd like to go. I've just told Renny that I can't go back to 'Varsity."

"How did he take it?" She was not surprised because they had talked of that together. But she could not speak of Renny without all her being quivering into oversensitiveness.

"Just what you'd expect. We had a row."

"Oh, I'm sorry! What a shame—on your birthday!"

"Well—now he knows. One unexpected thing happened. Piers took my side."

She wondered why Piers had taken his side. She suspected him of being shrewd, and she could never be unconscious of his dislike for her, though it was concealed behind an air of heartiness. He had welcomed her even less as mistress of Jalna than he had welcomed her when she had first come there as Eden's wife. He would have liked Pheasant to be the only woman in the house, his wife, a young girl and docile, though she had been wanton once.

Alayne said—"You must go to England. You must!" She took him by the lapels of his coat and gave him a quick kiss. It was the first time she had ever kissed him. She realised his

Checked out item   for
SCHIEDEL, MARY
02-04-2019 3:28PM

BARCODE: 33420013285508
LOCATION: wf
TITLE: The building of Jalna / de 1
DUE DATE: 02-14-2019

BARCODE: 33420009352601
LOCATION: wf
TITLE: WPL Interlibrary Loan
DUE DATE: 02-15-2019

BARCODE: 33420000029
LOCATION: wf
TITLE: A Day in the
DUE DATE: 02-25-2019

BARCODE: 33420000189085
LOCATION: wf
TITLE: Where she has gone / Nino Ricci
DUE DATE: 02-25-2019

BARCODE:
LOCATION:
TITLE: Nino Ricci
25-2019

spiritual hunger, and the kiss was a gesture, not only of comfort, but of urge to the fulfilment of that hunger.

He felt a high excitement. His eyes shone. "How beautiful you are to me," he said, taking her hands in his.

"Do you know," she said teasingly, "I believe Aunt Augusta has it in her mind to make a match between you and this Sarah Court."

"Nonsense! She looks on me as a boy."

"Yes, but boys grow into husbands. Especially in a house with an attractive cousin."

"I don't like the sound of her."

"She's musical."

"I don't like the sound of that."

"Well, don't think I should want you to marry. You ought not to marry till you are fully matured. Not for years and years."

The luncheon bell sounded, and almost at once they heard voices in the sitting-room. They found the others there, standing about eating roast-beef sandwiches and drinking tea. Wakefield, excited by the novelty, darted here and there, half a buttered scone in each hand. Not since his grandmother's funeral had there been such excitement in the house. Not since then had there been a meal that was not a meal, and the opening of the doors to invited guests. And all about Finch! Wakefield, for the first time in his life, regarded him with respect. He found a chair and, hooking his arms beneath its arms, dragged it towards him.

"Here!" he cried exuberantly. "Here's a chair! Sit down and rest yourself."

There was an outburst of laughter at Finch's expense. He pushed child and chair aside, and went, with a sheepish frown, to the table where the viands were spread. He picked

up a sandwich, and, before he remembered to offer the plate
to Alayne, had taken a large bite from it. He attempted to get
tea for her, and slopped it into the saucer. He was in despair
with himself.

Renny was in despair with him too. He stood watching
his fumbling movements with brooding disapproval. What
the devil was the matter with the fellow? He was always
wrought up over something. And this latest! This wanting to
throw up his studies the very moment of coming into his
money! It was the spinelessness of him, that was what was
so exasperating. If only he were wild, reckless—but this
shrinking from things! Were these half-brothers whom he
had reared to be one disappointment after another? All but
Piers! He'd no fault to find with Piers. But Eden... Never
able to earn his own living, and yet somehow able to keep
that girl, Minny... He hadn't married her though, which he
ought to have done... Now Finch was coming on... And little Wake, who was like his own child, what would he make of
him? He looked gloomily at the undersized boy, with his
sensitive dark face, his long-lashed, brilliant eyes, too big for
the face... he'd been caught lying, he'd been caught stealing... well, life was a queer, mournful thing, and this was a
queer, mournful occasion, though the others might stand
about grinning with their sandwiches like a lot of schoolchildren at a feed.

Nicholas thought, with an inward chuckle—"Renny
might have put a better face on it, seeing that Ernest and I
have achieved a festive air. After all, the party was his idea."

Finch could not get enough to eat. As usual, when he was
mentally disturbed, he found the cavity within more difficult
to fill, especially with a scrappy meal like this. No number of
buns spread with damson jam would do it. He was the last in

the room. He had hoped that Renny would linger, giving him a chance to propitiate him; but, after bolting two sandwiches and a cup of tea that might well have seared insides of less tough fibre, he had stalked out.

It seemed that the afternoon would never pass. Finch hung about the house watching the preparations, playing snatches at the piano, teasing Pheasant, and, when possible, having moments of serious conversation with Alayne on that subject of never failing interest—himself.

He and Wakefield went to the kitchen in the basement and surveyed the fowls all trussed up for roasting, and the wineglasses all polished up for filling, and the moulds of jelly, and the buckets filled with chopped ice into which were thrust the containers holding the Neapolitan ice sent out from town. They had never seen Mrs. Wragge's face so purple, or Wragge's so pallid, or Bessie's arms, as she scrubbed the celery, so mottled. All were atwitter with excitement. They looked at Finch with wonder in their eyes, to think that he had attained this pinnacle.

Long before it was time to dress for dinner he was in his attic room. The night had turned cold. He got into his dressing gown, a gaily coloured one that had once been Eden's, his bedroom slippers that had once been Renny's, took his bath towel, one of a pair given him by Meggie at Christmas, and descended to the bathroom. There was a chill there too, but he had told Rags to fill the tin tub with very hot water, and it was hot enough in all conscience. Hot enough to boil him. When he ran upstairs again he was pink from heat and in a state of high excitement.

Already he had laid his evening clothes on the bed. They had only been worn twice before, once at a dance at the Leighs' and once at the recital. The jacket became him well, he thought, surveying himself in the small glass. Alayne had given him a white carnation to wear. He brushed his moist hair, giving special attention to the lock that had a habit of dangling on his forehead. He polished his nails and wished that his fingers were not so stained by cigarettes. A shiver ran over him which he did not know whether to attribute to excitement or the change from the hot bath to the cold room. God! How well the new cufflinks and the new wristwatch looked! He glanced at the face of the watch… It was an hour and a half before dinnertime!

What to do! He could not go downstairs at this hour, looking like a fool, with a carnation in his buttonhole. Yet he should die of cold if he spent the intervening time up here. He cursed himself for his stupid haste.

Still, if he chose to go down and sit for an hour and a half in the drawing-room, whose business was it but his own? He supposed he could do as he liked on his own birthday… He was halfway down the attic stairs when he heard Piers ascending the lower stairs, whistling. They would meet in the passage, or Piers, glancing up, would see him on the stair-way. One look at him in those clothes, at that hour, would be enough to make Piers humorous at his expense for the evening. He could hear him greet an early arrival with— "Too bad you couldn't have got here earlier. Young Finch has been waiting, all dressed up, for an hour and a half to welcome you!" No, he must never risk that! Not risk being seen by any of the family.

He turned back and re-entered his room. He looked at his watch. Five minutes had passed. Somehow or other he must put in the next hour and a quarter in that cavern of coldness. He looked longingly at the bed. If only he might lie down and cover himself with the quilt and keep warm! But his suit would be ruined by wrinkles in no time. The next best thing was to wrap the quilt about him and find something to read. He folded it carefully about his shoulders, keeping one hand curved above the carnation to protect it. He felt utterly miserable… What hell coming of age was!

From his shelf of books he took a volume of Wordsworth's poems. It was handsomely bound, the only prize he had ever got at school. The support he craved, the something of pride in achievement, might be in that book, he thought. Something to fortify him in this hour. He sat down, opened it and read: "Presented to Finch Whiteoak for the excellence of his memorising of Holy Scripture." And the date, nine years before. He had been a small boy then, at a small school. Nine years ago… He was getting on!

He thought of the numerous prizes each of the others had won at school, for they had each had a subject or two in which they excelled. As for prizes for athletics… They had been put to it to find places for all the silver cups and urns… Well, at any rate, he had got one, that was better than nothing. He read stolidly for what seemed a long time, dividing his attention between his new cufflinks and watch, and the poetry for which he did not much care. But the rhythm of it eased him somehow, the quilt comforted. It was no easy matter to keep it around him, protecting the carnation with one hand and holding up the book of poems with the other. He did wish he had a cigarette; yet he was afraid of disarranging himself to get it, lest in the rearranging the carnation might be injured. It might be better to take the carnation off for the time, but there was the danger in pinning it on again.

He heard Wakefield running below and gave a piercing whistle to attract him. He came flying up the stairs. Finch concealed the poems under the quilt.

"Hello," said Wakefield, "what are you wrapped up in a quilt for?"

"Been having a bath and got chilled. Look in that top drawer and hand me the package of cigarettes, like a good kid."

"I say," exclaimed Wake, as he handed him the cigarettes, "how funny you look! You're wrapped in a quilt, and yet I can see your pumps and pants underneath!"

Finch scowled at him in what he hoped was a terrifying way, but he dared advance no more than his fingers from the quilt toward the cigarettes because of his cuffs. Yet Wake held them just out of reach.

"Give them here!" snarled Finch out of the side of his mouth like a stage villain.

"I am giving them," Wake's tone was meek, but his eyes were on a narrow aperture in the quilt and he brought the cigarettes no nearer. "Here they are. Why don't you take them?"

"How the hell can I take them when you hold them away off there?"

"It's not away off. It's just a little bit of a way. What's the matter with you? Do you feel sick? Because, if you do, perhaps you'd better not smoke."

Exasperated beyond endurance, Finch shot forth his hand from the quilt and snatched the packet of cigarettes, instantly drawing the quilt once more tightly about him. "Now," he said, "clear out of here and no more of your cheek!"

Wakefield seemed to drift out of the room and down the stairs, so pensive was his mien. Finch felt hot all over. He let the quilt slide from his shoulders and put a cigarette between his lips. He reached for a match, but, just as he struck it, he heard Wakefield and Piers talking in the passage below. He held his breath and heard soft steps ascending the stairs. Like an arrow from the bow he leaped to the door. Just as Piers reached the landing he threw himself against it. He shot the bolt. Smothered laughter came from outside.

"Look here, Finch," came Piers's voice, "can you let me have a cigarette?"

"No," growled Finch, "haven't got any up here."

"The kid says you have."

"He's a little liar."

"Well, look here, I'd like to speak to you a minute."

"Sorry. I can't just now. I'm busy."

"Is anything wrong? The kid says you didn't seem very well when he was up before."

"Let me alone!" roared Finch, and he showed, furthermore, that the example he had had before him in the matter of swearing had not been entirely lost.

When they had gone he looked down at the carnation. He had flattened it against the door... He looked at his wristwatch... The fracas had done one thing for him, at any rate. It had made time fly.

The Vaughans were the first to arrive: Meggie, a little plumper, a little more exuberantly the wife and mother; Maurice, a trifle greyer, his masculinity a trifle more muffled. She clasped Finch to her. Oh, the lovely depth of that bosom! He was never taken to it, but he wished he might burrow into its tender depths and remain forever enfolded there. She gave him three kisses on the mouth, and put a packet into his hand. "With *our* love and many, many good wishes." Wake crowded up beside him to see. It was a white evening scarf of heavy silk. "Oh, thanks," Finch murmured; and Maurice shook him by the hand.

Maurice had been warned on the way by his wife not to make any reference to Finch's inheritance, but he could not resist saying:

"Well, enjoy it while you're young!" And his glance did not indicate the scarf.

Meg caressed Wakefield, remarked his delicate looks, and went up to Alayne's room to lay off her things. The men stood about with the conciliatory air worn by them in the presence of female antagonisms. They knew that Meggie and Alayne disliked one another, that there was no love lost between Meggie and Pheasant. They would be glad when other guests arrived.

They soon arrived in a stream. The Fennels: the rector, thickset, beaming, his hair and beard tidier than was usual even on Sundays; George, resembling him; Mrs. Fennell, long-backed, hatchet-faced, with eyes always searching for a vacant seat into which she might drop; Tom resembling her. Next, the two Miss Laceys, whose late father had been a retired Admiral, and the elder of whom had been after Nicholas forty-seven years ago. After these Miss Pink, the organist, prematurely aged by being rushed, year in and year out, through the hymns and psalms by the combined impetuosity of the Whiteoaks at a speed which she thought little short of blasphemous. She was in a flurry at exposing her shoulders in a seldom worn evening gown, and had veiled them by a scarf, though they were, in truth, the best part of her. These were the old, old friends and neighbours.

Considerably later, and from Town, came the Leighs. They were mere acquaintances to the rest of the family, but Finch thought of Arthur Leigh as his best friend. Mother and daughter in their sheathlike gowns of delicate green had the appearance of sisters. He could scarcely wait to have Arthur alone that he might tell him of his contemplated trip, with all the more eagerness because Arthur himself had spoken of spending that summer in England.

The party was now complete except for two people. These were neighbours, living in a small, rather isolated house, but comparative strangers. About a year and a half before, Antoine Lebraux had brought his wife and daughter from Quebec and acquired this place with the object of going into the breeding of silver foxes. He had been in the Civil Service, and, his health having broken down, he was advised to turn to an outdoor life. His wife, who had relations in Upper Canada, wished to be near them, and, within fifty miles of a brother, she had discovered this small and neglected property for sale. Lebraux, with the enthusiasm of his race, had thrown himself heart and soul into the new life. Reliable parent foxes had been bought, and he had read every book obtainable on the subject of their breeding and care.

Renny had met and liked him. He had ridden over frequently to see how the foxes were progressing. The first litters were admirable. The change of climate had done Lebraux good, and his malady had shown signs of improvement. But good luck did not follow in good luck's train. His most valuable vixen had somehow dug her way out and was never seen again. The later litters were weakly, a vixen died, then, when fresh stock had been bought in the hope of raising the stamina, thieves had broken in and stolen the best of them. The bodies of the foxes had been found less than a mile away, stripped of their pelts. All this told on the health of Lebraux. He had become so irritable that Renny's heart had gone out to his wife and daughter. When Lebraux had at last been confined to the house he had begged Renny to come to him as often as possible. He could forget his sense of disappointment, of failure, of impending disaster in Renny's presence. "I like you!" he had often exclaimed. "I like you to be near me. You and I have an appreciation of the fine and sensitive things of life." Renny had never been told this before, and it pleased him. And so they had talked of horses and foxes and women.

Lebraux had taken to drinking brandy. He had had uncontrollable outbreaks of despair, during which he would threaten to do away with himself. Only the presence of Renny would calm him. Often Mrs. Lebraux had sent her young daughter all the way to Jalna with a note for Renny, begging him to go to her help. When, in January, Lebraux had died, Renny had spent half his time in the house. Her brother had kept out of the way as much as possible, for he shirked the responsibility that he felt was moving toward him.

It had been Renny's idea to invite the mother and daughter, an idea that had not met with much favour from the rest of the family. Mrs. Lebraux had called on Alayne soon after her marriage. The call had been returned, and there had been an end to intimacy. Alayne had felt pity and, at the same time, had been repelled by the family. The uncles had agreed with her that they were strange people. "Not at all the sort of people who *used* to settle here." Meggie had not called. Piers was contemptuous of Lebraux, his failures and, what Piers considered, his spinelessness. He made fun of Mrs. Lebraux's thick yellow hair, that was turning dark in streaks, her round, light-lashed eyes, and red hands. But Renny had his way. The poor woman had never been anywhere since her husband's death, and the little girl would keep Wake in countenance.

If Mrs. Leigh and Ada had looked like sisters as they entered the drawing-room, Mrs. Lebraux and little Pauline seemed of no relation to each other. She had a blonde, hardy, wholesome look, was the daughter of a Newfoundlander who had made a good deal of money in the fisheries, and somehow lost it, and she resembled him. Pauline was like Lebraux, a thin, dark child of fifteen, in white, with the promise of some beauty. Her parents had met on the great toboggan slide by the Château Frontenac, and had precipitately slid into matrimony.

It was an odd, mixed party, Alayne thought, as they filed in to dinner, but it was the first time she had entertained since her marriage, and she was rather wrought up over it, fearful lest all should not go well. But she need not have had any apprehension on that score. Where there were Whiteoaks gathered there was no danger of dullness. The family was all talking at once, as a garden of hardy flowers might burst into vigorous bloom at the first encouragement of the sun. A festive occasion, the prospect of a good dinner with plenty to drink with it, was sun enough for them. Ernest took in Mrs. Leigh; Nicholas, his old flame, Miss Lacey; Vaughan, Mrs. Fennel; Finch, Ada Leigh; Renny, Mrs. Lebraux, with the others distributing as congenially as possible down to the two youngest, who came last, smiling gravely at each other, she half a head taller than he.

Whatever Mrs. Wragge's faults might be, it would never be said of her that she was not a good cook. Fowls, under her hand, shed their earthly plumage and turned into glistening forms of celestial sweetness. Her vegetables were drained at the critical moment, the pastry was light. Only her pudding was heavy, and there was no pudding tonight. Wakefield could scarcely credit his own senses when he saw all the best china and silver on the table at once. Things that usually lived in cabinets, behind glass, were now on the table looking as though they were used every day. Several wineglasses were clustered at each place, even his own and Pauline's.

"Have you ever been to anything like this before?" he asked her, trying to feel not too important.

"No; isn't it lovely?" She smiled, and he thought how prettily her lip curled from her little white teeth. He noticed her long white hands, then stared at her mother across the table.

"You don't look a bit like your mother," he remarked, settling his chin above his Eton collar.

"No, I look like my daddy." She stopped eating, and withdrew into herself, a look of sad remoteness shadowing her small face.

"*My* father," he observed, looking hard at her, "died before I was born."

She was startled into regarding him with an almost fearful interest. "Did he really? I didn't know they *could*. I always thought you had to have both father and mother when you were born."

"I didn't. My father was dead and my mother died *when* I was born."

She breathed—"How awful for you!"

He agreed.

"Yes," he said. "I'm what is called a posthumous child. I think it has preyed on my mind. I think it is what has made me so delicate. I'm not able to go to school, you know. I go to Mr. Fennel for lessons, but I haven't been for weeks because of the weather."

"I wish I could go to him, too. That would be nice, wouldn't it?"

He looked dubious.

"Yes... but you're a Catholic, aren't you?"

She nodded. "But Mother isn't. I don't believe she'd mind. Do you think he'd have me?"

"Well, he might. If you'd promise not to try to convert me or anything. He'd not like to risk that."

"Oh, I'd promise!"

Around the table conversation flowed easily. Alayne perhaps was less at ease than the others. She was so anxious that things should go well, especially because of the Leighs. Rags was a constant irritation to her. His shabby trigness, his air of anxiety over the two hired maids, his bending over Renny to whisper to him with an expression of portentous significance. And why did Renny grin up at him in that way? She did wish that Renny wouldn't talk to Rags at mealtime. Rags seemed always to be hovering behind his chair like an evil genius, and Renny never looked more like his grandmother than when he was grinning up at Rags. What was he saying to that Mrs. Lebraux? She strained her ears to catch the words.

He was saying—"Well, I'll be very grateful if you will let me have the use of your stable. I could keep two horses there. We're terribly short of room, as it is."

Mr. Fennel, on the other side of Mrs. Lebraux, joined in. "I am glad to hear that you are staying on in your house, Mrs. Lebraux. I do hope you are comfortable."

She turned her round pale-lashed eyes on him. "Comfortable! No, I'm not very comfortable. But I'm getting along somehow—"

Then Ernest's musical voice came to Alayne. He was saying to Mrs. Leigh:

"Yes, I'm doing a work on Shakespeare. I've been working on it for many years now. One can't hurry with that sort of thing. But I do feel that the result will be..."

Nicholas was booming to his old flame, Miss Lacey:

"He's never talked since she died. Isn't it extraordinary? There he sits on his perch, in her room, just brooding."

Then came Meg's voice, as she claimed Mr. Fennel's attention. "You'd never believe the things she does and says. Sometimes she quite frightens me. Only this morning, she said—'Mummy, I want to see God!'"

Pheasant and Arthur Leigh were laughing together. She was saying—"But, truly, I know a man who saw a two-headed foal…"

Finch's head was inclined toward Ada Leigh. Alayne caught just a snatch: "Oh, I dare say I'll travel round a bit. You can't stick in one place forever."

How the Whiteoaks loved to talk, she thought. From all about her their voices came, and yet their plates were the first to be swept clean of each course. They seldom asked a question. They took their world as they found it, without curiosity. Only Piers and Miss Pink, whom he had taken in, did not trouble to speak, but were devoting themselves to the business of eating and drinking. She lived alone, and her great economy was food. Now she had allowed her gauze scarf to slide from her shoulders, for even it had seemed to impede her progress toward repletion. Piers was drinking a good deal. His lips were taking on that sweet, mysterious curve they had when he was becoming oblivious of his sur-roundings, and only wished to be left alone that he might give his full attention to the pleasant phenomenon that was taking place inside him.

There was champagne. Nicholas had seen to that. Rags could not have been more solemn about the drawing of the corks if he had bought and paid for it out of his own savings. Something intangible but vital drew them all nearer each other. The fingers of their spirits touched.

Mr. Fennel rose, glass in hand, to propose Finch's health. Finch saw it coming, and drooped still closer to Ada Leigh for support. His hour had struck. He was twenty-one and Mr. Fennel was going to propose his health.

The confusion of voices sank into a gentle sigh. All eyes, made brighter or dreamier by wine, were turned on the Rector. All eyes, with the exception of Piers's, which were looking into a tranced and pleasing space. Mr. Fennel said:

"What I am about to do is very agreeable to me. That is to propose the health of a member of this household who today has reached the estate of manhood. It is not easy for me to believe this, because it seems only a few years ago since I held him in my arms at the font and baptized him in the church his grandfather had built. His grandfather had built the church in what was at that time a sparsely settled community. He established there the religion of his fathers. And his descendants have never failed in their support of that church. At Jalna he established a family which preserves today the traditions of a fine old English family, as few families do in these times of standardisation and irreverence for tradition... The memory of his devoted wife—whose presence I seem to feel among us tonight—will long remain fresh in the minds of all who knew her. Her faults—for none of us are perfect— were far outshone by her virtues... This member of her family who has just attained the age of twenty-one—an age that seems quite unbelievably fresh and glowing to me—has been the companion of my sons all his life. With them he has run in and out of the Rectory a thousand times on the mysterious quests of boyhood. In their room they have held with him innumerable conferences on the mysterious business of youth. He has enlivened many an evening for us with his music. We have known him in many moods, but none of us

have ever known him to do a cruel or shabby thing. I wish
him well from the bottom of my heart. I know you will all
join me in this. I give you the toast—Finch Whiteoak!"

Mr. Fennel sat down with the unruffled air of a man who
had just as lief make a speech as not.

Finch crouched between Ada Leigh and his sister-in-law
Alayne with the air of a man to whom the making of a
speech would be a task of appalling torture. The heads of
those about him swam toward him goggle-eyed like goldfish
in a round glass bowl. There was clapping of hands, glasses
clinked. The glass of the bowl shivered into splinters, and
Finch was left gasping, looking piteously like a stranded
goldfish himself, trying to rise to his feet.

Ada Leigh smiled soft encouragement. She said—"It will
be all right... just anything that comes into your head...
now!" She touched his arm with an impelling gesture.

Renny's voice came down the table, metallic and commanding. "Up you get, Finch!" and others added jovially—
"Speech, speech!"

But it was Alayne who got him to his feet. Her father and
her grandfathers had been New England professors, moni-
tors of the young. Out of the background of their authority,
her blue-grey eyes looked dominantly into his, saying—
"Rise and give tongue!" Her fingers clutched his under the
tablecloth so tightly that it hurt. He twisted his own about
them as he spoke.

How different this was from doing a part in a play! Then,
in velvet cloak or in vagabond tatters, he could abandon himself to the portrayal of another's moods. But now he was
simply his naked self, and a dozen words were harder to get
out than a torrent of talk on the stage. He heard his voice
with a curious kind of croak in it.

"It's frightfully good of you—all. I never had such nice things said about me before... in all my life... and I don't quite know what to do about it. Mr. Fennel and Mrs. Fennel couldn't possibly have been kinder to me if I'd been their own son... and, of course, everyone present... has been the same..."

"Hear, hear," said Piers, without moving his lips.

"I can't tell you how much I am enjoying... this occasion," he continued, looking the picture of despair. "If I should live to be as old as my grandmother—"

"You'll never do it," interrupted Piers, without any appearance of having spoken.

Renny threw Piers a fiery look down the table.

"I'd never forget this dinner... and... I do most heartily"—here his voice broke—"thank you. I hope no one here will ever be sorry that... sorry that..." Good Lord, what was he about to say? Sorry that what? Oh, yes, sorry that Gran had left him her money—but he couldn't say that—it would be horrible—but what could he say?—"Hope no one here will ever live to be sorry—" he stammered, and sought the ruddy sunrise of Piers's face for inspiration—"be sorry—"

"That we let you live till you were twenty-one," supplied Piers without seeming to utter a word.

There was a burst of hilarious applause. The hero of the occasion sat down.

He took a gulp of champagne.

"You did splendidly," whispered Ada Leigh, and Alayne squeezed his fingers before she uncurled hers from them. He was flushed, and happily conscious that he might have done worse. He had been delighted at the burst of applause and laughter, though he could not quite recall what he had said that was so witty.

After the speeches, voices rose to a babble. The faces about the table were changed to a noticeable degree. Those which were ordinarily vivacious became dreamy, those which were usually somewhat stolid were transfigured into liveliness. The two maids stood together motionless now, like black-and-white drawings of maids, unbelievably trig. Rags drifted ceaselessly around the table refilling glasses, the creator, it seemed, of this animation, these changes of expression, this babble. Ernest had got to the point of telling Mrs. Leigh of his life in old London, the times he and Nicholas had had. Nicholas had reached the point of intimating to Miss Lacey, by look rather than by word, that he wished he and she might have been joined together in wedlock, rather than he and that other from whom he was divorced. Renny and Mrs. Lebraux were engaged in a low, earnest conversation which excluded the existence of all others. Piers had picked up Miss Pink's gauze scarf from the floor where it had fallen and laid it about his own shoulders. He, only, did not talk, but his lips were curved in that same enigmatic, Mona Lisa smile.

The rugs had been taken up in the drawing-room and hall and the floor waxed, but it was late before anyone suggested that they dance. It was George Fennel who sat down at the piano, very square, very upright, his hands drawing insidious sweetness from the keys. The latest dances from the world of jazz were tossed by George as invitation to this mixed company, some of whom still danced in the style of forty years ago. And how gallantly they responded to the invitation! They thought it "queer stuff—very modern, you know—and not at all easy to keep step with." But somehow they contrived to do it, the couples moving in small circles, conversing lightly and gaily all the while. Nicholas and

Ernest with the two Miss Laceys, with whom they had danced the quadrille, the polka, and the schottische on this very floor when they were young men and girls. Mr. Fennel had Pheasant tightly clasped to him, his beard, now and again, tickling her bare shoulder. Like a captive bird she cast wistful glances at her mate, wishing she might fly down the room with him, in long graceful strides, their bodies as one. And there he was dancing with Miss Pink, who was quite old enough to be his mother!

The younger men had no flowers of speech to offer to their partners. Up and down the drawing-room, in and out of the hall, they moved, their faces as void of expression as a clean slate, their very souls set in the mould of jazz.

Miss Pink had been afraid she could not do it. But when once Piers had got hold of her she found that she could, and not only that, but she wished she might go on doing it forever. As for Piers, he scarcely knew whom he was dancing with—old or young, skilful or amateurish, it did not signify. She had been at hand when his forceful body had responded to the inexorable call of the dance.

Alayne was dancing with graceful Arthur Leigh. Wakefield had almost more than he could cope with in Meggie's solid frame. Meg had an eye on Maurice and Mrs. Leigh, who seemed to her to be dancing altogether too well.

Finch had been going to ask Ada Leigh to dance, but had turned away as he saw Tom Fennel loping towards her. He must not be selfish at his own party. With whom would he dance then? He looked rather vaguely about the room. There was Mrs. Fennel in a comfortable chair near the fire, with a dish of crystallised fruit beside her. And, in the farthest corner, on the settee, was Mrs. Lebraux in her black dress, with Renny keeping her company, his back half turned to the

dancers. And staring into the cabinet of curios from India
was the Lebraux child, her skirt too short, her legs too long,
and the back of her head looking as though it needed comb-
ing. Her hair stuck out in thick black tufts, giving her an odd,
elfin look. He went to her and said:

"Would you like to dance, Pauline?"

She glanced at him over her shoulder and shook her
head. "Can you dance?" He felt a stirring of curiosity about
her.

Her gaze had returned to the cabinet again, but she
answered in a low voice:

"Yes. But I don't think I should. Mother isn't."

"I see. But you're such a kid I don't think she'd mind.
Shall I ask her?"

She turned and looked at him searchingly, as though
wondering whether or no she should like to dance with him.
Then she went sedately to her mother and bent over her.

She came back smiling and put her hand into Finch's.

"It's all right. Both Mother and Mr. Whiteoak say to
dance." Her face lit up and she moved her shoulders as
though eager to begin.

She was so thin that she felt nothing more than a wand
in Finch's arms, yet there was a wild strength in her movements. He thought she was like a little breeze-blown boat
tugging at its anchor. The music was swift, even feverish, for
this second dance, but not swift enough for her. He bent to
look into her face. He had scarcely seen her, yet he had the
impression of beauty. He saw the thick hair above the low
forehead, with its pencilled brows, the eyelids that had a foreign look, the half-closed eyes, of which he could not make
out the colour, the childish nose, the wide, rather thin-lipped
mouth with its upward curve at the corners, the little white

chin, the long, graceful neck. He could not tell where the beauty was, but he was satisfied that it was there or would be there.

"Who taught you to dance?" he asked.

"Oh, I had lessons in Quebec. Daddy and I used to dance a lot together. I can dance alone too. Solo dances, you know."

"How splendid! I wish you'd dance one tonight."

"Oh, no, I couldn't!"

"Not to please me? It's my birthday, you know."

"I couldn't *possibly*!" There was a note of hurt in her voice.

"I'm sorry," he said. "But perhaps some other time you will. You're going to stay on here, aren't you?"

"Yes—if we can make it pay."

"The fox-farming, you mean?"

"Yes. And we may go into poultry, too."

"Aren't you afraid the foxes will eat the poultry?"

"That shows how much you know about it! They're kept absolutely separate."

"It will mean a lot of work."

"We don't mind that, if only we can make it pay." Her slender body seemed to tighten with resolve. She swayed and dipped and turned like a bird, he thought. And she had a hard time before her, he was afraid. He would like to help them if he only knew how to go about it. This having of so much money opened up new channels to one, gave one a troubling sense of responsibility toward one's fellows.

"Mother and I do all the housework," she was saying—"dish-washing, sweeping, and everything. She does outdoor work too. She's awfully strong."

"Do you really?" He was astonished, for he had never seen his sister do anything but take care of herself; and Alayne and

Pheasant were very much the same, except that Pheasant looked after Mooey, and that none too well, he thought.

He saw Ada Leigh watching them, and he wondered what she thought of the child. When, at last, they danced together, and he had reproached her, as he had a feeling she wanted him to do, for having eluded him, he asked her.

"I could not help being amused by the pair of you," she answered; "you looked so odd together."

"Did we?" He was a little nettled. "Well, I suppose I look odd at any time."

She gave him one of her challenging looks. "Not at all! You don't look odd dancing with me, I'm very sure. But that girl is almost ridiculous, with her hair and her terrifically long, thin legs. And that sort of do-or-die look."

"Well, she may look queer dancing, but it's like heaven to dance with her!"

"I'm so glad, because one gets so little of heaven here on earth, doesn't one?"

Finch observed solemnly—"I'm afraid she's going to be one of those women that other women don't like."

"Oh, I don't think you need worry about that."

"I'm not worrying. Why should I worry about it?"

"I don't know, I'm sure. But you are."

"No, I'm not."

"Yes, you are."

"All I feel is a great pity for her and her mother. They've had a hard time, and, I'm afraid; they'll have a harder."

"What a *strange-looking* woman Mrs. Lebraux is!"

"Yes, rather. Piers calls her 'Dirty-locks—' Lord, I shouldn't have told you that! But her hair is rather queer, and he has a brutal way of putting things. I notice that women don't like her either."

"I do," said Ada. "I love her."

"For heaven's sake! Why?"

"Because she lets you alone and devotes herself to your brother."

"But she's years and years older than I am."

"How clever of you to have found that out! I should have expected you to insist that she was younger, you're so chivalrous."

"And you're so detestable!"

They stopped dancing. They were in the dark end of the hall, alone. They clung to each other a moment, motionless. Then he took her in his arms and kissed her again and again on the mouth. She lay there acquiescent, the perfume of her going through all his nerves as the champagne had. She was like champagne, cool, softly stinging, potent to the senses.

They began to dance again as smoothly as though they had never lost a beat, when Renny, with the Little Lebraux, glided into the hall. It seemed to Finch that Renny cast a sharp look at Ada, as though he suspected her of something, and he had a curious feeling that Ada had rather have been kissed by Renny than by him, even though she had been more than acquiescent, had kissed him back. Pauline's lips were parted in a joyful smile, showing her very white teeth; she clutched Renny's sleeve in one thin white hand. Her expression was that of a young creature that has been unhappy far too long, and snatches at some sudden pleasure with almost fierce desire.

She and her mother left early. Then the Leighs, with a long motor ride before them. Somehow or other the Fennels packed the Miss Laceys and Miss Pink into their car. The Vaughans were the last to go.

"And I really don't care very much about trusting myself to him in a car, the way he is," Meg said.

Renny looked his brother-in-law over.

"He'll be all right after a breath of fresh air," he assured her. "I'll open the windows on him."

Maurice watched this move for his revivification with interest. As soon as the window was opened he started the car, and it sped across the lawn, scraping the end of an ice-covered garden seat, and on three wheels gained the drive.

Nicholas was declaiming in the drawing-room.

"I might never have had gout in my life, I was so free from it tonight. As lively as a three-year-old."

"And I," said Ernest, "never thought of my dinner again. And I ate everything!"

"It's remarkable what exhilaration does."

"If only there is no evil reaction!"

"Mrs. Leigh," declared Nicholas, "is the prettiest woman of her age I have seen in years."

"But that daughter of hers!" cried Pheasant. "I can't stand her. She takes care to let you know that her gown comes from Paris."

"Yes," agreed Alayne; and she referred to London as 'my London!'"

"Such swank!"

"Still," protested Ernest, balancing himself on the balls of his feet, "they are a charming family, the Leighs. And really intellectual."

"I don't agree," said Alayne. "To me, they seem very superficial."

"To me, too!" cried Pheasant.

Finch interrupted, hurt for his friend's sake. "Not Arthur. Arthur's absolutely sound."

"I'd like to give him a sound hiding," observed Renny, lighting his pipe, "and knock some of the effeminacy out of him."

"Listen to the he-man!" exclaimed Pheasant.

Renny took her by the nape and rumpled her hair into a brown crest.

"Mrs. Leigh," said Ernest, "was greatly interested in my annotation of Shakespeare."

His two nieces by marriage looked at him pityingly.

The two young women went, as with one impulse, to the mirror above the mantel that had reflected so many of the scenes at Jalna, and examined themselves in the glass. The five men regarded their backs and the reflection of their faces with incurious interest. They were interested, as always, in this manifestation of sex, but they knew them too well to feel the sting of curiosity.

Alayne said, turning round to them:

"It was rather a nuisance Mrs. Lebraux not dancing. It kept one of the best dancers always at her side entertaining her."

Neither Nicholas nor Ernest had sat by Mrs. Lebraux, consequently they felt a little irritated by this remark. Ernest said:

"I talked to her for a moment, but she scarcely took the trouble to answer. I can't say I admire her."

"I shouldn't have minded sitting by her for a bit," said Nicholas, "but she seemed not to lack attention." He looked at Renny.

Renny looked back. "Someone had to be decent to the poor woman. The girls were awfully cool to her."

"I scarcely know her," said Alayne.

"That is no reason why you should be cool to her," returned Renny.

"She's one of those women," asserted Pheasant, sagaciously—"who don't care a bit about other women. She's
simply *mad* about men!"

"How unjust you are," said Renny. "She's been in great
trouble. She only liked to talk to me because she is used to
me—I've been a friend of Lebraux."

Piers said—"I shouldn't mind the looks of her so much,
if only she'd darken her eyelashes and touch her hair up so
it would be all one colour."

Renny turned on him angrily. "She'd never do anything
to her hair. She's not that sort. She never thinks of her personal appearance."

His wife and his sister-in-law looked at him scornfully.

"Well, she spent about ten minutes on her face in the
dressing-room!" cried Pheasant.

"Dear me," said Ernest, "what was she doing to it?"

"Wiping her tears away," suggested Piers.

"Tears!" scoffed Pheasant. "Mrs. Patch, who helped nurse
Mr. Lebraux, told Mrs. Wragge that they quarrelled half the
time and the other half they didn't speak."

"You've little to do," said Renny, "to be gossiping with
the servants about Mrs. Lebraux."

"I wasn't gossiping. She just told me. And besides, you
often repeat things that Rags told you."

The master of Jalna gripped his pipe and drew back his
lips from his teeth. He could think of nothing to say, so he
glared at her.

"She looks healthy," said Nicholas.

"Such crude health lacks charm for me," said Ernest.

"Renny only danced once this evening," observed
Pheasant, "and that was with her child."

"I had hoped," said Alayne slowly, "that no one had noticed that."

"Heigho!" said Piers, in an endeavour to imitate his grandmother. "I want something more to eat. I want it right away."

His Uncle Ernest looked at him reprovingly. "Is it possible, Piers, that you are mimicking my mother?"

"Oh, no," answered Piers, innocently. "Not consciously, at any rate. But I was thinking, just a moment ago, how much she would have enjoyed tonight, and I suppose the thought of her stayed in my head."

Ernest smiled at him. No one could help it, with his face so pink and that enigmatic smile on his lips. He led the way to the dining room and got a decanter of whiskey and a siphon of soda water from the sideboard. He sat down by the table, which had been cleared and reduced to its normal size. Nicholas, Ernest, and Finch followed him. Pheasant stood a moment in the doorway before going to bed. She said:

"I do think it was rather a shame, Piers, the way you whirled poor little Miss Pink around. She looked positively dazed."

"You're just jealous of her," said Piers.

She ran over to him and bent her head to his ear.

"Don't be silly, darling! And please, please, don't drink much more! It's bad enough for me to see my father going home in the state he did without seeing my husband come to bed in another..."

"Another what?" he mumbled against her cheek.

"Another state. Of intoxication, of course."

"All right, little 'un. Run along now."

Renny had discovered Wakefield sound asleep on the settee in the drawing-room and had carried him up to bed.

Alayne had followed, angry with herself for being irritated by the sight of the child's legs dangling, his arm tightly around Renny's neck.

She went straight to her own room. She felt definitely unhappy, tired in spirit yet restless in body. She fidgeted about the room, exposing, with a touch of self-pity, her bare arms and shoulders to its chill air. How often during the day she had looked forward to dancing with Renny that evening! And he had danced only once, and then with a child. Then, when the guests were gone, he had taken on that protective tone about Mrs. Lebraux. Just because she had chosen to lean on him! And there was Wakefield to be carried to bed, who should have been sent there hours ago... She heard Mooey whining in the next room as Pheasant took him up... She heard Wakefield's voice raised complainingly in Renny's room... Children were too much in evidence in this household...

She was getting cold, yet she could not go to bed. She thought she would go to Pheasant's room and talk to her for a little... Really, Mrs. Lebraux was a strange-looking woman... something animal about her... lucky for the child that she had taken after the father... She went into the passage, but, instead of going to Pheasant's door, she went to Renny's. She laid her two hands against the panels, and stood motionless there.

Very soon Renny came out, drawing the support of the door from her. But she still retained her posture, and stood before him, hands raised as though in wonder. His brows flew up.

"Well—you here, Alayne!"

He took her hands and drew them together at the back of his neck, looking with solicitude down into her face.

"Tired, old girl?"

She nodded her head several times, frowning and pushing out her lips. Never during her married life with Eden had she shown him this mood of childish petulance. In truth, she had not in all her life shown it to anyone but Renny: had not known it was in her to frown and pout, and be at once both angry and clinging, and, if she could have seen the expression of her own face at this moment, she would have felt mortified, angry with herself.

He kissed her. "Were you long at the door? Why didn't you come in?"

"Not very long... I didn't want to. What was the good?"

"What do you want?"

"You."

"Well, you've got me, haven't you?"

"You're going downstairs to the others."

"Not if you don't want me to."

"Yes, do go, please! I don't want you to stay with me." She tried to push him from her.

"Yes, you do!" He tightened his arms about her.

"Well, I don't see why I should. I'm not at all necessary to you."

"What rot you talk!"

"How am I necessary, then?"

"You know without my telling you."

"You will make me hate you!"

"Why should women always think of only one thing!"

"I suppose they know the truth."

"My dear child, you make me tired!"

"I know I do." Her voice broke.

He picked her up, as he had picked up Wakefield, and carried her into her room. It was lit only by moonlight. The new mauve silk bedspread caught and held the light like a dreaming pool in a wood. The moon was sinking.

Its last rays were shining into the dining room too. Its light was enough for the business they had in hand there. Nicholas, unmindful of gout, had given himself up to it. Ernest, unmindful of indigestion, had given himself up to it. Piers, forgetful of wifely admonition, had given himself up to it. Finch, mindful of his new estate, entered heart and soul into it. The decanter and the siphon, with amber and cold white lights in their respective parts, moved slowly around the table. The moonlight blotted age out of two faces and stamped age into two, so that the quartette appeared to be all of one age, and that was ageless.

Finch said: "I wish one of you would tell me what it was I said that was so funny. They were making such a row when I sat down that it knocked it clean out of my head."

"I can't remember," answered Nicholas, "but I know it was damned witty. In fact, I've never heard a better after-dinner speech."

"Nor I," agreed Ernest. "Just the right amount of sentiment mixed with real wit. It's a special talent in itself, this after-dinner speaking."

"I thought the Rector spoke very well," said Finch judicially.

"Yes, he spoke very well. But you were better. I only wish I could remember just what it was you said at the last."

"Something about the joy of living," suggested Piers.

"Well, that's not very new," said Finch, rather disappointed.

"Seems to be new to you!"

"Life," said Nicholas, "is experience."

"I don't agree," said Ernest. "I think life is work."

Finch said gravely—"I suppose you have all heard of my decision"—he rolled the words "my decision" on his tongue—"my decision not to go on with my University course."

"It would have been better," said Ernest, "if you had made up your mind to go to England and take a university course there."

"No, no," interrupted his brother, "the boy's quite right. He knows what he's fitted for. And I say that he is a musical genius." His eyes, glittering strangely in the moonlight, were fixed on Finch.

"I'm so glad you think so, Uncle Nick! And you thought my speech was all right, didn't you?"

"Absolutely. From the moment you rose to your feet, you were, as the Italians say, *pere bene*."

"Meaning," said Piers, "full of beans."

"Exactly."

Finch half filled his glass with Black and White and aimed a squirt of soda at it. "I think, just among ourselves, that I may say that my aim is to live an unselfish life."

"You couldn't have a better," commended Ernest.

"From my own experience I know that bringing happiness to others brings happiness to oneself."

"What form," asked Nicholas, "is your unselfishness going to take?"

"I should suggest," said Piers, "making a pool of it."

Finch turned toward him somewhat truculently. "What do you mean?—a pool of it?"

Piers pondered a moment, and then said: "Your unselfishness, of course. Sunshine idea. A brighter Jalna."

"Don't be silly," said Finch. "I'm in dead earnest. I want to do something for each one of you, and that's a fact."

"Say it in writing," put in Piers.

"My word is as good as—"

"Of course it is," said Nicholas. "We all know it is."

Finch proceeded—"I'm very glad that Renny hasn't joined us, because he never seems to see eye to eye with me in anything."

"Where is he?" asked Ernest. "I hadn't missed him before. Indeed I quite thought he was here." He peered about the room.

"Been sent to bed," said Piers; "he was a naughty boy, poor fellow!"

Finch said—"Uncle Nick and Uncle Ernie, if I were to invite you to come on a trip with me to England at my expense, would you accept?"

"Delighted to accept," answered Nicholas instantly.

Ernest reached across the table and took Finch's hand and shook it. "Dear boy—dear boy—" was all he could say.

"Me, too!" said Piers. "What are you going to do for me?"

"What should you choose?"

"Give me time. Let me sleep on it."

"It's settled then, is it? You two are coming with me to visit Aunt Augusta?"

Ernest squeezed the hand he held, the hour, his condition, the invitation, filling him with an almost overwhelming emotion. Nicholas accepted airily, as though he were bestowing a favour.

"I will take you to some of my old haunts in London," he promised, straightening his shoulders and drawing his chin against his collar.

Both uncles then began to talk about the years they had spent in England, repeating, at first, incidents that the nephews had heard before, but, as the night drew on, and as the decanter emptied, drawing from remote places in their memories events unrecalled in years, like forgotten birds' nests dragged forth from an old belfry, or rusty anchors drawn up from the deep.

Some of these memories were disgraceful, and, in the telling of them, the two elders became more and more youthful, breaking into sudden uncontrolled laughter, their speech falling into the catchwords of their day. The young men, on the contrary, grew graver and more judicial with each glass, looking as though they did not quite approve of the levity of the others, Finch even going to the length once of giving some sound advice. In order that he might hurt no one's feelings he addressed the advice to the siphon in a kind of chant, and when no one gave any heed to him he shed a few unnoticed tears.

But, when the moment came when sing they must, he was ready. Ernest, who loved very old songs, ballads, madrigals, and the like, began "Summer is acumen in," in his still excellent voice. A tenor, a lusty baritone, and a bass joined in with:

> Loudly sing, cuckoo!
> Grows the seed, and blows the mead,
> And grows the wood anew,
> Sing cuckoo!
> The ewe is bleating for her lamb;
> Lows for her calf the cow.

The bleating and the lowing, so loud and mellow, brought a fifth member of the family on the scene. This was Renny, clad in dressing gown and slippers. He stared at the revellers with ironical amusement.

"Well," he said, "you're a lovely looking lot!"

The moon was gone, and the dawn creeping in showed them wan and dishevelled in their evening clothes.

"You'll wake the women and the kids," he said. "They've been asleep for hours. Don't you think you've had enough?"

"I've made serious decision," said Finch.

"What?"

"To go to bed."

V

THE DEPARTURE

To ERNEST it seemed positively portentous that Sasha should die just before his departure for England. It was as though she had comprehended what the state of his mind must be at the thought of parting from her. She was fourteen years old, and though she seemed to be in perfect health she required certain luxuries, certain attentions, to keep her so. On whom could Ernest have depended to care for her? Alayne had promised, but her attitude towards all animals was detached. Pheasant might have done very well, but there was Mooey, always at hand to lift her up by the wrong part or to roll on her as she slept before the fire. That left a choice among Wakefield, the Wragges, and Bessie the kitchenmaid. Ernest shivered before the choice and almost felt that he should not go.

As he fondled her with concern he noticed the look of understanding in her translucent amber eyes. She was standing on him, rhythmically kneading his stomach with her forepaws, as she so often did. He fancied, half-whimsically, that she was aware of his weak digestion and that she held the belief that gentle massage, such as she gave him, would benefit him. The benign expression she wore, when she kneaded him thus, encouraged the belief. Now to the expression of benignity was added the look of understanding.

The very next morning he had found her dead on his eiderdown. Curled up, as though sleeping, with a look of blissful peace—but dead. It was as though she had not been able to bear the anxiety in his eyes and had willed her spirit to depart in the night, setting him free from the claims of love.

He had lain back again, pulled the covers over his head, and felt much shaken. He remembered the morning she had had her last kitten on this very bed. Just given one yell, as of triumph (for she was then old), and had it, about six o'clock in the morning. He remembered when she had been given to him by one of the Lacey girls fourteen years before, a tiny golden ball of sportiveness. He had been rather bored then at the thought of owning a kitten, had not much wanted her... a dog had killed her last kitten, and now she was gone...

Everyone was sympathetic. They had dug a grave for her in the prettiest corner of the garden, just where the old stone urn marked the spot. Wakefield had filled the grave with marsh marigolds and had curled her beautiful tail about her like a plume.

Ernest thought that Nicholas was very callous in the leaving of Nip. Nip, to be sure, was not so fine fibred as Sasha, but still he merited something more than the brief injunction thrown off by Nicholas at the supper table, on the night before departure—"For heaven's sake, look after Nip!" That had been all. But it was Nick's way.

The two months just passed had flown for them all. The spring had been backward, then forward. Their spirits had been up, then down. It was such an upheaval. At first the mere stupendousness of it had been exhilarating. But later, the thought of how they would be scattered was like a hovering cloud. Augusta was in England; Eden was in France or England—no one knew which; and soon Nicholas, Ernest, and Finch would be on the ocean. They felt afresh the blank left by the death of Adeline.

When old steamer trunks were carried down from the attic, rubbed up and new labels written for them, all felt definitely that the moment was at hand. New luggage was bought by Finch.

He had paid much more for it than he thought was necessary, but Arthur Leigh had been with him when he bought it and had insisted on the best. Finch was afraid of what Renny might say about such expenditure, but he had said nothing. Since the day Finch had announced his intention of going no more to the University, Renny, after his first outburst, had been cold towards him. Piers, on the other hand, had been warmer than ever before. But neither one would give him any advice about his money. If he approached Renny with—"I say, George Fennel thinks I ought to invest something in New York stocks and not be satisfied with such a low rate of interest," Renny would shrug and say—"It's none of my business. Do as you like with it." And he would turn away.

If he sounded Piers on the same subject, Piers would laugh and say—"You're going to have the time of your young life, aren't you?" And, if Finch persisted, he might add—"Well, George ought to know something about it; he's in the business. I should think it would be rather fun to speculate a bit."

Finch felt like a half-fledged bird suddenly pushed from the nest. After being constantly supervised in his spending, ordered here and there, sometimes tyrannised over, this sudden thrusting on him of responsibility bewildered him, skimmed the cream of his pleasure in his inheritance.

It was as though they had formed a conspiracy against him. His uncles never referred to the money in his presence.

It was as though they said—"By hook or crook he got what we should have had. Now let us see what he will do with it."

He had been almost frightened when the bank book had been put into his hand, when he had interviewed the bank manager and been shown the list of Gran's solid and conservative investments. But George had scoffed at them. George had said that, aided by one versed in the fluctuations of the market, Finch might with "speculation" double his fortune.

His head was in a whirl. It felt hot most of the time. He found that he could not quiet his nerves by playing the piano. The virtue seemed to have gone out of it. His spirit, like a captive bird that had been wont to sing in captivity, now found itself baffled in its freedom, beating itself against the walls of change.

Alayne realised something of his bewilderment, his loneliness. They had several long talks. She felt anxiety at the thought of his giving up old Adeline's safe investments for more spectacular ones, on the advice of George Fennel. Yet, like Finch, her imagination was captured by the thought that he might greatly increase his capital by careful speculation. George had offered some tempting suggestions, and she had heard from American friends who had made large sums of late. She wrote to the head of the New York publishing house for which she had been a reader, and asked his advice. His reply was an effort to stress cautiousness, but he could not conceal jubilation over the result of his own recent investments. In the same week came a letter from Miss Trent, with whom she had shared an apartment in New York, telling joyously of her own good luck. Renny and Piers, the two uncles, Maurice Vaughan, were children, she thought, in matters of business. To be sure, the first two exhibited a certain shrewdness in their own province, but she had seen and heard so much of mismanagement at Jalna. There was no use in consulting them. And added to their incompetence was their disinclination even to speak of Finch's inheritance. If in some unexpected way the subject of the grandmother's money came up, a feeling of tension was at once apparent. They shied at the mention of it, as skittish horses will shy at their own gatepost.

Alayne took her own small capital, left her by her father, out of the Government stocks where it had been invested, and bought Universal Autos with it.

When the stock began to rise steadily she could not resist telling Finch what she had done, and, after that, it was impossible for her to restrain him. But she made him tell Renny of the project. "Invest it as you like," Renny said curtly. "I don't know anything about stocks. I've never had anything to invest." Finch knew that it was not jealousy that made him curt, but anger that he should have, at the instant of attaining his majority, refused to return to the University. This prompt refusal had symbolised to Renny the rejection by Finch of all further authority, of supervision by him as the head of the clan.

How bitter Meg Vaughan would be, Alayne thought, if Finch were to lose even a small amount of money by following her example. Meg had always regarded her as an interloper, and to have some tangible injury to lay at her door would give her real satisfaction. Finch must go, therefore,

and talk the matter over with the Vaughans. He was not loth
to do this, even though he was afraid they would discourage
the investment. He was in a condition of sensitiveness which
made him desirous of discussing his affairs with anyone who
was willing to do so. Himself and the hundred thousand dollars that were his seemed to him of vast importance, looming above all other subjects. Within an hour after it was
decided that he should go to Vaughanlands he was on his
way.

There was no doubt about the arrival of spring, but as yet
no manifestation of it was visible in the landscape beyond an
indefinite swelling of tiny leaf-buds which gave the trees the
appearance of being seen behind a veil. Or, like love unrecog-
nised, it had come, causing the heart to turn, but as yet making little difference in the outward life.

It was midday, and the cup-like formation in which the
house stood had caught and held the sun. The windows were
open to it, and certain pillows, curtains, and draperies piled
on the sills gave evidence that spring-cleaning was in
progress.

He found his sister covering a cushion with new cretonne
in a design of tulips and delphiniums. Her white hands
moved softly above it like two plump pigeons in a gay bit of
garden. She wore a pink-and-white chintz cap in Quakerish
shape, which, she fancied, gave her the appearance of being
hard at work. Vaughan, who made no pretence of working,
lay stretched on a sofa reading a book on fox-breeding. Since
Lebraux had died, and there was a good chance that Mrs.
Lebraux would give it up, he had entertained thoughts of
buying her stock himself.

"Well, Finch dear," exclaimed Meg, "so you thought you
would come to see me! It's about time. When I think how lit-

tle I see of my brothers it makes me quite sad." She held up her smooth face expectantly.

As Finch bent to kiss her his unruly forelock fell across her eyes. He kissed her repeatedly, smelling the warm sweetness of her flesh and the peculiar stinging odour of the new cretonne.

"How untidy you look!" she said, surveying him.

"I always do, don't I? Hello, Maurice! You seem pressed for time."

Vaughan answered good-naturedly—"I'm digging into the question of fox-breeding a bit. I hear that Mrs. Lebraux is going to sell her stock."

"I haven't heard that. I think she really has nothing else to do for a living. Between the rent and the doctor's bills I guess she's had a pretty hard time."

"I feel frightfully sorry for her," said Meg. "She's a thoroughly nice woman. So sensible, and not spoiled a bit by having married a Frenchman. And settling down here with her child as though she'd always been—" She bit her thread with a certain sharp tooth she used for this purpose. She had been quick to perceive that neither Pheasant nor Alayne liked Mrs. Lebraux, and her own feeling toward her had warmed accordingly.

Her husband and her brother watched her with wonder and approval. Meggie was perfect, mysterious, richly feminine, kind.

"That's a funny little girl of Mrs. Lebraux's," remarked Finch. "All legs and hair."

"But how she can dance!" Meg's mood held warmth for daughter as for mother. "You and she were like two fairies dancing together!"

"Thanks so much, Meggie. It's pleasant to hear that I look like a fairy."

"Well, you do, dancing." She plumped the cushion with soft thumps, held it up for admiration, then sank back to rest. "Now tell me just what is going on at home? Getting ready for the trip, I suppose. To think that I have never been across to the Old Country, and now you—at your age! Able to travel as luxuriously as you like. And Uncle Nick and Uncle Ernest at their age! And all their expenses paid. And here are Maurice and I with the mortgage falling due!"

"Oh, well," growled Vaughan, "it can be renewed."

It was not an auspicious moment, Finch thought, for asking advice about his own investments. He pulled at his lip doubtfully, then made up his mind not to broach the subject.

After a silence Meg said wistfully:

"I suppose you would not care to take over the mortgage yourself?"

Finch stared, startled. "Me? I've never thought about it."

"Of course not." She looked into his eyes, smiling at his boyishness. "But mortgages are a good investment, aren't they, Maurice?"

"I wish I owned a few," answered Maurice.

"What interest do you pay?" asked Finch.

"Seven per cent."

"Great Scott! I get only four per cent on some of mine!"

"How much happier I should feel," cried Meg, "if you held the mortgage in place of the old wretch who does!"

"There would be no need for sentiment to enter into it, on Finch's side," put in Vaughan quickly. "This is a valuable property. And bound to be more valuable. Look at the old Paige place that the Golf Club bought. They gave a fancy price for that. One of these days we shall be able to subdivide this and sell it in town lots."

"Good heavens, you wouldn't do that! Renny would never speak to you again."

"Well, I might never do it. But Patience might when she grows up."

Finch asked, nervously—"What is the mortgage?"

"Fifteen thousand. At seven per cent—one thousand and fifty a year—paid half-yearly."

Meg sighed—"And the old wretch is so detestable always!"

"Why?" asked Finch.

"Oh—I don't know—"

Maurice interrupted her. "Meggie's too critical. He has rough manners; that's all that's really wrong. He's not such a bad old fellow." Maurice dropped the book from the hand which had been crippled in the war and it fell to the floor. Meg frowned as he bent to pick it up.

Finch felt a glow of affection toward them as a couple, quite apart from his brotherly love for Meg. "I'll do it," he exclaimed. "I'll take the mortgage over. But, look here, I'll not accept seven per cent. It's exorbitant. I'll not take more than five."

"You darling!" cried Meg. She made as if to rise and go to him, but, even in a moment of emotion such as this, the effort was too great. Instead she said again—"You darling!" And held out her arms to him.

Finch crossed to her rather shamefacedly. He did not want to be thanked. But it was wonderful, this doing things for people and benefiting himself at the same time.

Again Meg embraced him, pressed her plump lips on his. "I don't believe we'll tell the others a thing about it," she said. "I do like privacy about my own affairs, don't you?"

"Rather," said Finch.

They made all the arrangements, and, when they were complete, Finch sought advice on the subject of the New York stock. Meg and Maurice threw themselves into the discussion of it with enthusiasm. He would be a fool, they said, not to take advantage of such an opportunity. Why should Americans have all the money in the world? And if they had got it, why should they be allowed to keep it? Finch could not do better than to bring some of it here where it was so badly needed. He might become a rich man. And there was surely little danger when heads of publishing houses, who were right on the spot, considered it a good thing.

"If Alayne," said Meg, "is going into it, you're safe. I never knew a more calculating person. To me she's the very embodiment of shrewdness."

"She wasn't very shrewd when she married Eden," observed Maurice.

"Maurice, how can you say such a thing! If ever she showed shrewdness it was then! Who was she? Nobody! He took her out of an office and brought her to Jalna—to a life of ease. He made a *Whiteoak* of her!"

"He nearly broke her heart," said Finch.

"Hearts like hers aren't so easily broken! They're too calculating. For my part, I think she had her eye on Renny from the first. Poor lamb, he hadn't a chance against her!"

The two men sighed simultaneously in the effort of picturing the red fox, Renny, as a helpless lamb.

Patience, now within a few months of three, came running into the room. She was vivacious as Mooey was grave. Her light brown hair lay sleek on her head, her frock was bright blue.

"Baby, darling," said Meg, as Finch picked up the child, "you must put your arms right round Uncle Finch's neck and give him a perfectly 'normous hug! He's just done something so nice for Mummy."

Patience pressed Finch's head against her stomach. "Oh, my Finchy!" she cooed.

"Who's got a pretty new dress?" asked Finch, to cover his embarrassment.

Talking to Piers that afternoon, Finch could not forbear dropping a hint about the taking over of the mortgage on Vaughanlands. Piers was curious, and, after binding him to secrecy, Finch told all. Piers thought it a very good thing for both parties. "But mind you make them toe the mark with the payments," he advised. "Maurice is more than a little slack in money matters. He owed me for two years for a Jersey bull he bought, and I only got the money lately by keeping right after him."

Finch felt a little depressed at the prospect of keeping right after Maurice. The responsibility of wealth was beginning to weigh on him. He said:

"You've never told me what you would like in the way of a present. It would please me awfully to give you something. I hate not dividing things up a bit."

"Oh, I'll think it over," and Piers turned away.

Finch strode after him. "You're not going to get out of it like this. Just tell me something you'd really like."

"I've got everything I need."

"But there *must* be something." He went on complainingly—"I don't know what's the matter with you chaps! You'd think the money was tainted or something—you're so shy of it!"

Piers stopped, and turned to Finch. "Well, if you want to make me a present that won't break you, buy me a new motor car. The old one is literally falling to pieces, and, as

long as the engine has a kick in it, Renny won't buy a new
one."

"Good!" cried Finch. "I'm awfully glad you thought of
that. And Pheasant will enjoy it too. Shall we go in tomorrow and choose one?"

Piers made short work of choosing a car. He knew exactly
what he wanted, down to the smallest detail. How amazing,
Finch thought, to know all that when you had had no earthly
prospect of getting a new car.

They had taken the train to town and come home in the
car. It would be hard to say which of them enjoyed the drive
most—Finch, sitting with folded arms, feeling, he could not
have told why, rather like a self-made man, rich enough at
last to indulge in the pleasure of philanthropy; or Piers, with
a small, set grin on his face, entranced by speed.

They talked little on the way, but, by the time they
reached Jalna, Finch had promised to reshingle the barn for
Piers, and to build him an up-to-date piggery. It was understood that Piers was to repay the cost of this when he was able.

Everyone came out of the house to admire the new car.
Pheasant and Mooey danced round it. He must be lifted into
it and must sit with his little hands on the wheel. Pheasant
put her arm about Alayne. "You must share it too. The old
car is a *disgrace*." Nicholas and Ernest were delighted at the
thought of driving in such style to the train on their departure. There was nothing cheap about the car. It was a beauty,
they agreed. But Wakefield was dubious.

"I don't believe," he said, "that my grandmother would
approve. She never liked the old car. She thought buying it
was a great waste of money."

Piers answered—"She's not here to worry over changes,
and, as for you, you shan't ride in it, just for being cheeky."

"Still, I don't think Gran would like her money to be spent on motor cars."

"Would you like your seat warmed?"

"No." He edged away.

"Well, shut up, then!"

As they reached the garage they saw Renny standing in the door of the stable. When he saw the new car he turned sharply away and disappeared.

At dinner, in the face of his forbidding expression, no one referred to the purchase. Only Wakefield, in every pause, made some pensive remark relating to the likes and dislikes of his grandmother.

The day of leaving drew inexorably near. Then it dallied in a spell of heavy rainfall, seeming unreal and far off. Then it rushed upon them, giving them scarcely time for their last preparations.

Nicholas and Ernest had taken tea with each of their old friends in turn. Ernest's cheeks were flushed by excitement. Years seemed to fall from him with every day. The death of Sasha, which in moments of quiet saddened him deeply, made him feel in the moment of departure singularly free from responsibility. Nicholas, on the contrary, was intensely irritable. Gout danced about his knee, always threatening him, always making him feel that, at the last moment, he might have to postpone the trip. He found it hard to tear himself from the four walls of his room where he could do just as he liked and need pretend to be in no better humour than he was. And, though he would not acknowledge it, he was worried by the pleading look in Nip's eyes. Toward the last Finch could do little but play the piano. From morning to night he played. And, when the family would no longer endure it, he went to the Vaughans' or the Rectory and played there.

He was up before the sun on the last day. A gale from the west had blown all night, making him wakeful. He rose and leaned out of the window, letting the coolness of the wind refresh him. Daybreak, like a silver sail, was raised in the east, behind the darkness of the wood. To him it seemed the swelling sail of his adventure into a different world.

But he wished his old world had been less lovely on this last morning. He wished that the birdsong that seemed to be shaken from the boughs by the wind had been less heart-rendingly sweet; that the silver sail of daybreak had not turned to gold, and then to rose, before his eyes. He would have liked to take away with him a homely, comforting remembrance of the place, not the etherealised aching beauty of this May morning. The green of the new leaves was too translucently green, the shadows in the ravine slept in too rich a bloom, the mating birds called from tree to tree with too tranced a longing.

He dressed, in a kind of dream, and went out, taking old Benny, the sheepdog, with him. One by one he visited his old haunts. The rustic bridge across the stream, the apple tree in the old orchard, in whose crotch he had spent many hours reading. He went to the inmost part of the wood and lay down on the ground beneath the white-stemmed birches, pressing his face there, drinking in the smell of the soil. He crushed the young grass in his fingers and smelled it. He cut his initials and the date on a smooth white bole. He wondered what he would experience before he saw this place again. The old dog trotted seriously about, investigating, sniffing for a while, then settled down in a sunny space to doze.

The three who were going away took dinner at the Vaughans. Meggie could not bear to part with them till tea

time. When they returned to Jalna the new car was before
the door, the hand-luggage already placed in it. Everything
was in a rush now. They were annoyed with themselves and
Meggie for detaining them so late. Pheasant had on her
tweed suit and little brown hat. Mooey, though he was not
going, was dressed in his best. Between slices of bread and
honey Piers looked at his watch. Alayne was tying up a package of books she had bought for them to read on the voyage.
Meg had packed a hamper with plum cake, currant jelly, the
last of the russet apples, "because Finch loved them so," and
a jar of cough mixture made of rum and honey, which she
thought infallible. From first to last the protection of this
hamper fell to Finch and was a constant source of worry to
him until, on shipboard, he scraped out and ate the last
spoonful of the cough mixture, just to get rid of it. How
could he throw away anything Meg had given him!

Renny had not come in to tea. Finch asked, rather anxiously, where he was. Ernest explained—"He said goodbye to
Nicholas and me before we went to Meggie's. He said he
might not be in to tea."

"But he did not tell me goodbye," stammered Finch.
"Surely he would not let me go away without seeing me?"

"Surely not!" Ernest looked much concerned. "But there
is no time for hunting him up. We must leave as soon as we
have had our tea."

"I don't want any tea!" He set down his cup and rushed
out of the house. He had a sense of panic.

Running towards the stables, he saw Wright in the act of
backing the old car into the garage. He hesitated, and Wright
called out:

"If you're looking for Mr. Whiteoak, sir, he's over at Mrs.
Lebraux's."

Finch halted. "Wright, what's the best time you can make to drive me there and back?"

"I can get you there in five minutes, sir."

Finch clambered into the car. He must see Renny! The others would just have to wait for him if he were late. There was plenty of time for catching the train... Wright was showing what the old car could do. "You wouldn't think she had it in her, would you, sir?" he grinned. A box that had been bumping about on the back seat fell to the floor. The door of the car jarred open and the box rolled into the road.

"Let it go!" cried Finch.

Wright drove on. "That was a mixture I'd just got from the vet," he said ruefully.

The place Antoine Lebraux had rented for his venture into fox-breeding comprised about twenty acres, a wooden house painted a dingy white, a small stable, a poultry-house, and the fragile outbuildings Lebraux had added. Finch had known it as the house of a retired tradesman who had built it ten years before, had spent his days in keeping the premises in unnatural order, and had been swift to complain of any intrusion on the part of the boys or dogs from Jalna. Several times Renny had had to pay him for fowls, the deaths of which were laid at their door.

Finch had always hated the ugly neatness of the place, hated the rows of white painted stones that lay on either side of the walk. As he ran between them to the door his swift glance took in the air of neglect that had replaced the smug tidiness.

He pressed the electric bell twice without answer. Then he saw, stuck above it askew, a card with the words "Out of order." He knocked loudly. The minutes flew while he waited for some response, then a step sounded in the passage and a bolt was drawn. Good Lord, was Renny locked in there? The door opened and Pauline Lebraux stood on the threshold. She looked half frightened at seeing him. She wore a black serge dress of scanty cut, and this, with her long black legs and dense dark hair standing out about her face, made her look strangely fragile and pathetic. On her arm she carried, like an infant, a sickly fox cub wrapped in flannel. Its bright eyes peered out at Finch with an expression abnormally intelligent. Her appearance was so singular to Finch that he forgot for a moment what his errand was.

"I'm going away," he said.

He thought a shadow darkened her face, but she only smiled a little and said—"Won't you come in?"

"Thanks, but I mustn't. I'm in a rush to catch the train. I came to see if Renny is here."

"Yes. He's with Mother. Helping her with the foxes. Are you going far?"

"To England."

"For a long time?"

"All the summer. Perhaps longer."

He thought it cruel of her mother to have put her into mourning. He heard himself saying—"I hardly knew you in that dress. You had on white the night you were at our place."

"This is one of my school-dresses. I went to a convent in Quebec."

He thought she looked exquisitely remote, half wild, with the fox cub in her arms. He had a sudden desire to touch her, somehow to bring her near him.

He said, almost in a whisper—"Will you kiss me good-bye?" She was only a child, but he reddened in an odd excitement of the nerves.

She shook her head. "No. But you may kiss my hand."

She was being affected, he thought, then remembered her French upbringing. He took the hand she offered, thin and white, with the immature wrist showing below the black sleeve, and raised it to his lips.

They repeated "Goodbye," shyly. He hastened to the back of the house and looked about, in the hope of seeing Renny.

He saw the foxes in their enclosures, their fur darkly bright in the lowering sunrays. He heard voices in the little stable. How could he go there and call Renny's name, as though he were a child? He had a feeling of hot anger against Renny. He had a mind to return to Jalna without seeing him. But he had been seen from within. Renny appeared in the doorway, then came slowly toward him.

"Looking for me?" he asked.

"Did you suppose I'd go away without saying goodbye?" blazed Finch.

"How was I to know what you'd do? You do what you like."

Finch was aghast. Was this the way they were going to part? If it was, it would spoil his trip. If he missed his train, if he missed the boat, he would stay here till he'd wrung something better than this taciturn coldness from Renny.

"What have I done? Why are you treating me like this?"

"Watch out! Mrs. Lebraux is in there, she'll hear you."

"I'm missing my train, do you know that? Yet you won't say a friendly word to me! God, we might never meet again!"

"I hate saying goodbye."

"But you said goodbye to Uncle Nick and Uncle Ernie. Why not me?"

"That's just it. I didn't so much mind saying goodbye to them."

Finch's eyes searched the lean red face before him. If that were the truth—and Renny was not a liar—and he was frightfully queer about some things.—Oh, perhaps it was not so bad after all—perhaps Renny didn't hate him—why, Renny had always kissed him when they parted, like a father! He looked into Renny's eyes, his face suddenly contorted in an effort to keep from crying. He put out his hand.

Renny took it and drew Finch toward him. He bent and kissed him in the old way. Finch sniffed the familiar smell of stable on him. A load rolled from his heart.

Mrs. Lebraux came out of the stable. She was bareheaded and wore a man's linen dust-coat. She was rather attractive out of doors, Finch thought, with her short hair in its strange stripes of tow colour and brown, blown back from her face, her blue-eyed boyish stare and her reckless-looking mouth. She showed him her hands.

"I can't shake hands with you, you see. I've been working with the foxes, and now I'm learning how to look after horses."

Finch murmured a few hurried words of greeting and farewell, threw a warm glance to Renny, and hastened back to the car. But he was still within earshot when she said in her deep, rather musical voice, with its Maritime Province accent:

"It was amusing to see you kiss that tall youth. I hadn't imagined—"

That was all he heard. But what hadn't she imagined, he wondered. And what had been Renny's reply? He would give a good deal to know. And why had Renny gone to the fox farm that afternoon? Had he spoken the truth when he said that he had been loath to say goodbye? Or had he just been nursing his resentment against Finch? Still, this was not the first time he had taken himself off at a critical moment. Finch drew a deep sigh as they bumped along the road.

At Jalna he found the others in varying degrees of perturbation at his delay. Ernest was almost in despair, not able to keep still for a moment. Nicholas, solidly settled in the car, was uttering wrathful ejaculations. Pheasant was distraught. Piers said that it was almost more than he could do to keep his hands off him. Wakefield had brought out a pair of binoculars the better to watch for him, though the road was quite hidden from the drive by trees. It was one of the moments when Alayne felt that the Whiteoaks were almost beyond bearing. With a controlled expression she stood holding Mooey in her arms. Mooey was dubiously sucking his thumb, only taking it from his mouth at intervals to say— "I'm not f'ightened."

They caught the train, and that was all. The porter had barely disposed of their luggage, Piers had barely shaken hands all round, Pheasant kissed all round and exclaimed, "Oh, how I wish I were going too!" when she and Piers had to get off. They stood on the platform together as the train drew out, their young faces upturned, she blowing a kiss to the three at the window; he bare-headed, a smile, in which there was a shadow of boyish envy of the adventurers, softening his face.

VI

THE VOYAGE

NICHOLAS AND ERNEST had arranged that they should sail from New York, returning by way of Quebec. Once, years ago, they had done this and had enjoyed the variety it gave. They would like to repeat the experience, and it would be interesting for Finch.

It was necessary that Nicholas have a cabin to himself. He was so heavy, he said, and could not bear the thought of others in the room with him. Ernest and Finch therefore shared one. The boat sailed at midnight. Finch felt beside himself with excitement.

To sail out of the harbour under the quivering brightness of the stars; to look back at the starry brilliance of the city that stretched out arms, as though to hold the ship; to gaze ahead into the unrolling obscurity of the sea, stirred the very pith of him. Up and up till he was on the highest deck, which he had almost to himself, there to lean against the rail, feeling the trembling of her through all his nerves, brought him a new joy unlike anything he had yet experienced.

He might have spent the night there had he not remembered that Uncle Ernest would be wanting to turn in. Down below he found that the confusion was lessening, but there were still groups of women in evening cloaks, carrying flowers, surrounded by too prosperous-looking men. Here and there were stewards, fetching vases to hold flowers, running errands. He had trouble in finding his stateroom in the intricacies of the passages. The door of the one next his stood open, and, on the floor just inside, he saw two flower-baskets and several open boxes filled with roses. Two women stood in the passage reading a telegram together, clutching other telegrams in their hands. "Telegrams," he thought; "trouble at home, poor things! Hard luck that, just as they're setting out."

He found his uncle tucked up neatly in the lower berth, his clothes unpacked and hung in the wardrobe, a little irritated at the lateness of Finch's coming.

"This is what comes," he remarked, "of travelling with someone your age!"

"But," returned Finch, peeling off his things, "I don't think you could have slept if I had been here, there's so much noise in the corridors."

"I could have had this glaring light turned out, at any rate."

Finch wasted no time. Soon he was clambering up the little ladder, snuggling on his swaying perch, rather like a wild-eyed young cockerel, half timid, half challenging toward the world.

He lay there feeling in himself the capacity for absorbing the essence of what surrounded him, not only the beauty or the tragedy, but the mere motion and sound, the thrusting of the ship's bow against what would restrain her, the foamy onslaught and the troubled retreat of the waves against her side.

The next morning the sky had clouded and the sea grown rough. Nicholas and Finch were sick men. But Ernest, in spite of his weak digestion, had not enjoyed his meals so well in years. For two days the others lay in their berths while he savoured the pleasure of new contacts. While they aged the years fell from him as he paced the deck or played bridge and sipped cocktails in the lounge. The invincible vein of youthfulness in him was rubbed bright. He strode out with the best of them on the promenade deck. He seemed more like a man of sixty than one of seventy-four.

The third day out, when the sky had become a merry blue and the sea was scarcely ruffled, the invalids reappeared, looking rather sallow, and feeling a little resentful of Ernest's state of well-being. Nicholas had the habit of looking down on him as something of a weakling, while Finch had been obliged to watch his cheery changes of costume from his own perch of suffering, for two days. Had been waked from his first restful sleep by Ernest returning flushed out of his bath, opening and shutting drawers, talking breezily to the steward.

Ernest's wish was to keep away from their melancholy presence and to make desirable acquaintance among the passengers. It was on the second day that he had discovered Rosamond Trent.

It was a moment before he recognised her as the friend with whom Alayne had shared an apartment before her marriage to Eden. Ernest had met her several times on his visit to New York and had admired her. Now he felt delighted at the re-encounter at such an auspicious moment. She showed an almost equal pleasure at meeting him. Her mind still brooded with passionate affection on Alayne. She felt pity for her and a kind of envy. Pity, because Alayne had buried

herself in a place so remote from New York; envy, because
she would have liked to reach out and grasp the varied experiences of those who existed outside that city. She had a certain greed for life, and, in New York, she thought she had her
ear against the beating of its heart, but was, at times, doubtfully conscious that she was not aware of what its extremi-
ties were doing.

They settled themselves in the prettiest corner of the
lounge and Ernest nodded toward the wine steward. He
remembered Miss Trent's fondness for cocktails. She was, he
noted, perfectly turned out, from her closely fitting hat to
her manicured hands and her shoes that, one felt, were spe-
cially designed for shipboard wear in the month of May.

"Now, do tell me," she said eagerly, "about Alayne! I was
just thrilled by her second marriage. But I'm so perfectly
devoted to her that I can't help worrying the least teeny bit
when she doesn't write often. I haven't had a letter from her
for three weeks."

"Alayne is very well. To my mind she grows more
charming. She and Renny are so deeply attached. They are
really like one being."

Miss Trent smiled happily. "Ah, I'm perfectly delighted to
hear that! I was so disappointed at not meeting him when he
was in New York two years ago. *Do* you think that Alayne is
ever going to invite me to visit her?" She hurried on, without waiting for an answer, asking questions about the family
(knowing most of them only through Alayne) as though
they were old friends. She was shocked to hear that Renny
had ridden at the New York Horse Show the autumn before
and had not come to see her. She and Ernest got on famously.
She told him that he looked younger every time she saw
him, and he told her that she looked handsomer every time

he saw her. And, after a couple of cocktails, he and she did indeed look even younger and handsomer still.

She had given up the profession of advertising, she told him, and had gone into the antique business with a friend. They had put all their capital into it. They were like two leaves swept along by a tide. They might arrive *anywhere* or be just *swamped*. The object of Miss Trent's trip to England was the purchase of more antiques.

"In my waking moments," she declared, "I think of *nothing* but antiques."

"How well I understand you," said Ernest, leaning toward her across the cocktails. "I am exactly like that about my annotation of Shakespeare. Waking or sleeping, it is seldom out of my head."

Miss Trent's eyes found the depths of his. "Do you think," she asked, "that you are going to realise your dream?"

Ernest said that he thought he was.

On the morning when Nicholas and Finch came on deck they found the two stretched side by side in their deck chairs. No other legs on the deck had been swathed so meticulously by the steward, as theirs. They exhibited a like fastidiousness. There was not a wrinkle in their rugs. On his lay his binoculars. On hers the latest available copy of *The Connoisseur*. Her head was thrown back, her lips parted, showing her fine teeth. She looked young for her fifty-five years.

Nicholas, who was leaning on Finch's arm, halted and stared. Finch stared too, recognising Rosamond Trent. He told his uncle that she was the New York friend who had, in a way, mothered Alayne.

Nicholas gave Ernest a poke with his stick and smiled ironically down on him. Ernest, a little self-conscious under his brother's eye, introduced him to Miss Trent.

Ernest arranged that they should sit at table together. So Rosamond had the felicity of being surrounded by three distinguished-looking men, distinguished, at least, by their dissimilarity from the other men aboard. Their contrast to their companion also was marked. The group was the subject of some conjecture. How had they come together? Rosamond, usually sociable, now became distant, determined to keep her little circle intact.

Nicholas took a quite unreasonable dislike to the good-natured woman. He was annoyed at having the isolation that he craved when travelling disturbed by imposed intercourse with her. He was annoyed by the sight of Ernest promenading the deck with her, discussing the menu with her. He hated the sight of the food she chose. He resented her knowledge of the affairs of his family, her knowingness concerning antiques. She even knew that at Jalna there were some fine Chippendale "pieces" brought over by Captain Whiteoak.

He decided that she was a fool, and told Ernest so.

Ernest decided that poor old Nick was only envious of the brisk time he was having. He did not say this to Nicholas, but he did say that Miss Trent was one of the best-turned-out women on board.

"That may be," returned his brother, "but she's not at all Alayne's sort. I can't see how she ever came to take up with her. There's something cheap about her."

Ernest smiled pityingly. "You don't understand New York life, or even modern life. Besides, Miss Trent comes of a good Virginian family. Her people used to keep slaves."

"It appears to me that she keeps one now," said Nicholas testily.

As Miss Trent and Ernest became more preoccupied with each other, Nicholas and Finch held more aloof from them.

Finch was too shy to make friends with other young people on board. He would stand in the doorway of the saloon watching them dance, choosing an imaginary partner among them. One girl, with a rather heavy face but with movements of sustained rhythm, attracted him. Through an entire dance he would follow the graceful swaying of her body, mentally pressing it against his own, then turn away and find some isolated spot on the deck where he could watch the dark rhythm of the waves.

Once he found the saloon deserted when some amusing contest claimed the attention of all, and he sat down at the piano. He played the Prelude in A softly, for fear of being heard, bending over the keyboard as though with his body to muffle the sound. Before he was finished he was conscious that there were others in the room with him. He kept on, but, when he had touched the last notes, he rose and, assuming the sullen hangdog expression he often wore at home, he hurried out. The girl with the heavy face and graceful movements was in the doorway as he brushed past. She had been playing the piano through him, as he had danced through her.

His Uncle Nicholas complained a good deal to him of his Uncle Ernest.

"He's acting like a simpleton," he said. "There's nothing he won't do. He and that woman went into some idiotic contest as partners and actually won first prize. I've just been in the lounge seeing them get it. I don't know what your grandmother would say if she could see him. Upon my word, I shouldn't be surprised if he'd end by marrying her, if she were fool enough to have him."

Finch was horrified. The thought of Uncle Ernest as a husband, the husband of Miss Trent, caused his world to rock. He gasped:

"Is there nothing we can do to stop it? Couldn't you give him a talking to? Couldn't you remind him what Gran would think if she knew? He's always quoting her opinion himself."

"He'd probably make out that she'd quite approve of Miss Trent. Spirits always say just what you want them to, you know."

"Well, look here, Uncle Nick—do you think I might try to cut him out?"

Nicholas looked him over with amusement. "He's twenty years older than she is, and you're about thirty-five years younger. You might have a go at it though she seems to be out for antiques."

Nicholas was not so much worried over Ernest's behaviour as irritated by it. But Finch was very much worried.

On the last night out a fancy dress dance was given. Nicholas, after watching the changeful pattern of the dancers for a while, went early to his berth. Finch, lurking outside a window, saw two figures in dominoes which, he made sure, were those of Rosamond Trent and Ernest. The thin one in mauve was Ernest. Mauve! The very tentative blithesomeness of the colour sent a stab of apprehension through Finch. He felt weighed down by a sense of responsibility for his uncle. How to save him from Miss Trent!

They were undressing in their cabin when Ernest remarked:

"Rosamond Trent is a very brilliant woman, Finch. A very vigorous yet very sympathetic woman."

Finch's head was concealed in his shirt and he left it there, feeling more comfortable thus sequestered, while Ernest went on.

"She has rare business acumen combined with understanding of those of more reflective bent."

Finch thought—"It's coming! God help us!" And he kept his head inside his shirt.

Ernest proceeded—"She never succeeded in her advertising enterprise because it gave no scope for her really ardent temperament."

Ardent! Oh, this was too much! He struggled out of his shirt and stood in his bare pelt, crimson-faced, glaring at his uncle.

Ernest sat down on the side of his berth and fixed his eyes on Finch's. "But this collecting of antiques is another affair—"

"Antiques," mumbled Finch; "you don't mean—"

"Mean *what?*"

"That you're going—" He could not get it out.

"What I was going to say is that it seems such a pity to see a woman like Miss Trent handicapped in her new enterprise for lack of funds."

"Oh," said Finch, relieved, "is that all?"

"Isn't that enough?"

"Uncle Ernie, I thought you were going to tell me that you were in love with her."

Ernest's face turned almost as red as Finch's, but he did not look ill-pleased.

"I hope I've too much sense to be falling in love at my age," he said. "And if I were going to do anything so foolish, it would be with quite a different sort of woman. A woman more like Alayne possibly."

Finch felt boundless relief as he hurriedly pulled on his pyjamas.

"Miss Trent has put all her capital into her business. It is tied up. She has not sufficient ready money to invest in antiques to ensure a large profit. She is sadly hampered. If she had, say, ten thousand dollars to invest at once, she could, with her skill, double, even treble it."

Finch climbed up to his own berth. He hung over the edge of it, looking down on Ernest, feeling somehow that he had saved him from some danger. But it turned out that it was Miss Trent whom he was to save, and, in saving her, make a splendid investment for himself. To the muffled throbbing of the engine they discussed the intricacies of her affairs, with which Ernest was astonishingly familiar, far into the night.

VII

LONDON

THERE they were, crowded into a taxi, making their way through the traffic of the London streets, Finch on one of the drop-seats, almost dislocating his neck in the effort to see out of both windows at once. It was too unreal, seeing the places he had heard of so familiarly all his life. Westminster Bridge, the Houses of Parliament, Trafalgar Square, the lions, Buckingham Palace! They thundered at him like a series of explosions. It was too much. It was overwhelming.

His uncles simultaneously pointed out places on opposite sides of the street. They were amused and touched by the expression of his face. It was nearly twenty years since they had been in London. They perceived changes even in that hurried drive. Old landmarks gone, new buildings towering in their place. A certain depression tempered the pleasure of the return.

They had engaged rooms at the same hotel where once they had been familiar guests. It was no longer a fashionable hotel and had lost something of its air of elegance. But they were delighted to find that the hall porter was the same, scarcely changed except for greying. He recognised Ernest, after a moment of hesitation, but Nicholas only because he was in the company of Ernest. This heavy old man with the drooping shoulders, the sombre face where, only in the eyes, the old light smouldered, was a very different gentleman from the former Mr. Nicholas Whiteoak.

Finch leant across his window ledge and looked down into the street. Tawny yellow sunlight gave it mystery. The shadows of pedestrians were elongated. A flower-seller with his barrow of spring flowers had taken his stand below. Three disabled returned men were at the corner playing the Londonderry Air on two violins and a sort of legless piano held on the knees. A fourth man timidly held out a hat toward the passers-by. From the position of the piano-player's head Finch guessed that he was blind. He closed his own eyes and listened to the wild plaintive strain. Beneath the music he heard the turgid rumble of the city's life. London… It was too unreal to be here. He could not believe it.

He wanted to buy violets from the flower-seller, to give money to the musicians, to do something for the terrible-looking old woman in the feathered hat, shuffling along the opposite side of the street. He wanted to make a gallant gesture to the plump lady in the flower-boxed window across the way as she paused in her conversation with her parrot to look at him. He must go out again. He could not endure the indoors. They had been out all afternoon, had just come back in time for tea, but he must go out again, this time uncleless.

They were to be only a week in town before going on to visit Augusta. The fine weather might not hold, so Nicholas and Ernest had decided to go to the Park on that first afternoon. They had sat in the little green chairs watching the riders cantering in the Row. Finch had sat between them, and they, hands clasped on their sticks, had leaned forward to talk across him. Their quiet tones had broken into excited exclamations once when they had recognised a burly purple-faced rider as an old acquaintance. They had been more or less certain of the identity of half a dozen others. A handsome girl riding a black horse was so like another handsome girl, sat her mount with so like a grace, that she must surely be a daughter. It was most exciting.

They had walked through the gardens, shown Finch the Serpentine and the waterfowl, the flaming rhododendrons, the rosy foam of the hawthorns in bloom, pointing out this and that to him with their sticks as though he had been their little boy. But the new apartment houses in Park Lane were horrible to them. Strange, they said, that nothing could have been done to prevent that. They were disgusted with Finch for thinking that Park Lane was still a fine street.

To go forth uncleless was now his idea of happiness. He got his hat and went down to the street. Before he could stop himself he had bought a bunch of violets from the flower-seller, and so had to set out with these inadequately wrapped in paper in his hand. He dropped a sixpence into the hat for the musicians. He stood listening as once more they played the Londonderry Air. Sensitive as his nerves were to music, they did not shrink before the discords. He was no more affected than a skylark might be affected by the oddities of other singers. But the look in the eyes of these men hurt him deeply.

He went past densely crowded corners, crossing streets in the jam of evening traffic. He found himself in a little bar in North Audley Street with a whiskey and soda before him. He longed to talk to the barmaid, for he thought she looked interested in him, but had not the courage. He had never been in a bar before.

He strolled along the street, looking in the shop windows. One, in which works of art from the East were displayed, held him. He saw a blanc-de-Chine figure rather like the Kuan Yin that Gran had given him. The little white hands of the goddess were like the half-opened buds of some night-blooming lily. Her tiny feet, set wide apart, were like resting white birds. He should have liked to lay his violets at them.

He entered the shop and enquired the price. He was astonished to find how high it was. He told the attendant that he had one very much like it at home. He did not say where his home was, but he was aware as they continued in conversation that the man knew he was not an Englishman, and he wondered how. Finch told him that he was not going to buy anything, but the man's interest did not flag. He seemed willing just to stand and talk about the various objects admired by Finch. Although he had barely arrived in London, he began to think of what presents he should like to take home to the others. The years that his grandparents had spent in India, the things they had brought from there, had created in their descendants an interest in things oriental. He should like to take that wicked-looking scimitar to Piers, who had a fancy for old weapons, and had been given his grandfather's long cavalry sword. And for Meggie that embroidered screen. And Wakefield would like that carved ivory pagoda. He thought of Wake with sudden tenderness. Poor young devil—he had never been anywhere, seen anything. And, for that matter, where had Piers been, and what had Piers seen? And here was he seeing and doing so much!

When he had left the shop he looked again into the window and saw a picture of a snow-white cockatoo, with a coral-coloured crest, and he suddenly remembered Pauline

Lebraux, and thought he should like to take the picture to her. He saw her clearly for a moment, with her dense dark hair and long black-stockinged legs, standing before the cockatoo, hands clasped in rapt admiration.

Either the things he had seen in the shop, the kindness of the man, or the thought of little Pauline, he did not consider which, gave him a feeling of deep elation as he went on his way down the street.

He stopped before the window of an elegant saddler's to choose the perfect saddle for Renny.

He walked on and on. It seemed that he would never tire. At a corner, surrounded by a few stragglers, he came upon an old man, standing bare-headed, reciting Shakespeare. He had a grand old head, a battered face, and a voice hoarse from declaiming in the foggy air.

"Speak of me as I am, nothing extenuate,
Nor set down aught in malice."

As he was! Finch looked at him, tattered, broken, despair in his eyes. Speak of him as he was! Oh, who could do it? Who could bear to think of him as he was?

He stood listening to the voice that was sometimes drowned by the passage of an omnibus, broken by the jeering interruptions of one of the stragglers. Yet once, Finch was sure, he had been a good actor. He had the artist's instinct of knowing when he was appreciated. He finished, with his eyes full on Finch. He bowed, with a fine mixture of humility and tragedy, above the half-crown dropped into his hat.

"Well, it was a good deal to give him," Finch thought, as he walked away, "but I've paid more to see poorer acting."

He wandered on, losing all sense of direction. He was in streets of small shops and cinemas, frequented by the working class. They were a slow-moving, respectable-looking lot, with knobbly features, under the electric lights. They were exactly like crowds he had mingled with at home, when he had stayed in town for the night, and he and George Fennel had been members of an orchestra. Different from the New York crowd with its predominance of foreign faces.

He had bacon and eggs and coffee in a Lyons shop, sitting at a table next a young couple with the most stunned expression he had ever seen. He wondered what they had done, or were going to do, that they should have that expression. The woman did not eat, but just nibbled the tip of her finger, while the man poked squares of bread into his mouth, where they were consumed, apparently without chewing or swallowing, like letters dropped into a pillar-box.

The week they were to have spent in London lengthened into two. Nicholas and Ernest renewed old acquaintances, and were alternately elated and depressed by the revivification of their past. Finch went with them to dine at the house of the magenta-faced rider in the Row, who, after some conversation with the boy, came to the conclusion that the Whiteoaks were degenerating.

Ernest took Finch to Westminster Abbey, and he stood awestruck, his forelock drooping, above the wreath which the Sultan of Zanzibar had lately laid on the tomb of the Unknown Warrior.

Finch went on the Sunday morning to Hyde Park and stood among a group of tattered Welsh miners, listening to Socialistic and anti-Socialistic orators. He heard the latter turn the mettlesome force of an obscene vocabulary on an Irish interrupter.

He listened to the arguments of a young lady, who looked half frozen in the wind, on behalf of the Catholic

League. She spoke well, and he was moved by the sight of the crucifix upright on the ground beside her.

He pictured himself as a leaf blown back across the sea from a root transplanted. Here, in England, his grandfather, Captain Whiteoak, had been born. Here his mother, daughter of a London journalist who was always hard up, had been born. Here she had wandered about, distraught, after her father's death, wondering what to do, before she had decided to go to Canada as a governess. Three-quarters of him were English. All but that fourth quarter. That had come like a stormy wind out of the West—a fierce gale from Ireland—in the person of Gran.

VIII

NYMET CREWS

AUGUSTA had dressed herself with even more care than usual on this afternoon. She arranged with even greater exactitude her hair, still worn in the fashion of Queen Alexandra, that curled fringe upon which her nephews had so often speculated, going to the length of making bets with each other as to whether it were her own and natural in colour, her own and dyed, or a transformation. Not one of them had ever found out. And, if her brothers knew, they loyally kept the knowledge to themselves.

She surveyed herself in the long glass in her bedroom with inward satisfaction, but, if an onlooker had been present, he would have supposed that her reflection met with her complete disapprobation. She drew in her chin, stiffening the back of her neck, and widened her eyes into an expression of surprised offence. But this aspect was as natural to her as one of bold dominance had been to her mother. Her gaze appeared to be a defence against the object upon which she turned it, as old Adeline's had been one of challenging curiosity.

Augusta was little changed since her mother's death. She had, in truth, improved in appearance.

The last visit to Jalna, which had been prolonged to three years, had been something of a strain, enduring, as she had, the old lady's caprices and quips at her expense, and continually expecting that so long delayed death. The lively commotion of the household had also been rather exhausting to a woman herself long past seventy. The return to the serenity of her own house, where there was no one to contradict her, without running the risk of losing their situation, and nothing more exciting than the misbehaviour of maids, was a benefit to her health.

So, with inward satisfaction and outward disdain, she put the finishing touches to her toilette, noted her still shapely shoulders, and the unimpaired arch of her Court nose. Her complexion had always been bad, so in that respect she had had nothing to lose.

She went the rounds of the rooms prepared for her brothers and nephew, saw that the ewers were full of fresh water, clean towels on the racks, and sniffed the pleasant scent of lavender from the bed-linen.

She descended to the drawing-room, where the tea table, an hour late in agreement with the arrival of the train, had just been arranged by the parlourmaid, Ellen. She had been with Augusta many years, and, having made up her mind, on the day after her arrival, that her mistress's look of offence was directed at her, had acquired an apologetic, scuttling air with which she efficiently performed all her duties. Augusta, however, thought Ellen was an admirable servant, and was constantly singing her praises to friends.

She looked doubtfully over the tea table. Would there be enough scones? Was one square of honey in the comb sufficient? She remembered Finch's appetite, how she had always tried to put flesh on him and failed. Well, at any rate, there was plenty of bread and butter, and the fruitcake was unusually deep.

She went to a window and looked across the spring greenness of the lawn and park to where she could see the road climbing upward from the village. Only one vehicle was in sight—the cart of Jim Johnson, the carrier, returning after one of his two weekly trips to Exhampton. She waited there a few minutes, but she could not be quiet for long. She was too restlessly awaiting the arrival. It would be so nice to see them. A week ago she had had all ready to receive them, when a telegram had come to say that they were remaining another seven days in London. It was so like Nicholas to have sent it at the last minute. He and Ernest had not been to visit her since her husband's death. On that last visit they had quite tired out Sir Edwin by talking so much, and being so late to meals and disagreeing with him, as he said to her afterwards, on every subject he brought up. Well, he was safely at rest in the family vault now, and the years had made her brothers more amenable. As for Finch, he was now her favourite nephew. Eden had been once because of his charm, his good manners, his talents; but he was behaving altogether too badly. She loved Renny, but he had inherited several of Mamma's most regrettable traits. Piers was a splendid young fellow, but sometimes surly and with quite rough manners caused, she supposed, by association with grooms and labourers. Wakefield was a darling and quite companionable for his years, but there was something about Finch that made her feel almost maternal.

She began to be really annoyed at the lateness of the arrival of her relatives. She sat down by the table, however, and held herself together. The firelight (an unnecessary extravagance, for the afternoon was still warm) played over the folds of her black satin dress and maliciously accentuated a dark mole on her left cheek.

A step sounded in the hall and a small spare woman appeared in the doorway. She was Mrs. Thomas Court, Augusta's cousin by marriage. Her husband had been a son of old Adeline's youngest brother. She had lived, since her marriage, in Ireland, but had remained in all aspects English, as Augusta was inherently English though brought up in Canada. She advanced into the room in a quick, jerky walk like a little wound-up figure. Her hair, dragged back from the forehead, vied with Augusta's in purplish darkness. She had a complexion even more sallow, but she brightened it with two spots of rouge, and her dress, though ornate and old-fashioned, was sprightly. Her features were small, her light grey eyes intense, and the expression of her thin-lipped mouth one of unyielding conceit. Mingled with these qualities was a kind of jaunty good humour. She wore a black tailored suit, with a hairline stripe, the skirt of which reached her instep, just disclosing her rather heavy black boots that squeaked irritably as she walked. She walked straight to the window, with a side glance at the tea table.

Outdoors a shadow had fallen.

"Is it raining?" asked Augusta.

"Just beginning to spot," replied Mrs. Court, her eyes on the paved terrace.

"I wish it would rain. The flowers need it."

"I hope it doesn't. Dry weather agrees with me much better. It suits my ear."

"How is your ear?"

"Going chug-chug, the same as ever."

Augusta deepened her contralto tones. "Dear me, how very aggravating!"

Mrs. Court wheeled and stared at her. "Aggravating doesn't express it at all; it's maddening."

She advanced, with a businesslike air and squeaking boots, to the tea table. She pointed with a knuckly forefinger at the plate of scones. "Give me one of those and a cup of tea, and I'll carry them to my room. Relations don't want outsiders poking noses into their reunions."

"I haven't rung for the tea yet. And your leaving us is quite unnecessary."

"Very well." She sat down on an unyielding chair with buttoned-in upholstery. "But you'll not be able to make so free with each other."

"There is no need to make free," said Augusta, rather stiffly.

Mrs. Court played a tattoo on the floor with her heels. "It makes me jumpy," she explained, "to go so long without my tea."

Augusta regarded her with disapproval. "Where is Sarah?" she asked, in order to take her cousin's mind off her stomach.

Mrs. Court tattooed harder than ever. "Out in the rain. The girl's mad. She quite likes to get wet. And when the sun is shining she's as likely as not moping in the house. I call her Mole. My pet Mole." She wagged her head, in recognition of her own wit.

"She is a very sweet girl," said Augusta, "mole or no mole. And I only hope she and Finch will make friends."

"No boy of twenty-one will ever give a second thought to her. She's too quiet. Boys like romps. Sometimes I call her Mouse, my pet Mouse."

Augusta was listening to a sound outside. "Here is the car!" she cried, and hurried to meet them.

Mrs. Court squeaked, with even more alacrity, to the bell-cord and gave it a tug.

"Bring in the tea," she said to the maid, "and we'd better have an extra pot." She stood stock-still then, in the corner, watching the embraces of the family.

Augusta turned to her at last. "Oh, you have rung for tea! Now you must come and speak to my brothers and nephew. Of course you remember Nicholas and Ernest."

They shook hands, recalling how the last time they had met had been in London during the Coronation ceremonies of King George.

"Dear Edwin was alive then," said Augusta.

"Thomas was alive too," said Mrs. Court, not to be outdone.

They settled about the tea table, and Augusta noted how well her brothers looked, but she was a little disappointed in Finch's appearance. He had the same half-starved look. It was rather hard to reflect that this lanky youth was the possessor of her mother's fortune, when it would have graced so well Ernest's courtly presence. Not a large fortune, but how important in a family of such restricted means! Yet, when Finch, sitting close beside her, on a chair too low for him, gave her one of his affectionate looks, her heart warmed towards him and she plied him with buttered scones. She could hardly believe she had him here. A young man. And it seemed only yesterday when he was in his cradle! Finch, with even greater wonder, stared about the room with its innumerable ornaments and framed photographs. On the walls hung watercolours of Scottish scenery painted by Sir Edwin. On the mantel was a photograph of him looking out of pale eyes, between thin whiskers. There was a photograph of Wake, in the starry-eyed beauty of five. There was one of

Eden and Piers in white sailor suits, with a dog between them. On the piano, a large one of Renny on Landor, the year he had won the King's Plate. Then there was a pretty one of Meg with Patience. And a still prettier one of Pheasant with Mooey. Everywhere he looked he saw photographs of Whiteoaks. Nicholas, Ernest, and Augusta in their young and middle-aged days. Gran, as a handsome woman of fifty, in evening dress. And what was that on the small table just beside him? *Himself* at wild-eyed thirteen! It had been taken just after his first day's shooting, and he held the gun, in the picture, with a terrified look. No wonder he had looked terrified, for the very next week he had tripped with it, when out with Piers, and nearly sent a bullet through Piers's back. He had got a licking for his stupidity, and the gun had been taken away from him. It was nothing short of an insult to be faced with that picture in the moment of his arrival.

"I want you," he whispered, "to burn that awful picture of me."

"But I like it, dear. It's the only one I have of you."

"I'll have one taken for you while I'm here."

She gave him more tea, and again he whispered:

"I say, where's the girl?"

Augusta looked mysterious. "She's like you; she's devoted to Nature. She forgets all about her meals!"

"That's a lot like me!" And he helped himself to more honey.

"I hope," he added, "that she doesn't look like her mother."

"Sh."

"But they're talking to her, one in each ear. She couldn't possibly hear me."

"That is her aunt by marriage. Sarah is an orphan and has been brought up by Mrs. Thomas. I must tell you about her father later."

A shower was now beating against the panes. As though coming directly out of it, Sarah Court appeared in the doorway and came slowly toward the group about the tea table.

What had Finch expected? An impetuous Irish girl, late for tea because she liked being out in the wet? A curly haired sprite, dancing in with rain-dappled cheeks? A sturdy matter-of-fact young person? Whatever he had vaguely expected, it was certainly not this.

She came with a long slow gait, that imparted almost no motion to the upper part of the body. That part, held with an erectness unknown to the present generation, moved like the torso of a statue carried on a float. Her dark dress was open at the throat, but buttoned tightly down the front with the effect of an old-fashioned basque, having also the effect of that garment in a short continuation below the waist. Her skirt was too long for fashion, and was arranged at the back in a manner suggestive of a bustle. Her arms were held rigidly at her sides, her hands had an extraordinary pallor. This pallor was equalled in the profile turned toward Finch. Her black hair was brushed back from her high forehead in glossy smoothness, and worn in a heavy braided coil at the nape.

Finch saw that she had the Court nose, but that was not what held his gaze with a sense of something remembered. As she was being greeted by his uncles, who apparently had seen her as a small child in Ireland, his mind flew here and there among his recollections of the past, striving to fix on something that would explain this strange sense of having seen her before. It had fastened on nothing, when he heard his aunt's voice introducing them.

He still stood staring at her, unable to detach his mind. She came, however, to him holding out her hand. Something in the gesture gave him what he was looking for. Even as they shook hands he did not see her. His consciousness was occupied in the attic at Jalna. He saw himself in the lumber-room on a rainy day, crouching by the window, absorbed in old copies of *Punch* taken from a toppling dust-covered pile that year by year increased, for none were ever thrown away. He was looking at the picture of a Victorian drawing-room in which a whiskered gentleman was bowing over the hand of a lady. Other ladies were standing by. They were all alike, and each and all bore a striking resemblance to Sarah Court.

That was it! She was like a drawing by du Maurier.

He was so relieved by the discovery that he smiled delightedly at her. She smiled back, and he saw how the thin, delicate lips parted, showing unexpectedly small, even teeth. He thought he had never seen an upper lip so short, a chin so jutting.

Mrs. Court was saying:

"Well, Mole! So you've come out, now that the sun is gone!"

Sarah Court's lips closed tightly. She fixed her eyes on a ring with a large green stone, which she began nervously to twist on her forefinger.

Her aunt leant forward, as though she would pry under the lowered lids.

"Well, Mouse! Quiet as ever?" She turned to Ernest. "I call her Mouse, she's so silent. It's very irritating to me when I've no other companion."

Nicholas said—"Many years ago there was a girl we called Mouse. She was a ballet dancer."

"Was she quiet?" asked Mrs. Court eagerly.

"No, she was rather noisy. But she'd a peaky little face, and small bright eyes."

"I enjoy a good ballet," said Mrs. Court, "but I've no pleasure in the Russian ballet. I hate Russian music. It's nothing but a fantastic noise compared with Bach, or Handel, or Mozart. When Sarah begins to do the rough-and-tumble of it on her fiddle I get out of the room. It gives me the fidgets." And she played a tattoo with her heels to show how really fidgety she could become.

Her niece had seated herself and continued to turn the green ring on her finger until Finch carried a cup of tea to her. She helped herself to bread and jam with something of the concentration of a child. Finch was so conscious of her withdrawal, he hesitated to speak to her. However, there was no need for conversation. Mrs. Court only stopped talking long enough to snatch a mouthful of scone or tea, and her harsh, yet somehow not disagreeable, voice required no encouraging response.

"Do you keep up your music?" she asked Nicholas.

"I play a little occasionally, but I notice that my hands are getting stiff."

"Is that rheumatism?"

"I daresay."

"And you've gout, too?"

He grunted.

"Now, I wonder if your blood pressure is high?"

"Shouldn't be surprised. Nothing my body does surprises me now."

She turned to Finch. "We must get you playing. We'll make a musical time of it."

She talked of music she had heard in the principal capitals of Europe. "But I can't afford to travel now," she said. "I just stick at home in Ireland. Mouse and I make our own music. Don't we, Mouse?"

How ludicrous, Finch thought, to call that remote-looking girl Mouse! He got up his courage and said:

"You play the violin awfully well, I expect."

Her aunt had received no answer to her question and had apparently expected none, for she continued to talk without hesitating; but Sarah turned to Finch with a peculiar smile, with a certain elfish mischief in it, and answered:

"You'll know that when you hear me."

It was the first time he had heard her say more than a monosyllable. Her voice, he thought, was the very distillation of sweetness, all the more noticeable following, as it did, the gruff tones of her aunt. And it had a muted sound, as though a secret being within her spoke for her. He tried to draw her into conversation, but he was awkward and she was either shy or aloof.

He was glad to escape into the garden when the others went to their rooms. He stood on the drive drinking in the air that was so fresh after London, his eyes opened wide, as though they would take in, at one extravagant glance, the scene that lay unrolled before him.

The shower had passed and a light wind was blowing the rain clouds from the upper sky. In the west the sun had emerged from behind piled-up masses of snowy vapour, the fantastic shapes of which were outlined by his brilliance. But some of this triumphant radiance was reserved for the earth where fields and trees, wet with rain, showed their own colours intensified to celestial brightness. ·

The house stood on a hill overlooking the village of Nymet Crews and, beyond that, the fields, woods, and pastures that stretched to the edge of Dartmoor. From the village, with its square-towered Norman church and white cottages, there was another rise of land toward the moor, and on this stretch every irregularity of field and meadow was outlined by the flowering hedgerows. The pattern of it was unrolled before him like a rich tapestry. The deep red earth of one field lay beside the pale red of another. The tender green of pasture against the silver green oats. The darkness of a spinney next a field of corn that held the sun. He could see lanes, between tall hedges, threading their way to the open moor, there to be lost. He could see, looming above all, the hyacinth-blue contours of the Tors. The air held an almost palpable sweetness, unknown to him, of garden flowers, of new-mown grass, of the thousand wild flowers of the countryside and hedge, of Dartmoor itself.

Lyming Hall was an unpretentious house of no particular period, but its gardens, lawns, and small park were kept in excellent order. Augusta was proud of the commanding view over the countryside. The fact that there were no large landowners about and few people of wealth gave her a pleasant feeling of superiority.

Finch wandered among the flower beds, discovered the tennis court, the rosery, and walked down the drive, which sloped steeply, to the gate. There was a small gabled lodge half hidden in roses, so much like a picture of a little English house that Finch had to grin with delight as he looked at it. He turned away when he saw a woman in the door and cut across a corner of the park to where he could see the stable.

In the stable he found only a pony which had just been given its evening meal by a boy a couple of years younger than himself. He put his knuckle to his forehead when he saw Finch. He had sombre black eyes and a rich tan on his cheeks.

"Good evening," said Finch. "I came in to see the horses."

"There's only this one, zir," answered the boy. "Her ladyship just keeps him for the lawn-mower and garden work.

Her hasn't kept more than this 'un since I've worked 'ere. His name's Bobby."

Finch patted Bobby's fat flank. "I suppose he's all she needs. But aren't there any dogs about?"

"No, zir; we had one, but he was took bad one day and died."

"Have you worked here long?"

"Two years, zir. I help Ash, the gardener."

What a nice-looking boy he was, Finch thought. He said—"I should think you'd like a dog about."

"Yes, zir."

Finch wished he wouldn't call him "sir" quite so often. It made him feel silly. The men about the stables at home did not treat him with great respect. He scarcely seemed grown up to them.

"An old English sheepdog is a nice dog," he remarked. "We have one at home."

"Yes, zir. An old English is a very nice kind of dog."

"And Irish terriers are first-rate companions. We have one of them too."

"Yes, zir. An Irish terrier is a nice kind of dog to have."

Finch remembered Nip. "My uncle has a Yorkshire terrier. Clever little fellow, too."

"Yes, zir. A Yorkshire terrier is a very nice kind of dog." His dark eyes looked earnestly into Finch's. He seemed satisfied that he was carrying on an animated conversation.

"There are spaniels too," went on Finch.

"Yes, zir. A spannel is a nice kind of dog."

Finch looked at him excitedly, trying to bridge the gulf that separated them. "My brother has two Clumber spaniels," he said.

"Yes, zir. Two Clummer spannels must be very nice to have."

They smiled at each other. Finch turned to go. Then he stopped. "I say, what kind of dog was the dog you had here?"

"He was a spannel, zir."

"Oh… was he a good dog?"

"Yes, he was a spannel, zir."

"Well, I think I'll be off. What's your name?"

"Ralph Hart, zir."

Finch repeated the name to himself as he prowled among the shrubbery, thinking how well it suited the dark interesting-looking boy. But what a conversation! He should like to go back and do it all over again and see if it would turn out the same way. He'd wager it would.

He found the kitchen garden. He found strawberries under netting, and gooseberries like eggs. He came upon a door in a wall, almost hidden in ivy, and pushed it open. He found himself in a walled flower garden.

He went up and down the box-bordered paths, a lanky figure filled with the joy of being alive in that warm sweet-scented enclosure. He squatted to look into Canterbury bells. He held moss-roses in his hand. He put his long nose to the very earth to smell the mignonette. The pear trees, trained against the wall, were beautiful to him. At that moment the orchard of pear trees at Jalna, that carelessly covered the ground with golden fruit every fall, seemed a poor thing. He could not decide which roses were the most beautiful—the newly opened ones, their inner petals still resisting the fingers of the sun, or those at that mysterious moment of perfection, just before they fade and fall, when they seem to be offering their essence in a final surrender so complete as to have something of delicate vehemence in it. He thought he should like to carry his breakfast to this garden one morning, and eat it with no one about but the birds and Ralph Hart.

When Ellen showed him his room, he was glad to find
that its windows overlooked the walled garden. There was a
can of hot water and his clothes were laid out ready for him
on the bed. He felt very happy. He had had no idea it would
be so nice at Aunt Augusta's. He wished that Mrs. Court and
her niece were not there so they might have been just a family party… Still, after all, Sarah Court was his cousin. But
how strange and unapproachable she was! And she had a
baffling charm for him. As he stood looking out of the window his thoughts, like curious birds, hovered about her.

He was still looking down into the garden, where a vio-
laceous shadow had tempered all the brightness, when a light
tap sounded on the door. Augusta's voice asked:

"Are you dressed, dear? May I come in?"

He threw open the door and stood guiltily before her.

"I say, Aunt, I'm awfully sorry! I haven't begun to dress;
I've just been staring into the garden. You shouldn't have
given me a room with a window overlooking it."

She sailed with kindly majesty into the room.

"I am glad you enjoy your view. It is not as pretty a room
as I should have liked for you. But you see how it was. There
were four others to be considered before you."

"Look here," cried Finch, with a violent wave of the arm,
"I'd rather have this garden under my window than a
Turkish rug and a Louis Seize bed and a Turner landscape in
the room!"

"I am so glad you like it," said Augusta; but she spoke
abstractedly. She went back to the door, closed it, then sat
down on the settee at the foot of the bed. She had on a black
dinner dress and wore her old-fashioned jewellery that was
beginning to be fashionable again. She raised her large eyes
to Finch's face and said, in a tone almost tragic:

"Finch, I am in great trouble." Her voice sounded a baritone depth.

The thought of anyone's being in trouble terrified him. He was used to trouble, Heaven knew, but his hair seemed to rise at the mere mention of it. "Oh—what's up, Aunt?"

"Eden," she boomed, "is sitting on the doorstep."

He had an instant mental picture of Eden, rather down-at-heel but debonair, with that insolent, veiled smile of his, lounging on the door-sill. He could only make incoherent sounds expressing a state of being staggered.

"That girl," proceeded Augusta, "is with him."

So Eden and Minny were both sitting on the doorstep! He could only get out—"Well, well."

But his look of consternation was sufficient to satisfy his Aunt of his sympathy.

"They are," she said, "living in the lodge."

The lodge! And he had walked down to it not an hour before! Perhaps the woman he had seen in the doorway was Minny.

"But how did they get there?" he asked.

"By effrontery. As they get everywhere. You know I am attached to Eden. I cannot help being attached to Eden. But to have him come and sit on my doorstep, when I have Mrs. Court and Sarah in the house, is too much."

"But how did they come there? And when?" Life seemed one long surprise for him. Now he asked himself, as he had asked himself about so many things, can this be true?

Augusta said—"They have been there a week. Eden turned up a month ago alone. She was somewhere in the offing, awaiting her chance to creep onto my doorstep. He told me that he was completely out of funds, and he asked me if he might not come and live at the lodge. I told him that the widow of the late lodge-keeper lived there alone. She paid me no rent, but he had been very faithful, and after his death I let her live on there. She often came and helped about the house. Now what do you suppose Eden's remark was after I had told him all this? His remark was—'Can't you turn the widow out?' Did you ever hear of anything more cold-blooded?"

"It was terrible," agreed Finch.

"It was barbarous; not only the words, but the way he uttered them. Just a casual—'Can't you turn the widow out?' As though it were the turning of a hen out of a coop. I spoke impressively to him. I said—'Eden, I never thought that I should live to see the day that a Whiteoak and a Court should suggest that a widow be turned out of doors. Whatever our faults may have been, we have been benevolent.'" She pressed her middle finger where her eyebrows all but met.

"What did he say to that?"

"He said nothing. He just gave that rather tired smile of his and began to talk about his poetry. He does write really beautiful poetry, you know."

"And what then?"

"After he'd had tea he went away. What was my astonishment, in less than a fortnight, when the widow's daughter, who lives in Plymouth, wrote to her mother asking her to come there to live. She is going to have another child, and takes in lodgers, so it was altogether too much for her."

"And did the widow go?"

"She went. And she had only been gone two days when Eden sauntered into the garden, where I was cutting roses, and said 'Well, we've settled in.' 'Settled in!' I almost shouted it. 'Who has settled in?' 'Me and Minny,' he said.

Just like that, without grammar or consideration. Then he said—'We heard the widow had got out, so we've moved in.' I shouted—'*You've moved into the lodge! You?*' And he said—'Yes, Minny and me.' And there they've remained."

"What are you going to do about it?"

"I don't know, I'm sure. I thought perhaps you could help me. I'm afraid that, if I tell your uncles, they may be too severe with him. He is such a sweet boy. Clever, like you—only so much more—" She hesitated.

"Yes, I know," said Finch.

"I shouldn't mind their occupying the lodge for a time, in the least, if only they were married, though Minny does look very odd since she's taken to painting her ears."

"Painting her *ears*!"

"Yes. She puts a dab of paint on the lobe of each ear. I suppose it's living in France."

"Well, well," said Finch again. He felt as though life were really crowding too furiously on him. He asked—"Do the people about here know that they are not married?"

"No one knows but Mrs. Court. We have, so far, kept the fact of their existence from Sarah. Her aunt is very particular about Sarah's acquaintances."

"She is rather a strange girl, Aunt Augusta."

"You will not think her so strange when you are used to her…"

But her strangeness was even more pronounced at dinner. When she spoke to him, asking him a question or two about his home, he could only feel a sensuous pleasure in the beauty of her voice. Her words, he was sure, revealed nothing of her. She seemed scarcely conscious that she uttered them. Not once did she turn to look him in the face. He could

study, as often as he chose, that pale profile with the drooping, sensitive mouth encamped between the conspicuous
nose and chin. He noticed how the candlelight lay on her
breast and touched her arms as though it loved her.

He heard Mrs. Court's voice across the table as she talked
with gusto to Uncle Nicholas. "Fred thought he would be
better off if he took the other church as well. But it just
meant that he had to get a curate; and what with the curate,
and the glebe lands being worth so much less, I think he's
worse off. He rents his fields for half what he used to, and his
hearing grows worse every year."

He longed to hear his cousin play the violin, but he could
not make up his mind to ask her. However, the evening was
not far advanced when Augusta said to Mrs. Court:

"I am hoping that you and Sarah will play for us. My
brothers are too tired for whist, but they would delight in
some music. Wouldn't you, Ernest and Nicholas?"

They would, and said they would, both addressing Mrs.
Court, as though she were to be the sole performer. She got
up at once in a businesslike manner, and hurried, with her
effect of being wound up, to the piano.

"Come, Sarah," she commanded, "and get out your
fiddle."

Her niece rose impassively and followed her. On a window seat near the piano lay her violin case. She took out the
instrument and began to tune it. Mrs. Court had seated herself and removed several bangle bracelets.

Finch did not know what he expected, but his curiosity
had in it the quality of pain. There was a subtle sense of distress in the thought of these two women, so antagonistic in
spirit as he was sure they were, attempting to produce the
exaltation or gaiety of music. He could not tell which he

despaired of most—the self-assured little marionette at the piano or the resolute, ice-cold girl with the violin... That chin of hers... God, she seemed fairly to dig it into the violin! He glanced nervously at his aunt and uncles to see if misgiving might be evident in their faces, but there was none. Augusta sat upright, wearing an expression of almost overwhelming benevolence. Nicholas was frankly sprawling in the deep chair he had chosen, his handsome hands dangling over its padded arms. Yet, in spite of his attitude of indolence, he was very much alive. A vivid interest was bright in his deep-set eyes. Ernest looked suddenly wan and tired.

They played one of Handel's sonatas. The slow, gracious music rose from the violin and piano in harmonious accord. Aunt and niece were not only skilled performers, but they were in complete understanding.

Yet Finch's sense of pain did not diminish, but rather increased. On Mrs. Court's side he felt too much cold energy; on his cousin's a too docile perfection. Mrs. Court was, he felt, not playing Sarah's accompaniment; she was dragging her by the hair of the head through the starry realms of sound.

As they went from one piece to another (Mrs. Court never seemed to tire) Finch became convinced that Sarah could play the violin very differently if she had a different accompanist. Now the door of her senses was shut fast. She was only going through certain tricks she had been taught. If only the door were opened and her spirit set free to rejoice and to suffer in the music of her violin! He had a scarcely controllable longing to lift Mrs. Court bodily from the piano-seat and himself take her place. He pictured himself as cutting Sarah's bonds, and the two of them free, soaring together.

But it grew late and he was not even asked to play.

IX

A Devon Day

1

Morning

FINCH was woken the next morning by the sound of a man's voice shouting orders to a dog, by the dog's barking, in his turn, orders to a flock of sheep, by the troubled baaing of the sheep themselves, and by a gust of wind blowing in at the window and flinging on his face the gathered sweetness of the garden and the fields.

His eyes flew open and he saw the bright chintz of the bed curtains, the wallpaper with its prim birds pecking prim cherries, the white mantelpiece with the china figure of a little lady riding a pink horse, and two framed photographs so dim that he could not tell what they represented.

He was in Devon, he realised, in the very depths of its deep, rich, luxuriant roundness that lay on the earth like a nest on a bough. He was in Devon. He was in England. He must make himself believe it, though it seemed impossible to believe. Here he was, Finch Whiteoak, in the middle of one of Aunt Augusta's beds, in the middle of one of her bedrooms, in the middle of Lyming Hall, in the heart of Devon. He had travelled by train the six hundred miles from Jalna to the New York pier. He had crossed the ocean on a liner. He had stopped a fortnight in London. He had travelled the nearly two hundred miles into Devon. And he had not only done that but he had brought his two old uncles with him, paid all their expenses out of his own money that Gran had left him, and had set them down, safe and sound, beside Aunt Augusta. He lay still, feeling flabbergasted at his own achievement. He wondered if other fellows felt so surprised at the happenings of their lives. There was Piers—he had got married, got a kid, gone through a good deal, yet he never seemed surprised. He might look in a rage at things but not surprised. George Fennel never seemed surprised, nor Arthur Leigh. Still, he supposed, they kept it to themselves if they were. Just finding himself alive was often a rather frightening surprise to him. He wondered when he would outgrow it and rather hoped he would not, for there was something he liked in it.

Suddenly he jumped out of bed and went to the window. It was framed in a yellow climbing rose, the buds clinging there as thick as bees on a honeycomb. Down in the garden, where sunlight and shadow had the sharp distinctness of early morning, he saw Ralph Hart trimming a box border. He wore corduroys and leggings, and his black head was glossy in the sun. The stone wall had a peculiar golden bloom on it except where there were patches of greyish lichen. Ivy lay thick along its top and clumps of yellow stonecrop.

The fields beyond the wall were let to a farmer. Finch saw him now, astride of a stout brown cob, wearing a clean linen Norfolk jacket and breeches, a pink wild rose in his button-hole. He was so short and stout that his legs stuck out on either side of the horse. Beneath his hat, set at a jaunty angle, showed his round earnest face, red as a peony. In gruff hearty tones he gave directions to two men who were trying to keep several bullocks separated from the sheep which the dog was endeavouring to herd through the open gate into the next field. The men ran here and there waving their arms, the bullocks blundered, with unexpected agility, among the buttercups, the dog barked, half beside himself with importance, and the sheep, uttering the same cry in a variety of tones, bundled themselves here and there, but always managed to evade the gate. It was a vivacious scene, of which all the participants, from farmer to buttercups, looked shining, well nourished, and in good humour.

"Devonshire cream," murmured Finch, lolling on the sill. "Devonshire cream, that just expresses it. Gosh, if only the others were here to see this!"

One of the others was, he remembered, just down the drive at the lodge. If he walked down that way now he might get a sight of him, before Minny was about, for Eden loved the early morning. He had not seen him for more than a year and a half. Eden would be quite a cosmopolitan after all that time in Europe. Would he be changed, he wondered. Rather embarrassing to meet Minny under the conditions. Hot stuff, Minny; no doubt about that.

He slid into his clothes and went downstairs. No one was about but Ellen, industriously dusting. The door stood open and warm sunlight had already taken the chill from the hall.

The gardener was mowing the terraced lawn. Finch stood for a moment to watch the little white heads of the daisies leap from their stems and fall like spray before the knives of the mowing-machine. He went to the gardener and spoke to him, just for the pleasure of hearing the singsong of his

Devon speech. He was a thin, youngish man with very blue eyes, a fair skin, and not a tooth in his head. He stopped the pony and let his eyes wander over the sweep of fields, woods, and mist-wreathed tors that Finch had admired.

"Ay, it's a lovely voo," he said. "It's a lovely voo in all seasons. But 'tidden quite so pretty now as 'twere an hour agone when that highest tor had just put un's head out o' mist."

"What is the name of that tor?" asked Finch, to draw him out.

"Ah," his eyes moved slowly to Finch's face, "I couldn't tell 'ee that. He's got a name. They'm all named; but I've never seen un close by, and I've never heerd tell."

Finch stared. "Have you never been on the moor, then?"

"No, zur. My work has allus been about here. Us sticks pretty close to own parts hereabouts."

A heavy cart, drawn by three horses harnessed head to tail, and carrying a forest tree, rumbled along the road below. The gardener watched it till it was out of sight, then he said:

"Him's one of Squire Varley's trees. They'm cuttin' down a fine lot there. Six souls are hard at it, day in, day out. Cuttin' trees."

Finch felt that if he stayed longer talking to the gardener he would not have the strength to walk to the lodge. That rich singsong voice, those meditative eyes, produced in him an exquisite weakness. Soon he would have to lie down among the daisy heads...

The whirr of the mower began again as he went down the drive. The rumble of the cart faded in the distance. The grey trunks of the beeches on either side of him were dappled with sunshine, and, here and there along the hedge, a tall foxglove shook out its bells. The ground fell away so abruptly that he looked down on the lodge. Someone was astir within, for a blue spiral of smoke rose from the chimney. He followed the curve of the drive to the gates and stood looking timidly at the house. He felt very shy of meeting Minny. At last he got the courage to go up the flagged walk, between borders of petunias and pinks, and peer in at the window.

He saw a table inside set for a simple breakfast, the sunlight falling on a half loaf of bread and a glass pot of raspberry jam. He saw a small room with beamed ceiling and a large fireplace. A figure he recognised as Eden was bent over something in a frying pan. He was almost inside the fireplace.

Finch entered without knocking, his canvas shoes making no sound on the stone floor. He went and stood almost behind Eden. The room was filled with the smell of frying bacon. A pot in which tea was brewing stood on the warm hearth. Eden wore loose grey flannel trousers, a shirt open at the throat, and rolled-up sleeves. Finch could see the gleam of short golden hairs on his rounded forearms. His face looked full and healthy but retained a certain delicate sensitiveness of expression that prevented its acquiring an aspect of well-being. His brows were drawn upward, as he blinked against the smoke, and the inherent melancholy of his mouth was perhaps accentuated by the cigarette that drooped from its corner. His hair was, as always, well brushed, with the gleam of a metal casque.

Finch had time to take in these details, over-emphasised by the glow of the fire, before he was discovered.

Eden, with difficulty, kept himself from overturning the bacon. "Well, I'll be damned," he exclaimed, "if it isn't Brother Finch! So you've come to breakfast with me!" He stood smiling at Finch. The frying pan tilted in his left hand, he extended the right.

"Oh, no," protested Finch, shaking hands limply. "I really mustn't! Aunt Augusta will be expecting me. I shouldn't have come in on you like this, so early—I think I'd better not stay." He felt flustered under Eden's eyes.

"Sit down," said Eden, pushing him onto a chair. "You're just in the nick of time. I'm getting my own breakfast, as you see. We'll start on what bacon I've cooked, and I'll put on some more to fry while we eat."

He carefully divided the bacon and made his other preparations in a businesslike manner. Finch cut thick slices of the sweet crusty bread, and felt ferocious hunger rage within him. He saw that Eden had dumped all the bacon from the paper packet into the pan, and he thought—"Lord, he hasn't forgotten what a pig I am!"

So they sat facing each other across the breakfast table—another marvellous happening to Finch. He watched a bee drift in through the open diamond-paned casement and settle on the rim of the jam-pot. He said:

"I say, Eden, isn't it funny that you and I should be eating breakfast here together? To think that we'd both cross the ocean, and you'd go to France and then come to England, and then I'd come to England and we'd sit down at a breakfast table here in this lodge, just like we've had breakfast together many a time at home!" He took a large mouthful of bread, and his young face was so thin that it made his cheek jut out ridiculously. His eyes were bright with excitement.

"I don't see anything funny in it, except you," said Eden. "Certainly you are Finch, wherever you go."

"Don't you think I've changed?" Shyly he hoped that Eden would say that he had improved in appearance. Eden had never seen him in such good clothes as he wore this morning.

Eden looked him over critically. "No, you've not changed, except for a better haircut and a few glad rags. You're the same callow youth. But"—he added quickly as he saw Finch's face fall—"believe me, you're the flower of the flock, Finch."

"I don't see why you must pull my leg the moment we meet."

"I'm not pulling your leg. And I don't know exactly why I say it. It's not because of your music. Perhaps it's because it seems to me that you have the faults and virtues of the rest of us sublimated in you. You're more of the coward, more of the hero, more of the genius, more of the poet—"

"The poet!"

"Oh, I don't suppose you'll ever get it down on paper. And, unless I miss my guess, more of the lover—when your time comes."

Finch drowned his embarrassment in a cup of blazing hot tea. Yet he liked to hear himself described, especially in such extraordinary terms as these.

"You're the peculiar flower of our peculiar flock," continued Eden. "It looks to me as though our forebears had rampaged down the centuries for the sole purpose of producing you, as their final flourish. Their justification, perhaps."

There was no doubt about it now, Eden was talking to hear himself talk. Finch glared at him. "What about you?" he demanded.

Eden smiled faintly. "Well, perhaps me too. Let's hope so."

"We're not half the men Renny and Piers are!" burst out Finch.

"No? Very well, I don't suppose we'll produce so many young. Breed so many foals. Jump so many hurdles."

"I'd a thousand times sooner be like them!"

"Of course you would. And they'd a thousand times sooner be like themselves. The world might have reached a state of civilisation ages ago if that weren't always the case. People without imagination are always cocksure, and they've been given the power of intimidating and exhausting those who have. The man with imagination is frightened at what he sees in himself. The thought of trying to govern others is abhorrent to him."

Eden emptied the remainder of the milk from the jug into his teacup and drank it. "Ever since I had that beastly lung trouble," he said, "I drink whatever milk comes my way."

Finch had finished the bacon. He remembered Minny. "Why, look here," he cried, "what's Minny going to have?"

"She eats scarcely any breakfast. She's getting fat, poor soul!"

"I hope she's well," said Finch timidly.

"Absolutely fit. Sleeps like a log—sings like an angel—and talks like a fool," answered Eden, turning the loaf crumb-side down to keep it fresh for her. "Let's go for a walk, and not waste the best time of the morning indoors. I'll show you my favourite nook. Only mind you keep out of it unless I'm with you."

They went through the gate into the road, two tall bare-headed figures. Finch angular, rather slouching; Eden moving with the grace that made people turn to look at him.

The road curved frequently, so that they seldom saw more than a short distance ahead of them, and the height of the hedges combined to produce in them the feeling that they were traversing one of the very veins of summer through which flowed the energy that produced her efflorescence.

They met no soul on the road, after they had passed a man sitting sideways on a white horse, with a basket on the crook of his arm. The tangle of holly and ivy in the hedges glittered as though lacquered, and against this background a thousand spring and early summer flowers were fluttering their bright petals: pink and waxen white hedge roses, the cuckoo flower, bird's eye, the bee-shaken bells of the foxglove, and, clustering beneath them, the tender spears of ferns. The road was a changeful dusky red, paling on the rise of a hill, darkening on its fall. Above it, the sky changed without rest, white cloud and translucent blue moving, arching, giving at one moment the impression of tranquil nearness, at the next the aching pallor of unbounded space. A flock of starlings cast a shadow on the road, and the beat of their wings as they passed was like the break of a summer wave.

They had to stand close to the hedge to let a herd of red Devon cows go by. The sweet warm smell of newly milked udders came from them, and their humid eyes turned in indolent curiosity toward the brothers.

Eden opened a gate into a meadow across which a footpath wavered among buttercups and clover. In a boggy corner rose the yellow spears of the iris, and a great oak tree made a shade already sought by sheep pink from the dipping.

They followed the path through a spinney where some young rabbits at play paused, staring and startled for a space, before scampering to cover. They crossed a stream by stepping-stones, and then the path joined a lane so narrow that the trees, almost meeting overhead, turned it into a green moist tunnel where the colours of flowers and fern were intensified into an unreal and dreamy brilliance.

They talked little as they went, Eden pointing out this and that in broken sentences. But, when they reached a certain gap in the hedge, he said—"Here we are! This is my own particular spot. You see, I must rather like you or I shouldn't have brought you here."

They passed into a grassy dell that lay at the foot of a series of fields of barley, oats, and wheat that rose, fold upon golden fold, to the rounded hills on which the bosoms of the clouds seemed to rest. They stretched themselves upon the grass, and it was as though they lay at the foot of the rich tapestry of June, unrolled on the hillsides above them. Here were the last of the bluebells, their tender stems bending beneath the weight of their blossoms that seemed the very distillation of nature's thought of blueness.

Finch lay with his eyes on a level with them, as still, as empty of remembrance as he could make himself, letting, in this instant, their beauty pour into him. As with a catch in the breath of his being he was suspended, knowing nothing, feeling all, as he fancied.

"I am thinking," Eden said, "of the ecstasy that bluebell must feel in its colour—how it must push out each fibre into the soil to get more pigment for it—how it spreads its leaves like hands to catch the sunrays, and, before it flowers, how it holds up its pale green bud like a mouth towards the rain. And all of this with just one idea—colour!"

"And yet, after all those thoughts," said Finch, "you have picked it!"

"That is my way of reaching out to get colour for myself."

"Eden, you're a queer sort of fellow."

"Yet I shouldn't be surprised if I have more pure thoughts in the twenty-four hours than some of the people who complain that I am immoral."

"Just what do you mean by *pure thoughts*?"

Eden rolled on to his back and let the sun shine on his face. "I mean thoughts of men and women as happy natural beings, making the most of every hour of their short stay here, like these flowers do or those birds overhead—satisfied that there shall be any number of varieties of their kind, not trying to force themselves to one dun colour or one self-righteous squeak."

Finch grunted acquiescence. "That's just the way I feel," he said. "Only I think you're wrong when you say that Renny has no imagination. I think he has lots of imagination. Only he's like a spirited horse and, I think, his imaginings rather startle him."

"Do you really? That's interesting... By the way, how do he and Alayne get on?"

Finch wished that Eden hadn't asked that question. Discussing Alayne and Renny with him was too difficult. "They get on very well," he answered hesitatingly—"that is, as far as I can tell."

"I can't imagine their getting on. No Whiteoak that ever lived could satisfy Alayne's ideal of what a husband should be. All those cold-blooded New England ancestors—with a few stolid Dutchmen thrown in—are too much alive in her to make it possible for her to understand us."

Finch felt suddenly frightened for Alayne. "But Renny's not a bit like you!"

"Yes he is! Only where I am weak he is strong, and where I am strong he's as weak as water."

"I've never seen any signs of weakness in Renny!"

"Have you seen any signs of strength in me?"

Finch laughed, but did not answer.

Eden went on—"Well, when you begin to look for the one you'll perhaps stumble on the other."

"The only trouble I have noticed is that she doesn't see enough of him. I think she often feels hurt because he spends so much time with his horses." It was easier to discuss them with Eden than he had thought.

Eden laughed. "She may thank her stars that he does. Let them remain distant acquaintances and passionate lovers and they may get on. Renny couldn't be a companion to a woman of Alayne's sort. She's too exquisitely precise. She's a very sweet-pea-ish kind of woman."

"I think that's rather good," Finch said. "There's something delicate and alert and fragrant about her—rather like the sweet-pea, though I know you don't intend it as a compliment."

"A woman shouldn't be like any particular flower. It grows monotonous. She should be like a whole garden of flowers—indefinite, restful, drugging the senses, not stimulating them to irritation."

"Is that what Minny is like?" He reddened then at his own boldness.

"Minny is like a vegetable garden—nourishing, wholesome, a kind of roughage for the soul."

"She sings beautifully."

"Doesn't she! I sometimes think when she is singing to me in the evening that, if only she would pass away as she sings, I could adore the memory of her forever!"

Finch considered this remark in silence. He could not follow the swift, erratic changes of Eden's mind, the mystery of his relations with women. He felt pity for any woman who loved Eden... Pity, too, for a woman who loved Renny... And was not there something in young Pheasant to stir one's compassion? Perhaps then it amounted to this—that any woman who gave herself in love was to be pitied. What then of the woman who would perhaps one day love him? Would she move another heart to pity?

He lay in the increasing warmth of the sun, his eyes gazing into the tangle of grass blades as into a forest. At that moment it had to him the impenetrability of a forest, above which leant the perfumed globes of the bluebells. His lips parted and he drew the sweet air into his mouth... A long sigh came from Eden. Was it of content or longing?

The face of his cousin, Sarah Court, rose in his mind, fixed there as though in a trance. Dreamily he examined it, feature by feature... the high white forehead under the drawn-back hair; the eyes that repelled all warmth, yet held the light of some inner fire; the high-bridged, narrow-nostrilled nose; the mouth, small, secret, withdrawn between that nose and jutting chin; the full white throat developed like that of a singer.

Hotly he wished that he were alone that he might meditate on that face, its potentialities, in this solitude. He turned his back on Eden and lay face downward, pressing against the tender growth of grass and flowers.

Then, with hidden face, he experienced the sensation that had come to him at intervals for years. A form, mist-like, opaque, yet the shape of himself, drew out from his breast, and when its entire pale length had emerged, and it had sprung free of him, it floated near him, leaving him empty as a sighing shell, but with a strange feeling of power, as if he were at that moment capable of doing unimagined things. As it left his breast it drew all sense of the *I* away from him, and, at the same time, all weakness. The impersonal being that was left held an undirected, elemental strength. The strange feeling of power was there, but with no desire to exercise it.

The sensation passed like a breath from a mirror, leaving him the reflection of his normal self. He found his mind still dwelling on the thought of Sarah Court. In a muffled voice he asked Eden if he had ever seen her.

Eden answered drowsily that he had.

Had he spoken to her?

No. The old aunt saw to that. He was an outcast.

Had he really seen her face?

Yes.

What did he think of her?

Eden sat up, clasping his ankles. "Think of her? Why, I think that by the time she's fifty her nose and chin will meet."

Finch remembered how the lamplight had glimmered on the point of her chin, turning it to porcelain, as she stood beside the piano. He remembered how she had held the violin a prisoner with it, seemed to dig it into the very wood of the violin.

He said huskily—"She'd be a funny sort of girl to kiss, wouldn't she?"

"God, you'd never be able to tear yourself away from her!"

"There's something very beautiful about her too." He turned over and faced Eden, half-shamefacedly.

"Is there?" A troubled look came into Eden's eyes. "I wish I might meet her. I have had nothing but glimpses of her passing the lodge. She's always going off alone. Minny can't bear the sight of her, yet she's always routing me out of my chair to see her go by. She cries, in a stage whisper—'For Heaven's sake, come. That old-fashioned creature is mincing past. What a dead-and-alive profile! What skirts!' And we peep between the curtains."

"If only you two were married, we might have some good times together. There's a tennis court that could be made into quite a decent one."

Eden gave a grimace that made his handsome face grotesque. "No! I tried it once; it doesn't suit me. Talk of prostituting one's art—better that than smothering it in the marriage-bed... I was only twenty-three when I married Alayne. Perhaps when I'm thirty-five I'll try it again. No man should marry before that... Don't you do it, young Finch!"

"This situation," said Finch, "is very worrying to Aunt Augusta. Here you are, one might say, on her doorstep—"

"Her very expression," shouted Eden. "You've been talking me over."

"Well, that's natural, isn't it?" But he got very red. "Anyhow, there are you and Minny at the lodge, and Aunt can't invite you to the Hall—she can't even speak of you to her guests—"

"Because we're living in sin!" interrupted Eden. "Whereas, if we went to a registry office where some old gaffer, probably of the most disgusting habits, would say a few words over us and have us sign our names in a book she'd perhaps invite us to play tennis! No—we'll play tennis on our own kitchen-table, with two spoons and a lump of sugar, and we'll cry—'Love all and marry none!' But I'm damned if we'll get married for the sake of an introduction to old Mrs. Court!"

"I see," said Finch. "But it would be nice, all the same, if you were married... Well, since this not being married is so good for your writing, I suppose you've done a lot of poetry this year."

Eden looked at him suspiciously. Was this youth making fun of him? But Finch looked serious, as few can look serious.

His expression was indeed lugubrious. Eden answered, rather sulkily.

"Not a great deal. I got some good material from the libraries in Paris for my poem of New France. But I believe my natural bent is toward lyrics. I've had a good many published in magazines this year. Have you seen any of them?"

"No, I scarcely ever see magazines. I'd like awfully well to hear them though."

"Very well. The first evening you are free come in and I'll read some of them to you... Sometimes I think I'll attempt a novel, but I don't believe I'd succeed. There's something in a poet turning novelist like a beggar turning highwayman."

He offered Finch a cigarette, and they smoked in silence for a space. The sun beat down on them hotly now, and from the hedge an unseen bird uttered a prolonged *sweet, sweet,* then broke into a gushing warble.

Eden said—"As you know how hard up I am, there's no need for me to tell you that I can't pay you what I owe you yet. But when this long poem's published—"

"Look here, you're not to bother about that! I've just been wondering if I couldn't help you a little more."

Eden's eyes, as they returned Finch's gaze, had in them a look almost of sadness. The boy had such a kind of idiot-generosity in him, such inimitable silly kindness, that it almost hurt one!

"That's awfully good of you," he said. "Perhaps you may. And would you mind telling me if you've been doing things for the others too?"

It was difficult for Finch not to look proud as he replied—"Well, I brought the uncles over here, did everything quite decently. And I'm putting up a new piggery for Piers. And I

bought a new motor car for the family. A Dodge, this year's
model. But Renny won't get into it. And I've taken over the
mortgage for Maurice and Meggie though, of course, that's
nothing, because they pay me a higher interest than I get
anywhere else. Oh, yes, and I paid for a new iron fence for
the plot in the graveyard. The old one was falling to pieces of
rust."

Eden considered these various financial activities in
silence while he calculated roughly what they would amount
to. He said:

"I hope you're not going to overdo this fairy godfather
business, or you may find yourself sitting on someone's
doorstep along with Minny and me."

Finch laughed. "No danger of that. I've changed Gran's
investments to much better ones. I had a frightful row with
old Purvis over it. He was for refusing to let me take it out
of the Government Bonds. They brought about four and a
half per cent. Fancy! But George Fennel—he's in a broker's
office you know—advised me to put a good deal into New
York stocks. Purvis was awfully disagreeable until Renny
wrote to him and said that I was to do just as I liked. Then he
gave in."

"Hmph! I don't believe Renny would care if you lost it—
I shouldn't be surprised if he were glad—if only it would
bring you to heel. He'd rather support the entire family, till
they drop like rotten plums from the tree, than have such a
rival as you are now. He's extravagantly paternal; yet here
are you taking the whole family under your wing. Snatching
his role from him. No wonder he won't ride in the car you
bought. He'd acknowledge himself as one of your pension-
ers. Old Redhead isn't greedy for anything but to be chief of
the clan. What else have you invested in?"

"Nickel, and some Western stocks. And I lent ten thousand to that Miss Trent—Alayne's friend, you know—at nine per cent. She insisted on paying an exorbitant interest. It really makes me feel uncomfortable. She's in the antique business. Over here to buy things. She has a stock in New York, so there's no risk. She crossed with us, and we saw something of her in London. She and Uncle Ernie were rather too thick to please Uncle Nick and me. We were quite worried about him."

Eden rose.

"I think I'd like to go home," he said. "This is too much for my little brain." He yawned and stretched his white bare arms. "But it perceives one thing with awful clarity. You are going to sneak back to Jalna dead broke, world-weary, with nothing but the rags you stand in, and Renny is going to receive you with open arms. The returned Prodigal. It will be a return quite after his own heart."

"I suppose you're remembering how good he was to you when you came back," said Finch.

2

AFTERNOON

That afternoon, when Augusta had carried off her brothers and Mrs. Court to pay a call at the Vicarage, Finch went into the drawing-room and sat down at the piano. His fingers ached to play, for he had not done so since the day on the boat. Soon after lunch Sarah had disappeared into the park carrying a book. The day was warm and there was a feeling of tranquillity on the countryside, now that the first passion of young growth was over. The trees, the fields, the flowers, the birds and beasts had given themselves up to the sustained bliss of their fruition with no thought of its evanescence.

Finch had drawn aside one of the curtains just far enough to allow the sunlight to slant across the dimness of the room. He sat with his hands on the keyboard waiting for the moment to come when he must play. The black keys, he thought, were like black birds perched in a row on a marble balustrade. Soon he would scatter them into flight. They would be scattered, singing sweetly and mournfully.

He played Moszkowski's Habanera. He played with a dreamy joy. As he finished he was aware that someone had come into the room, but, instead of the irritation that he usually felt at an intrusion, he was glad of this new presence. He did not look round, but sat motionless while the harmony still lingered in the room. He was not surprised when his cousin's voice came almost in a whisper from behind him.

"May I come in and listen?" she asked.

"Please do," he answered, still without looking round.

She came in and seated herself, her hands folded in her lap. She gave him a little smile, but after that fixed her eyes on the scene beyond the open window. He was able to study her face as he played.

He had never seen a face so still, so repressed, yet with a strange eagerness. He could not decide where this eagerness was shown. Not in the eyes with their withdrawn look. Not in the small sweet mouth with its almost sucked-in appearance. It seemed to come from some luminosity within or from her attitude, the posture of her arms suggesting folded wings, aquiver for flight. Her expression did not change as he played piece after piece, but when he ceased she said:

"Will you play with me one day?"

She spoke with the simplicity of a child, and again he was conscious of the caressing sweetness of her voice. He thought there was a look half frightened in her eyes as she spoke, and he had a sudden sensuous desire to say something brutal to her to startle her into betraying herself. Instead, he said:

"I should like to accompany you now, if you will let me."

She got up without a word and went to the window seat where her violin case lay. She bent over it, taking out the violin and dusting it with a piece of silk that lay in the case. Then she put it under her chin and began to tune it. She did this in a manner so aloof that Finch began to feel nervous, wondering if he could accompany her.

"What shall we play?" he asked, turning over her music.

"Anything you like."

He found something by Brahms that he knew, but at first the going was not easy. The rather frozen beauty of her playing seemed impossible to merge with the fluid grace of his. It was as though a frozen lake had said to a running stream—"Come, merge with me."

They almost gave up in despair. Then, suddenly in a waltz of Chopin, they achieved the flow, the union of spirit for which they had been striving. Something seemed loosed in her. A delicate flush came in her cheeks. Finch delighted in the sense of power this gave him. They played on and on, speaking only in hushed tones between the pieces. It was miraculous to him that there should be such a change in her playing, and he wondered if a corresponding change would take place in her attitude toward him.

But this was not so. As soon as the music was over she was as remote, as monosyllabic as before. When they heard the others returning, though, she whispered:

"Do not tell them we played together." As she said this her face wore the expression of mischievousness sometimes seen in the faces of women painted by medieval Italian artists.

"And you will let me accompany you again?" he whispered back.

She nodded, her lips folded close, her greenish eyes glittering. She was like a child, he thought, full of playful malice against elders who repressed her. He heard Mrs. Court holding forth on the tepidity of spirit displayed by the Vicar on the subject of Prayer Book Reform. "Upon my word," she was declaring, "you might think, to hear him, that one Prayer Book is as good as another." He heard Augusta suggesting that they play bridge that evening. Might not he and Sarah be alone for a while? He was going to ask her, but found himself saying instead:

"I think Sarah is a beautiful name."

She raised her brows and repeated the name after him. He thought her way of saying it was delightful. "Sair-rah." The syllables were like sweet stressed notes.

He continued rapidly then—"I don't believe you care for bridge. I hate it. Would you come out to the garden for a while?"

"Perhaps."

"Why perhaps?" he insisted.

"It's always *perhaps* with me."

"Because of…?" He gave a little jerk of the head toward her aunt.

She nodded.

"But, if she's playing bridge—"

"There's letter-writing. We have thirty-two regular correspondents. I write most of the letters."

He was too astonished for words. He came of a family who seldom wrote letters except on business. It had frequently been a matter for dispute who was to write the monthly letter to Augusta. He had sent a picture postcard to each member of the family from London. He had had no word from home. Ernest had had a letter from Alayne, and often said that he must answer it.

"If there's nothing to do I'll come," she said. Then she moved away and went to Nicholas, listening attentively to what he had to say.

When Finch and Nicholas happened to be alone for a moment before dinner, Nicholas said

"That girl has her father's face; but Dennis Court was a devil, and I'm afraid the aunt has brought her up to be a prude."

3

EVENING

They entered the garden through a door in the wall that was half hidden in ivy. The door was not easy to open, and, when they were inside, Finch left it ajar. It was not dark, nor would it be that night. Across the clear primrose yellow of the west were two bars of purple cloud fringed with crimson. The pale new moon stood aloof, like a young singer standing in the wings timidly awaiting her summons to the stage. An ancient oak tree, its trunk embowered in ivy, its every branch and twig hoary with lichen, towered just beyond one of the garden walls. In it a number of rooks were gathered and seemed to be enjoying the wind from the south that tossed its lesser boughs. The birds leaped into the air and, after a few powerful

strokes of the wing, allowed themselves to drift or tumble
back into the green shelter. A linnet, perched among the
branches of a peach tree trained against the wall, sang a thin
plaintive strain that could be heard when the rooks silenced
their cries for a space. The flower beds seemed to have drawn
closer together, as though in a concerted effort to overpower
by their perfume the senses of any who walked in the garden.
And above the scent of the rose and the heliotrope there
ascended the heavy somnolent sweetness of the nicotiana.

Sarah Court wore a flame-coloured shawl, the deep
fringe of which almost touched the ground behind. The
shawl made her look proud and Spanish, he thought, and he
remembered having heard his grandmother say that, in the
days of Queen Elizabeth, one of the Courts had married a
Spanish woman. He suddenly had a picture of Renny in his
mind—Renny with a pointed beard and a high ruff that
suited him well. He smiled to himself and saw that she was
peering around at him with curiosity. He had wondered what
he could talk to her about. Now he said:

"I was thinking of my eldest brother. I wish you could
know him. He's such a splendid fellow. It is strange that just
now there was something in you that reminded me of him."

"Something *splendid*?" she asked.

"Yes. Something very proud and rather splendid."

"But I'm not proud!"

"But you have a look of pride."

"I have nothing to be proud about." After a moment she
added—"And every reason to be humble."

She was walking slowly along a narrow box-bordered
path, and Finch, following her, was conscious of pride in her
every movement, in her manner of wearing the Spanish
shawl, and in the restrained musical tones of her voice.

When they reached the end of the path he looked into her face. "I'm glad you were able to come out," he said. He was glad that she had come, but, in truth, he would have been still more glad to be in the garden alone at this hour, or with some companion of whose presence his nerves were not so aware.

Her lip curled in the same smile of a malicious child as when in the drawing-room. "My aunt gave me enough letters to write to keep me busy till bedtime."

At that they were drawn nearer each other. She began to caress the flowers of a yellow rose bush and to press her face into them with an almost cruel eagerness.

"What a lot of hair," he thought, looking down at the mass of glossy braids covering the back of her head. "And she holds the roses to her exactly as she holds the violin." He remembered what Eden had said about being kissed by her.

He would have liked to summon the romantic valour to make love to her. He could not even picture the possibility of doing so in the future. Her air was too self-concealing. She was too exquisitely removed from him.

Through the door in the wall he saw two figures passing, hand in hand. He recognised the gardener's boy, Ralph Hart, but the girl's face was just a disc of white.

The boy dropped the girl's hand and came to the door. It was supposed to be bolted at that hour, and he was surprised at finding it ajar. Finch went to him.

"I shouldn't have left that door open. But I'll not forget to shut it when we leave. Perhaps you'd better shut it now and we will go out by the gate."

As he spoke he tried to see the girl's face, curious to know what sort of sweetheart the boy had chosen. But she drew away, shyly averting it.

"I'm sorry I came to the door, zir," said Ralph; "but in the dimsey I didden see 'ee in the garden. Us thought it were left open by mistake." He touched his cap and went after the girl.

Finch shut the door. The noise of its closing frightened the rooks, and, with hoarse caws, they rose from the oak and sailed in close formation toward the afterglow. The linnet in the peach tree hushed his song, listening till he believed all was well again, then once more his pipings and flutings filled the garden, not in the intervals of the clamour of rooks, as before, but in full and confident possession.

There was a seat like a tall, narrow church-pew between two clipped yew trees, and they seated themselves on it. Finch began to tell her about his family. She listened with absorbed interest, and, as he described each one in turn, his heart warmed to them, their imperfections dwindled, and he could hardly find words to describe Renny's spirit, his horsemanship; Piers's courage, his knowledge of farming; Wake's gentleness and precocity; Meg's—oh, well, Meggie was perfect! He almost made himself homesick talking about them. Eden alone he did not mention.

"You have so many," she said, "and I have no one. I mean of my very own."

"Will you tell me something of your life?" he asked gently. "I'd like to be able to picture you in Ireland."

She made a disdainful movement of her shoulders under the bright shawl. "My life is nothing but practising, paying calls, and writing letters."

He was hurt by her inclusion of practising with calls and letter-writing. He said—"But you love music, don't you?"

"Never till today."

He felt what this implied through all his nerves. Yet—to have learned to play so beautifully, and not have learned to

love it, to find sanctuary in it... The thought almost repelled
him. He felt something insensate in her. What had today's
awakening signified then? That she had suddenly become
conscious of the sensuous release in music? He asked:

"Didn't you care for it before you went to live with your
aunt?"

"I never thought about it."

She talked so little he was driven to catechise her.

"Were you left an orphan young?"

"My mother died when I was seven."

"Mine, too."

"How strange."... Her tone was musing, rather than
impressed by the coincidence.

"And your father?" Well, she was his cousin; he had the
right to question her!

"When I was thirteen." She turned towards him (the
moon was now giving just enough light to etherealise her
features) and began to speak rapidly. "He was drowned. He
and I had lived alone after my mother died. Our house was
on the sea coast. He was very fond of horses—like your
brother Renny—but he drank a good deal. And he brought
strange people to the house. I don't mind telling you that I
liked them. Much better than Aunt Elizabeth's friends.
Father was always boasting about his horses. Especially a
mare called Miriam which had saved his life in a flooded
stream once. When he had been drinking, he'd boast of the
great distance she could swim. One night he and his friends
began making bets about it. To prove what she could do, he
led her to the shore, and his friends went with him. He
mounted her and rode her out into the sea. It was like glass,
and there was moonlight. She swam on and on, with him on
her back, and he shouted and sang. At last his friends were

frightened and screamed to him to come back, but he only sang the louder. They heard the mare whinny. Before morning a storm came up, and the next day his body and the mare's were driven ashore by the waves."

"How appalling! And were you alone in that house?"

"Yes; but I watched the people on the shore from a window. The peasants said it was a terrible sight to see the great waves dash the mare against the cliff. My father's feet were caught in the stirrups. They said the mare would rear and her hooves clatter against the rocks, as though she were alive."

Finch remembered having heard the family talk of this tragedy when he was a child, but he had thought of it as having happened many years before. The story had seemed too fantastic. The Dennis Court, of whom he remembered his grandmother exclaiming, "Ah, there was a real Court!" had seemed almost a myth... And now here was he, Finch, sitting on a garden seat beside Dennis's daughter, while she repeated the story of his death in unemotional tones.

Keeping his own voice as level as hers, he said:

"And after that you went to live with Mrs. Court, I suppose. It was a great change."

She answered, with a touch of bitterness—"Yes. A change for the better everyone thought. No one seemed to remember how I had adored my father. It's true enough that I can never repay her for all she's done for me. All the lessons, the travelling. But she made me practise six hours a day, and, when we travelled, I never had a moment to call my own. Now we don't travel. She can't afford it. And, if I'm quiet or go off by myself, she calls me *Mouse* and *Mole*!"

He had not hoped for any intimate companionship such as this, had not dreamed that she would reveal anything of her inner self to him. Now he found that he could not keep pace with her careless and cold revelations. He would have liked to escape from her at that moment to brood on her mystery without the necessity of making talk. Yet she seemed not to expect comment from him, and, when he uttered a lame sentence or two, she made no reply but withdrew into her former immobility.

The young moon had passed behind a tall elm, and, as the branches were tossed in the wind, moonlight fell fitfully into the garden, illuminating now one flower bed, now another, now casting its silver veil on Sarah's face and hands.

Looking at her hands, like the hands of a silver statue, and remembering how they drew the music from her violin, he longed to touch them. Timidly he laid one of his own upon them. They were very cold.

"I'm afraid you are cold," he said nervously. "I think we had better walk about. Would you like that?"

She rose at once without answering him. They went through the garden gate, along a stone-paved passage, and crossed the tennis court.

"Do you play tennis?" he asked, and he wondered if her reason for rising so abruptly had been her desire to put aside the touch of his hand.

"A little. I wish I played better."

"I will see if I can get Aunt Augusta to have the court put in order."

She gave one of her small malicious smiles. "Perhaps we could get the two at the lodge to join us. I'd like that."

He looked round at her, startled. "Would you really? I didn't think you knew of their existence."

"I only wish I could meet them! I've passed the lodge time and again, wanting to speak to them. But all I saw was the curtain moving, as though they were peering out at me, thinking how horrid I was."

"Well," he said, frowning in anxiety at what he was going to suggest, "we might go and call on them now, if you're not afraid of offending your aunt."

"I don't mind offending her in the least," she replied coolly, and turned in the direction of the drive.

She walked quickly, as though she were doing something eagerly anticipated. They passed in and out of shadow and moonlight, her bright shawl flaming and darkening like the plumage of an exotic bird.

Halfway down the drive he offered her a cigarette, which she at first declined, then suddenly accepted, saying—"Yes, give me one! I'll do everything tonight that Aunt would hate."

He had only to see her put it in her lips and light it from the match he held to know that she was well accustomed to smoking.

He looked at her almost sternly, for he felt something devious about her. "When do you do it?" he asked.

"When I am being Mole." And she held up a thin fore-finger with a swarthy stain on it.

They found Eden sitting in the porch of the lodge on a tilted chair, like a workman after his day was done. He regarded their approach with an incredulous smile, then got to his feet.

"I've brought our cousin, Miss Court, to see you," said Finch, feeling suddenly daredevil and at his ease. Was it the support of Eden's presence that produced this feeling?

They shook hands gravely, and Eden led the way indoors. Finch had heard Minny scampering upstairs to tidy herself. Yet, when she came down, he wondered what the process of

tidying had been, she looked so far from neat. He came to the
conclusion that she had gone to powder her face, which had
the pink bloom of a peach in the candlelight. Her milk-white
neck looked thicker than when he had seen her last, her
crossed legs, under her too-short skirt, stouter. But her slanting eyes held the same challenge and gaiety, and her lips
looked ready as ever to part in laughter or song. She had on
an orange-coloured jumper, a blue skirt, and "nude" stockings. Finch wondered how Eden could tolerate this combination of colours. But then, Eden seldom seemed to notice
things.

Minny made Sarah sit in the one comfortable chair, close
to the fire, because she looked so pale. Minny's own cheeks
glowed beneath the thick layer of powder. Her generous
mouth smiled welcome, and this astonished Finch after what
Eden had told him of her feelings toward Sarah. Sarah spread
out the long fringe of her shawl and inhaled the smoke of her
cigarette as though she were inhaling the very sweetness of
life. She preened herself like a bird, and Minny was apparently delighted to entertain her. Eden too was delighted. He
was beginning to feel the need of some society other than
Minny's. He heaped dry faggots on the fire, which crackled
into swift ruddy flames. He sat down on the narrow ingle-
seat facing Sarah. He thought Finch's description of her very
superficial. He read her with a far more subtle understanding.

Minny talked a great deal, directing almost all her conversation to Sarah, who sat motionless, seeming to drink in
all that Minny said. She told of amusing things that had happened to them abroad, now and then appealing to Eden's
memory to supply some foreign name which she invariably
mispronounced. Before long she began to speak of Eden's

poetry, of which she was very proud. It was the only poetry, she said, that she had ever been able to read, even though so much of it was hard to understand. Finch reminded Eden that he had promised to read him some of the poems he had written since leaving home.

Eden took a candle and went up the stairs that ascended from a corner of the room. Minny said—"He keeps everything he has in such perfect order." Soon he returned, carrying a folio of papers. Hot wax had dripped on his hand, and he went to Minny like a child to show it.

He sat again in the ingle-nook and read by the light of the flames. His voice, always musical, took on new, full tones when he read his poems.

"These are some bits from the long poem 'New France.' I can't read all of it. It's not in order," he said.

He read fragments which he called—"Indian Braves as Galley Slaves," "The Loves of Bigot," "A Countess of Quebec," and "Song of the Ursuline Nuns."

The two young women made little murmuring noises of approval after each poem. Finch liked them immensely and said so. He was almost overcome when Eden said suddenly to Sarah—"Do you know, this boy has been paying my way for a year and a half. If it had not been for him I don't know what I should have done."

"That was good of him," she said simply. "But how he must have liked doing it!"

"Did you like doing it?" Eden asked of him.

Finch assented, uttering the sudden guffaw of his hobbledehoy days, which still came from him in moments of embarrassment.

"These," said Eden, taking up some sheets of paper clipped together, "are some things I wrote in Italy."

"In Italy!" gasped Finch. "Why, I didn't know you were in Italy!"

"Yes, I had to go. It was beastly cold in France and I'd got a cough."

"We went on a cheap excursion," put in Minny, easily.

"How splendid!" sighed Finch. "How I wish I might go!"

"Don't be a silly young blighter," said Eden. "You can go where you like."

"Perhaps I'll go with Arthur Leigh. He's over here."

Sarah looked expectantly into Eden's face, waiting for the poems. He read three. The last one was "To a Young Nightingale Practising his Song in Sicily." His listeners agreed that this was best of all.

"It's beautiful! It's beautiful!" said Sarah, clasping her fingers tightly together. The shawl fell from her, as she leaned toward Eden, and her bare shoulders and arms were exposed to the firelight.

Eden was made happy by this approval. Soon he and Minny went to the larder together. Their whispers and the clink of china could be heard by the other two.

"Do you like them?" whispered Finch. "Are you glad you came?" He was worried lest her aunt might have missed her.

She nodded composedly.

Eden and Minny returned, he carrying a bottle in each hand, and she a large dish on which were arranged several sorts of cake, the icing of which, chocolate and pink and white, had crumbled and were intermingling.

Eden was hilarious at having company. Nothing was too ridiculous for him to say or do. Finch and Minny filled the room with their laughter. Sarah Court sat upright, sipping wine, nibbling cake, seeming to absorb with passionate intensity the gaiety of the moment.

As they hurried home along the drive they faced a strong warm wind from the moor. She had to grasp her shawl tightly to hold it about her. Their elders were still playing whist and they entered undiscovered. She glided up the stairs, while he lounged into the drawing-room and leant against Augusta's chair, asking her what luck she had had.

X

Old Love And New

THE DAYS strung themselves out like pearls warmed on the sunburnt throat of summer, till Finch and his uncles had been a month in Devon. The time had passed quickly for the two old brothers, with no incident more unpleasant than a wrangle at the bridge table to shadow their enjoyment. There was so much to do in the way of garden parties, paying calls on old acquaintances, drinking tea in the rose garden, and having the *Times* to read when it was a few hours instead of two weeks old, that the day was all too short. The change had done them a world of good. Nicholas had not in years been so free from gout. Ernest was almost frightened by the power of his digestion. There seemed something sinister about a stomach that, from rebelling at a piece of seed cake at tea, turned to the consumption of strawberries and Devonshire cream without a qualm. Ever since his meeting with Rosamond Trent his digestion had improved, and it had crossed his mind that if such meetings could be arranged once in, say, six months, the benefit to him would be immense. He attributed his improvement to nothing else than the exhilaration of contact with this vigorous and highly efficient personality.

He and Nicholas were both fond of music, and they delighted in the violin and piano playing of Sarah and Mrs. Court. Nicholas thought the girl's playing was without soul, and it was he who insisted that Finch should accompany her one evening. But the performance was a depressing failure. Finch was unaccountably nervous, and Sarah more soulless than ever. Mrs. Court had sat delightedly tapping her heels on the floor while they had spiritlessly executed a Polonaise by Chopin.

At the end she had exclaimed:

"Sarah can't play with anyone but me! And Finch is far too nervous to play accompaniments. You've got to have nerves of iron to play accompaniments. I've never heard you do so badly as you did tonight, Mouse."

The little woman had trotted eagerly to the piano, scarcely waiting till Finch had risen from the seat before she settled herself on it and instructed Sarah to repeat the Polonaise with her. Sarah had repeated it to the brilliant exactitude of her aunt's accompaniment, and after that no one again suggested that the boy and girl play together.

But they did play together. Every afternoon that their elders went out to tea, and they went about four out of the seven, Sarah and Finch glided like two conspirators into the drawing-room. They went as though to indulge in the taste of some forbidden wine. He trembled as he sat with bent back above the keyboard while she tuned her violin. As they lost themselves in the indolent beauty of a Tchaikovsky waltz the world about them dissolved. Their life came into flower. But no word or sign of love passed between them beyond the expression of their love for music. On the days when they were not alone together she seemed to go out of his life, leaving him scarcely a thought of her beyond the fascination her face and her attitudes always had for him. Even sometimes when they had played together he left her presence with a feeling of relief, drawing a deep breath, as though he had come from an atmosphere too close for him. But at times he was so susceptible to her nearness, to something captivating and strange in her, that he would find it hard to restrain himself from some open expression of his emotion. Once a mist came before his eyes when he was accompanying her, and he could not see the notes. He stopped playing, and, after a wild cascade of grace notes, she stopped too.

"I lost my place," he muttered.

She bent over him, her violin still tucked under her chin, and looked into his eyes with a gently curious expression. Yet he thought he detected the same hint of malice in her that he had encountered before. He stared steadily back without speaking, but his heart was beating wildly, and he was on the point of taking the violin from her hands and possessing himself of them when she straightened herself and, pointing to the place with her bow, said coldly:

"Please don't waste our time! It goes so quickly."

He wondered whether she were really repelling him or regarded these meetings only as an outlet for the sensuous enjoyment of music.

Once Nicholas did not go with the others as they imagined he had. Coming down from his room he turned, with a feeling of anticipation, towards the drawing-room at the sound of music. He opened the door softly, not wishing to interrupt them, but, after listening for a few moments and studying the expressions of the two, he withdrew as quietly as he had entered, standing outside the closed door until the piece was finished, with bent head and a look of sardonic gentleness on his lined face.

Though he had been conscious of the uneasy joy within the room, he never made any reference to their playing together. He never intruded on them again, and he often suggested afternoon excursions that would set them free.

Mrs. Court would have liked to insist on Sarah's accompanying them, but to have taken her would have meant discomfort in the car. She gave her endless letters to write, and stuffy, old-fashioned dresses to alter to keep her busy in the evenings. These Sarah did, sitting up late in her room, having previously put out her light and pretended to go to bed.

Augusta, at this time, began to be a little tired of her guests. The constant strain of ordering meals, to say nothing of the expense of providing them, was beginning to tell on her nerves. She had thought that Mrs. Court would see eye to eye with her in her hope for the union of Sarah and Finch. She had broached the subject before his arrival, and it had been received with Mrs. Court's customary jaunty good humour. But now Augusta was driven to believe that Mrs. Court did not approve of the match at all, that she selfishly wished to keep the girl unmarried in order that she might have not only a companion whose salary consisted of her clothes and keep, but one of striking appearance and artistic attainments. The young pair themselves were not very satisfactory. They seemed to have nothing to say to each other, and the music which she had hoped would draw them together was apparently a barrier between them. His attempt at accompanying Sarah had been a failure, and when Sarah and Mrs. Court made music Finch sat drooping in a corner, the picture of gloom.

Nicholas, too, was on her nerves. They could not be long together without his having this effect on her. His untidy hair and slovenly habits irritated her as much as Ernest's

neatness pleased her. More than once he had caused her dismay by his apparently unconscious imitation of their
mother. He had made sops of his cake in his tea. He had rumbled at table—"I want gravy. More dish gravy, please," in
their mother's very tone. She and Ernest had given each
other a look. Another time he had said—"Why doesn't that
young whelp at the lodge come up to see me? I want to see
Eden!" At this Ernest and she had been positively frightened. Ernest had counselled her to pay no attention to this
vagary of Nick's. "Just ignore him," he had advised, "and
he'll grow ashamed of himself." But they had an uncomfortable feeling that Nick knew their ignoring was a pretence
and that he was unashamed.

When whist was being played in the evening it became
the custom for Sarah and Finch to meet in the garden. They
entered it by the door, and Finch usually left it ajar so that he
might see the gardener's boy and his girl pass, hand in hand.
Ralph no longer troubled about the closing of the door. A
quiet understanding had arisen between the two youths. No
day passed without their talking together for a little. Finch
learned that Ralph's mother was a Cornishwoman and that
the men of his family had followed a seafaring life. Sarah had
found out that the girl was a kitchenmaid, thickset, round-
faced, stolid. She had spoken to her once, but could scarcely
make out what she said, for she came from a farm and spoke
in broad Devon.

The rustic love affair had a peculiar fascination for the
two who sat on the garden seat. They discussed the lovers,
their regular walking out together; and Finch repeated fragments of his conversations with Ralph, trying to imitate the
singsong of his speech. They would sit silent in the dusk,
thinking of the other two in the dusk somewhere unseen,

perhaps kissing, embracing, and they took a sensuous mournful pleasure in reflecting on their attachment.

Sometimes they went to the lodge, where they were very welcome to Eden and Minny, who were often bored by each other's society. They would gather about the fire, and Eden would throw pine boughs on it that burst into a vivid crackling blaze, illuminating their faces and the black oak beams of the ceiling, then die down, leaving the pine needles like fiery wires. The twigs would writhe in worm-like agony, pale, turn grey, and crumble. Then Eden would throw on fresh boughs.

Before the fire he read his new poems to them, directing his voice towards Sarah, but Minny showed no sign of jealousy. She seemed perfectly sure of Eden. He said once to Finch, as they lay talking on a hillside—"Minny is kind. That's the beautiful thing about her. Alayne is unselfish, but she isn't really kind; and love without kindness is like a garden without grass..."

One evening a knock came at the door, and they looked at each other like frightened children, fancying it might be Mrs. Court in search of Sarah, for Finch had told Eden of her tyranny. But it was Nicholas and Ernest come to call. Nicholas and Augusta had had words over the whist-table, and the game had been broken up. The two ladies had gone to Augusta's room, and the two gentlemen, feeling rather reckless, had marched down to the lodge. They showed no surprise at seeing Finch and Sarah there.

Minny was delighted by so much company. Nicholas and Ernest found the society of the young people so exhilarating that they felt aggrieved at the time they had lost on the evenings at whist. They asked Minny if she still could sing. She denied that she could, laughing a good deal. But, persuaded at last, she threw back her head and sang one piece after another to them. She had an endless repertory of old favourites. Her face was tilted as she sang, so that it was partly in shadow, but the full light of the fire fell on her white, throbbing throat, the skin of which was like the inner petals of a rose.

On the way back to the house Sarah whispered to Finch that now her aunt would find out everything and their evenings would be spoiled. Luckily for them a change in the weather came that night, and for several days they had driving rains and a gale from the moor. In the evenings the uncles asked for nothing better than a game of whist by the fire.

One morning Ernest announced his intention of going into Dorset to visit some old friends. That same day Finch had a letter from Arthur Leigh, and, remembering how much Augusta had admired Arthur, he conceived the idea of having him down for a visit during his uncle's absence. He might have Ernest's room, which was really the best guest room. Augusta, wondering if she would ever have the felicity of feeling somewhat lonely again, agreed. Inside a few days Ernest had gone, his room had been "turned out," and Arthur had taken his place.

The friends were joyful to be with each other again and with an opportunity for intimacy they had hitherto not known. Finch had forgotten how subtly attuned to his surroundings and how full of charm Arthur was, and Arthur felt anew the curiosity and sympathy Finch roused in him. He thought the household rather a strange one, including its offshoot in the lodge. Most of all, he was interested in Sarah Court.

At his coming she had withdrawn into her former aloofness, and it was difficult to make Arthur believe that she had gone on secret visits to the lodge, continually deceiving the aunt to whom she now seemed so devoted. But one afternoon, when the three young people were left alone, Finch persuaded her to play her violin for Arthur. And from that time there seemed to be engendered in him, almost against his will, a passionate interest in her. From being highspirited and gay he became meditative and morose. She appeared to be unconscious of the emotion she had roused in him. This change in his friend, taking place so soon after his advent into the house, was bewildering to Finch.

Augusta had had the tennis court put in order, and the daughter of the Vicar was invited to make a fourth at tennis. She was an athletic girl, with a blistered skin, who moved in long strides. Beside her the rigid yet gliding movements of Sarah seemed singularly out of place on the tennis lawn. Mrs. Court viewed with delight her incapacity for playing even a fairly good game.

"I never saw such a girl!" she would cry. "There's nothing spry about her. I call her my puppet." And sometimes she would exclaim—"Well played, Puppet!"

Sarah seemed as impervious to her aunt's ridicule as she seemed unconscious of Leigh's feeling for her. He and she always played on opposite sides, and the games usually turned out to be only a contest between Finch and the Vicar's daughter.

After the game he and she would discuss the various plays while the other two sat silent, Arthur hitting at the turf with his racquet, while his large grey eyes were fixed on Sarah's profile, as she sat gazing straight before her into untroubled space. She had been taught never to sit on the grass without something beneath her. She carried to the court a red woollen shawl, which Arthur spread out for her, and on it she sat isolated while the rest sprawled on the grass.

Finch was so conscious of Arthur's unease that he scarcely knew what he said, still he managed to talk in a desultory fashion while his mind was occupied with the problem of his friend's sudden infatuation. Was it really love that Arthur felt for Sarah, or had she merely exercised on him the peculiar fascination that seemed to be the very core of her personality? Finch himself had felt it. He had seen its effect on Eden. But in their case the spell was volatile, intermittent. Once Sarah had entered a room, neither the room nor its occupants remained the same. By the power of her chiselled remoteness she subdued their atmosphere. By the suggestion of hidden malice she produced a sense of foreboding. The more Finch observed aunt and niece, the more sure he was that Mrs. Court felt both the fascination and the foreboding. He began to think that her jeering attitude toward Sarah was assumed in an effort to reassure herself, as young Mooey reiterated—"I'm not f'ightened!"

He was angry with Arthur for allowing himself to be so speedily enslaved. He was angry with Sarah for being the enslaver. He felt in himself a stirring of jealousy that clouded the clear waters of his friendship for Arthur. Sarah and himself, who had been drifting in a shadowy and devious intimacy that might have led to strange and lovely revelations, were separated by Arthur's intrusion, for as such Finch began to regard his visit.

In the mornings, when Sarah was in attendance on Mrs. Court, Arthur Leigh sought out Eden, and they spent hours wandering in the flowery lanes, over the hillsides rich with ripening corn, and into the gorse-grown borders of the moor. Arthur could not say enough in praise of Eden. He confessed

that with no one else had he ever experienced such a sensation of magnetic accord. As for Eden's poetry, if Eden
belonged to any other country he would have met an appreciation not yet given him. He was worried over Eden's
future, and was too appreciative to please Finch when Finch
said that he would never let Eden suffer for lack of funds.
Eden was his own brother, and he did not see why Arthur
should take such a possessive note toward him. He began to
pity himself. Eden did not want him, Arthur did not want
him, Sarah no longer sat with him in the garden. He took to
sitting there alone, and had long conversations with young
Ralph, who confided to him that one day he hoped to marry
the kitchenmaid with whom he walked out. "But," he had
confided, "her's the oldest of a long family and must help her
mother for a bit, and I'm the youngest of a long family and
must help my mother till one of my brothers can afford to
have her live with he."

Nicholas planned an excursion, in which he invited the
three young people to join him. It was supposed to be merely
the revisiting of a hamlet in the moor that had once pleased
him. It was a rough drive that neither Augusta nor Mrs.
Court cared to undertake. In reality he did not want them to
know what he was about. This was to revisit the old home of
the wife from whom he was divorced. He had heard of the
death of her brother, who had lived there, and that the contents of the house were to be privately sold. He had spent
some of the happiest days of his life in this house, when he
was courting Millicent, and he had a sentimental desire to
walk through its rooms once more. He confided his intention
to his companions, with a half-cynical air, and yet with
enough seriousness to make them feel both compassion and
a romantic interest in the visit.

It was a day of alternate brilliant sunshine and flying cloud shadows. Their road lay, for the greater part of the way, along the ridges of rolling hills from where they could see a wide stretch of country where the green and gold pattern of the fields was blotted here and there by rounded clumps of woodland. High Willhayes and Yes Tor rose, alternately purple against the clouds or dim blue beneath the sunshine. The house where the Humes had lived was in a remote spot on the edge of the moor. Bracken and gorse grew to the very edge of its lawn, and behind it a small but noisy cascade rushed down a miniature gorge.

The house and all its outbuildings were of grey stone, very old, but quite bare of ivy and unsoftened by protecting trees, so that it gave the impression of bleakness. The many windows were small and the front door was sunk inhospitably between stone projections.

As they left the car and went toward the house the sun passed under a cloud. A wind from the moor began to whistle above the tumble of the cascade. Arthur and Finch showed their disappointment in their faces. They did not see how there could have been much jollity in that house. Even Nicholas, whose eyes had been alight with eagerness, looked rebuffed. He knocked on the heavy brass knocker. The door was opened by a tall stout man with a ruddy face, who had the place in charge. He was expecting them. He led them into the dismantled drawing-room. Surviving relatives had taken what they wanted from the house, and on tables were displayed in forlorn groups the ornaments and silver for sale. Light patches stood out on the wallpaper where pictures had been taken down. Furniture that had been long ago consigned to the attic had been carried downstairs by the agent in charge as being valuable, and the pieces thus reunited stood about the rooms, with the sad, hopelessly estranged air of old friends who have not met for half a lifetime.

The last Hume had been dead for only a month, yet there was an accumulation of dust in the house that might have been collecting during the seven generations of their occupancy. As they moved from room to room it seemed that some gloomy revelation of the past might be presented to them at any moment. Nicholas became more and more depressed. In a small room that had apparently been used as a study he found a framed photograph of a cricket team at Oxford wearing striped blazers, flat straw hats, and little side whiskers. He drew Finch to it and pointed out himself and his brother-in-law, the Hume who had lately died. Finch thought he should like to have this for himself, and bought it from the agent for three shillings. With it under his arm he followed Nicholas through the dining room into the kitchen. They left Leigh and Sarah examining an old brass-bound writing-case. A new intimacy seemed to enfold them.

The kitchen was the largest room in the house. The low ceiling was heavily beamed, the floor was of uneven stone, and the deep windows gave on a cobbled yard beyond which were the gabled stone stable, the shippen, and linhays. A long table, with benches on either side, filled one end of the room. At the other end was the fireplace and, at right angles to it, a high-backed settle. On the hearth lay a pair of heavy boots stained with mud, and on the settle a worn leather coat and a hat. These garments, belonging to the dead man, added the final touch of desolation to the scene. For the first time in his life Nicholas felt that he heard the portentous creak of the gates of death.

The agent and two people, a man and a woman, were talking in subdued tones before a cupboard filled with china. They were half hidden by the settle.

Suddenly the woman raised her voice on a note of energy and exclaimed: "I really must have those adorable glass bottles, and, of course, the Toby jugs! What do you say; do you think I ought to buy the cupboard itself?"

Nicholas reared his head as might an old lion who hears the voice of the hunter. He listened and heard what he expected—the mellow tones of his brother Ernest! Ernest and Miss Trent were there in quest of antiques! It was too horrible. His gorge rose at the thought. Ernest must have got wind of the sale, sent word to Miss Trent, and the two come post haste after bargains. Finch heard too and could not help approving of their sagacity, considering what he himself had at stake in Miss Trent's enterprise.

Nicholas grasped him by the arm and dragged him from the room. In the passage he glared at him, the deep downward lines of his face accentuated. He growled:

"I'm off upstairs to hide. Try to keep out of their way, but if they see you, don't let them know I'm here! When that woman takes herself off, come upstairs and find me."

Heavily he ascended the stairs. At the top he took off his hat and wiped his forehead, above which the iron-grey hair still grew strong and thick. "A damned close shave," he muttered. "I wouldn't have met that woman and that flibbertigibbet brother of mine for worlds." He peered in at the principal bedrooms, finding no remembrance there but only distaste for the fly-blown mirrors and beds heaped with mounds of linen and pillows. Drawers of writing bureaux stood half-open, the yellowing papers within revealed.

He felt half-stifled and longed for the moment of escape. He turned from each with a sigh and wondered where he would be safest from Miss Trent. He thought he would go into the room to which one descended by two shallow steps, and, if he heard them coming, he would simply put his back against the door and keep them out. He thumped down the two steps, opened the door, entered and closed it softly behind him.

A sun blind, yellow with age, hung askew halfway down the window, dimming the light in the room to a sallow twilight. He was astonished to find that he was not alone there. A woman was sitting by the bureau looking over some papers she had taken from it.

He would have escaped, but she looked up and their eyes met. He stood quite still, returning her gaze, with that peculiar feeling of having done all this before, of enacting a scene which he had previously rehearsed. Apart from that feeling his brain had ceased to function. He looked at the woman, saw that she was well dressed, elderly, distinguished-looking, but he was uncertain as to whether he and she were really existing in the world he knew.

The sound of her voice dispersed this trancelike condition. She said—"Why, Nicholas, how strange to meet you here!"

Her words came as the breaking of ice in a frozen stream, setting free a flood of memories. He saw clearly now that she was Millicent, the woman who had divorced him, and he realised that they were face to face, alone in a room of her dead brother's house. He had the painful sense of returning reality that comes after the oblivion of an anaesthetic. Her voice sounded far away, yet it beat on his ears. Her face was the face of a stranger, yet the eyes pierced the intimacies of his heart.

She had got up and come to him. "I'm afraid I gave you a start," she said. "Hadn't you better sit down? You look pale."

She too looked pale, and her voice, for all the coolness of her words, trembled with emotion.

"No, no," he said. "I'm quite all right. But you did give me a start. I was feeling rather despondent, as it was, finding everything here so changed. The rooms, where we'd been so happy, torn up." The muscles about his mouth twitched and he looked at her almost pathetically.

"I know, I know. I was feeling badly too. I had no idea you were in England."

"Ernest and I are over here on a visit to Augusta. We've got a young nephew with us. He and another boy and one of the Court children are downstairs."

She was rubbing her palms with a wisp of a perfumed handkerchief. Good God, it was the same scent she had always used! How it brought things back to him! She asked—"Is Ernest here?"

"*Ernest!*" he repeated wrathfully. "Don't speak to me of Ernest! He's down in the kitchen with a woman who is in the antique business. I believe they're buying up the pots and pans for her shop."

"I hope they are. I'll be very glad of the money."

"Did this place come to you?" he asked, his tone taking on the matter-of-fact note of intimates.

She nodded. "I should have put the whole house in order and had a proper sale. But I really hadn't the energy. I'm just letting this agent sell things off as best he can."

"I've a rich young chap downstairs. Perhaps I could get him interested in something."

"That would be good of you!" And she added, with the flicker of a smile—"You were always so kind, Nick!"

His grey eyebrows went up. "It's never too late to hear good news," he said.

"Oh, I never accused you of unkindness... except in court!"

"Well, it's about the only thing you didn't accuse me of!"

She gave a little laugh. "When I look back on it all it seems to me that we were very silly."

"Do you mean," he asked, "that you think we might have got on?"

"Yes, I do."

He eyed her suspiciously. She wasn't trying to make it up, was she? At this time of life! He said gruffly:

"No, no, no. We never could have got on!"

"No, I suppose not," she sighed.

"May I open the window?" he asked. "It's very close here."

"Please do. I tried, but it was stuck. Isn't this room terrible? The whole house depressing? Henry lived here alone for the last two years, with only a woman coming in by the day to look after him. He drank himself to death. He refused to see me."

He had let in the air and he took deep breaths of it. The door of a cupboard standing open revealed a mound of decaying apples on the floor and shelves crowded with empty spirit bottles. He sat down and gazed mournfully at her. "A bad business," he said. "Apples and whiskey, eh? Well, well."

"I should have had the place tidied up," she sighed again, "but I really was not fit for the effort."

"Is your health pretty good, now?" He remembered that she had always been complaining.

"Better than it used to be," she answered defiantly.

"You hold your age well. You're a good-looking woman."

"You're a handsome man still."

"No, no, I'm a wreck."

"Nonsense!"

"No nonsense about it."

"You're a distinguished-looking man, and always will be."

"Do you wish me well, Millicent?"

She put out her hand and just touched his. He noticed her white, rather clawlike fingers, with the large, curving nails. They were just the same. He had intensely disliked her hands.

He tugged at his moustache. His nerves felt shaken by this strumming on them of a half-forgotten tune.

"I wish you very well," she said. "And I'm glad we met—this last time." No doubt about it, there was a note of sentimentality in her voice.

"It's odd," she went on, "that you did not marry again."

"No desire."

"I suppose you know that my husband is dead."

"Yes, too bad!" He had liked the young Irish officer for whom she had left him, and whom she had married after the divorce. Nicholas had allowed her suit to go undefended. She had had good grounds.

Finch came hurrying up the stairs and into the room. Nicholas introduced him. "My nephew, Millicent. Finch, Mrs. O'Flynn, an old friend of mine."

They had trouble in finding Arthur Leigh and Sarah. At last Finch discovered them—she sitting on a stile that led into a field where there was a flock of sheep; Arthur standing, with one of her hands in both of his and an expression of joyous excitement on his sensitive face.

XI

ARTHUR, SARAH, AND FINCH

As SOON as there was an opportunity Leigh drew Finch into the privacy of the little outbuilding where the lawn roller and the tennis net were kept. The sun had gone and the dew was falling, but the heavens were still transfused by a tender rose-coloured light. A chestnut tree shaded the outhouse, and the fallen petals of its bloom lay thick about the door, trampled by those who entered.

Arthur sat down on the lawn roller and looked up at Finch with a half-pleading expression. He said:

"Now all the misery and uncertainty of it is over and only the beautiful part is left, you'll forgive me, won't you?"

"Forgive you what?" Finch asked in a hurried, nervous voice. He hoped that Arthur was not going to tell him of his feelings, disclose the spiritual distress that had been torturing him during all his visit.

"You know quite well. I've been a perfect beast ever since I came. Honestly, I don't believe I can ever remember having been so morose and so brutally selfish in all my life before. Especially to you, Finch, who mean most of all to me!"

"More than Sarah?" asked Finch, trying to speak lightly.

Arthur answered seriously—"Yes, more than Sarah, in some ways. Because you're my dear close friend and she's the woman I worship, and dearness and closeness don't seem to go with that someway."

"I scarcely know anything," said Finch. "Won't you tell me? Of course, when I saw her sitting on the stile and you beside her, with that look, I knew there was something pretty serious. Arthur, is she going to marry you?"

"She is! I can hardly believe it. I've been like a man lost in a forest, giving up all hope of finding his way out. I've felt half mad sometimes; it was all so sudden, so unexpected." In spite of his reassurance, his new-found joy, there was still a look of distress on his face. "How can I make you understand? You've never been up against this kind of thing."

Finch looked at him compassionately and yet with a feeling of being himself hurt. Arthur had rushed into the midst of their scene, gathered into his own hands the strands of the tapestry Finch had slowly been weaving, and, in a kind of panic of passion, was changing it into a pattern all his own. Finch believed that it was the first time in Arthur's life that he had ever been frightened by his own feelings, felt the possibility of being thwarted in a desire. Arthur had always worn the bright, silky look of youth that had never been crossed!

"I can imagine something of what you are feeling. I've seen how unhappy you've been. But it couldn't last. Things were bound to come right. How could any girl keep from loving you if you loved her?"

"Oh, but you don't know Sarah. A man might prostrate himself at Sarah's feet and howl of his love till the stars were shaken, and it wouldn't move her. Not unless she loved him too!"

"But she does love you. It must be splendid to realise that."

"I can't realise it! You know, I didn't intend to speak of love to her today. All I intended was to ask her if we might meet sometimes. To tell her that I simply couldn't bear to think that everything would end with my going back to London... She was sitting on the stile, with a big holly bush behind her, looking divinely distant... You know that little secret look at the corner of her mouth. Well, it maddened me, because I felt that, if she were thinking of me at all, it was only as a far-away mortal whose hopes or despairs could never mean anything to her... I said what I had meant to say about our meeting. She said that she very seldom came over to England. It had been three years since the last visit. I said then that I'd go to Ireland to see her, if she'd let me. She turned and looked at me with the most adorable smile, but she didn't answer... There was something in the smile that made me lose my head. I poured out all my feelings. A regular flood, it must have seemed to her... At the end I said that if she would not marry me I'd not answer for what I might do. She said, very gently, that she'd marry me... Oh, that voice of hers! Did you ever hear a voice like it, Finch?"

"It's very sweet."

"Sweet! It's as though a star spoke! And the way she moves! Like a lily on its stem... And the way she won't look at you, and then turns and looks into the very depths of you! She is like the angel that troubled the waters and brought out all that was potent in them. It's that way with me. Now I know she loves me, I feel as though I have a new power for living."

"I'm frightfully glad for you, Arthur."

"I know you are! And to think it all came through you! I wonder how her aunt will take it?"

"She likes you. I can see that."

"Well, like or not like, she can't stop us. We're going to be married right away."

Mrs. Court raised no difficulties. In fact she seemed to be delighted with the idea of having Leigh for a nephew. She told Augusta that she believed she herself had brought about the match by her tact and understanding of the young people. Augusta was offended because of her plans for Finch and Sarah. She had an inward conviction that Mrs. Court was making the best of a bad job. If she had to lose an unpaid companion, she would get what credit she could out of the affair and trust that Sarah, in her future affluence, would not forget her kind old aunt. She took a motherly tone with Leigh, was anxious about his paleness. She was having a course of cod-liver oil and begged him to join her in it. Leigh, always nervous in regard to his health, was persuaded. After each meal Ellen carried a small tray to her on which was a bottle of the oil and a tablespoon. The rest of the party watched fascinated while she measured out the nauseous dose; turned away as she opened wide her thin-lipped mouth and gulped it; turned back again, with sickly smiles, to see her lick the spoon.

"It's all in getting used to it," she declared. "Once you are used to it, it grows on you."

The moment Leigh consented to try it she ordered two tablespoons to be brought. She poured out his dose herself and trotted round to his side, balancing it on the spoon. He opened his mouth. She thrust it in. His expression of heroic suffering delighted Sarah. She threw one of her malicious looks at Finch.

Inside of a few days Mrs. Court could perceive an improvement in him. "Isn't he getting a pretty boy?" she cried. "I call him my poppet! My pretty poppet."

It was arranged that Mrs. Court and Augusta should take Sarah to London to buy clothes for the wedding. Arthur was to accompany them.

When Nicholas and Finch found themselves alone at Lyming for a space they were pleased rather than otherwise. Nicholas had been finding it increasingly difficult to get on with Augusta. He was tired of Mrs. Court, her passion for whist and playing accompaniments, her habit of taking cod-liver oil in public. He was tired of hearing her extol the virtues of Thomas Court and condemn the habits of Dennis, for he had disliked one and liked the other. Besides, he wanted an opportunity of seeing something of Eden and Minny. He resented the fact that, because of Mrs. Court, he could not have Eden come to see him at the Hall.

Finch had been living under a strain since Arthur's arrival. Now he could relax and let the days pass in indolent succession. He would get up in time to see the sun rise, watching its face, red as a garnet, push up out of the meadow mist till it swam above the church tower into the clear sky. He would spend most of the day in its warmth, his neck turning a deep brown, until the sunset faded in a glory of dying wings behind the tors. In the heat of noon he lay on the short grass in the shadow of the ivied wall, with a book or just dreaming. The form of Sarah glided in and out of his dreams, both waking and sleeping, sometimes seeming to flee from him, at others to beckon him. In the evenings he fancied he could see her on the garden seat in her poppy-coloured shawl. When she had been in the house with him he had forgotten her almost as soon as her physical presence was removed, but, now that she was gone, he could not forget her for a moment. Arthur he seldom thought about, except to wonder how much Sarah really loved him. He conceived the idea that the intensity of Arthur's passion had evoked a response in her, and he wondered whether, if he had burned with love for her, she would have responded. But no girl could help loving Arthur, if he set about making her love him. For himself, he fancied he would be hard to love. He would be blundering even in that relation.

Once he followed Ralph Hart and his girl along a winding lane, across a field, over a stile, and across another field. All the way they had held hands. It was the bell-ringers' evening for practice, and during the walk the ecstatic chime and clamour of the bells had not ceased. From every hedgerow the sweetness of flowers had come, and from the dark clump of woods the hoot of owls. Above all other scents, and intermingled strangely with hoot of owl and chime of bells, rose the smell of new-mown hay.

Finch had a feeling that this life would go on forever. Himself and Uncle Nick alone in the house, himself and Ralph Hart talking in the garden, himself walking alone at night under the moon. The sensation of the shadowy form that left his breast, leaving him void of personality but strangely strong, came to him more often. It was drawn like a bolt from his body, the door of his being flew open, and he was one with the moor and the wind on the moor. For the first time he attempted to compose for the piano.

Nicholas suggested that they ask "the lodge-keeper and his lady," as he called Eden and Minny, to spend the Sunday evening with them. The maids, excepting Ellen, would be out, and Ellen knew how to hold her tongue. "Even if Augusta finds out that they've been here, I don't believe she'll mind much. Though she does wear a Queen Alexandra fringe, she dates from before Victorian days." And, looking hard at Finch from under his shaggy brows, he added—"I want to see Eden. I want to see Minny. I like the young folk about me." Finch thought—"Good Lord, he's at it again! It's a good thing Uncle Ernie isn't here. It upsets him so to hear Uncle Nick being like Gran." He agreed that it would be jolly to have a little party.

The two from the lodge arrived looking tidier than Finch had yet seen them. Minny, poor girl, had got a new frock of summer silk, purchased through the advertisement of a London shop's July sale. Eden had himself trimmed her thick hair. And, surely enough, there were the dabs of rouge on her ears!

"I've turned barber," Eden exclaimed. "How do you like Minny's hair?"

"I like her ears," said Nicholas, and pinched one.

Minny caught his hand. "May I call you Uncle Nick?"

"My dear! What else should you call me?"

There was hilarity at supper. Eden swore that it was the first good meal he had had in months. Minny cooked so badly, he said, that he had to do most of it himself. But it was impossible to offend Minny. Like the yielding fulfilment of hot July itself, she opened her mouth, and laughter and breath as sweet as clover issued from it. Nicholas was generous with Augusta's best wine.

After supper Nicholas and Eden talked, and Finch and Minny listened. Then there was music, and the talkers listened.

On the way back to the lodge Minny said, holding tightly to Eden's arm—"Oh, darling, wouldn't it be thrilling if we owned a place like that!"

"We never shall, my child," he answered. "You and your poet must sing on other people's doorsteps."

When the others came back from town all was haste and preparation for an early wedding. Leigh was nervously intolerant of delay. The pangs of his love could not brook the loss of summer weeks with Sarah as his bride. His mother and sister were in British Columbia. His mother had had an illness, and it would be some time before she could make a long journey. He would have liked to be married in a registry office, but neither Augusta nor Mrs. Court would hear of any such thing. The wedding might be simple, the guests few, but it must be properly done. Augusta thought it augured well for their happiness that Renny and Alayne had been married from her house the year before. Only people from the neighbouring houses and a few friends of Leigh's from London would be present.

Since Sarah's coldness had melted into love under Arthur's passion, Finch wondered at his friend's feverish unrest. He looked tired after the week in London. Suddenly one day he confided to Finch:

"I often feel as though she were slipping away from me. I've never been quite so near her again as that first day by the stile. I feel half-frightened... And irritated... Then I'm angry at myself. She's so absolutely sweet and adorable. Yet she puzzles me. I think when I've had her in the flesh it will be different. We've disagreed about the honeymoon. I wanted to go to Norway; but no, she wants to go to the sea. Some place quite near here. She hates society. She scarcely spoke to my friends in London when I brought them to see her."

"Has she ever told you about her childhood?" asked Finch.

"Nothing except that she was orphaned at thirteen, and that Mrs. Court adopted her then. Educated her, took her travelling. My feeling is that Sarah has no spark of gratitude toward her for what she's done. I think she's an old dear."

Finch hesitated as to whether or not he should tell
Arthur of the manner of Dennis Court's death. A longing to
keep something of Sarah secret to himself prevented him. If
she had wanted Arthur to know of her strange childhood she
would have told him. In any case, his conversations with her
in the garden were his own to forget or to meditate on as he
chose. He was glad that she had told Arthur nothing. He said:

"I agree with Sarah. I can't think of anything better than
a honeymoon on the seacoast here. Renny and Alayne had a
cottage in Cornwall for a month, and they were awfully keen
about it. He's often spoken since of the hours he spent with
fishermen."

"Well, that's a funny thing to remember out of one's
honeymoon!"

"Oh, I suppose there were other things. But he's that sort
of chap; and then she was always going about to the old
churches making rubbings of the brasses. She's got quite a
lot of them at Jalna now. But that sort of thing would bore
Renny horribly."

"I wonder if we could get their cottage."

"It's rather late for that. They had it in June, before the
rush."

"I like the idea of a cottage. I must speak to Sarah about
it."

Finch thought that Arthur, in marrying Sarah, was
bound to an enterprise that would leave him less time for
self-analysis than formerly.

They hired a motor—for the keeping of one was an
extravagance Augusta did not allow herself—and went into
Cornwall. They sought out agents and had one disappointment after another. All desirable places had been let months
ago. It was within a few days of the wedding, and Leigh was in

despair, when an agent in Polmouth told him of a house
belonging to a well-off retired Cornish farmer. It was a fine
house, he said, vastly superior to the places that were usually
to let. The two youths rattled off in their hired car to inspect it.

It stood on the outskirts of the town in its own garden—
a square, ugly house, with white sun blinds and curtains
gleaming frostily behind each polished pane. Not a fallen leaf
lay in the spruce garden, not an atom of dust within. They
were shown into the dining room, where, seated on the
mahogany chairs upholstered in crimson plush, they were
critically interviewed by the lean husband. With a hard,
quizzical gleam in his small eyes, he sat entrenched behind
the dining-table, tapping on it with his spectacles while the
rent was discussed. The plump wife, a yearning beam in her
large eyes, sat silent, with submissively folded hands. Finch
soon discovered that her chance of visiting her married
daughter in Scotland depended on the letting of the house.
Something in the Cornishman roused a feeling of antagonism in Leigh. Finch was astonished to hear him haggle over
the rent. There were periods of terrible silence while they sat
at grips, the old man tapping with his spectacles, Leigh looking stony. By the time all was settled and the rent had been
reduced by twenty-two and six a week, Finch and the wife
were in a state of abject depression.

Leigh and the Cornishman were suddenly beaming,
pleased with each other. Finch thought—"I begin to see why
Arthur's people all made money." Yet, Arthur was so extravagant. Finch and the wife smiled at each other and drew sighs
of relief. A final survey of house and garden was made. Leigh
was told that the apples on the wall were not included with
possession unless blown down by a gale. But the runner
beans were. The Cornishman was almost jubilant in the

throwing in of the beans. He ran into the house and fetched a kitchen knife that he might demonstrate the most effective way of preparing them for the pot. Leigh, who had probably never seen an uncooked bean before, looked on attentively while one was meticulously sliced. The wife showed them just how reverently the electric suction cleaner must be manipulated, and promised to engage a capable cook and housemaid for them.

In the car Leigh threw himself back with a gesture of dismay.

"To think," he ejaculated, "that I should be taking my lovely Sarah to such a mausoleum! It seems too bad to be true! Did you see the dreadful whiteness of the bedrooms? Why did you let me do it?"

"I don't think it will be so bad," comforted Finch. "After all, the house is only a shelter. Look at that, and you'll see how little the house matters." He pointed to the sea stretching to the blue horizon in an incalculable multitude of advancing foam-fringed waves. "You should worry," he grinned, "about lace curtains and texts on the walls!"

Arthur looked out, his face brightened. "Isn't it glorious! Oh, if only you were going to be with us to enjoy it, too." His eager eyes turned to Finch with a compelling look. "There is no reason on earth why you shouldn't." He smote Finch on the leg. "You must! You must! Think of those fine white bedrooms! Don't refuse me this, Finch! You've no idea how much I want you."

"Well," said Finch, "it's the rummiest suggestion I ever heard. To want to take your best man on your honeymoon. Why, Sarah'd never stand for it. It would be awfully upsetting for her. A honeymoon is about enough for a girl to take on, let alone a groomsman thrown in!"

"Rot! Sarah would love to have you. She likes you tremendously, she's told me so. And it's not only that we'd like to have you... there's something more... I can't quite explain... Finch, darling, I want your support... You may think that my love for Sarah has come between you and me. You're wrong. I think more of you than ever. And I want to have you near me in these weeks. I want the woman I love and the man I love beside me. I want the two different loves merged into one beautiful whole. I want our love to be as clear as the brightness of a three-pointed star. Do you understand?" He held one of Finch's hands tightly in his.

"But—hadn't we better begin it a little later?" asked Finch. His very flesh and bones seemed to melt into some ethereal substance at Arthur's words, Arthur's touch, but he was assailed by doubt at the thought of sharing the honeymoon.

"No, we can't!" Arthur returned fiercely. "It's begun already. Now is the time to hold it to us. Cherish it. Make it part of us, don't you see?"

Finch felt rather bewildered, but he agreed. "You won't want me right at the first, will you?"

"Of course we shall!" Arthur pulled his hat petulantly over his eyes. He relapsed into a brooding silence.

The day of the wedding was a day of soft rain. Everything felt warm and damp to the touch. The pensive air held the sound of the wedding chimes as though reluctant to let it go. The chimes beat, quivered, pulsed through the patter of the rain, and died at last in the mist of the moor. Arthur was delighted at the thought of giving money to bellringers at his wedding.

Mrs. Court annoyed Augusta excessively by beating a tattoo with her heels throughout the service. Augusta shed a dignified tear or two, since there was no one else to do it. She had also done this for Renny and Alayne.

That part of the church not occupied by guests was filled by curious villagers and country people. They agreed that the groom was a pretty young man and that the bride was proud and cold. They thought that the best man was a kind-looking young man, but sad. An aged Court, almost stone deaf and with an appetite even greater than Finch's, came over from Ireland to give Sarah away. He evidently mistook her for some other great-niece, for he continually addressed her as Bridget.

At the first Augusta and Mrs. Court had thought the idea of taking a third person on the honeymoon a far too unconventional one. Arthur persuaded them, however, that, on the contrary, it was one of really arch-propriety. Sarah was acquiescent. The thought of a house near the coast pleased her, for her aunt's house was inland and she longed for the sea.

By the time they and their belongings were stowed in the hired car and had gained the macadam highroad to Polmouth, the rain that had been lightly falling from a sky of pale, shifting cloud-forms, began to beat fiercely on the pavement, rebounding from it in large silvery drops. The drenched hedgerows seemed to draw nearer the road, abundantly green and starred by a multitude of flowers.

Finch sat with the driver nursing Sarah's violin. The case was clammy in his hands, and he thought of the violin inside as a sensate thing, troubled by the tide of life that flowed about it. He clutched it, staring at the streaming glass of the windows.

Mrs. Court had explained—"Sarah cannot play without me! No use in taking her fiddle that I can see."

Arthur had answered silkily—"Sarah must learn to play with Finch, for my sake."

Sarah had agreed to take it, but she doubted if she would play it when she had the sea to play with.

When they reached Polmouth, the rain was a deluge. When they stopped before the gate of Penholme, they saw the house behind a leaning wall of rain. The dash from motor to porch was a scurry under a wave. The maids ran here and there with the luggage. Leigh was glad that he had told no one in the place that he was newly married.

As they sat about the square expanse of the mahogany table, eating their tea, his eyes roved distractedly about the room.

"I can't bear it," he kept repeating. "I simply can't bear it."

"Don't glare about so," advised Finch. "Keep your eyes on Sarah."

"But what a blasphemous setting for her! I can't and won't bear it."

"What shall you do?"

"Turn half the things out of this room. You'll see. Just wait until I've finished this preposterous saffron cake!"

Sarah, appealed to, thought the room was very nice.

When tea was over and they had got the servants out of way, Arthur linked arms with the other two and made the rounds of parlour, dining room, and little morning room. Each, he declared, was more contrary to art and nature than the other. The walls of all the rooms, including the hall, were hung with gilt-framed oil paintings by an artist named Stephen Gandy. They were all of Cornish scenes. Cornish cows stood footless in tangled meadows. Cornish waves poppled against turgid Cornish cliffs. Enormous, stiff-tailed setters gazed upwards at a falling bird. Sheep were lost in snowdrifts. Ships were wrecked. All, all Cornish.

"Oh, Stephen Gandy!" cried Arthur. "If only I had you by the throat! Tomorrow's sun would rise on one Cornishman the less!"

Sarah said she liked the pictures.

"My adored one," he explained, taking her hand, "if you like them it is because you see them in a golden mist of love for me! Don't you think that is so?" He looked at her in a way Finch thought was strange. His eyes had an excited glitter in them, his mouth looked strained, as though his smile were forced. He looked afraid.

Finch thought—"This is terrible. Why am I here?"

Arthur said—"I will bear with the pictures, but I will not endure the mats and the tidies!"

Scattered over the floors and in the doorways they counted thirteen mats, and, on the chair backs, nine tidies. Finch and Arthur carried them by armfuls to an upstairs room. To it also they carried innumerable glass and china ornaments of tortured shape. The furniture must be all changed about. Arthur discovered an old table and some chairs that pleased him, and brought them out of their retirement into the light. He swathed the glaring electric globes in coloured scarves of Sarah's trousseau. He was in despair over three grim aspidistras in ornamental pots until Finch offered to keep them in his bedroom.

"You're sure you don't mind having them? They won't keep you awake?"

"Oh, hell," said Finch. "What do you take me for?"

"If I slept in the room with them, do you know what would happen? In the morning they would be more overgrown, more disgustingly green, more macabre. But I should be dead!"

"I know," returned Finch solemnly. "But you're so frightfully sensitive, Arthur, and I'm not."

"Listen to that rain! Do you think it's a bad omen?"

"Of course not."

"Do you think Sarah cares very deeply for me?"

"I'm sure of it."

"Finch, will you play to us tonight?"

"As long as you like…"

The three sat smoking about the red and green tiles of the grate. There was a blazing fire. The little German inlaid clock chimed the hour.

"I shall now make my Cornishman's prayer," declared Arthur. "'From ghosties, and ghoulies, and long-tailed gandies, Good Lord deliver us!'"

XII

By the Sea

THEY WERE TAKING their first picnic to the shore. After three days of wind and rain the sun shone warmly and a period of tranquil summer weather was foretold. The wings of the gulls shone between sea and sky of equal blueness. All the life of Polmouth that had retreated, damp and discouraged, to the shelter of its slated roofs now leaped out rejoicing. On the links the figures of golfers were dotted with upraised bare forearms. On the downs the black-faced sheep exposed the dampness of their wool to the sun. On the porches of the boarding houses appeared rows of drying bathing suits. Soon after sunrise the hardiest strode to the sands, towels hung about their shoulders. All day long the bathing continued. In the heat of the day the throng of bright-coloured figures glowed like tropic flowers in the surf. Strong-limbed boys and girls hurled themselves on painted surfboards and were carried, half-smothered in foam, to the gleaming sands. They were careless of the changeful currents and gave little heed to the coast-guardsman who shouted warnings to them through a megaphone. As he wiped his mouth after each brazen warning he would growl to himself, in his natural voice—"Let 'un drown then! And serve 'un right! What do they think I am? A nursery-maid? Next time I'll let 'un drown and no mistake." Little bronze, half-naked children scuttled here and there carrying tin pails and spades. Elderly ladies clutching reticules walked gingerly in the advancing foam, their upheld skirts showing plump white legs, while they kept a wary eye on their black stockings and shoes perched on some shell-encrusted rock. In gravelly recesses between the jutting cliffs little groups lay basking in the sun or reading novels with its light full on the page.

Along the edge of the cliffs, high above these scenes, Finch and Arthur were carrying baskets for the first picnic on the shore. Behind them, so that it was necessary for them to wait every little while in order that she might overtake them, came Sarah. She glided empty-handed on the smooth turf, frequently pausing, on the very edge of the cliff, to look below.

"Do be careful, Sarah!" Leigh would cry, in sudden fright. "Don't you see how dangerous it is? One slip, and you'd be flying down that precipice!"

For a time she would be careful, but soon again she would be hovering like a seabird on the edge of the cliff. She seldom spoke, but once she pointed across the sea and said—"Over there is Ireland."

The youths felt so full of life that they would have liked to run up and down the sweeping roll of the downs. But there was Sarah to be waited for, watched over. In all his aching curiosity about her, Finch discovered no slightest change in her attitude either toward himself or Arthur since her marriage. She spoke in the same sweet, almost inaudible tone. She listened to their conversations and laughter in silence. Occasionally, Finch fancied, she threw him a look of

evasion. At times Arthur showed an almost agonised desire
to understand her. At other times, he appeared to strive to
ignore her and to delight in the presence of Finch. His attitude towards her was at once protecting and tormented
because of his inability to draw near to her.

Her most urgent need seemed to be, as before her marriage, the need for solitude. Finch could not help recalling
Mrs. Court's nicknames of Mouse and Mole. But, as the
month drew on, she had moments of wild gaiety. This was
evinced, not by laughter or movement, but by change of
expression. Her look of detachment would vanish and her
aspect become one of untamed joy in wind and sea.

Although so often they must wait for her as she glided
over the smooth undulations of the downs, it was she who
urged that they go on and on, always seeming to see in the
cliff just beyond, the perfect view, the perfect place for rest.
At last, on the tallest cliff, on the one that pressed farthest
out to sea, she stopped and, taking the red shawl from
Arthur, spread it for herself on the grass. He and Finch set
down their baskets and stretched themselves at full length.
No bathers were visible here, only, far below, a man was leading a plunging team across a stony ridge cast up by the sea
to where he would fill his waggon with stones for building.
The stamp of hooves, the rattle of rolling stones, rose sharply
above the languorous wash of the midsummer sea.

Finch lay still, listening. He felt the magnetic draw of the
dark cliff beneath him. He felt the vibration of the sea
through the interminable congregation of rock and earth and
subterranean spring that formed it. He watched the seagulls
like wind-tossed lilies drift above him. He felt conscious of
the beating of the hearts of his companions. Like the beat of
an advancing tide he felt their nearness. He remembered

what Arthur had said about their love being clear and bright… a three-pointed star… He wished that he could put the thought of Sarah from him.

After a while Arthur began to unpack the basket. He was eager to see what the cook had given them. He set out the plate of sandwiches, the tomatoes, the cakes, the box of raspberries, the bowl of Cornish cream. Finch had carried some bottles of Somerset ale.

"I'll be hanged," ejaculated Leigh, "if we haven't forgotten the opener. How are we going to open the ale?"

"I'll knock the heads off the bottles," answered Finch blithely.

He crept to the edge of the cliff, carrying a bottle, and peered over the side. The dark plane of shale and slate swept down into the black shadow of a cave guarded by jagged pinnacles of rock. What would it be like, he wondered, to drop over the edge of the cliff, end all, discover all, in one brief moment. He saw himself sinking, not plunging, downward, into the translucent greenness of forward-sliding waves. Ah, but it should be done at high tide, not to fall on those black pinnacles!

Arthur's voice recalled him. "What's the matter, Finch? Can't you find a rock to hit it on?"

Finch struck the neck of the bottle on a sharp projection. A swirl of small birds rose from the face of the cliff. Foam spurted over his hand and spattered his face. He returned to the others, grinning. Flakes of foam made his grin ridiculous. Arthur shouted with laughter but Sarah said coldly:

"You have cut your wrist." She took her handkerchief and pressed it on the cut.

"Oh, I'm sorry, old man!" exclaimed Leigh. He filled three glasses with the ale.

"It's nothing," muttered Finch. He sat very still, as Sarah bound the handkerchief about his wrist, his nerves strangely aquiver.

"It's too small," she said. "Look, the blood is coming through!"

"Don't ask me to look," said Leigh hastily. "The sight of blood makes me sick."

"It doesn't me," said his wife. "I like it."

Leigh gave her a horrified look. "Sarah! You don't know what you are saying, darling."

"Yes, I do! It stirs something in me."

"What sort of something?"

"Old and fierce and wicked."

Leigh gave a forced laugh. "Take your hand away from her, Finch. She's dangerous!"

She put the hand away from her. "Finch understands."

"Do you, Finch?"

"I think I do."

"Explain then. She frightens me."

"I can't explain."

"Why?"

"It's just a feeling."

"Well, I'll explain for you. You're both Courts, and you have the same bloodthirsty old ancestors behind you."

Down below the man had loaded his waggon with stones. The horses were struggling across the stony ridge with it. They plunged, with scraping, clattering hooves and straining flanks. Patches of sweat appeared on their heaving sides. The man, cracking his whip, stumbled beside them. One of them stumbled, fell, was up again. In a last savage and despairing effort they dragged the load over the ridge, across the shingle, and halted on the grassy sward. For a few moments they relaxed, the horses with drooping heads, the man nursing a strained elbow.

The three on the sunny cliff-side reclined watching the scene below in silence. Delicate spirals of smoke curled above their heads. The white clothes of the young men and the red of the shawl on which Sarah sat were very distinct to the driver of the team when he raised his eyes in their direction. The tide advanced murmurously in a long rippling line, its advance scarcely perceptible until it gained some new outpost of the shore.

"What a pity," said Leigh, "that we have no bathing suits! We must buy some in the town."

After that they went bathing almost every day, the limbs of Arthur and Finch turning a ruddy brown, and Sarah's coffee colour. She bought a black bathing cap that fitted closely about her face, so that it looked like a strange pale flower appearing from its dark sheath. They had almost to carry her down the steep steps cut in the rock. She relaxed in their arms like a young child, seeming to give no thought to the difficulty of the descent. The cave was assigned to her for a chamber while they undressed in a sand-strewn crevice of the cliff. Then she must be guided among the small sharp rocks jutting from the sand. Finch cast a shy look at her legs, wondering that she was not able to make better use of them. They were thin but shapely. When she was safely on the sands, that gleamed like wet brown satin, she glided at her accustomed pace to the surf. The sea looked far away, glancing in the sunlight, tossing up its foam, singing to itself. The footprints of the three slowly filled with water. Then suddenly they were in the sea. They took hands and danced up and down. They splashed and were half blinded in the translucent singing world of the waves. Sarah fell and they caught her up, holding her in their wet arms, expecting her to scream, to be joyously frightened, but she lay in their arms as she had lain when they carried her down the steps in the cliff. They left her and dashed forward breasting the waves. When she was left she lay down on the rim of the foam, letting it wash over her.

On calm days they tried to teach her to swim. Obediently she made the strokes, as they commanded, but the moment they relinquished their hold of her she sank.

"There is no use in trying, my angel!" cried Leigh. "You'll never be a swimmer!"

"If I could find a proper place," she replied, "I think I could."

One day, when they had swam out farther than usual, they returned to find the shore empty.

"God in Heaven!" chattered Leigh, turning ghastly. "She is drowned!"

Beside themselves with fright they ran up and down the shore looking for her, shouting her name. "Sarah! Sarah! Oh, my darling!"

Between their shouts they heard a faint answer. They flew shoreward from where the sound came. They found her in a large tranquil pool, made tepid by the sun, swimming round and round.

"I knew I could do it," she said, "if only you would let me be."

Mole! Mouse! Ignoble Fish! Crafty Crab! They hurled these names at her.

They lay on hot slabs of rock to dry themselves.

"But I cannot lie down with nothing under me," objected Sarah.

"Darling," cried Arthur, "that rock is as hot as blazes! You couldn't possibly take cold."

"I'd like my shawl, please," returned his wife.

"I'll get it," said Finch. He made the ascent to the top of the cliff and found the shawl. He stood motionless, for a moment, holding the shawl in his arms then he buried his face against it, kissing it.

"That was nice of you," said Sarah, when he had spread it on a rock for her. And he knew, by the fleeting malice of her smile, that she had seen him on the cliff-top.

When it was too cold to bathe they built a fire of drift-wood in a sheltered coign of the cliff and boiled a kettle for tea. It was at these times only that Sarah attempted to give any assistance. She would stand sheltering the fire from the wind with her shawl until it began to crackle and the flames lick about the kettle. They would sit smoking, while Leigh talked happily, watching the sun sink into the sea, cloud-flakes, like a flock of butterflies, drifting above it.

As the sultry days passed their gaiety was tempered by pensiveness which grew into a faint melancholy, making them sit silent in each other's company, feeling troubled, they knew not why.

Toward the end of the month they were caught in a sudden squall. It was a Sunday, and there were many people abroad. In order to escape these they walked to a point more distant than any they had reached before. They sat on the brow of a cliff enjoying the new view of headland beyond rocky headland stretching northward. Vast cloud formations were reared like cities gilded and glorified by the sun's splendour, then were disintegrated, dissolved before their eyes, leaving the sky a tranquil arch of unbroken blue.

The sun went down, a flaming red sphere whose colour was reflected in a thousand varying tints by clouds and wisps of vapour, by long, slow-moving waves, by swift ripples that crisped along the sand, by the ripples set in the sand itself, by pools left by the tide, by streamers and thick clumps of sea-weed, by the jagged surface of the cliffs, by the rounded smoothness of pebbles, by the delicate hollows of shells, by the wings of birds, by the fleeces of sheep, by the faces of the girl and boys on the cliff. From the moment when the sun's lower rim had touched the horizon he had transformed the world into an embroidered tapestry for his couch.

The squall, the driving rain, were on them before they had time to do more than collect their belongings and run to the shelter of a hedge. They huddled together while wind and rain beat on them. Nearby a flock of sheep took shelter.

When the worst was over they set out on the walk back, wet but rather exhilarated by the experience. The twilight was silvered by rain. Dense clumps of furze loomed black as pools before them. They ran down the long slopes of the downs with Sarah between them. She ran, as she walked, with a peculiar gliding motion that left her upper part immo-bile. Finch had the fancy that she was on wheels and that he and Arthur were drawing her. His nerves were intensely alive.

As they were passing through a gap in a high hedge, they made out the figures of two people who had found shelter there. They did not seem to be in a hurry to leave the shel-ter. The woman lay with her head toward the hedge, and the man, raised on his elbow, beside her. They were oblivious of the three who were passing. Finch saw the bulk of the man's shoulders and the movement of his arm as he caressed the woman. They were shadows thrown against a wall of rain. The woman half sat up. The man's head, bent above her, was as motionless as the head of a gargoyle on a church tower. She sank back.

"Heavens, what a night!" exclaimed Leigh, when they had passed through the gap. "What a night, and what a place for love!"

"I can think of worse nights—and worse places," said Sarah.

"I wish we were back at Penholme. It's a long way yet."

"Have you my shawl safe, Arthur?"

"I have it, and it's as safe as anything is."

He spoke crisply, feeling suddenly irritated by her, irritated by Finch, by the rain that was trickling down his neck.

Finch thought of the two by the hedge. They must be soaked through, but they would be unaware of the discomfort. They were lying there wounded, shot through by the fire of love. The man's head had been still as the upraised head of a snake about to sting. The woman had been supine as a snake basking in the sun. They were natural, that's what they were. People weren't intended to go into houses, to hide themselves away from the rain and the blown spray of the sea. He gloried in it wetting his cheeks, plastering his hair on his forehead. For the first time in his life he gloried in his maleness, feeling it strong and untamed and bitter within him. He gloried in the feel of Sarah's fingers caught in his, clinging to him for support and guidance, in the jolt of their bodies together as they passed over a rough bit of ground. He felt a creeping antipathy for Arthur. It crept through him like a slow fire through grass, sending a choking feeling like smoke through his being. He would like to order Arthur to go on alone, to leave Sarah and himself together. They would crouch somewhere together, watching the stormclouds disperse and the young moon show through. They would search for the reflection of its crescent in each other's eyes... He would kiss the raindrops from her face. He would know

what it was like to be kissed by her... Heavy hatred for
Arthur surged through him. He was afraid of himself. Afraid
of what the storm and the sight of those two in the hedge
had done to his mind... He remembered Arthur's saying—
"You are both Courts. You have the same ancestors behind
you." That must be the explanation of something wild in
them both... If only he might talk to Sarah alone!

He was not watching where he was going. He stepped
into the opening of a burrow, hidden in grass, and fell head-
long, almost dragging the others with him. When he gathered himself up he found that his ankle was strained. He
could walk no farther. He sat down on a low crumbling wall
and nursed his ankle. The rain was ceasing and the faces of
Sarah and Arthur were pale discs in the glimmering moonlight.

"You must stay here while I go and fetch a car," Arthur
said in a flat voice. He felt no sympathy for Finch's suffering,
only irritation. The three had been isolated too long in each
other's company.

"Sarah will wait with you." He was glad to leave Sarah
behind, to put down the heavy basket on the wall beside her.
He set off gloomily toward the blurred lights of the town
below.

They listened to the soft suck of his retreating steps.
Sarah took her shawl from the basket and wrapped it round
her. Finch forgot the ache in his ankle. Her nearness, the consciousness that they were shut in by the walls of the night,
was a pain that obliterated all others.

She said: "This is like it used to be—in the garden."

"It's not at all like it was there."

"Why isn't it?

"Because now I'm mad about you."

"And you weren't then?"

"I don't know. Perhaps I was. But I didn't realise it. Now it's too late."

"I've loved you all along. From the first day you played my accompaniments."

"Sarah!" His voice broke. He tried to see her face. "You loved me, and married Arthur!"

"You did not ask me."

"You didn't give me time."

"You never made a sign. You say yourself that this is different—that you don't know what your feelings were then."

"But you! You knew yours!"

"What could I do?"

"Couldn't you have made a sign? Don't women let men know? Never once—never once did you give me any intimation that you cared for me!"

"I met you almost every night in the garden. You knew I was deceiving my aunt."

"But a word—a look! You were as cold as ice! I don't believe you love me! You just want to torture me." He buried his face in his hands.

"I love you more than you love me."

He gave a bitter laugh. "What do you know of love? Marrying one man—loving another!"

"What do you know? It's new to you. It's partly the night. The storm. Those lovers we saw. You're excited."

"You're as cold as ice. As cruel. And what a shame for Arthur—if what you say is true!"

"He need not know."

"He will know. He's too sensitive not to find you out. Even now—he's not happy."

"Did he tell you so?"

"No, but I feel it."

"He will be happy again when we are away from you."

"Yet it was Arthur who insisted on my coming! And you let me come... loving me!"

"You said just now that you do not believe I love you."

"I was wrong! You do love me, Sarah! Oh, my darling, beautiful Sarah! Tell me you love me!"

She put her arms about him. In the darkness they kissed. A mighty primeval urge rose to them from the earth. The triumphant beating of their hearts almost stifled them. A great wave thundered on the beach and filled the night with its murmuring.

Finch tore himself from Sarah's arms. "We must not," he gasped. "Arthur... my best friend... never again... We must forget all this—never let him guess—that I—that you—"

Sarah folded her arms under her shawl. She gave her small, mysterious smile.

XIII

RALPH HART

MRS. COURT surveyed them critically. "Arthur is the only one," she said, "who looks the better for the stay by the sea. But probably it was that dosing of cod-liver oil I gave him that put flesh on him. Finch's cheeks look more hollow than ever. As for Mouse, she looks exactly the same. Let her bask in the sun or live in a hole, she's always the same—Mouse and Mole!"

The young people stood looking down at her, the youths rather shamefaced before her scrutiny, her niece as aloof as ever.

"Did you play your fiddle much, Mouse?"

"I did not play it once."

"Not once! I told you how it would be!" She turned triumphantly to her contemporaries. "She cannot play unless I accompany her. I inspire her. Isn't that so, Mouse?"

Sarah nodded, curling her lip in her malicious child's smile.

"And Finch depresses you—isn't that so?"

"Yes, Aunt."

Mrs. Court was delighted. She sat down in order that she might beat a tattoo with her heels.

"It was the house, not Finch, that depressed Sarah," said Arthur. "If you had seen the house, you would not have wondered that she could not play in it. But it didn't affect Finch. His music is its own roof and walls. He used to play to us in the evenings while we sat by the fire." He told them then how they had changed the aspect of the house in the first hour of arrival and of how they had forgotten the original position of things when they set about restoring it at the last.

"You can picture Finch and me," he laughed, "running distractedly about with antimacassars in our hands trying them first one place, then another, discovering that they looked natural no place. There was a door-mat with 'Watch and Pray' on it and we tried it in seventeen doorways before we found the right one."

"And which was the right one?" demanded Augusta.

"Ah, Lady Buckley, don't ask me. Let me tell you about the aspidistras! There was a large one in a glazed pot in each of the principal rooms. Finch agreed to take them all into his bedroom. I don't know what he did to them but they grew so that, when we carried them out they would scarcely pass through the door. His room looked like a jungle."

"In my house," observed Mrs. Court, "I have three aspidistras, nine begonias, and fifteen cactuses."

"Cacti!" boomed Augusta.

"I call 'em cactuses. Funguses, cactuses. I never did like la-di-da pronunciations."

"What is the plural," asked Ernest, "of candelabrum? I mean the sensible, unaffected plural."

"Brums," answered Mrs. Court, curtly, but she eyed him with suspicion.

Soon she carried off Sarah and Arthur to another room where she could question them without interruption.

"Well," said Nicholas, when the door had closed behind them, "I can't imagine what young Leigh saw in that girl."

"She is certainly a very strange girl," agreed Ernest. "She says almost nothing, yet one feels she thinks too much. She seems to be amiable, but one wonders what is behind it all. One feels baffled."

"Perhaps that is what attracted Arthur Leigh," said Augusta. "Many men admire deep women. My husband invariably admired a deep woman."

Her two brothers stared at her incredulously.

"Well," said Nicholas, "he wasn't very deep himself."

"Not deep?" cried Augusta. "Why, he was as deep as the sea!"

"How do you mean, deep as the sea? Do you mean deep intellectually or just devious?"

Augusta answered firmly—"I mean both."

"I always thought," put in Ernest, "that Buckley was one of the most transparent fellows I ever knew."

"So he was," agreed Augusta. "Transparent where he should be transparent. Deep where he should be deep."

"And devious where he should be devious, I suppose," continued Nicholas.

"He could see as far through a stone wall as anyone," said Augusta, with a hint of chill in her voice. Her tone implied that he had seen through both Nicholas and Ernest.

Finch asked—"Have you heard from home while I have been away?"

"Yes," answered Nicholas, "and not good news. Meggie has not been well. It will be necessary for her to have an operation, the doctor says."

Finch was aghast. "An operation! But wh—what's the matter? I hadn't heard of anything wrong with Meggie."

"Well, I don't think it's anything very serious. Something that has been troubling her since Patience was born. But it will be worrying for them."

"Yes, indeed," said Ernest. "Poor Meggie!"

Poor Meggie? Finch's heart contracted with fear for her. And there his uncles and aunt had sat discussing this and that as calmly as though all were well at home! How callous, how self-absorbed they were! And they had no secret trouble such as he had. He had had no peace of mind since the scene on the downs. He had suffered shame, wild desire which there was no hope of assuaging, and an unreasoning, bitter anger against both Sarah and Arthur. He had not gone with them on any of their excursions that last week. His strained ankle was excuse enough. He had kept to himself, longing for the day of departure but not having the initiative to return to Lyming without them. He had sat by the hour brooding on what had passed between himself and Sarah, trying to recall their very words in the conversations in the garden. In tacit understanding they had avoided each other, but one look into that face, mysterious as a closed flower, was enough to set his nerves on fire. Feverishly he would recall the moment when the flower had opened to him. And not only opened but pressed backward its petals, as though to absorb the extreme measure of his passion.

And now there was this worry over Meggie! No love could make him unheedful of Meggie, so tender, so unselfish, so kind. Did Eden, he wondered, know of it? He did not ask the others whether they had told him, but set out at once toward the lodge, moving slowly with the aid of a stick.

As he limped down the drive he noticed how things were beginning to take on the appearance of late summer. The berries of the thorns were becoming a light red. Hips shone like coral in the wild rose bushes along the fence. The swarthy harvest fields drew the last glance of the sun. He noticed its light on the smooth grey trunks of the double row of beeches, and how each beech had its own delicate embroidery of ivy on the side exposed to the sun. The climbing roses that half hid the lodge had attained their full growth of the season.

He stood listening at the door. There was no sound inside, and, after a moment's hesitation, he entered without knocking. He would like to see Eden alone. In some mysterious way he felt that he was nearer Eden than he had been when he last saw him. Yet nothing would have induced him to tell his brother of his experience.

He found him alone, stretched at full length on the floor, writing hastily on a pad by the light of the fire. He had been disturbed by the sound of Finch's stick and threw him a furious look over his shoulder.

"Oh, I'm sorry," stammered Finch, backing, "I'd no idea you'd be writing."

"Why in hell shouldn't I be writing?" snarled Eden, his gaze returning to the suspended point of his pencil.

"Why, of course, I'm glad you are! I'll take myself off. I do hope I haven't made a mess of your poem."

"You blasted young swine, you've ruined it! Minny's in the garden. Go and find her. I wish you'd do each other in and that would be an end of you both."

Finch limped, as hastily as he could, through the back door into the garden. He found Minny swaying indolently in a hammock hung between two apple trees. The lichen-covered trees were so old and bent that they tottered under the weight of Minny's fresh, exuberant form. She looked up at Finch smiling, mirth in her oddly coloured slanting eyes.

"Did he drive you out, too?" she whispered. "I think he must be doing something awfully good because he's been like this all day—scarcely able to bear the sight of me. But he's quite capable of tearing it up tomorrow."

"I'm sorry I came at such a bad time, but I just wanted to see how you were getting on."

"Oh, we're getting on well enough. But we missed you." A mocking light came into her eyes. "Did you enjoy yourselves? Was it a nice honeymoon?"

Finch answered seriously.

"Yes, I enjoyed it very much. The sea bathing was glorious."

"You didn't find yourself *de trop*?"

Finch gave a little laugh and began gently to swing the hammock. "You'd better ask them that."

"Even Eden," said Minny, "thought you were an unconventional lot."

"I suppose we are, but Arthur and I are such pals. He's a curious fellow. Very sensitive and easily upset."

Minny burst out laughing, then pressed her hand to her mouth, glancing fearfully at the lodge.

"Minny," asked Finch, rocking her a little harder, "what do you think of my cousin? Do you like her?"

"Very much. I think she's the most striking girl I've ever seen. But I don't think they're suited to each other. I don't think she'll make him happy."

Finch turned away his face. He watched a flock of rooks wheeling above the park.

Minny continued—"You and she would have been much better suited in my opinion. I know I shouldn't say that, but I'm hopelessly candid." She looked curiously into his face, but for once it revealed nothing.

"I strained my ankle," he said, tapping his boot with his stick, as though forcibly to attract her mind from the dangerous subject of Sarah.

"Oh, what a pity!"

"It's nothing. What is worrying me is some bad news about my sister. She's not well. She's got to have an operation."

"I have heard of that already. You mustn't worry. I'm sure she will be quite all right. She complained when I was with her, but I don't think it was anything serious."

She was made for the comforting of men, Finch thought. Her very tone gave him reassurance. The relaxed curves of her body gave him a feeling of tranquillity.

"How kind you are, Minny!" His hand dropped to hers. She clung to it, swinging herself by it, smiling up at him.

Before he returned to the house he thought he would walk through the walled garden where he and Sarah had been used to sit in the evenings. He opened the door in the wall and looked about cautiously before entering. If she were there he would not go in, would not risk the danger of meeting her there. But the garden was empty except for the figure of Ralph Hart, the gardener's boy, trundling a barrow along a walk. Finch was surprised to see him at work at this hour, for it was the time when he and his girl walked out together.

"Hello, Ralph," he said, strolling over to him, "you're working late tonight."

Ralph touched his cap. "Gardening, zir. I thought I might as well finish this job up. It'll be raining tomorrow by the look of the sun. He's gone down in a proper stormy sky."

Finch inhaled a deep breath of the garden scents. "But it's a lovely evening. You should be having a stroll with your girl."

"Her's had to go to nurse her mother. Her folk live down Clapwithy way, near Beddelcoombe. 'Tis a long way, zir."

"I expect you miss her."

The boy gave a dreamy smile. "I feel fair mazed without her, zir. 'Tis the first time her's gone off with hersen since we have been keepin' company."

The interest with which Ralph's love for the stolid little maid had invested him in Finch's mind was now greatly intensified by his new feeling for Sarah. He wanted to say to Ralph—"How much better off you are than I! You love a girl that you may one day marry, while I love one who is already possessed by another." Instead, he asked:

"Have you ever been to Cornwall, Ralph? I remember that you told me your mother came from there."

"No, zir. I've never been to Cornwall. Yet 'tis a nice place, my mother says, with the sea and all."

"But you've seen the sea!"

"No, zir. I've never been to the sea. And the sea is very nice, so they tell."

"But it's only a short distance away!"

"Yes, zir. I've been told that tidden far." He raised his eyes to the purple tors that bounded his world for him.

Finch became excited. "Look here, Ralph, I'll tell you what you must do! You must take your girl to the sea for your honeymoon, and I'll pay for the trip."

"Thank you, zir. Her 'ud like that."

"But I suppose your marriage is a long way off. We can't wait for that! You must take her the first fine Sunday. I'll hire the car for you." He wished he might go with them, watch Ralph's face when his eyes first saw the might of the sea and the granite cliffs. Yet Ralph would probably say—"It's very nice, zir," and the girl stare stolidly without a word.

He no longer talked to Sarah of the pair. He avoided her, when it was possible, enwrapping himself in isolation. He had no desire to experience again the passionate emotions she had aroused in him.

When, after a few days, Arthur persuaded her to go on a motor trip and they left for London to buy a car, Finch said goodbye to her almost apathetically. Between him and Leigh an inexplicable coolness had arisen, in which each felt that the other was the withholder of confidence. Two days after their departure Mrs. Court returned to Ireland. She already had in her mind another niece to take Sarah's place.

One night Finch found Ralph stretched on his face on the long orchard grass through which ivy pushed its way in its search for new trees to climb. It was almost dark, an hour when the boy, if he were not walking out with the maid, had always returned to his mother's cottage in the village. He lifted a tear-stained face.

"Why, look here," exclaimed Finch, "wh-what's the matter?"

"I've had a master stroke of ill-luck, zir," he answered, in a husky voice. "Her's written that her won't walk out with I no more." He lay looking up at Finch in his young bewilderment like a wounded animal.

"But what is wrong? Have you had a quarrel?"

"No, zir. There was naught wrong when her left. I went to station with she, and her kept sayin' what a fine do we'd have together when her came back, with so much to tell me and all."

"What do you think has happened?"

"I don't know, zir. I feel mazed in the yead. But perhaps her's found another lad."

"She'll never get another like you, Ralph! And see here, you mustn't take her too seriously. Just wait till she comes back and have it out with her. She'll come round, I'm sure."

Ralph hid his face on his arm. Finch saw that he wanted to be left alone. He left him, but he could not get the thought of him out of his mind. The dark, pale face, so different from the ruddy faces of the other village youths, came between him and those in the house. Ralph and he were linked together, tormented by their longing and despair.

For several days he saw Ralph only when working in the garden. He asked his aunt when the girl was to return. The next day, Augusta said. He told her of the trouble between the two, and she said that she wished Ralph would get over his attachment for the girl, as she was not good enough for him.

The next morning Finch found him in the vegetable garden sowing the seed of winter spinach. He was squatting on the dark loam dropping the seeds with an expression of almost tender melancholy on his young face. Autumn sunshine gilded to a still beauty every object that it touched. In the shadows there was a peculiar hush as of waiting.

"It's a lovely morning, Ralph," said Finch, with forced cheerfulness.

"Yes, zir. It's a lovely morning."

"It's as hot as July. I like a day like this."

"It's your luck you can enjoy it, zir."

"I wish I might see you as you were when I came here, Ralph."

"There's only one thing that'll make me like that again, zir."

"Well, she's coming home tonight. It isn't much longer to wait."

"No, zir, 'tidden long."

"Tomorrow you'll be a different man."

"Ay, perhaps." He sat on his heels and looked up at Finch with something of his former serenity. "I know where I can get you a very nice spannel, zir, if you'd like one. Her's just gone three months and comes of a rare good stock."

"I'll ask my aunt. She ought to have a dog here."

"You don't think you'll take it home with you then?" His tone was wistful.

"It's a long way to take a dog."

"I suppose it is, zir. But this yere's a spannel."

"Yes, of course, that makes a difference," said Finch gently. "A spaniel is a very nice dog to have. If you can get her for me, I'll take her home." He could not resist the look of entreaty in those eyes. It seemed to him that Ralph thought to get a little happiness through making him happy.

That evening he saw him standing just outside the kitchen door talking to the girl. His back was turned, but the girl's face showed white in the dusk. Finch lingered near for a few minutes hoping to see them walk towards the lane as before, but they stood very still talking in low tones. Finch could just hear the rise and fall of the Devon tongue.

He lay awake that night thinking about Ralph and the girl. It was the first night since his return from the sea that he had been able to lie awake without the torment of Sarah's face before him.

When he had had his breakfast next morning, he went to the garden to find Ralph. He was not there, and Finch was walking along the flagged path towards the tennis court when he met the gardener running towards him. Ash's fresh-coloured face was pallid, his mouth was wide open, showing his smooth, toothless gums. He was gasping as though he had run a long distance.

"Oh, zir," he managed to get out, "whatever shall us do? Ralph Hart's lying over in the shed there poisoned! He's killed hissen!"

"He's not dead, is he?"

"I'm not sure; I think so. Will you come with me, zir?"

They ran together to the shed. Ralph was lying, curled up, in an attitude of agony. They bent over him. Finch, shaking from head to foot, peered into his face. It was a greenish colour, the mouth contorted and stained with something. Beside him was a tin half filled with a liquid, some of which had been spilled on the floor. This was the place where garden implements were kept and where Arthur had told Finch of his love for Sarah.

The gardener knelt down and felt the boy's heart. "'Tidden beating! He's dead as can be!" Tears began to run down his face.

"We must tell my aunt," said Finch, with a feeling of numbness in his limbs and throat. Could he move? Could he run to the house? He found that he could, but he moved lurchingly. Ash, either because he was eager to tell the news or because he was afraid to stay with the dead boy, ran after him. They stood before Augusta, while behind her stood the cook and the parlourmaid, who had followed her out to the drive. She had been giving them their orders when, looking out of the window, they had seen the two white-faced running figures approaching the house.

Augusta's self-control was admirable. She drew herself up and surveyed them with a look of command.

"Are you sure he is dead?" she asked.

"Ay, that I am, my lady. There be no breath of life in un. I'll warrant he were dead a quarter hour when I found un. He come to me hissen and asked me for the poison spray us uses for plants, and I don't rightly know the sense of why he swallered it, but swaller it he did. And it's took he off proper!"

"Fetch the doctor as quickly as you can, Ash," said Augusta. "I must go and break the news to his poor mother. But Ralph must not be left alone there."

"I will stay with him." Finch said it between set teeth.

He stayed with Ralph's body until the doctor came. He stayed until it was put on a hurdle and carried down to his mother's cottage. Augusta spent most of the day with the poor mother, went with her to order Ralph's coffin, interviewed the vicar, urging him to appeal to the bishop for permission to have the boy buried inside the churchyard.

It was said that the little kitchenmaid cried aloud when she heard of Ralph's death, declaring that it was not her fault, that she'd never given him any encouragement:

"You've got to turn that girl out," said Finch savagely to his aunt. "We can't have her staying on here. She's a beast. She killed Ralph."

"No," answered Augusta, firmly. "I cannot dismiss her. Any girl has the right to change her mind. She wrote to him, quite kindly she tells me, saying that he no longer attracted her."

"Little bitch!" sneered Finch.

"Finch! Not one word more of such language! I'm surprised at you. At such a time too! I blame Renny very much for the language you boys use."

Finch muttered—"Renny's not to blame. A saint would use bad language about that girl!"

A newspaper reporter came to Lyming and interviewed Ralph's sweetheart. An article appeared in the local paper in which it was stated that Miss Muriel Slater denied having ever been engaged to the suicide. She had walked out occasionally with Hart, but that his company had of late been distasteful to her and that he had tried to create a scene when she had informed him of this.

The day of the funeral was the most beautiful day of the season. The village, with its surrounding fields and meadows, appeared as tranquil as a village in a dream surrounded by fields of powdered gold. Even the dark Tors looked gold today, their heads hidden in a golden mist. In striking contrast to this pervading colour in the landscape, the thorn trees, covered thickly by scarlet berries, stood out in vivid procession along the roadside.

Nymet Crews was one of those villages the centre of which is a level green. Around it the whitewashed cottages gathered as though for sociability, and, on the green, a loose horse and a cow or two were almost always to be seen cropping the grass. The thatch of the cottages also was transformed to gold on this day, and their drawn blinds, and the closed shutters of the little shops, gave an air of great tranquillity to the scene. Even the ducks on the pond seemed less noisy today, floating in a peaceful group on its unruffled surface. Nymet Crews had its idiot, and he, no larger than a boy of five, though he was in truth past twenty, pushed himself about on his toy velocipede, rolling his enormous goggle eyes in wonder at the unaccustomed air of the street.

It was very hot for September. When Finch reached the foot of the hill he took off his hat and wiped the sweat from his face and neck before entering the village. He was embarrassed by the groups of women who stood in doorways talking together. He felt that they were saying—"Here comes her Ladyship's nephew. It was he that found the body... It was he that stayed with the body while the gardener fetched the doctor."

The cobbles of the narrow pavement felt hot beneath his feet. It was easy to distinguish the cottage where Ralph's mother lived by the knot of people standing at the door. Two women in black were hurrying across the green towards it, as though fearful of being late. He went to the door, and the group of people separated to let him pass. He saw the room crowded, the coffin standing in the midst. He could not force himself to enter. He turned hurriedly away, his face growing crimson under the gaze of those about. He turned quickly back along the street till he came to a lane where about twenty young men, friends of Ralph, were collected. They wore their Sunday clothes of navy blue serge with bowler hats or tweed caps. Their faces and hands looked hot and sunburned in this apparel. Finch joined the group, but stood a little to one side. They glanced curiously at him, then went on talking together. Talking among themselves their dialect was so strong that only a phrase now and then was intelligible to him. He made out something about a football match. Evidently they had said all there was to say about Ralph's death, and now their thoughts turned to other things.

He had feared he would be late, but it seemed a long time that he stood there waiting. He saw his aunt come down the road and cross the common into the narrow street that led to the church. She had put on black clothes for the occasion. That was nice of her, he thought. She looked tall and dignified and very tired, for it was the second time that day she had taken the steep dusty walk.

Soon after she disappeared in the direction of the church the bell began to toll. Nineteen solemn knells, one for each year of Ralph's short life. Soon the funeral procession appeared from the cottage and made its way slowly along the road.

The coffin was carried by six young men, four of them Ralph's brothers. It was stained a light oak colour and highly varnished. It must have been heavy, for the young men showed that they moved under a strain. On the top of it were wreaths of bright flowers. The idiot boy moved his velocipede on to the roadside so that he might miss nothing of the procession. Following the coffin were relatives of the dead boy. Women and young girls in black, carefully kept in drawers for occasions like this. Men, some of them quite old. One of those, Finch thought, was the grandfather. He was leading Ralph's mother. She looked bowed down by her black and her grief, a stout thickset figure, holding a handkerchief to her eyes.

All the young men left the shelter of the lane and hurried across the cobbles to join the procession. Their heavy boots made a clumping, sinister sound to Finch's ears, as he went with them. Augusta had wanted him to accompany her to the church, but he had been determined to follow behind Ralph's body.

XIV

Eden and Finch

The stars had never seemed to hang so low in the sky as they did that night. The various heavenly patterns which they formed stood out in burning brightness. The full moon, when it swung clear of the hills, appeared to be too large for the earth which lay flooded in its light. The earth dwindled beneath the moon, overflowing with brightness, as a green goblet held beneath the foam of a cascade. The moorside fields were almost white, and, in contrast, the intricate design of the hedges and copses was black as ebony. The silence was so deep that Finch, standing on the dew-drenched lawn, could hear the murmur of the stream beyond the orchard, the movement of sleepy birds on the bough.

Down below he could see the church tower rising out of the trees, and about it clustering the village. Down there was Ralph's mother in her cottage. Down there was Ralph in his grave. From the tower sounded the four quarters, then slowly came eleven strokes. Soon the orange squares of the drawing-room windows were darkened.

A white figure appeared out of the park and came toward him. It was Eden. Since Mrs. Court had left he had come

several times to the house. But Augusta had not asked him
to bring Minny. What she was really afraid of was that if
Eden once got Minny inside the house he and she would settle down for a visit. Eden had remarked more than once that
he was tired of Minny's attempts at cooking.

On the one hand Augusta felt that it was her duty to
force the young couple into marriage by forbidding her
house to them. On the other hand she feared the responsibility of pushing Eden into a permanent union for which he
seemed by his temperament to be unfitted. Every time Eden
came near her he put his arm about her long sloping waist
and remarked:

"Darling Auntie, you are the only one who understands
me!"

"What about Minny?" Augusta had asked once, somewhat sternly.

And he had replied: "Minny is not intellectual. She is
natural. She doesn't need to understand. But you are both
intellectual and natural."

She had looked dubious, but it was hard for her to resist
him.

Now he asked:

"What are you looking so tragic about, Brother Finch?"

"Strange if I wouldn't," answered Finch heavily.

"You mean because of that boy who killed himself. But
why feel tragic about him? Sooner be envious of him. How
much better off he is than we are! He'll never get tired. His
hair will never get thin and grey or the sap dry up in his
bones. He won't see his girl turn into a sloven or a shrew, and
his children turn out wrong. He's as bright and fixed as one
of those stars. Let's choose a star for him and name it Ralph
Hart."

Finch raised his eyes to the stars. "Do you believe in life after death, Eden? Do you believe that somewhere Ralph is conscious?"

"I shouldn't be surprised. Perhaps he is walking about a garden at this moment. Perhaps he is looking in his girl's window trying to tell her how glad he is she let him out of all that."

Finch exclaimed—"Eden, you contradict yourself! That time I tried to drown myself and you stopped me—you said that life was better than death, no matter what the suffering! You said that nothing you had ever gone through had made you desire death for a moment. Life, life, life, that was what you kept drumming into me. If everything else is gone, you said, there is always the wind on the heath." He turned his troubled young face to Eden's.

"I know. And I still think so. Whatever happens is best. This is a glorious tree, isn't it, but if the next gale takes it down we shall have a better view." He put his arm into Finch's. "Let's go for a walk! We haven't had one together for a long time. Let's be jolly glad we are alive and drink the moonlight like wine." He tugged at Finch, laughing as though he had a joke hidden from the rest of the world.

Something magnetic in him drew Finch along. They went through a gap in the hedge, through the park, and into the meadows. An immense sweetness and purity enveloped them. Finch's mood of melancholy left him. A wild joy in life surged through him as though it rose from the earth into his body, rained down on him from the stars.

"If there's anything better than this," cried Eden, "I should like to know it!" His hand slid down Finch's arm till their fingers were linked. They strode along a winding shepherd's path hand in hand.

Each moment brought them new delight, made them more carefree. They were flooded, as the earth was flooded by moonlight, with joy in their own bodies. They went till they reached the moor. On its shaggy vastness, among its silvered ling and bracken and gorse and heather they laughed and sang. They felt swept clean of all the grief that had ever been in them. Their bodies felt new and strong and sinless.

They threw themselves flat on the ground and stared at the moon.

"I give you back stare for stare, old moon!" shouted Eden. "I'm not afraid! I'm alive! I had rather be Eden Whiteoak than anyone on earth!"

"And I had rather be Finch!" shouted Finch. "I'm alive! I'm alive! And you, old moon, you are alive because the sun is kissing you!"

They were only on the skirts of the great waste of Dartmoor which stretched beyond, its rolling hills that climbed upward to the hoary heads of High Willhayes and Cawsand Beacon and Yes Tor. The fastness of its granite, its bogs, its dark cushions of furze turned by the moonlight to silver and amethyst. They could look back on newly thatched ricks, on the shapes of hillside fields which crept to the edge of the moor, but they felt that they had left civilisation far behind them. They felt that life must continue with them forever.

XV

Aunt and Nephew

Nicholas and Ernest decided to return to Jalna while the fair weather held. They went to London, intending to spend ten days there before sailing, but the ten days became a month and they ended by making the voyage in heavy gales toward the end of October. By the time all their expenses had been paid Finch found that his present of a trip to them had been a costly one. But he did not regret it. He scarcely felt interested in the fact.

A curious numbness had descended on him since the death of Ralph Hart. After the night that he and Eden had spent on the moor he had experienced an almost hallucinated happiness for several days. It had seemed enough for him that he was alive and young. He turned from one of the primitive pleasures of life to another, savouring each as though it were the last time he was to enjoy it. He wanted to be alone in order that all his senses might have unhampered play. He shunned Eden as though fearing that the fire of his presence might shatter the clear crystal of this mood.

He had gone to church on Sunday, sitting in the high carved pew with his aunt. In the church he had felt a return of the sickness of spirit that had shaken him during the funeral service. He could scarcely make himself believe that Ralph's coffin was not in the church. He knelt, pressing his knuckles into his eyes, trying to shut out the sight. The musty smell of the old church became the smell of a grave. He perceived the innumerable wormholes in the end of the pew and was filled with loathing. His mind turned to the thought of Ralph in his grave, and tore at it savagely like a persistent dog unearthing foulness. The hymns became howls of mourning to him. He saw, near the back of the church, all Ralph's relations in deep black. They had come in a body as was the custom, on that first Sunday. Ralph's mother knelt during the entire service, a bulky mourning figure, her face covered by her hands in black cotton gloves.

Nicholas had remarked to Ernest that afternoon:

"The boy seems very down in the mouth. I think he should come up to London with us. He's really wasting his time in the country when he ought to be seeing life."

"He's a strange, moody boy," Ernest had replied. "One never quite knows how he will take things. I thought he was very callous about that young gardener's death. He scarcely spoke of it. But this morning, after service, when we passed the boy's relations all gathered about his grave, Finch's face was working as though he were going to cry."

"He ought to come up to London with us. He needs a change after the shock he had. He's a bundle of nerves like his poor flibbertigibbet mother." The shadow on Ernest's face, caused by his anxiety over Finch, deepened to gloom at what he could only consider Nick's mimicry of their mother.

But when they approached Finch on the subject of accompanying them, he said that he wanted to remain in Devon. While Augusta was flattered by his desire to remain, the thought of being entirely rid of visitors was not unpleasing to her. She was afraid, too, that if Finch stayed behind she would see more and more of Eden and Minny. It was becoming the problem of her life how to get them to remove from the lodge. But she could not definitely ask Eden to go, since he had no money to go on. Really, she thought, what with two difficult elderly brothers in the house and a fidgety friend like Mrs. Court, and a moody boy, and a marriage, and a suicide, she needed a rest.

Well, what was Finch going to do? Was he going to London later? Was he going to Paris or Rome? It was usual for young men to sow a few wild oats in these places, the elderly men suggested.

Yes, he would see those places later. Just now what he wanted was to be let alone. Soon after this Nicholas and Ernest left for the return journey.

He took long walks about the countryside. The ankle he had strained at the sea was still weak, and he learnt to ease it by the carrying of a stick. Soon the figure of the tall, thin boy with the stick was familiar to all in the neighbourhood. Many a time he thought of the spaniel bitch Ralph Hart had been going to get him. He began to picture it as trotting at his heels.

Once at dusk when he was returning from a walk he was just about to enter the drive when he saw the figures of two girls in cap and apron. They had been speaking to a young man on a bicycle, and they now stood giggling together at some remark of his. Finch saw that one of them was the kitchenmaid, Ralph's girl. He was suddenly aflame with anger at the sight of her on the roadside making free with a passing youth. Her round white face, which he had never seen in any but this dim light, was widened by a smile. He went up to her, raising his stick.

"I should think you would be ashamed of yourself!" he said loudly. "Go into the house and never let me see you out on this road again!"

The two girls fled in terror from him. He strode along the drive, swinging his stick, bristling with rage. He expected to hear next day that the girl had given notice, but that was the end of the incident. After that, when she saw him coming, she scurried out of sight.

It was the first time he had ever spoken in a tone of authority to anyone but Wakefield, and Wake gave little heed to any authority of his. The fact that the girl was not his servant, that he had no right to speak to her so, did not trouble him. He only felt a fierce satisfaction in the thought that he had made her afraid of him. He strode up and down the floor of his bedroom, taking a fierce pleasure in the fright he had given her. He said aloud:

"I stopped bang in front of her and raised my stick and said—'I should think you would be ashamed of yourself! Go into the house and never let me see you on this road again!'" His face again reddened. He raised his stick, imitating his own gesture.

The thought of Sarah had been put out of his mind by the shock of Ralph Hart's suicide. Her face, which had come between him and all he saw, was replaced by the horribly contorted face of Ralph as he lay on the floor of the shed. That face had glared at him out of the garden loam, out of the flying clouds of autumn, out of the wallpaper in his room, out of the darkness of his own closed eyelids.

After his encounter with Ralph's girl another change took place in him. By degrees the image of Ralph's dead face faded, and once again he was haunted by the face of Sarah. A remarkable peculiarity about this change was that, day by day, the dead boy's expression grew less agonised, until he finally appeared in brown-throated serenity, his eyes darkly bright, and that Sarah's image, in a like degree, frequently assumed the dreadful contortions of the suicide. This expression troubled Finch most deeply when he had gone to bed. He would dig his face into his pillow, trying to smother the terror of it.

He came to hate the thought of Sarah. He came to imagine that she had served him as cruelly as the kitchenmaid had served Ralph. He coupled the thought of the two females together. Ralph's girl had driven him to suicide, and Sarah was driving him to insanity. He pictured her as deliberately haunting him with that terrifying expression. Her power so to torment him at will was borne out in his mind by the strangeness he had always felt in her. He remembered his own attempt at suicide, and, in some mysterious manner, he began to blame her for that.

When the subject of Sarah came up between him and Augusta he now disparaged her. "She's a queer sort of girl," he said once. "I'm afraid poor Arthur has made a big mistake. I think he's going to find himself up against it. I should hate to be in his shoes."

"I shall be very sorry if the match turns out badly," said Augusta. "He's such a nice boy. And I'm fond of Sarah too. You know, dear, when you first came I thought you and Sarah might be drawn to each other, but I see how mistaken I was. You never would have got on with her."

"Get on with that girl! Never! I'm attracted by an entirely different sort of girl. I like a girl that can be a pal to a fellow."

This expression, as a matter of truth, was repugnant to him. The thought of a woman he loved being a pal to him was distasteful. He only used the word because it implied something so different from what Sarah was or ever could be.

Another time he said—"You should have seen her walking on the downs, Aunt! There was no more freedom in her movements than in the movements of a Chinese woman. I don't know what's the matter with her, but she seems to be too tightly put together." And almost at the next moment, a pang of cruel lust for her went through him.

Leigh wrote to him dilating on the beauties of the Lake country, then, a month later, of France, where they were going to spend the winter. Finch read the letters greedily, noting how much Arthur wrote of what he was seeing and how little of what he was feeling. He fancied that Arthur wrote cautiously. He did not answer either letter. Leigh and Sarah both wrote several times to Augusta. Finch listened judicially, smoking his pipe, while Augusta read Arthur's letters aloud. But, when she began to read Sarah's letter to him, he exclaimed:

"Please don't trouble to read her letters to me! I know just the sort of boring thing she'd write."

"It's not at all boring," said Augusta, as she reached the end. "It's very bright." She folded the letter and put it in her writing bureau.

When she had gone upstairs after lunch to lie down Finch went to the bureau and took out the letter. He turned it over several times in his hands, then he opened it and read it. It was unexpectedly simple and girlish. He read and re-read it, his eyes dwelling on the words "Please remember me affectionately to Finch." He went to the piano and played almost noiselessly, so as not to disturb his aunt, some of the pieces he had played with Sarah.

He saw her with the utmost clarity standing beside the piano with her violin under her chin. He could hear the piercingly sweet notes of it as in imagination he accompanied her. He could see her sweet secret mouth, the pinched elegance of her nostrils. He held his breath for fear her face should contort in the expression of agony which it sometimes assumed for him. But, as long as he played, it remained steadfastly serene and as though lighted by some inner radiance.

In the late autumn he heard of the Stock Market crash in New York. He read the newspaper headings concerning it with very little emotion. Augusta was distressed when he told her that he had lost thirty thousand dollars. She blamed his brothers and hers for having allowed him to invest so much in a foreign country. Eden, too, was aghast. He told Finch that since it was his intention to throw away his money, he might as well throw some of it in his direction. Finch did not remind him that, when he had first told him of the investment, Eden had applauded his initiative.

Soon he had a letter bearing an American stamp. It was from Miss Trent and was almost hysterical in its reiterations. She had lost everything, everything. But she would repay the ten thousand she had borrowed from him, if she had to starve herself to do it. She wrote a five-page explanation of the crash, full of technical terms that showed what she called her "terrific intimacy" with the doings of Wall Street. She ended by being optimistic and declaring that she would be in a position to repay the loan in a year at the most. She had given Finch a promissory note which was due the first of December. He put her letter in a drawer of his dressing table but he did not answer it. Augusta heaved a sigh when Finch told her of this additional loss. Her mother's money, over which there had been so much discussion, so many hopes and disappointments, was fast disappearing.

The mortgage on Vaughanlands which Finch had taken over was fifteen thousand dollars. The interest payable twice yearly was now due. A letter in Maurice's handwriting arrived. He wrote—

I thought perhaps you would not mind waiting a bit for the money. Things have gone rather badly with me this year. And now this operation of Meggie's is giving me a lot of worry. I have had a large bill to pay to the doctor already, and the specialist who is going to operate will of course charge a big price. You can be certain that I care nothing about the cost if only he can bring her through it safely. They say the danger is not great, but one can never tell how those things will go. Meggie is as courageous as possible. She sends her best love. She would have written you long ago but she has been ailing all summer. Patty is growing prettier all the time. The other day Meggie asked her—Where is Uncle Finch? And Patty answered—In Heaven! Well, I suppose Devon is almost Heaven. You are lucky. I expect to be in hell for the next few days, at any rate. Meggie goes into the hospital tomorrow.

Will you give my kind regards to your aunt. Meg and Patty both send love and kisses.

Yours,
Maurice.

Finch folded the letter with shaking hands. His Meggie, his darling sister Meggie, in such danger! Perhaps he would never see her again... He remembered the time when he had been ill at Vaughanlands and she had sat by him and fed him as though he were a baby. He remembered the feel of her tender feminine hands on his hair, the ineffable sweetness of her smile. Oh, she was so loving, so unselfish! If only all the brothers had been like her, how happy they might have been!

He reflected, as his mind calmed a little, that if she had not come through the operation he should have had a cable by now. Perhaps, some day soon, he would get a letter to say she was doing nicely. In the meantime better not say anything to Aunt Augusta to worry her. Though she knew the operation was pending she didn't know of its imminence.

He went into her dressing-room, where he had seen a small bookcase, in search of something to read. More than any room in the house, this one was saturated with the personality of Augusta. Its sun blinds were always half drawn like drooping eyelids. Under them the room seemed to look out on the world with an air of offence. Finch now disliked being in there because the windows overlooked the tennis court, and beyond it the toolhouse where Ralph Hart had died.

He ran his eyes along the titles of the books—*The Scarlet Pimpernel, Robert Elsmere, The Prisoner of Zenda, The Lady of the Lake.* What books were these? Were they old favourites of his aunt's that she liked to dip into at odd times? Or were they relegated here because of their shabby binding? Nothing on that shelf. He glanced at the one below. *The Silence of Dean Maitland, Friendship, Chandos, Lady Audley's Secret, Cometh up as a Flower... Hypatia, Ben Hur, A Pair of Blue Eyes.* Five of Eden Phillpotts'. Well, Devon explained them. *The Heavenly Twins, The Gods, Some Mortals,* and *Lord Wickenham.* On the bottom shelf the books were so shabby that the titles were illegible. They were wedged in so tightly that it was not easy to dislodge the large one at the end, the size of which attracted him. He carried it to the window. It was a medical book for the layman. Perhaps he could find out in this book what might be wrong with Meggie. He read and read, listening at the same time fearfully for his aunt's step on the stair. The more he read, the more bewildered and more horror-struck he became. Why, there were a thousand things that might be wrong with Meggie! And each one of them worse than the last. His head pounding, his nerves unstrung, he forgot to listen for Augusta. Women, he thought, why, it was better never to be born at all than be born a woman! How had Meggie lived so long as she had without disaster? How had Grandmother achieved her hundred years? It was a miracle. As he read his heart bled for the mothers of men.

XVI

JALNA

RAIN was steadily falling on the old house. It was a cold rain for the end of May, and it fell, not in drops, but in a slanting sleet that beat against the panes and ran down them in rivulets to form puddles on the sills. The fact that the panes could not be seen through was a matter of no significance, for the eyelids of all in the house were closed in sleep. The changes worked on the flower beds, trees, and lawn by the rain, cold as it was, would not be observed until the morning sun revealed flowers from yesterday's buds, buds from yesterday's sheaths, leaves shaken out to full size, and grass in a thousand springing spears.

The rain entered the house at two points, the attic and the basement. Through rotted shingles it dripped into Finch's vacant room. Soon after Finch had gone abroad, Wragge had placed a basin on the floor during a heavy rain, to catch the drip. He had not been in the room since, so he had not observed that the basin was full. Now the drops falling from the ceiling struck the water with a clear musical note, sending tiny ripples to the brim that overflowed silently on to the worn carpet. The daylight would show this room with a bereft air. Its furniture, most of which needed repairing, had been the ramparts of Finch's world. In the cupboard hung his worn clothes, still showing the impress of his body.

The rain came into the basement through a crack beneath a window, outside which it collected from the soaking ground above. From the window ledge it dropped with a smart rapping sound to the brick floor beneath. This sound, entering Wragge's consciousness, caused him to dream that he was back in the trenches and that the Germans were bombarding the British position. His sleep became more and more troubled. His snores turned to gaspings, and Mrs. Wragge, woken by his distress, put out her hand to quiet him. The result was the opposite of what she intended. The instant the large heavy hand was placed on his head he imagined that a fat German had captured him and he uttered a yell of fright.

Old Benny, the bob-tailed sheepdog, who slept on a mat in the hall above, heard in his sleep the echo of the yell. He had been dreaming of a strange creature, half-tramp and half-sheep, that had been prowling about the shrubbery. He had been stalking it through illimitable spaces of time without its having perceived him. Suddenly it turned, peered at him with the face of a man, uttering at the same time the metallic bleat of a sheep. His hackle rose and, with a sonorous growl, he leaped and caught it by the throat.

Upstairs Nip slept in Nicholas's armchair. He refused to sleep anywhere but in his master's bedroom. He always had one ear cocked for the sound of the deep voice he loved. Now he was in his first sleep of the night and the sound of Ben's growl came up to him. It came as the voice of his master saying—"Nip, Nip, catch a spider, Nip!" He stood on the seat of the chair, quivering. He gave tremulous whines, part pleasure and part fear. His eyes were fixed on the door though the darkness hid it from him.

Wakefield, snuggled against Renny's side, was the only one of the family who heard Nip's whining. He opened his eyes, saw that it was black night, heard the little quivering sound again, and shivered all over.

"Renny," he whispered tugging at his brother's sleeve. "What's that noise?"

Renny grunted drowsily. "Nothing. Go to sleep."

"But I heard something strange. Like someone crying."

"Mooey. Having a bad dream."

Wakefield sat upright, listening. Nip, at that moment, jumped from the chair to the floor and scratched at the door. "There! Listen to that! There's something very queer going on."

Renny, to satisfy him, got up and went into the passage. He listened but heard nothing. Nip had gone back to bed. Then the growl came again, from below. Renny remembered a loutish stable boy he had dismissed that day for kicking a horse. He had pitched him bodily out of the gate and the fellow had gone off shaking his fist. It might be as well to see that everything was all right downstairs. He lighted a candle and made the round of the principal rooms. All was quiet, Benny curled up again on his mat wagging his stub of a tail to show that he was quite capable of handling the situation.

The light from Renny's candle fell across Piers's face as he passed his door. Piers's eyelids slowly raised and he looked sleepily about wondering what had waked him. He was deliciously comfortable. An earthy tenderness was diffused through all his being. Pheasant's breathing came quick and soft beside him like that of a sleeping fawn. He drew her to him, his lips touching her bare shoulder.

It might be considered then that the falling rain which opened new flowers in the garden that night was also responsible for the conception of a new Whiteoak.

XVII

Sextette

It had been many a long year since the family at Jalna numbered as few as six. It took those who remained some time to get used to the empty places at table. The vacancy left by the heavy figure of Nicholas was especially hard to get used to. Renny did not like it at all. It was like losing his grandmother over again to have her sons, whom he had always at his side, go off like this. Alayne suggested that they take the leaves from the table so that they might draw closer together about it, but the idea was abhorrent to him. So he and she continued to sit facing each other across the long stretch of tablecloth on which stood the ponderous silver that made even breakfast seem a weighty meal. On one side of the table sat Pheasant and Piers, on the other Wakefield, looking very small and self-important.

"I'll tell you what we'll do," ejaculated Renny one morning. "We'll have Mooey take his meals with us. He's plenty old enough. Have a place set for him at dinner, Alayne. He can sit beside Wake."

The thought of a child of barely three sharing the family meals was distasteful to Alayne. She pictured a crumby face and a baby voice reiterating demands for helpings of the grown-up food. She tried to keep her voice even and her expression unruffled but both failed her. Her voice had a little rasp of irritation in it, and a pucker appeared on her forehead as she answered:

"Don't you think Mooey is too small? I'm sure Pheasant does."

Pheasant's first thought had been—"Oh, how sweet to have the little darling at the table!" But, when she found that Alayne did not want him, she turned doubtfully to Piers and asked:

"What do you think? Is he too small?"

Piers, with a swift glance at Alayne's face, answered:

"Wake sat up at table when he was smaller."

Renny broke into laughter at the recollection, "Of course he did! I can just see him. All eyes. And Gran used to dip bits of biscuit in her wine and feed him."

Alayne could imagine the scene. The old woman, even then past ninety, popping wet morsels into the mouth of the baby boy. She said sharply:

"Perhaps that is the reason why Wakefield's digestion is not stronger today."

"Nonsense," retorted Renny. "Gran often said that she saved his life! He'd no appetite. It was only she who could tempt him."

"I remember! I remember!" cried Wakefield. "I'd be sitting between Meggie and my Grandmother, and I'd have no appetite at all. Meggie would be holding a spoon in front of me and I'd turn my face away and say—'No, no'—and then Gran would lean over me, and she'd look simply enormous with her cap and a shawl, and she'd say—'Open your mouth, Bantling'—and I'd open it wide, and she'd put the most *delicious* little blob of biscuit into it and the wine would run down my chin on to my bib!"

Rags had been an interested listener to the conversation. He was cognisant of every slightest change of inflection or expression. He now said, in his nasal voice:

"I hope you'll pardon me speaking, Madam. But I 'ad just arrived at Jalna at that time. And it was always my opinion that the little boy might 'ave pined away an' died if 'e 'adn't got the attentions 'e did from 'is Grandmother. Coming right after the sights I'd seen in the War, madam, I thought it was the prettiest picture I'd ever be'eld."

Alayne regarded him with icy disapproval. But Renny grinned up at him showing every tooth, resembling his grandmother to a degree very irritating to Alayne, though in this he was blameless.

Piers said—"Well, of course, there would be one advantage in having the kid take his meals with us. As it is, the kitchenmaid has either to look after him just when she's needed in the kitchen, or he has to be down there during mealtime."

"And always the dynger of getting scalded!" put in Rags.

Alayne looked into the marmalade jar. "Please take this to the kitchen and have it filled," she said sternly. "It's been put on the table almost empty, and you can see what the edge is like."

Rags gave her an astonished look as he took the jar, as though he would say—"Well, who comes 'ere ordering me abaht!"

Since her return to Jalna as mistress Alayne had been diffident about giving orders to him. It was easy enough to give orders to the cook or the kitchenmaid. They were respectful and friendly. But she felt a cold antagonism in Rags, a resentment, and a desire to thwart her at every turn. He was aware, she felt sure, of her dislike of his intruding into the conversation of the family, and consequently he intruded the more often. He was aware that she was sensitive to draughts, and it seemed to her that there was one in every room. In old Adeline's time she had felt stifled often for lack of air, but it seemed not to matter to the Whiteoaks whether the air they breathed was vitiated or a veritable whirlwind. Sometimes the presence of the little Cockney in the house was almost more than she could bear.

When he had gone she said:

"I think Bessie can easily be spared at mealtime to look after Mooey. She gets the vegetables ready for cook, brings in the fuel, and, after Pheasant goes to him, Bessie is ready to wash up. I can't see that she is needed in the kitchen at mealtime."

"That's quite beside the point," said Renny. "It's the servants' business to get their work done whether or no. I was talking about the look of the table. Too damned lonely."

Wakefield, responsive to Renny's mood, exclaimed:

"I think the table looks awfully lonely!"

"Well," said Alayne, "I think you're the most sentimental people I've ever known. For my part I think we could be very cosy, if only you would take the leaves out, as I suggested, Renny, and make the table smaller." She had longed to speak sharply to Wakefield, but had managed to restrain herself.

A chill breeze from the shady side of the house blew in on her off the wet lawn. Without a word she rose and went to the window and tried to close it. It was swollen by the damp and she could not move it. For an instant Renny watched her struggles, then he sprang up and came to her side.

"Why didn't you tell me you wanted the window shut?" he asked, bringing it down with a bang.

She gave a little shrug and returned to her chair. Piers and Pheasant exchanged a look. Wakefield saw the look and stared inquisitively at Alayne.

Piers said—"Where is the marmalade? It was here a moment ago."

"I gave the jar to Wragge to have it filled," said Alayne. Piers could not have failed to see her do it. He was doing his part to irritate her evidently.

Piers looked at his wristwatch. "Well, I must be off. I can't wait for it."

"Oh, don't go without your marmalade, Piers!" said Pheasant, holding him by the sleeve. "You're so fond of it. Do ring the bell, Wake, and hurry Rags along!"

Wakefield ran to the bell-cord and pulled it violently. It was seldom used now, and had become frayed and unable to bear strain. At the second tug it broke in his hand.

"Now, there," exclaimed Renny, "what are you trying to do?"

"There was no need to be so rough," said Pheasant. "Alayne, I do wish you had not sent the marmalade pot away before Piers had got some. There was plenty in it for him."

"Go to the top of the stairs and shout to Rags," said Piers.

Wakefield, waving the end of bell-cord, ran to the stairs, crying—"Rags! Hurry up!" Before he returned to the table, he ran twice round it waving the cord.

"Sit down!" growled the master of Jalna, and he gave an apologetic grin towards Alayne's end of the table. His eyes avoided hers.

Wragge came panting into the room.

"*Where* is the marmalade?" demanded Pheasant.

Wragge looked injured.

"W'y, I was just fetching it, 'm, when first came the ring of the bell, and right on top of that a shout. It gave me such a turn that I dropped it. I thought there must be something hurgent, 'm."

"It is urgent. Did you break the jar?"

"Well, 'm, I 'ope not. I know I was a bit long, but Mrs. W'iteoak"—he made a bow, half cringing, half impudent, to Alayne—"she complained of the way the jar was washed, so I 'ad to find Mrs. Wragge to get 'er to wash it—the maid being upstairs minding the little boy, 'm—and I was just fetching it when the ring and the shout came."

"Please bring some more, and hurry. Mr. Piers is waiting."

Alayne sat silent, sipping her tea, trying to control her irritation, to conceal her hatred of the little Cockney. She said to herself—"It is nothing. I must not be easily upset. This is my life."... A mental picture was presented to her of breakfast at her father's table. The little embroidered mats on the round polished table, the slender silver vase holding perhaps three roses, the fragile china, the grapefruit, loosened from its rind, sweetened and decorated with Maraschino cherries by her mother the night before, the delicious coffee. Her father reading an editorial from the *New York Times* in his slow, precise New England voice. Her mother exquisitely neat, with her special digestive bread and her dish of stewed figs before her. Before she was aware of it her eyes filled with tears.

Her thoughts were broken by the sound of Mooey's voice at the door. Wragge was standing in the hall with the little boy on his sloping shoulder.

"Oh, what a nish brekkus!" Mooey was saying. "Hello, Mummy! I've got a nish 'orsie to wide!"

Pheasant cried—"Hello, darling!" Then—"Why did you bring him down, Rags?" But she was obviously pleased.

Wragge answered—"'E was crying' 'is little eyes out, 'm, being left alone by Bessie for a bit while she went to answer the door, I being in the kitchen at the time, along o' the marmalade jar."

"He deserves a licking for crying for that," observed Piers, eating marmalade as though it were a delicacy he had never tasted before.

"Don't be such a harsh parent, Father," said Pheasant.

"Don't Father me!"

Pheasant continued—"But it is rather inconvenient taking Bessie from the kitchen to mind him when he'd be quite all right here, isn't it?" She cast a propitiatory glance at Alayne.

Wakefield exclaimed, through a mouthful of toast— "Come to your old uncle, Mooey!"

"I want to go to Unca Renny," said Mooey, holding out his arms.

Wragge sidled into the room with the child. Renny took him on his knee.

It was a small thing, thought Alayne, but it showed their attitude toward her. They had all known that she did not want the child brought to the table, but his presence was to be inflicted on her nevertheless. The presence of such a young child was an affliction, she persisted in her mind. There would be still less possibility of sensible conversation now. Not that the conversation at Jalna was ever intellectually stimulating to her. But now she foresaw that the cleverness or naughtiness of a baby would be its centre. Renny was already looking pleased, feeding the child from his plate, Wragge beaming down at them.

It seemed that they would never finish breakfast. Piers had forgotten his haste. Pheasant was leaning forward gazing at her child. Alayne noticed a long "runner" on the shoulder of her knitted jumper. Wakefield's hair looked as though it had not been brushed that morning. He was saying in a whining voice:

"I aren't very well this morning. I don't think I should go to lessons."

"You're perfectly well," returned his elder brother. "Get along with you! It's nine o'clock."

Alayne rose from the table. "I think you will have to excuse me," she said. "I must see Cook at once about the dinner."

Renny half rose, still holding the child. He caught her dress as she passed and drew her to him. She went rigidly like an offended little girl. The moment he touched her, dignity seemed to fall from her. Her intellectual clarity made her aware of this and, while she despised herself for her weakness, her resentment toward him increased. He held up his face to be kissed, his lips pouted, the darkness of his eyes deepened. She was in no mood to kiss him, still less in the presence of the family. She shook her head, compressing her lips.

His eyebrows went up. He formed with his lips— "What's the matter with you?"

"Kiss him! Kiss him!" cried Mooey, tugging at her.

Alayne kissed him instead. He had left a sticky mark on her sleeve where he clutched her.

"Don't mind us!" cried Pheasant gaily. "I've never seen you two kiss and I'd love to."

"Our form improves as the day wears on," returned Renny.

Alayne was offended and she did not trouble to hide it. Yet, as she descended the stairs to the basement, she had the feeling of having been priggish.

Mrs. Wragge usually came upstairs for her orders. She greatly preferred to do this, for, as she put it to her husband: "I don't want none of the ladies nosin' about in my kitchen. Miss Meggie, she stayed out of it. Mrs. Piers, she stays out of it. Now let Mrs. Renny stop out of it!"

Consequently Alayne received a very glum greeting from her when she appeared in the kitchen.

Looking Mrs. Wragge in the eyes, she asked—"Is anything wrong, Cook?"

Mrs. Wragge, rather taken aback by this quick pouncing on her unusual aspect, said:

"I ain't just myself this morning along o' my innards. I come over sick in the night. I should be in me bed, but I wouldn't ast for the time off, not with Bessie spendin' hours upstairs mindin' the baby and me 'usband smashin' marmalade jars on me clean floor."

"It was ridiculous," said Alayne, conscious that Wragge was within hearing, "for him to drop the jar just because the bell rang."

"Oh, Alfred's a bundle o' nerves, 'e is, along o' shell shock and worry over the way me innards took on last night." She folded her stout arms on her heaving bosom and regarded Alayne with something approaching defiance. "An' were you wantin' anything special down 'ere this morning, 'm?"

"I thought I would just have a look about the pantries. And I want to see how much canned fruit and jam is left, so we shall know how much to put up this year."

"There ain't none left," said Mrs. Wragge, following her into the larder, "nor 'asn't been for months. I could 'ave done down a lot more than I did, but there weren't no bottles to put it in."

"Then, why ever didn't you say so?"

"I did, 'm. I ast Mr. W'iteoak for more before he set out for England to 'is weddin', but 'e said that things were too easy broke in this 'ouse and that if there wasn't jam pots enough we must do with less jam."

Alayne felt that this remark was thrown at her with the intention of intimidating her. She felt that the three servants were aware that she was not used to dealing with servants and that therefore they intended to impose on her. She had, up to this moment, liked Mrs. Wragge, had thought her quite superior to her jaunty little husband, but now she began to dislike her. Holding her head high she preceded the cook into the larder and began to investigate conditions there with a rather quaking spirit.

First of all was the smell. She did not like the smell at all.

"I don't see what it can be, 'm," declared Mrs. Wragge sniffing. "There ain't nothing 'ere to smell. Bessie scrubs it out on 'er 'ands and knees every day of 'er life."

"What is in this crock?" asked Alayne, lifting its lid. It was half full of biscuits and small cakes tossed in together. She picked up a biscuit. It was as limp as a bit of flannel. "Don't you know," she said severely, "that biscuits should not be put in with cakes? After this, keep them quite separate."

She saw butter on three different dishes, all uncovered. She saw a large bowl which had held preserves and now was empty but unwashed, with a lining of green mould, across which a spider scuttled. She saw a cheese half-finished while a fresh one was cut into. She saw milk and cream at every stage from that morning's to wrinkled sourness. Lifting a heavy silver dish-cover she discovered a roast of meat that was unquestionably the cause of the smell. For all these things she reproved Mrs. Wragge. When she discovered an old Staffordshire bowl filled with leftover beetroot, her reproof was inflamed to denunciation of such practices.

From the larder she went to the china-closet and pointed out that the china was not properly washed. Instead of a glittering and pure surface, it showed a dull one; it was not smooth to the touch.

"Well, 'm," declared Mrs. Wragge desperately, "they're washed every blessed time in strong suds."

"I smell it on them," said Alayne. "They are not half-rinsed." Mentally she recalled the stark immaculateness of the china-closet in the house of her aunts, on the Hudson.

She went to the kitchen and drew Mrs. Wragge's attention to the blackened condition of the saucepans. She drew her attention to the fact that the glazing on every one of the platters in the big platter-rack was cracked from overheating.

Bessie was in the scullery plucking fowls. Their feathers whitened the floor like snow. They were even in her thick black hair and sticking to her plump neck. She was a pretty girl with a turned-up nose and full red lips. She got to her feet when Alayne appeared, looking rather frightened. She held the fowl by one leg, its ghastly beak touching the floor. Its fellows, already plucked, lay on the table beside her.

"Don't you think, Bessie," said Alayne pleasantly, "that it would be better if you were to have a box to put the plumage in?"

Bessie did not know what plumage was and she looked still more frightened.

Alayne remained a little longer trying to talk cheerfully and arranging with Mrs. Wragge to have a tour of inspection of the basement once every week. Next time, she thought, it would be much easier. Then she would penetrate into the mysterious bricked passage that led to the wine cellar. She longed to see the place in perfect order. It would help to fill in the time to keep it so, for time often hung heavy on her hands. On the way to the stairs she passed a dishevelled bedroom and had a glimpse of Wragge making the bed, a cigarette in his mouth.

She felt tired but not ill-pleased with herself as she went to her bedroom. She would show these servants that she was not a figurehead. She would show Piers and Pheasant that she was as much mistress of Jalna as Renny was master. She would show Renny...

She was astonished to find Mooey in her room. He was standing in front of her dressing table, and he had a tin of talcum powder in his hand. She saw that he was sprinkling all her toilet articles with the powder, that he had already whitened his hair, and that the rug and chairs showed what could be done with a single tin of talcum.

She was tired and irritated or she would not have been so sharp with him. "Oh, you naughty boy!" she said, giving him a shake, "don't ever dare come into my room again!"

He looked up at her, tears springing to his eyes. He made his mouth square and uttered a howl of woe. She hustled him to the door and pushed him into the passage. As she turned back she saw that old Benny was lying in the middle of her new mauve silk bedspread. He was curled up tightly, with one hazel eye rolled toward her, with an air that intimated that it would take more than her disapproval to budge him from this new-found nest.

It was perhaps the first time in Alayne's life that she had experienced the violence of primitive rage. She knew that he had fleas, for she often saw him scratching himself. And after last night's rain his paws were certain to be muddy. She snatched up a slipper and struck him sharply with the heel of it, first on the head, then on the stern. The effect of retribution on Mooey was as nothing compared to its effect on Ben. He screamed as though all the bad dreams he had ever had were come true. He jumped from the bed, leaving a dark moist imprint of himself, but instead of running out of the room he took refuge under the bed. From there, on hands and knees, she was obliged to dislodge him with the slipper. By now she was almost beside herself. She followed him to the door and threw the slipper after him. He bounded down the passage yelping hysterically. Mooey was still wailing. Pheasant appeared at the door of her room with him in her arms.

"Why, Alayne, Mooey says you hit him! Whatever had he done?" Pheasant looked very much the offended mother.

"He threw powder all over my room," answered Alayne hotly. "Really, Pheasant, he must not be allowed to go in there by himself. He's too mischievous."

"Was that all?" said Pheasant coldly.

Renny came up the stairs with Benny mourning at his heels. "What have you been doing to poor old Ben? I've never heard him make such a row." When he saw Alayne's face he burst into loud laughter. She had got the talcum on her hands, then on her nose and chin. Her hair, for once, was ruffled.

Quite unconscious of her appearance she regarded him with an air of hauteur. She said:

"You may think it is amusing but I don't. That dog has ruined my silk bedspread, and that child has made my room look no better than Bessie's scullery."

Pheasant said, patting her son on the back, while he stared at Alayne wet-eyed, as though she were an ogress:

"I think that cats and a canary would suit you better than dogs and a baby, Alayne." She returned to her room still comforting her child.

"I like dogs and children as well as anybody, but I like them to behave themselves and to know their place."

"Let's see what the damage is," said Renny, leading the way into her room. He glanced at the floor, the dressing table, and the bed. "That will all brush off," he said soothingly.

"It may off the rug," she returned, "but the bedspread is *ruined*!"

"Can't you send it to the cleaners?"

"Of course I can! And have it come home all slimpsey like my dress did. The cleaners over here aren't nearly so good as I'm used to."

He could not take her seriously, looking as she did. His face broke into a smile as he said—"Only look at yourself in the glass and you'll forget all your troubles."

She looked, and was angrier than ever.

Old Benny thought—"With my master here I think I'm pretty safe in getting on the bed again." Accordingly he hopped with airy lightness on to the silk spread, avoiding the spot he had soiled before. His legs were strung with little beads of dried mud. He began to lick the place on his stern where the heel of the slipper had hit him.

Alayne had barely turned from the survey of her face when she saw him. It was one of those things that seem too bad to be true. Snatching up the other slipper she flew at him, striking him again and again. Renny caught her wrist.

"I won't have him beaten like that," he said sharply.

"Keep him out of my room, then! He's a perfect brute!"

"Come along, Ben! This is no place for us."

"You talk like a fool!" said Alayne.

He stopped in the doorway to look back at her. "I think," he said, "that you are the worst-tempered woman I've ever known."

She watched him go and then sat down on a chair by the window, feeling suddenly weak. Her own voice echoed in her mind, repeating—"You talk like a fool!" She had actually said those words to Renny... And what was it he had said? That, too, was echoed in her mind... She was not filled with remorse for her words or cut to the heart by his. She just sat motionless, stunned by the sudden rift between them. It was as though a crack in the earth had suddenly separated them... Could that be bridged? Could she leap back, across the chasm of her words, and stand once more close beside him? "The worst-tempered woman he had ever known." And he had seen his grandmother in her passions! Had seen her draw blood from the boys with her stick! He had felt the sting of her tongue himself. Ah, but she was his grandmother! To be his wife was different. His wife must be meek. Well—if not meek—she must still not raise her hand against his dog. She leant out into the sunny morning air. She heard the cooing of a wood-pigeon. She heard the rumble of a farm wagon. Saw the pointed leaves of the birches shaken out in gladness to the sun. She remembered her first coming to Jalna as Eden's wife. Life here had seemed so mysteriously different from the life to which she was used. Now her maiden life seemed far away, mysterious, though it was only five years. It was like a street she had once known well. Her thoughts, her emotions, had been the buildings—airy, narrow white buildings of a proud simplicity. That street had crumbled during the first months of her life with Eden. How the contact with his changeful, sensitive mind had absorbed her! A new street had been erected for her spirit—a wide, richly coloured street, where the stars hung above the roofs and fountains danced before the doors. Then she had thought she would be an inspiration to Eden, be the means of his writing glorious poems. And how quickly those bright edifices had dissolved! Eden's faithlessness, her meeting with Renny—her living in the very house with Renny—What was it that had crumbled the foundations? Eden and she had never had such a scene as this. She had never felt such a blaze of anger against Eden. Why was it? Was it because her love for Eden had been so much less? That with her love was mingled a maternal feeling? Was it because her love for Renny had in it so much of passion—her hope of understanding him ever baffled? The new street rising out of her life with him was threaded by intricate dark passages, separated by closed doors which, when they were forced open, were swept by frosty air and the sound of galloping hooves.

It was long before she put such fancies from her, rose, and tidied her hair and washed her face. She called Bessie to come and sweep the rug, and she tied up the silk bedspread in a parcel for the cleaners.

Renny slammed the side door behind him, Ben still at his heels. He was glad to get out of the house, but no more glad than he had been a score of times after a family row, when perhaps old Adeline had followed him to the very door, raining recriminations on him. Certainly this tantrum of Alayne's had been rather a shock. He had thought she had one of the sweetest dispositions possible. And to have beat up old Benny like this, and then to have called him a fool! He gave a kind of hysterical grin as he thought of it. Whatever had got into the girl? Perhaps it was a child? Women got into strange states at those times, he knew. Had tantrums or wanted to eat raw carrots or common starch—anything to be unnatural. Well, he hoped to the Lord it was a child. Meggie and Pheasant had both had them in the year, and now he'd been married a year and never a whisper of one. He'd like a boy resembling himself, except for the red hair. He could do very well without that. If it were a girl he should like it to look like Alayne, only, on the whole, it would be better if it inherited Meggie's disposition. She'd been cranky from the first that morning, he remembered. The way she'd pounced on poor old Rags about that marmalade, and the look she'd given him when he went to put down the window for her. Everything had annoyed her, even such a trifle as Wake's waving of the bell-pull. And how peevish she had been about Mooey coming to the table! She had tried to hide that, but he could see through her. Of course, if she were going to have a baby, the sight of another kid at the table might upset her stomach; there was no knowing.

He was only a few strides from the door when he was intercepted by Wragge. In the bright sunlight his coat looked very rusty and his scalp showed through his greying hair. He looked up at Renny with a mournful expression, twitching his nose and upper lip before he spoke as was his way when his feelings were hurt.

"Well, what is it?" Renny demanded impatiently.

"I've come to give notice, sir. I think that me and me missus had oughter go since we're not giving satisfaction to Mrs. W'iteoak, sir."

Renny stared at him, thunderstruck. "Mrs. Whiteoak hasn't said anything to me about your not giving satisfaction. What is the trouble?"

"Well, sir, you saw 'ow it was about the marmalade at breakfast. I was that unnerved that I nearly jumped out o' me shoes when the bell rang, and I let drop the jar and smashed it. Not but w'at it was cracked already and our second best one. Then, after breakfast, she came to the kitchen and poured out the vitals of her wrath on Mrs. Wragge. There wasn't a pot, nor a crock, nor a drawer she didn't look into, and nothink was right. She even examined of the oven cloths and said they was tea cloths and had no business there. She was after Bessie for the way she plucked the fowls. Bessie's young and she can tike criticism calm, but Mrs. Wragge ain't herself this morning along o' her innards. She 'ad a fry o' some pork leavin's last night before she went to bed, and at three this morning we both thought 'er hour 'ad come. So she don't feel able to swallow Mrs. W'iteoak's unreasonableness, sir, and my nerves won't stand it neither, so I think we'd better be goin'."

"The hell, you will!" said Renny. "Get along back to your work. I never heard of such nonsense. You have a very good place here and, if your wife can't stand a little scolding, she ought to be ashamed of herself. Give her a dose of salts and don't encourage her in her tempers." He strode on, but Rags followed. "We appreciate the plice we 'ave 'ere. I 'ave it in me to be an old family retainer, but wat's the use, if we can never do nothink to please the mistress?"

Renny stopped. "Rags," he said, giving him a look of almost tender familiarity, "you and I were through a good deal together. I don't want to part with you and I don't believe you want to leave me. You know quite well how to pacify your wife. Probably what happened this morning may never happen again. I've overlooked things in you and you must show your good sense by putting up with a little criticism. Remind your wife of the dozens of times I've praised her sauces and her tarts."

Rags's grey little face was quite broken up by emotion. "Do you mind the time, sir, when we'd moved our position at the Front and we arrived in a God-forsaken plice just at dark and, inside of a hour, I'd cooked you up a four-course dinner out o' some bits o' things I'd brung along in tins?"

"Do I! I'll never forget that dinner!"

They stood together talking of old times. Rags returned to the kitchen and told his wife that the master was all on their side and advised them not to take the missus too serious.

"I could have borne with 'er fault-finding," declared Mrs. Wragge, "if she 'adn't started in about the glazing on the platters. W'y, that was all cracked afore she ever set 'er foot inside this 'ouse."

"My! she has a funny way of talking," observed Bessie. "When she began about the fowl's *plumage* I nearly burst out laughing."

"Silly!"—said Mrs. Wragge. "That's the American for *fevvers*."

Renny and the sheepdog went on toward the stable, but now he was genuinely angry at Alayne. It was all very well to be disagreeable to him—Good God, she had told him that he talked like a fool—She had beaten poor old Ben for almost nothing, and now he found that she had all but lost him the Wragges. He remembered how she had drawn away from him when he had wanted to kiss her after breakfast. He sighed in puzzlement.

Usually he visited each of his horses in turn on his arrival at the stables in the morning, but this morning he felt out of sorts. He went straight to his little office and sat down before his yellow oak desk. Things were not going well with him this year. He had lost money at the races. A horse he had backed rather heavily, feeling certain of its quality, for it had been bred in his own stables and later sold to a friend (he had watched its training from month to month), had fallen, thrown the jockey, and galloped riderless to the finish. A horse of his own, trained by himself as a steeplechaser, ridden by one of his own men, had given a far from brilliant performance. He had hoped to sell it for a large sum. That hope was gone, unless the horse retrieved its reputation in another race. He had sold two of his best horses to a prosperous broker, but for some reason the payment for them was not forthcoming. Renny did not want to sue him for the money but he needed it badly. Added to these misfortunes, a gale in the autumn before had taken the roof from one of the stables and blown down a portion of the wall. Luckily the horses had not been injured, but the carpenter and the mason were becoming anxious for their money. They must be paid somehow.

In the early spring he had had a letter from Eden asking for a loan. He was in France, where he had been working all winter, and he wanted to go to England. His health was none too good. He badly needed a change—they had had a dreadful winter of cold and rain on the Riviera. Minny was with him, of course. He couldn't imagine what he should have done without her. Might he have a thousand dollars? And Minny had joined him in sending love.

When Renny had come to that part of the letter he had cocked an eyebrow. There was something about the whole tone of the letter that he had not quite liked. It was an almost impudent tone, as though Eden had said—"Well, I cleared out with Minny and made things easy for you and Alayne.

A thousand dollars isn't much to ask!" He had called it a loan, but Renny knew that he would never pay it back, and Eden knew that he knew. The money had been sent. One could scarcely refuse it to a brother who had almost died of lung trouble. Renny had never mentioned the affair to the family.

He picked up a paper that lay on his desk. It was an account from Piers of the hay, straw, oats, and chop with which he had supplied Renny during the winter. He had been expecting this account for some time, and he had known that Piers put off the rendering of it because of the shortage of money. The farm lands of Jalna were rented to Piers at a moderate rental. Renny bought from him the supplies he needed for the stables at the regular market price. Piers also supplied the house with fruit and vegetables at a low price, as they did not need to be packed or shipped. This arrangement had worked out excellently, each brother giving the other a little time when necessary. Their love of Jalna, their love of horses, and their pride in their family was a strong bond between them. In the last two years Piers had been ready with his rent each quarter, on the day of its falling due. Renny, on the contrary, had been obliged to ask Piers for more time on several occasions. He felt chagrin at this. He wondered if he might put off the mason, the carpenter, or some other creditor, and pay Piers at once. He ran his eye over the items of the account. Certainly the nags had got away with a lot of feed. But they were worth it! He opened a drawer and took out the accounts that had come in at the beginning of the month. He had not paid the vet anything since the New Year. His was mounting to a large figure. He must be paid something. Urgent notes were attached to the accounts of the mason and the carpenter, begging for an

immediate settlement. Then there was the notice from the
bank telling of a note that had fallen due. He had not been
able to resist that lovely mare in Montreal, though he really
had not needed her... He lighted a cigarette and stared rather
blankly at the papers on the desk. A jubilant neigh came
from the stallion's loose box.

He looked out of the window as a car drew up outside,
and saw Piers alight from it. Since he had got the new car
Piers seemed always to have some business that took him on
the road. Renny went out and joined him.

"I'm sorry," he said rather stiffly, "but you'll have to wait
a bit for the money for that fodder account. Money is
awfully tight with me just now, and the mason and carpenter are pressing. Other things too."

Piers's face fell. He had done the decent thing, he
thought, in delaying the rendering of his account. "Could
you pay me half?" he asked. "I need the money."

"No," returned Renny irritably; "you'll have to wait till
next month."

They had walked past the barn to the new piggery for
which Finch was paying. The work was proceeding well. It
was an up-to-date, solid-looking building. Piers had it in his
mind to breed pigs on a large scale.

"That thing is going to cost a lot of money," observed
Renny, eyeing it disapprovingly.

"More than young Finch expected, I'm afraid," answered
Piers, grinning.

"He shingled the barn for you, too, didn't he?"

"Yes. It needed it badly."

"It appears to me that, if you go on as you are
doing, you'll get more out of Gran's money than anyone else."

Piers's lips hardened. If his elder were going to throw Finch's present to him in his face, he could be disagreeable too. He said:

"When all is said and done, Finch is really doing it for you. The land is yours. The buildings are yours. I only have the use of them. You don't care what condition the farm buildings are in so long as the stables are kept up. These improvements Finch has made are for Jalna—not for me."

"I should never have asked for them."

"Of course not. As I said before, you don't care a damn about the farm buildings."

"Well, you'll have the use of them all your life. You'll likely outlive me. They don't mean anything to me."

"They mean that you get your rent the day it is due."

"I suppose that's a shot for me because I have to put you off." Renny's red face became redder.

Piers's eyes were prominent as they always were when his temper rose. But he spoke quietly. "No—but I don't like your tone about these buildings. You have known what is being done from the first and you've never said a word against the improvements until now."

"It was none of my business. I don't care what Finch does with his money."

Piers answered hotly—"But you resent his helping me."

"No, I don't. But I don't like your saying that he isn't doing it for you but for me."

"I didn't say that! I said he was doing it for Jalna."

"I'll look after Jalna—without anyone's help."

"Good lord! Then you would sooner he had squandered his money? He was bound to do that if he had been let alone."

"I don't want any of it spent on me; that's all. You will be saying next that he bought the car for me."

"Well, I acknowledge that was a present to me."

"It would have been better," said Renny, "if he had helped Eden a bit. He's not strong. I had to send him a thousand dollars in March." He had not intended to tell of the loan, least of all to Piers, but he felt himself forced to tell by what he considered Piers's surly attitude toward his delay in the payment of the account.

They were standing beside a small grassy enclosure where three sows, soon to farrow, were exposing their matronly forms to the sun. One of them trotted up briskly to the brothers and raised her small quizzical eyes to Piers's face. She recognised him and, like all animals, liked the looks of him. He carried a smooth, wandlike stick that he had picked up where the carpenters were at work. Wood had a fascination for him, whether in its natural state or polished. He would stop where a pine was being felled, pick up a smooth rosy chip, pass his hand caressingly over it, and hold it to his nose, drawing in its sweetness as though it were a flower. In the same way Renny would sniff when he entered the saddle-room and smelled the polished leather. It was Piers who most appreciated the Chippendale furniture brought out from England by their grandfather. Renny was proud of it, attached to it because it was a part of Jalna. He would have starved sooner than sell a piece of it.

Piers scratched the sow's back with his stick, rubbing it along the pink corrugated skin of her back on which white bristles stood up like a bleached forest. Her moist muzzle twitched. She put one huge ear forward as though listening to the rasping of the stick on her back. Her white eyelashes blinked rapidly, half-concealing her roguish eyes. The men stood silent as the spell was worked on her, then as, with a grunt, she rolled on to her side, Renny gave a short laugh, half amusement, half embarrassment. He wondered why Piers had made no reply to his confession of the loan to Eden. He repeated then:

"I had to send him a thousand. I couldn't refuse him."

Piers returned, still scratching the sow:

"Well, all I can say is that you were a fool to do it."

It was the second time within an hour that he had been called a fool, but he felt more hurt than angered.

"What would you expect me to do?" he asked. "Let him starve?"

"That's what he deserves." Piers turned away, as though he could not trust himself to speak on the subject of Eden.

The sow was unconscious that he had desisted from his attentions. She lay with closed eyes; her great side, under which dozed eleven little pigs, gently heaving, her small hooved feet sticking straight out.

Renny stood, with arms folded on the gate, looking down on her, old Ben sat close beside, pressing his hairy body against his legs. Renny thought—"Why, even when I tried to kiss Alayne at breakfast, she pulled herself away. Whatever is the matter with the girl?"

Piers went to the orchard to speak to the men who were giving the trees a final spray. He watched the misty fall of spray, glancing green in the sunlight, shroud the trees in its protective vapour. He examined the blossom from which the petals had now fallen, and reckoned that the crop would be a good one. He saw Pheasant walking among the strawberry beds with Mooey by the hand, and he could not resist a word of gossip with her, even though it was a busy time for him.

"Hello, Piers! We're hunting for ripe strawberries. Mooey has found three. Isn't he clever? There's a tremendous crop."

"You never can be sure of strawberries," he said, looking at the plants critically. Certainly the greenish-white berries were plentiful and looked large for early June. Here and there a pink one twinkled against the moist leaves, and Pheasant held to his mouth one that was actually ripe. His eyes smiled at her as he ate it.

"What do you suppose," she said breathlessly. "Renny and Alayne have been having a quarrel! They've been married a year now, and it's the first time I've heard them having words. And, Mooey, tell Daddy what Auntie Alayne did to you."

Mooey advanced between rows of strawberry plants, his cheeks berry-stained. He said gravely:

"Auntie Alayne f'owed me out of her room."

"What?" His father looked at him sternly.

"She f'owed me," he repeated, "out of the door. And I ran to Mummy, and I wasn't f'ightened."

"He is so brave," cried Pheasant. "He pretends he wasn't frightened, but he simply howled. I was in my room and I was positively terrified. He came running to me with his mouth wide open and his eyes tight shut and talcum powder all over his head. I was so annoyed."

Piers stared at her dazed. "But what had happened? Had she put the talcum on him?"

"No, silly! He had got into her room and sprinkled it on himself. She found him there and put him into the passage. Ben was in there too, and you should have heard her shout at him. One moment Mooey says that she hit him, and the next that she just pushed him. I think the poor darling was so terrified that he wasn't conscious of what was going on."

Piers looked down at his small son. "Did she hit you?" he asked, speaking very distinctly.

Mooey was filled with a sudden self-pity. His eyes swam with tears. "She f'owed a slipper at me," he said.

"I'll speak to her about this," said Piers. "I won't stand it."

"Oh, I don't believe I'd say anything," advised Pheasant. "It will only make a bad feeling. The more I see of life, the more I find that you must make allowances for people's complexes and frustrations and all that sort of thing. I think if all three of us are just a little cool to her for the next day or two it will make just as much impression as having words."

"Did you say that she and Renny were quarrelling?"

"Yes. I couldn't hear what it was about; but their voices were raised, and she followed him to the door and simply hissed after him—'You talk like a fool!' Isn't it terrible? Well—she's a brave woman. There's nothing on earth would tempt me to call Renny Whiteoak a fool."

"What did he say?"

"He said she was the worst-tempered woman he'd ever known."

Piers grinned. Then his face darkened and he said sombrely:

"I never had any hope of that marriage turning out well. I wish to God he'd never cared for her!"

Pheasant cried—"Oh, I like Alayne! She's really quite a sweet thing. But I won't have her doing things to my baby." And she snatched up Mooey and kissed his berry-stained mouth.

"Well, I have my bit of news, too," said Piers. "I put my account for feed on his lordship's desk this morning. He tells me he can't pay it for another month. Where he is going to get money in the next month I can't imagine."

"What a shame!"

Piers lifted a soft lock from Mooey's forehead. "There's a mark there! A bruise. Do you think she did that!"

"No. That's where he fell down the steps yesterday." She kissed the bruise.

"Anyway," said Mooey, "she f'owed her slipper at me."

Pheasant shook her head at him. "Don't let your mind dwell on unpleasant things, my child! I must teach you that poem of Longfellow's about the world being full of such a number of things, I'm sure we should all be as happy as kings. Smile, Mooey! Smile itty bitty at oo mummy!"

Mooey smiled waveringly, his eyes full of tears.

"Don't talk baby talk to him," said Piers.

"Oh, Piers, you don't realise what a delightful thing it is for a young mother to talk baby talk to her tiny boy in a strawberry bed on a June day. Only smell the air! Isn't it sweet? Excepting, of course, when one smells the Bordeaux mixture. And even it looks lovely over the treetops. And those big white clouds flying. And that oriole singing. And the sound of the carpenter's hammer! And Mooey's hair all fluffy on his temples!"

Piers looked at her with a little twisted smile. How funny she was... how long her lashes were... How he loved her!

He said—"Well, Renny will never get anyone else to take the interest in the farmlands that I do. Ever since I've taken them over I've improved them. Even when I managed them on a salary, when we were first married, I was improving them. Of course, this way is better for me, even though I pay a good rent."

"We get our living as well, don't we? Three of us, and Bessie does quite a lot for Mooey."

"Why, yes, we do." The thought that their living cost them nothing came as a mild surprise to Piers. He had always taken that for granted. Two or three extra people meant nothing to Jalna.

"Renny wouldn't have it otherwise," he said. "He gets nervy when the house isn't full of people. Look what he was like at the breakfast table. Wanting this fellow brought down. Be sure you fetch him to dinner, Pheasant. We'll see what Mrs. Alayne has to say to that!"

XVIII

THE FOX FARM

RENNY drew in the restive young horse he had been exercising and looked over the white gate into the fox farm. He was undecided whether or no he should go in. Before the death of Antoine Lebraux he had been in the house every day. The sick man had become more and more dependent on him. When Lebraux's periods of drinking had rendered him violent it was to Renny that his wife had come for assistance. After his death Renny had gone to the house constantly, trying to create order out of the disorder of affairs they discovered. He had helped Mrs. Lebraux through the cubbing season. He had got Piers to buy some purebred Leghorns for her with which to stock the poultry house. He had sent old Noah Binns to dig the garden for her. He himself had gone about the house putting the rollers of window shades into order, tacking up sagging wallpaper, tinkering at the kitchen tap that dripped. He had interviewed the retired farmer who held a mortgage on the property and persuaded him to give her more time. It was the same man from whom Finch had taken over the mortgage on Vaughanlands.

In return for these kindnesses Clara Lebraux had insisted that he make use of her stable, for his own were overcrowded. It was all she could do. The horses were company, she said. She gave them their evening meal and bedded them down herself. Between her and Renny had arisen the peculiar intimacy that is created between a man and a woman when he has seen her through distressing times, seen her looking her worst, red-eyed and unattractive or engaged in rough work, has done things about the house for her that a husband or a male relative ordinarily would do. They were as natural in the company of each other as two labourers on Piers's farm.

Things were going a little better with her now. She did not need his help so often, and a casual word from Piers had made Renny feel that there was some gossip in the neighbourhood about his frequent visits there. It was characteristic of him that he should dislike being gossiped about. He was overbearing. He could taciturnly ignore criticism. But he did not like to think that the Miss Laceys, Miss Pink, and Mrs. Fennel were giving sly hints over their teacups. He did not like to think that the grooms and stablemen nudged each other when he turned his horse in the direction of the fox farm. It was not fair to Mrs. Lebraux that he and she should create even harmless gossip. Before his marriage he had conducted his casual affairs of the heart with capable secrecy. Since his marriage he had given no thought to any woman save Alayne. His former amorous proclivities had been consumed in the generous fire of his love for her.

But in Clara Lebraux he had found what he had never known before—friendship with a woman. He could spend hours in her company without remembering her sex except as an intangible something that enriched their intimacy. He never forgot Alayne's sex. It hung about her as a cloak, clouding his vision of her. It lay about her feet as a magic circle beyond which he had neither the power nor the will to press. His nature was intermittently sensual. At times when Alayne was talking, giving her opinion on some matter with the somewhat elaborate detail natural to her, he would watch her with a look that was both admiring and baffled, and that had in it, as well, something hostile. He was aware that his impregnable masculinity was often irritating to her.

As he hesitated before the gate the front door of the house opened and Pauline Lebraux appeared. She ran toward him between the dingy white stones on either side of the path, her legs in their black stockings looking excessively long and agile. She threw back her head as she reached the gate to free her face from the uncared-for dark hair that hung like a mane about it.

"Aren't you coming in? Oh, please do!" she entreated, gaspingly, as though in excitement.

He noticed her low white forehead with its pencilled brows, the foreign-looking eyes, the wide, rather thin-lipped mouth with an upward curve at the corners. He said:

"No. I don't think I shall go in. Just tell me how you are getting along."

"The very same. There's nothing new. But you haven't come for three whole days! We're so lonely. We think you are annoyed with us."

"Open the gate, then."

She threw it open with a grand gesture.

"Noah Binns is here," she said, as though she had searched in her mind for news.

"Is he? I'll stir him up a bit then before I go into the house." He alighted and tied his horse to the fence, and it began eagerly to crop the uncut grass of the yard, taking swift mouthfuls with impatient jerks of the head.

Pauline Lebraux passed her long thin hands over its smooth sides. She ran to where the grass was mixed with moist Dutch clover beneath an apple tree, and, grasping all she could, carried it to him. She watched him solicitously as he munched, repeating to him endearments in French. Renny went to where he saw old Binns digging. "Hello, Noah," he said, "how much have you got done today?"

The old man leant on his spade and turned his dim eyes on Renny. Like Pauline's, his mind sought for news, but, instead of swooping on it and tossing it to the newcomer as a morsel to excite his appetite, he let his eyes travel the length of the garden, taking in every lump of earth, every weed and every vegetable growth, then, painfully wrenching his morsel of information from the soil, he threw it half-indignantly as a sop to this tyrannical being whose presence was an urge to activity. As his eyes reached Renny's face he said:

"Carrots be up!"

"So I see. And pretty thick too. Not so bad—but you've left a lot of thistles along the far end!"

Noah slowly turned his head so that at last his gaze was focussed on the weeds.

"Thistles be always up," he observed.

Mrs. Lebraux appeared at the side door of the house. She did not speak, but stood there waiting. Renny at once went over to her and they entered the house. They went into the sitting-room that had become so familiar to him. He was used to high ceilings at Jalna. Here he always felt inclined to stoop for fear he should strike his head in the doorways. He looked about the room, which had changed somewhat since he was last there, and said:

"It looks nice here. What have you been doing?"

She gave a shrug. "Cleaning house. Making things look different so it will be less depressing. Pauline made that lampshade. Do you like it?"

He looked at it seriously. It was a parchment shade, somewhat crudely painted with red flowers.

"It looks nice when it's lighted," she said. "It gave her something to do."

"What's this?" he asked, touching a gold-embroidered table-runner.

"She cut that out of an old evening gown of mine. I must let her do things." She pushed a box of cigarettes towards him and, striking a match on the under side of the table, lighted one for herself. She stretched out her feet, encased in worn brogues, leant back and clasped her hands behind her head. Her hair, streaked in gold and drab, looked as though it had just been hastily brushed. She stared straight before her out of her round light-lashed eyes and smoked in silence.

He looked at her, only half seeing her. But he thought she had improved the looks of the sitting-room. The brightness of the table-runner and the lampshade pleased him.

"Did you have a woman in to clean for you?" he asked.

"I did it myself. Skinned all my knuckles."

He frowned. "It doesn't cost much to get a woman for a few days."

"It costs enough to buy us new shoes, and we both need them."

He looked at her shoes, then noticed the hand she extended as she knocked the ash from her cigarette. She had not spoken with exaggeration, either of shoes or knuckles. She was made of good stuff, he thought.

"I'll tell Binns to clean out the poultry-house for you."

"I cleaned it out myself before breakfast."

"Hmph! How's the poultry doing?"

"Awfully well, but, of course, the price of eggs is low now. But we eat them twice a day. I give the child a raw one in a glass of milk; she's growing so fast."

"It's too bad the incubator went wrong that first time. I think it's rather a pity you set it up again. From what I hear these late chickens aren't up to much."

"I used Plymouth Rock eggs this time. They'll develop quickly into broilers. The lamp acted rather funny last night. I thought the first experience was going to be repeated, so I stopped up half the night with it."

"Look here," he exclaimed, "you're going to overdo it, you know."

"Oh no, I'm not! I'm feeling a thousand times better than I did in the winter. I'm worried about the child, though."

He looked at her enquiringly.

"Her education. She simply isn't getting any. Her father used to teach her, but I can't. In the first place, it isn't in me to teach. In the second, my own education was sketchy. Pauline knows more about literature and more Latin that I do. And, naturally—French."

"You never learned to speak French from Lebraux?"

"No. What was the use? He could speak English. He used to laugh when I'd try my schoolgirl French on him. But he always spoke French to Pauline. Now she'll be forgetting it, I'm afraid."

An idea came to Renny. "Why, see here, my wife reads French very nicely! She and Pauline could read some French books together and it would do them both good. Alayne has really no way of passing the time. I'll ask her."

Mrs. Lebraux's eyes looked blank, but she said:

"Thanks very much. I'm afraid it would be too much trouble for her."

"Not at all. She likes children. She has always been very keen about my young Wake."

"Well, I should be very grateful... Pauline wanted to go to Mr. Fennel with your small brother, but she's a Catholic, you know, and I'm sure Tony would have objected. What do you think? Do you think it is fair to her to hinder her education because of a prejudice?"

"I think her father's wishes should be respected. But among us we'll give her a start. Then, when things are a bit better with you, you can send her to a convent."

"She's going on for sixteen."

Renny knit his brows. "Uncle Ernest will be glad to help. I'm sure of that. He's an Oxford man. Then, my wife for the French... and poetry. She knows all about modern poetry. If you want Pauline to study that. I think myself she'd be better without it... I'm afraid I can't do much myself. It's amazing how I've forgotten everything I learned at 'Varsity. Just in one ear and out the other. Money wasted. It was all athletics with me. An amusing thing about my education is this—the little I learned from the governess who taught my sister and me when we were kids is all that sticks with me. I know the dates of all the English kings and of the principal battles. You simply couldn't catch me up on them. I might teach them to Pauline. It would be something to go on. Not one of my young brothers has hung on to them as I have. I've asked them suddenly—perhaps in the middle of their pudding— what are the names and dates of the battles in the Wars of the Roses? Do you think they could get them right? No. Or perhaps—what were the dates of King Stephen? They were sure to be wrong. I couldn't possibly forget. Eleven thirty-five to eleven fifty-four. Wakefield is pretty good at the kings. I've said them to him to send him to sleep when his nerves were rocky. It's the only use my education has ever been to me."

Clara Lebraux listened to all this with serious interest. She puffed at her cigarette, scowling intently at him through the smoke. Alayne had heard him say the same words with detached amusement, wondering at his ingenuousness.

"The governess was afterwards your stepmother, wasn't she?" she asked.

"Yes."

"Were you fond of her?"

"Not particularly. I didn't think much about her. She was often ill, I remember. She'd large blue eyes that she kept half shut, and yellow hair. Eden's rather like her... She taught me poetry too. Can you believe that? Tennyson. And I have forgotten every line of it. If Eden had inherited a love of dates from her instead of poetry, it would have been better."

"I suppose. I can't read poetry at all. It bores me."

They smoked in silence, he gazing thoughtfully at her brogues, thinking how worn they looked; she, at his boots, admiring the soft glow attained by the leather after many polishings.

Pauline came in, her small face flushed pink by the sun, her black frock worn at the elbows and too short for her. Renny said:

"Now, let's see what you know about history! What are the dates of Henry the Seventh?"

She stood before him startled. She shook her head. "I don't know."

He grinned triumphantly at her mother. "I told you! She doesn't know." Then to Pauline: "Fourteen-eighty-five.

Fifteen-nine. Now, Pauline, tell me the names of the kings from William the Conqueror." His fierce eyes ruthlessly compelled hers, but he prompted—'First William the Norman, then William his son, Henry, Stephen, and Henry...' By George, I'm telling them all to you!" He drew her to his side on the sofa. "Never mind! I'll teach you them. We're going to educate you among us. How will you like that?"

She thought he was magnificent. She laid her head confidingly against his shoulder. "I shall like to have you teach me. Will you come here to do it, or must I go to Jalna?"

"I think I'll come here. But my wife will read French with you at Jalna." By this time he felt sure that Alayne would acquiesce in the arrangement. How could she refuse?

"I know French already," said Pauline rather haughtily.

"Don't be ungracious," said her mother. "It will be quite a different thing to read French literature."

"Papa read French books to me." Somehow she did not think she would like to read French with Mrs. Whiteoak. There had been something in her cool gaze when they had met that had given the child a sense of being repulsed. However, she had been taught to be polite, so she added— "But, I suppose, these would be grown-up books. Quite different. Thank you, Renny."

Both mother and daughter called him Renny, as Tony Lebraux had done, but he had pronounced it René.

Between Pauline and her father there had been a love, and an understanding almost extravagant, such as occasionally exists between father and daughter. She was only a small child when she realised that her parents were opposed in character. Long before she understood what their disagreements were about, she was on the side of her father, her heart

aching in sympathy when she had thought his sensibilities
were hurt. The fact that they spoke together a language her
mother did not understand, that they were separated from
her by religion, gave their love a strange and precious quality. It had been ecstasy to her to lie in his arms, her cheek
against the soft cloth of his coat, gazing up into his olive-
skinned face, admiring the full curve of his lips beneath his
little black moustache, the hairs of which were strong and
glittering, and were twisted at the ends into two little spikes,
so sharp that they pricked you if a kiss were misdirected.
Then, as she lay in his arms, they would whisper endearments and plan what they meant to do in the future. She
would never leave him; never, never leave him. She would
not marry because he would have all her love. She felt that
his love for her made her inviolate against change or disaster. Even when he became ill, when he began to drink too
much French brandy, his love still enfolded her. Nothing terrible could really happen to them. Yet she knelt before the
crucifix in her room and prayed for him in ever-increasing
foreboding of the spirit... She was spared nothing of the
despair, the agony of his last days. In the small house nothing could be hidden.

It was then that she had learned to look on Renny
Whiteoak as a tower of strength. The sight of his tall figure,
his lean red face in the room with her filled her with a wild
timorous joy in these days of early summer. She lifted up her
heart to be filled with the strength of his presence.

She liked to listen to her mother and him talking
together as they smoked endless cigarettes. It was strange
how, even when they talked of worrying things, there was no
sense of fear or irritation in the room. Sometimes they
laughed, laughter sounding strange in that house. Pauline

liked to hear it—Renny's abrupt loud bark of a laugh, her mother's deep, sputtering chuckle. After he had gone the child would throw her arms about her mother and exclaim —"Oh, Mummy, isn't he nice?" Now that Tony Lebraux was gone, Clara and Pauline were drawing closer together.

When Renny looked at his watch, Pauline exclaimed:

"Oh, do stay for lunch. He must, mustn't he, Mummy?"

"Yes, do stay! You haven't had a meal with us since January... But I'm afraid there isn't much to tempt you."

"I'll make an omelet! I can make a splendid one. And there's ham!" She was willing, eager to use their supplies for the day to spread a feast for him.

She tied a white-and-blue checked apron under her chin and turned back the cuffs of her black frock. He stood beside the stove watching her as she frowned anxiously at the mixture in the frying pan. What if the omelet would not rise? she thought. What if it rose and fell again?

No need to worry. It rose in a yellow foam; at its height it attained just enough firmness to support it; it turned a golden brown. She laid it on the heated platter and Renny went to the garden to get parsley to garnish it. Old Noah Binns was seated under a tree, eating his lunch from a package wrapped in newspaper. He tilted his head to drink cold tea from a bottle, pointing his white beard heavenward and exposing the activities of his Adam's apple. A dog fox had climbed to the roof of its kennel the better to observe him. It sat there fiercely erect, aware in every nerve of his slightest movement. The bright eyes of the vixen peered from the opening of the kennel. Noah Binns grew restive under their gaze. He shied a bit of pork rind he could not swallow against the wire netting of the run.

"Go to earth, dang you!" he shouted.

Renny turned, with the bunch of parsley in his hand.

"Never do that again," he said sternly. "Don't you know that Mrs. Lebraux makes pets of her foxes? Don't let me ever catch you frightening them."

Noah twisted his beard in his fingers, looking like a strange old man in a play.

"Fox himself!" he muttered at Renny's back. "Pet fox? Whose pet fox? *Hers!* Dang 'em both!"

Renny had brought enough parsley to garnish a roast young pig, but Pauline would use it all. So the omelet came to the table resting on a bank of green, resembling a verdant mountain capped with the gold of sunset.

Pauline felt a quivering sense of pride in her achievement, elation at the presence of a guest—and that guest Renny. She smiled, lifting her lip and showing her small white teeth. They talked of foxes, and Pauline told of the habits, the knowing tricks, of each. The man who worked for them had made her a seat in one of the shady trees about which the enclosures were built, and there she sat by the hour watching the foxes. They were become so used to her that even the shyest no longer scurried into his den when she climbed the steps to her seat. The boldest knew her. They knew (she said) the names she had given them. The cubs loved her. They were wonderful foxes, no two of a like disposition.

"She knows more about them now than I do," said Clara Lebraux.

"Experience shows," Renny said, "that the more foxes are handled as tame animals the better they thrive. Better cubs. Better fur."

"If only," cried Pauline," I might keep them all! But I have my pets and they must always be kept for breeding."

"You must not be sentimental," he said. "I would sell any horse I own."

"But not to be *skinned*."

"Well, perhaps not. I agree that that's hard."

While Mrs. Lebraux cleared away the luncheon things, Pauline led Renny upstairs to the vacant room next her mother's where the incubator was kept.

"What do you think I do?" she exclaimed, squeezing his arm when she had him alone. "I steal eggs from the poultry-house and feed them to my baby foxes!"

"But that is wrong," he said, looking down at her as severely as he could. "Those eggs are worth something."

"Bah, a few eggs!" she cried, with the exact expression of her father.

"But look at these! See what they are doing!" He pointed through the narrow glass door of the incubator.

An egg next the glass was rocking like a little boat on the sea. Another showed a dark triangular chip. Through a third was thrust a gaping yellow beak. Far in the twilight, at the back, staggered a pitiable object, wet, goggle-eyed, half-fainting, hemmed in by the rows of uncompanionable spheres in which slept, cheeped, chipped, or lay dying, his contemporaries. His woebegone expression showed his consciousness of being hatched too soon.

Renny had struck a match and held it near the glass. They peered in, rough black head and red head touching.

"Isn't he a sight?" breathed Pauline in ecstasy.

"Poor devil," said Renny. "That's what it is to be born the eldest of a family."

XIX

The Outsider

Since the departure of Nicholas and Ernest, Rags had been laying tea in the dining room instead of carrying it to the drawing-room as was the custom in old Adeline's day. Her sons would have resented the change, but the younger members of the family enjoyed having their bread and butter, cakes, and jam spread out before them, and sitting around the table to it.

Renny had not returned until tea time. He entered the house in rather a propitiatory mood towards Alayne. In spite of her hard words to him he felt that, as a sensitive and fastidious woman, she had probably had a good deal to annoy her that morning. He knew that the servants were not what they should be, but he felt quite sure that nothing she could do would change them. He knew that he and old Benny the sheepdog were not all they should be, from her point of view, but he hoped that in time she would become accustomed to them and their ways. He rather admired the spirit she had shown that morning. He had never seen her in a temper before. To think that she would hit the old dog with her slipper! And tell her husband that he talked like a fool! He

grinned when he thought of it. He was elated by the idea of
getting Alayne to read French with little Pauline. He felt
that, if she would agree, it would be the means of drawing
her and Clara Lebraux together. It would be good for each of
them to find a friend in the other. It would be especially good
for Alayne to have an interest outside Jalna, for he realised
that often time hung heavy on her hands.

He went up to his room and changed into another suit,
after having scrubbed his face and hands till they were red
and flattened his hair with a damp brush. This was done in
order that she should today have no complaint that he
brought the smell of the stable with him.

She was pouring tea when he went into the dining room,
sitting at her end of the table with a book she had been reading open beside her. Piers and Pheasant were talking with
rather ostentatious good spirits to each other. Mooey had
been brought to the table and was perched on the large volume of British Poets on which Wakefield had been used to
sit. As he ate his bread and butter his eyes were fixed on
Alayne with a wondering look as though he expected her at
any moment to attack him. As his parents were present to
protect him he would not have been altogether sorry to see
her make some such demonstration. He smiled up at
Wakefield, who sat beside him, and whispered—"I'm not
f'ightened of Auntie Alayne."

"Of course you're not," said Wakefield, patting his head.
"So long as you do just what Uncle Wakefield tells you,
nothing can harm you." Renny grinned at the children, then
went and sat near Alayne. She had given Wragge a few roses
for the table, which he, in a conciliatory mood, had placed in
a vase beside her plate. As he entered the room with a fresh
pot of tea for Renny he cast his eyes on the roses and then

on Alayne, emphasising the fact that they were his gift to
her.

She looked up from her book and smiled at Renny—a
somewhat forced smile—then lowered her eyes again,
abstractedly eating a small iced cake while she read. With her
book, her roses, and her cake she was separated from the other
members of the family in a kind of frosty seclusion. At tea
Renny liked a pot to himself, which Wragge always ostentatiously placed beside him. He was very hungry after the lunch
at the fox farm, accustomed as he was to a solid one o'clock dinner. He ate in silence for a time, feeling himself in rather an
uncomfortable position midway between the opposing factions
at the table. Vaguely he wondered what he could do to please
Alayne, to show her that the words she had cast at him that
morning had not rankled. He discovered the roses and drew the
vase across the table to him. Glancing at Alayne from under his
thick dark lashes to make sure that she was observing him, he
sniffed each rose in turn, thrusting his handsome bony nose
into the heart of each like some enormous predatory bee.

"These smell awfully nice," he said. "Out of our own
garden?"

"Yes," she returned, closing her book on her finger. "You
had better put them in the centre of the table. I don't know
why Wragge should have set them by my place."

Piers and Pheasant had ceased their animated talk long
enough to listen to this exchange of words. Now they began
to talk again, their eyes dancing. They paid no attention to
their child, who sat gazing in astonishment at the large piece
of cake Wakefield had put on his plate while he still held
another piece in his hand.

Alayne returned to her book and Renny set the vase of
roses carefully in the middle of the table. His first effort had

failed. Wragge had come into the room and was gazing at him with an adoring expression. He came and bent over him, whispering:

"Is your tea all right, sir?"

"Oh, yes, it's quite all right." He looked up into Rags's pale eyes as though for inspiration.

It might be well, he thought, to show Alayne that he was definitely on her side regarding Mooey's misbehaviour of the morning. He fixed his nephew with his gaze and said:

"What's this I hear about you? Going into Auntie Alayne's room and flinging her powder about. Let me catch you in there again and I'll warm you so that you'll not want to sit down for a week."

Mooey's eyes overflowed with tears. He laid down the cake he had been eating beside the piece he had not yet begun, and clutched his head in both his sticky hands. He made his mouth square and emitted a wail. Piers shook his finger at him.

"None of that!" he said. "Sit up and take your medicine. Take that cake off his plate, Wake."

Mooey gulped back his woe and wiped his eyes on a corner of his bib.

"It's pretty hard," exclaimed Pheasant, "always to restrain a small child so that he'll never get into the least little bit of mischief!"

"You must manage it somehow," said Renny.

"If only Alayne would keep her door shut! Mooey can't manage doorknobs yet."

"Alayne can't keep her door shut. She doesn't want it shut. She likes the air to stir through it."

"But she's always complaining of draughts!"

"A draught in the sitting-room and a draught in her bedroom are two very different things."

Alayne sat listening with the feelings of one engaged in a lawsuit who sits silent, made to writhe alternately by the attorneys for and against. She had come to tea scarcely knowing how to face Renny. She had brought her book to the table as a protection. Now Renny's attitude of aggressiveness on her behalf gave her an agreeable sense of power. For the first time she felt the possibility of influence over him. If only she had him to herself! But how little likelihood there was of that since even now he was fretting at the smallness of the family! While he was in his present mood it might be timely to introduce the subject of a nurse for Mooey.

She said, looking down the table at Pheasant and speaking gently—"I know it is quite impossible to keep babies out of mischief. Don't you think it would be better if you had a nurse for Mooey? It would give you so much more freedom. Mrs. Patch has a young niece who might easily be got to come by the day."

"I can't afford a nurse for him. Pheasant has nothing else to do, and Bessie takes him off her hands sometimes," said Piers.

"One could see this morning," returned Alayne, still looking at Pheasant, "how well Bessie looks after him. He might easily have got into danger."

"I quite agree," said Renny. "We'll engage the Patch girl, and I'll pay her wages."

This was not at all what Alayne had intended. It was not fair. Already he was doing far more than was necessary for Pheasant and Piers. Alayne sometimes wondered if they or he realised what the cost of keeping three people amounted to in a year. In spite of her effort to control it, her face fell, the corners of her mouth went down. Piers's eyes were on her. He smiled triumphantly as though at a victory beyond mere matter of money, and said:

"Thanks awfully, old man! There's no doubt that it will be a relief for Pheasant, and we shall all feel reasonably sure that the kid won't be upsetting Alayne. For my part I think it would be much better if he didn't come to the table."

"He shall come to breakfast and tea but not to dinner or supper," said Renny dictatorially.

Mooey did not like this discussion about his meals. He laid his forehead against the edge of the table and wept. Piers got up, threw him across his shoulder as though he were a parcel, and carried him out.

Before she followed him Pheasant said:

"Thank you very much, Renny. It will be nice having a nurse. I'm not going to be excessively grateful though, because I think you are doing it much more for Alayne than for me."

They were alone, except for Wakefield. How often it seemed to Alayne that they were alone except for him. He had grown quieter of late. He was growing taller too, and he often had a brooding, half-sulky air. Then, again, he would be his mischievous precocious self.

Renny turned sideways in his chair and crossed his legs, regarding her with a pleased air. "I've got something nice for you to do," he said. Wakefield also turned sideways in his chair, crossed his legs, and folded his arms. Alayne drew the vase of roses from the centre of the table toward herself, withdrawing her hand just at the spot where the roses and their foliage would intervene between her face and Wake's. This was an unpremeditated gesture. It was simply that she must do something, though it were merely symbolic, to shut him off from herself and Renny.

"What is it?" she asked, trying to look pleasantly eager.

"I've arranged for you to read French with the little Lebraux girl. You see, she has no one to speak it with now."

"But why should I? I suppose she reads French better than I do already. And I speak it very little."

"Then it will be a help to you as well."

"But I don't want to do it!" The thought of reading or speaking French to a child whose native tongue it was, bored and intimidated her. She would not have minded teaching a child ignorant of the language, but that the child should know it better than she, should perhaps go home to criticise her accent to her mother, was not to be endured.

"Don't be silly! I've promised for you."

"It is impossible."

In exasperation he poured down a cup of scalding tea. "That's because you dislike Clara Lebraux."

"So her name is Clara!"

"Why not?" He had nothing to conceal, but the colour of his face deepened at the implication of intimacy in her tone.

"No reason at all. It is a name I've never cared for. And I do not feel attracted to Mrs. Lebraux. But that has nothing to do with my refusal to read French with her child." Her voice wavered. She picked up a morsel of bread and began to pulverise it between her finger and thumb. "Renny, can't you understand? It would be embarrassing for me to attempt to teach that girl!"

"Not to *teach*! To *read* with. There's a vast difference."

"I am sorry, but I can't make the effort."

"Not to please me?"

"To please you!" she repeated, raising two blazing eyes to his face. "Why should it be so necessary to your pleasure?"

"It's not. But I hope I have some compassion in me... Give me one sensible reason why you won't do this and I'll try to understand."

"I have explained."

"If anyone else offered such an excuse I can imagine what you'd say!"

"Can you?" She turned her head aside indifferently.

"Yes. You'd say they were being self-conscious and self-centred."

She directed a hurt and angry look at Wakefield, then rose from the table. "Not before an outsider, please," she muttered, and left the room.

Renny took out his cigarette case, extracted a cigarette and lighted it. He smoked in silence, his face twisted into a peculiar grimace which, if it had been observed by one of his kin, would have been translated by them as expressing a mood of defiance and chagrin. No one saw it. Wakefield was sitting with his elbow on the table, his head resting on his hand. The last of three sighs drawn from the depths of his being disturbed Renny's reflections. He shot an enquiring glance at the boy, noticed the despondent droop of the smooth dark head and the thinness of the childish wrist.

"What's the matter, kid?" he asked gently.

"Nothing." The word was scarcely audible.

"Aren't you feeling well? Are you tired?" A tone of anxiety at once came into the elder's voice. Behind the sheltering hand he saw the boy's mouth trembling.

"Come here," he said, and pushed his chair back from the table. Wakefield came round to him with averted face. Renny pulled him to his knee. "Tell me," he repeated, "aren't you well? Is it your heart?" He put his arm about him and pressed his thin muscular hand above the weak organ as though he would impart some of his vitality to it.

Wakefield shook his head. Then he said, twisting a button on Renny's coat:

"It's Alayne. She doesn't like me any more. Just before she went she called me an outsider. Did you hear her?"

Renny gave an embarrassed laugh. "That meant nothing! Married people call others outsiders sometimes—I can't just explain why."

"Well—if you can't explain—it's just as though you call me an outsider too."

Renny answered impatiently—"When married people make love or quarrel they generally like to be unobserved."

"You didn't mind my being here! And it wasn't only what she said; it was what she did. She pulled the bouquet so that it shut me out. She didn't think I noticed, but I did. She'd like to shut me out altogether, and there's no use in your saying she wouldn't, Renny." He began to cry softly, producing a ball of a handkerchief and rubbing his eyes with it.

Renny burst into noisy laughter. "Why, you damned little idiot, you know very well that a dozen wives couldn't come between you and me!" He hugged Wake to him and kissed him repeatedly. Wakefield's crying, from being soft, rose to almost hysterical sobs.

Alayne had left her book in the room and, thinking that by now Renny would have gone, she was returning for it. However, when she reached the door and saw the brothers, she quickly passed on toward the drawing-room.

"Alayne!" Renny called. "Come here!"

She returned to the doorway and looked in at them, with a self-controlled expression on her pale face.

"You have hurt Wake's feelings by calling him an out-sider. I explained that to him. Now he says that you moved the flowers so that they would shut him off from us!" He gave her an entreating look as though to say—"I can't have him worried! You must bear with his whims and with my love for him."

She saw the look and read in it only a repetition of his willingness to impose a disagreeable obligation on her that he might gratify someone who roused the protective instinct in him. The sight of Wakefield clinging about his neck, Wakefield's shuddering sobs, Renny's look of entreaty, filled her with cold anger. What Renny wanted her to do, she felt, was to come in and pet and reassure the boy. She could not do that, something reticent in her forbade the demonstra-tion. She felt that even to deny that she had moved the flow-ers for a purpose was a debasement of her dignity.

After an inward struggle she said—"I had no idea that I would hurt Wakefield's feelings. I'm sorry, if I did... But I can't help thinking it is a pity he hears so much of the grown-up talk. He's too introspective. He's becoming neu-rotic, I'm afraid... And isn't a boy of thirteen too big to be kissed?" She spoke in jerky, uneven sentences.

"I'm not thirteen! I shan't be thirteen till next week," objected Wakefield, in a choking voice.

Renny said—"His father was dead before he was born. His mother died when he was born. He's always been—well—I've often wondered if I should rear him. You can scarcely blame me—"

She interrupted—"But anyone who knows anything of child psychology knows that to talk that way before him is the worst thing possible for him. It puts into his mind the thought of forlornness, dependence, weakness. Cannot you see?"

"No, I can't," he answered hotly. He glared at her with the look of old Adeline. "If your father had been a horse dealer, instead of a New England professor, we might understand each other better."

"Renny," she cried, "how can you?" and she flew upstairs to her room.

Her room was to be her refuge more and more often in the following weeks. Her feeling of estrangement from the family increased rather than decreased. For Renny, to the springs of whose life she had joined her own, in faith and in passion, she experienced a strange numbing of the emotions. She waited till this darkness should pass like a trailing cloud, and the light of their love burst forth again. She withdrew herself spiritually as well as physically. On his part, he treated her with more than usual politeness before the others and avoided her in secret. Piers and Pheasant believed that harmony had been restored between Renny and her, but believed also that a delicate balance was being maintained in their relations which might easily be upset. Wakefield brooded on the scene in the dining room but repeated nothing of it to the other members of the family. At this time he acquired the curious habit of going to the room he occupied with Renny when Alayne retreated to hers. When she closed her door, she often heard the closing of that door, as though in mockery. Sometimes, as she sat writing, she heard the door open, then, after a space, close again, as though he had stood in the doorway listening. What did the boy do in there? She was convinced that he did nothing but brood or dream, that he went there for no purpose but to vex her.

The weather was hot and her room, shaded by a giant fir tree, was always cool and pleasant. Mr. Cory, of the New York firm of publishers for whom she had been a reader, sent

her several advance copies of new books from his autumn
list, asking for her opinion of them. He flattered her by
telling her that he had found no one adequately to take her
place, on whose judgment he could so rely. The books he
sent, the subjects of which were history, biography, and
travel, interested her intensely. She wrote him long letters
about them. So she created for the time an independent
world of her own within the walls of Jalna, in which she
recaptured some of the spirit of tranquillity and contemplation of her old life. It was a false tranquillity, a contemplation
born of her passion to conceal her real state from herself. A
word, a glance, would be enough to shatter her self-control.
But each day, as the heat increased, her face became more of
a cool mask. She became even more fastidious in her dress.
Renny, as though fastidiousness were a weapon which he
could use as well as she, became more and more careful of his
dress. Pheasant and Piers, in emulation, made themselves as
spruce as possible. Even Wakefield wore his best clothes
every day, and Mooey screamed for a silver napkin ring for
his bib. Piers had forbidden Pheasant to bring him to the
table, and Renny had not again expressed a desire to have
him there. A depressing quiet hung over their meals, often
only broken by Rags's whispered conversations with Renny.

In late July Alayne had a letter from her aunts on the
Hudson expressing their intention of visiting her. The
thought of a visit from them was both delightful and worrying. They had never been to Jalna, and she longed to show
them the old house and the rambling estate. Yet should she
be able to conceal from their shrewd and loving eyes the
present volcanic barrenness of her life? Might not an erup-
tion be possible during their visit? She was all the more
apprehensive because they had never met Renny. They had

met and given their hearts to Eden at first sight. The divorce and her remarriage to Eden's brother had been a shock to them. It was only now that they could make up their minds to visit her. She wished that the elder Whiteoaks were at home. The presence of Augusta, Nicholas, and Ernest appeared to her now as a protecting wall behind which she might conceal her own heartache. She had always thought how interested she should be if she could see her aunts, so refined, so whimsically proper, so gingerly perched above all ugliness in life, in the same house with the three elderly Whiteoaks, across whom lay the lusty shadow of old Adeline.

How she had welcomed the departure of Ernest and Nicholas for England! She had looked forward to a summer of greater freedom in her life with Renny, a summer of fulfilment, of spiritual development of their love. And it had come to this! If the Uncles had not gone away it might not have come to this. Even that thought came to her. Over and over again she lived through their misunderstandings and tried to see what she might have done to prevent them. She could not discover anything in her most self-accusing mood that would have prevented them except the humbling of her spirit to his and the absolute conforming to the life of the house. She believed that if she had it all to live over again that she would do just that. Humble her spirit and conform absolutely to the life of the house. Perhaps, if only she had agreed to read French with that unattractive Lebraux child, all might have been well. But the thought of the child brought the thought of the mother, and the thought of the mother brought a rush of anger and jealousy that drove all else from her mind. She discovered that she was bitterly jealous of Mrs. Lebraux, that she was even jealous of little Pauline. When Piers made a remark to Renny in reference to the fox farm, and Renny answered in obvious familiarity with its affairs, she dare not look at them lest they should read the anger in her eyes.

Looking back over her acquaintance with Renny she recognised that he had always irritated her, excited some latent antagonism in her, sometimes as though deliberately, more often by simply being himself. She and Eden had never quarrelled. From the first her love for him had in it a maternal quality. There was nothing maternal in her love for Renny. It was instinctive, violent, and without rest. And, though there was no rest in it, no peace in it, neither was there growth. It was like the sea, eternally beating against its shores, yet eternally bound by them.

What had they been quarrelling about? Old Benny—the sheepdog. Mooey—the baby. Pauline and Wakefield—children. Was their life together to be ruined by quarrels over dogs and children? If only she had a child of her own, things might be different. But Renny had never expressed a desire for a child of his own.

XX

BARNEY

ALMA PATCH was the girl who came as nursemaid to young Maurice. She was the niece of the village nurse, and her aunt was well pleased to be the means of installing her at Jalna. The village nurse was also the village gossip and, as the Whiteoaks were the mainstay of rumour and of tattle, Alma would be a conduit through which a continuous supply would flow.

She was a strong girl, with sandy hair, a freckled face, and she never raised her voice above a whisper except when she sang or laughed, which she did in a piercingly high soprano. She was as lazy as possible and very fond of children. To sit on the grass minding Mooey, while he trotted about her in his play, sometimes stopping to throw grass on her, or hug her, or even kick her, was Alma's idea of bliss. Then, to fill her stomach with the good food, and her mind with the rich gossip, and to return home at dusk an object of rare importance to her friends, constituted a life of such perfection as it is given to few to enjoy.

About the time of Alma's appearance at Jalna, Pauline Lebraux gave Renny a nine months' old Irish terrier dog,

named Barney. It had been sent to her for her birthday by a
friend of her father's in Quebec. It had been impossible for
her to keep him because he spent all his time in barking at
the foxes, exciting them to frenzy. So, though she loved him,
and because she loved him, Pauline presented him in turn to
Renny on his birthday. As though he needed another dog!

But he seemed to have unlimited room in his affections
for dogs and children. He looked on Barney as the one dog to
fill a long-felt want. But the terrier was the wildest, most
untamable creature that had ever been on the place. Piers
thought he was excessively inbred. Renny, who was an advo-
cate of inbreeding, insisted that Barney was the victim of a
system of raising dogs like wild animals. He guessed that he
had been brought up in an enclosure without a word of kindness. To make friends with him, to teach him what companionship of man and dog may be, this was a task after Renny's
heart. And Barney was beautifully set up, had, beneath the
untamed look in his eyes, a look of desperate need.

But he would not allow himself to be touched. He
scarcely knew his name. He carried his meals into a corner,
growling like a wild animal while he devoured them. He
slept in Wright's room over the garage, but he did not make
friends with Wright. From the moment he was released in
the morning he ran hither and thither as though half
demented by the multitude of strange sights about him and
the vast open spaces where he might run at will. The fields
of grain were tall and a deep golden colour. Barney spent
most of his days in them as in a jungle. Deep in a field a
movement might be seen stirring the ears of wheat or barley, and then stillness again, for it was sultry weather and no
breeze stirred the grain. Sometimes when Renny walked
past the fields, followed by his two Clumber spaniels,

Barney's face would appear watching them cautiously from the shelter of the grain. He would let them get a little way ahead, then, in his concealment, he would bound after them till he was again abreast, and again he would peer out with that same desperate look in his eyes.

The spaniels appeared to understand all about him. In his own way Renny had explained the situation to them. They would give a friendly look in his direction but no more, walking with dignity at their master's heels.

At last a day came when he emerged from the shelter of grain and ran in the open for a little way near Renny and the spaniels.

"Just watch," Renny advised Piers, who had been inclined to jeer, "and you will see a splendid dog in him yet. He's never had a chance till now, and he's responding to it every day."

"He's getting to look a little beauty, no doubt about that," acceded Piers. "He's grown a lot since he came. But I'm willing to bet that it will be cold weather before he comes of his own accord to you and lets you pet him."

"What will you bet?"

"A fiver."

"Done."

Renny won the bet by a wide margin. He was riding his favourite roan one morning at a canter along the path through the wood, when suddenly he came upon Barney, his head in a burrow. When he withdrew his head he seemed too astonished for movement. He stood sniffing the roan's legs, then raised himself to sniff Renny's boots. When horse and rider moved on he trotted close behind. From that time he followed the roan whenever and wherever he could. Inside of a month he had come to Renny of his own accord and laid his head on his knee.

Renny's pleasure in this achievement was so great that he boasted of it even to Alayne, who did not care for dogs, and for this dog less than others, since it had come from the fox farm. But she tried to soften her face, which felt rigid, into a sympathetic smile.

One day in late August, when a thunderstorm was pending, Renny and Piers, accompanied by Wright, went in the car to a sale twenty miles away. Pheasant was in bed that day, feeling ill. She had told Alayne that morning that she believed she was going to have a child.

Alayne wandered about the downstairs trying to settle herself at something, but the air was full of electricity; there was a sulphurous light in the sky which seemed uncomfortably near the treetops, and she felt disturbed, even shaken, by Pheasant's news.

A second child for her and Piers! Perhaps another son! And there were no signs that she herself might become a mother. She had not yet been married a year and a half, but she had a morbid premonition that she was to be childless. That she was to see Meggie and Pheasant rejoicing in their motherhood, see Renny carrying their children in his arms, and feel herself married without the fulfilment of marriage. She leaned against the window of the sitting-room, looking out on the side lawn where, in the sultry shade, Mooey lay stretched on his back idly, lifting first one leg and then the other. Alma sat beside him, her face a blank from contentment and heat. Alayne wondered what went on in that head under the sandy hair. She watched the girl's large pink hands pluck blades of grass and tickle her own lips with them.

As she was wondering this, Alma's eyes became round and prominent with terror. She opened her mouth wide and gave a piercing scream. The shock to Alayne was all the greater for never having heard the girl utter a sound above a whisper up to this moment. Mooey sat up and looked at Alma.

"Do it again!" he said.

As though at his bidding, Alma repeated her scream, and now Alayne saw what she was screaming about. Barney was flying round and round the lawn in a kind of aimless fury, his jaws snapping rhythmically, and foam whitening his lips. He passed beneath her window then, and she saw his eyes fixed in an hallucinated glare. From a window above came Pheasant's shrieks, then her agonised call to Alma to run with Mooey to the house.

"This way!" cried Alayne. "This way! Bring him to me!"

Alma snatched up the child and passed him through the window to Alayne just as the dog again flitted by like a creature from a nightmare. Somehow she managed to drag the girl in also.

She ran to the hall and met Wragge there. His pale face had become ashen.

"Did you know that that dog of Mr. W'iteoak's 'as gone mad, ma'am? Isn't it terrible?" He ran to the front door, shut and locked it.

Alayne could hear a commotion of voices in the basement. She could hear Pheasant frantically questioning child and nurse upstairs. One of the farm-labourers, named Quinn, appeared at the back of the hall. He said:

"Don't you think we'd better shoot the dog, ma'am? He's gone clean mad!"

"Yes, yes—we must have him destroyed! It's too terrible. Oh, I wish Mr. Whiteoak were here!"

"The cook said that if you would let me have Mr. Whiteoak's gun—I could use that."

"His gun..." She looked at him blankly.

"The cook says it's in his room."

"I'll fetch it, ma'am," put in Wragge.

"No, Wragge. I will get it."

She ran up the stairs, feeling electrified to strength and competence. Pheasant followed her to the door of Renny's room. "It's in a leather case," she said, "in the cupboard."

Alayne found the case, rapidly unbuckled the straps and took out the polished gun. Her hands were steady as she carried it down to Quinn and put it in his hands. She suddenly remembered Wakefield, and asked where he was.

"Oh, ma'am," cried Wragge. "'E's over there with 'is pony, and the dog has run to the stables!"

Quinn hurried off with the gun.

Pheasant called from upstairs—"Alayne! Come—quick! You can see him from my bedroom window!"

Alayne flew up to her, but when she reached the window, though the stables were visible, nothing living was to be seen but Quinn running toward them with the gun in his hands.

"Had you seen the dog today before this happened?" she asked.

Pheasant pressed her fingers to her temples. "Yes. I saw him following Quinn. Quinn was taking the roan and one of the farm-horses to be shod. Barney was following the roan. I thought it was funny, because I'd never seen him go out on the road before... There! Quinn has gone into the stable! Oh, isn't it horrible? Shall I close the window so we shan't hear the gun go off?"

Mooey shouted—"I want to hear the gun go off! Bang! Bang! I'm not f'ightened!"

"I don't think you had better shut it. It is stifling. The hottest day I have seen this summer."

They stood staring in the direction of the stables, of which only a part could be seen through a break in the row of firs that had been planted with the object of hiding them, as though they expected to see something frightful enacted there. Presently they heard shouts, and their fascinated eyes saw figures running past the open space. Then, between the firs, the terrier appeared and ran on to the lawn in a strange lolloping gait and evidently at the point of dropping. There was a tear on his haunch from which the blood dripped to the grass. He raised his head and looked up at the windows where they stood.

Quinn and two other men ran into view carrying hay-forks. One of them, a youth from a Glasgow factory, kept well behind the other two, his round face stupid with fear. Pheasant and Alayne did not realise what the men were going to do until they ran up to Barney and began to jab their forks into him. He fell, bleeding in a dozen places.

Then the Glasgow youth pressed forward and thrust his fork so deep into the body that he had to put his foot on it in order to pull out the prongs.

Alayne had Pheasant, fainting, on her hands.

Young Maurice asked—"Why did they do that? But Barney was naughty, wasn't he? Why does Mummy want to sleep?"

Alayne had got Pheasant back to her bed and had restored the child to his nurse. Wakefield had rushed into the room. His eyes were glittering with excitement.

"Did you see?" he cried. "Wasn't it terrible? I was standing quite close, behind the bushes. I saw everything, you know. Quinn didn't understand Renny's gun. He couldn't make it go off. They chased Barney round and round the stable, and Quinn managed to wound him, but he got away and ran toward the house. I believe he thought he'd find Renny here. Won't Renny be surprised when he comes home? I hope I can be the one to tell him!"

The car, in which rode Renny, Piers, and Wright, did not turn into the drive until late afternoon. They drove straight to the stable, and there were half a dozen men about eager to tell the news.

"You God-damned fools!" exclaimed Piers. "The dog no more had rabies than you have! He was hysterical. Nothing more."

Wright said—"If I had been here he'd never have been killed. We've had them like that before this and they got over it; didn't they, sir?" He turned to Renny.

Renny was staring at Quinn, who had told excitedly of his prowess but who was now looking slightly abashed. The Glasgow youth stood close by, eager for praise, if there were any, but disclaiming all responsibility in the act.

"Do you mean to tell me," said Renny, "that four of you chased that puppy through the stables with pitchforks, then rounded him up on the lawn and butchered him?"

"The gun wouldn't go off," muttered Quinn.

"What gun was it?"

"Yours, sir. Mrs. Whiteoak went and got it for me."

"Why didn't you shut him in the loose box?"

"Gosh, I wouldn't have touched him on a bet, sir. He looked something fierce."

"Where is he?"

They had buried him.

"Dig him up! I want to see him."

They led the way to the spot and the Glasgow youth, eager to put himself right, snatched up a spade and thrust it violently into the ground.

Renny took it from him. "Here!" he said, "do you want to crack his skull! I'd sooner see yours cracked."

He began cautiously to uncover the body. When it lay exposed he bent over it. He turned it on its other side, frowning at the wounds. He ran his hand along the spine in a quick caress, then straightened himself.

"You made a pretty mess of the job," he said. He added, to Wright—"Have the head taken off, Wright. I shall send it to be examined. He should never have been taken on the road in a heat like this."

He returned to the house. In the hall he met Alayne.

"Well," he said with a grin, "so you managed to murder my dog among you, while I was away!"

XXI

WHOSE FAULT?

THEY HAD not spoken since... News travelled fast at Jalna, and she had already heard, when she met him in the hall, an exaggerated account of all that had happened since his return. The Glasgow youth had run to the house to tell his friend Bessie. Bessie had run on tiptoe up two flights of stairs to gasp it out to Alma as she was giving Mooey his bath. Alma had repeated it with whispered embellishment to Pheasant when she carried some toast and tea to her. Pheasant had told Alayne... When Alayne and Renny met in the hall, she had already heard how he had gone into a terrible rage, threatened the men who had despatched Barney, insisted on himself unearthing the body, had caressed it, wept over it. The sight of him standing there with the light from the stained glass window turning his clothes into motley, falling on his red hair in a purple stain, was shocking to her. The frozen grin on his face was repellent. When he said what he said, she drew back, with a feeling of repulsion. She made no answer but stood rigid, her back to the wall, her palms pressed against it while he passed.

He went into the sitting-room, shutting the door behind him. A moment later she heard him draw the folding doors between there and the dining room with a bang. She was filled with bitterness and disillusion. And yet, she felt, she had always known he was like this. Had not her love for him been a fever that had turned the very blood in her veins to something alien, turned her flesh to the flesh of desire, made her pulses dance to the tune his maleness played.

As she climbed the stairs with heavy limbs she said to herself—"I never liked him. That is the trouble. I was mad for him. But I never have liked him."

In her room she sat by the window looking down on the parched garden. The flowers hung their limp heads. Their foliage separated, showing the dry earth beneath. Her own head ached so that she could scarcely hold it up. She pressed her fingers to the space between her eyebrows where there was a knot of pain. She felt as though she were going to be ill.

The face of Eden rose before her, smiling, with half-shut eyes. She remembered how he had come to her like a young god to deliver her from the humdrum of her life, to fill her heart that had been emptied of all love except love for the dead. How soon the presence of Renny had blotted out all that! Eden must have become aware in all his sensitive nerves of the change in her. He was not to be blamed, then, for turning to someone else. She saw Eden in a new light.

The face of old Adeline rose before her feverish eyes. She saw her standing in the hall, under the stained glass window, as she had seen her on the first day she had set foot in Jalna. Bright patches of colour were spilled over her, a purple stain across her forehead, and she was grinning at all the family standing about. But there was only savagery in the grin. She was going to say something terrible... Alayne thought, pressing her fingers to her forehead—"Is there no ease of spirit in this house? What am I to do? If I go on feeling as I do, what is to become of me? If I go on making him hate me, how can I live here? Even now I am having strange thoughts... confusing him and his grandmother in my mind..."

She sat with drooping head, going over incident after incident in her life with Renny, trying to discover if she had been at fault in the marked change in their relations. She could not see where she had failed him. She had managed to live peaceably in the house with Piers, who hated her, but she could not live peaceably with Renny, who—but did he love her? Or had he felt for her only a desire for her body, while she stretched out her hands for the satisfaction of her soul? She could not blame herself. Something stubborn in her refused to accept the blame. Again the jealousy of Clara Lebraux surged through her like a racking pain. She felt it in her back, in her throat, in the nerves of her stomach. That woman—with her streaked hair, her pale eyelashes, her bony hands—what fascination was there in her that drew him to the fox farm when he might have been with his wife? The thought came to her with a shock that, because Barney had come from the fox farm, he was doubly dear to Renny—that he even suspected her of agreeing only too willingly to his destruction because of that.

When she went down to supper she found that places were laid for only herself and Piers. She was not surprised that Pheasant was unable to come to the table, but where was Wakefield—where, that other? Piers, looking at his plate, muttered that Pheasant was still feeling rocky and that young Wake had had a turn with his heart—too much excitement—and was sleeping. He did not speak of Renny, but soon she saw Wragge pass through the hall carrying a tray. He went into the sitting-room and shut the door cautiously behind him. She saw Piers frowning, the corner of his mouth drawn to one side. Wragge, when he returned to the dining room, wore an expression of profound secrecy, as though torture would not induce him to reveal what was taking place on the other side of the folding doors. Alayne remembered how Meggie had had most of her food carried to her on trays by Wragge. Was Renny going to follow Meg's example? She had a hysterical desire to laugh. She could not choke down the cold roast beef, but nibbled a little cress and thin bread. Piers stolidly consumed beef and peaches and cream. Now and then he cast a frowning look at the door of the sitting-room.

She made no attempt to talk to Piers. She did not know what his attitude toward her in the affair was, but she supposed he blamed her. If he brought up the subject of the dog's death she did not think she could endure to remain at the table. However, he did not; but, when he had half-finished his meal, he began to talk about the sale which he had attended. In a muffled voice he gave her a description of the animals on which he and Renny had bid. He carefully described a Clydesdale stallion he had bought and a nice cobby mare, for general use, purchased by Renny. The stallion had cost a pretty penny, but he hoped to get it out of him again. She answered in monosyllables, but she was grateful to him, for she saw that he was trying to make things easier for her. When he had finished the glass of ale he always had for supper, he held his cigarette case out to her and, for the first time during the meal their eyes net. She saw that the look in his was kind, and her own filled with tears. He began gruffly and hurriedly to talk of the crowd at the sale, the intense heat, and to describe the mannerisms of the auction-eer. He knew she did not smoke, but he had offered her a cigarette as though he wanted to do something for her. She accepted and puffed at it awkwardly. It was the first time they had ever sat for a while together talking.

Now five days had gone by and she and Renny had not spoken. She lived in a kind of haze. Sometimes, when she was dressing in the morning, her mind became confused. She would hesitate, look blankly about the room, and begin to take her clothes off again, thinking it was night instead of morning. Then, seeing the sunlight, she would remember and shamefacedly continue her dressing. She had always been proud of the clarity of her mind, of the fact that she could keep her wits about her. She had often been intolerant of Eden's bemused ways. There had been a break in the weather, and now the nights were wet, but with each morning came bright sunshine that was continually being darkened by moving clouds. A forlorn look had descended upon the flower beds.

She had never before been in a house with anyone with whom she was not on speaking terms. She was not able to remember a shadow in the cheery attitude of her parents for each other. Renny addressed all his conversation to Piers, seeming to include Pheasant in his resentment. He was even less indulgent to Wakefield and insisted that he go to his lessons, though it was plainly to be seen that he was not well. Pheasant seemed absorbed in her own musings. She, too, was ailing and several times had to leave the breakfast table. On three days of the five Renny did not return to dinner. In the relief of his absence Pheasant and Wakefield chattered continually, while Wragge regarded them with disapproval. Though Alayne discovered that Renny had, in these absences, dined with the Vaughans, she still believed that he spent much of his time with Clara Lebraux.

On the fourth day Wragge brought the post to Renny at the breakfast table. He tore open a letter and, having read it, handed it to Piers.

"You see," he said, "it's just as I said. It was scarcely worth the trouble of sending it, but I wanted to prove that it was nothing but callous cruelty."

Piers read the note and gave a sympathetic grunt.

"Show it to Alayne," said Renny, looking at his plate.

Piers slid the paper along the table to her. She picked it up and read. It was the report from the Government Analyst, stating that the head of the dog had been examined and that no evidence of rabies had been present. She read it dully, feeling nothing more than a quickening of her sense of injury.

"Let me see it, please!" cried Wakefield. "Is it something interesting?"

Alayne passed on the paper to him.

"I don't think," said Piers, "that anyone was to blame for that. The men did just what was natural—seeing a dog in that condition. Alayne did just what was natural. She wanted him put out of the way with the least possible pain. And it wasn't Quinn's fault that he didn't understand the gun... If it had been my dog, I'd just try to put it out of my head— forget the whole thing!" He began to draw horizontal lines on the tablecloth with his knife.

"Yes, indeed!" cried Pheasant, revolting against her silence of the week. "If ever I saw a terrifying object it was that dog! If he wasn't mad he'd no right to act as though he was and frighten darling little Mooey and Alayne and me almost to death!"

"Don't bring me into it, please," said Alayne coldly.

Renny sprang up from his chair. "Christ!" he exclaimed, "you make me sick, the lot of you!"

He gave a wild look about the room and then flung out of it and out of the house.

Those who were left exchanged one startled look. Then Piers slit open a letter to himself, Pheasant bent her head over the newspaper, casting a sidelong look at Alayne. She, summoning all her will, picked up a letter in the handwriting of the younger of her aunts and forced herself to read it.

Wakefield kept repeating to himself, over and over, in a gabbling tone—"You make me sick, the lot of you... You make me sick, the lot of you."

Piers, suddenly becoming aware of this, scowled at him. "Shut up!" he said curtly, "or I'll put you out."

To hide his chagrin Wakefield examined his reflection in the hollow of a spoon, making grotesque grimaces at it.

Alayne thought—"What if Aunt Harriet is writing to say that they are coming at once? I never can endure that with things as they are!" But there was no word of a visit. Helen, the elder aunt, was ill. Her sister was greatly troubled.

Alayne's first sensation was one of pure relief. Then anxiety for her loved relation swept relief away. There was a note of foreboding in the letter very unlike the cheerful tone with which Aunt Harriet was used to face life's worries. A rather shaky postscript said that, if there were any change for the worse, Alayne had better come. She could not bear the responsibility alone.

All her life Alayne had been accustomed to make sudden decisions. There was nothing of wavering in her at such moments as this. She would wait for no telegram. She would go at once—today. For a moment she considered the idea of allowing the others to believe that Renny's behaviour was unendurable to her—of punishing him in this way. But she put that aside. She was too proud for pretence.

She took Pheasant aside after breakfast and told her of her aunt's serious illness. Something sceptical as well as compassionate in the girl's expression made Alayne give her the letter to read. Pheasant threw her arms about her and kissed her.

"Darling Alayne! I do hope it will be only a little visit! I shall miss you so! Jalna isn't really very comfortable for a prospective young mother these days. Oh, I do wish Uncle Nick were here! I'm sure he could have kept us out of this tangle!"

At one o'clock Piers came in with the news that Renny had gone off somewhere on business with Maurice. He did not say what the business was and Alayne was of the opinion that Renny was simply spending the day at the Vaughans. Meg had not been well, and she knew he was worried about her. She packed clothes to last her for a month's visit. She sat down at the writing-table in her room to write a note to Renny. She wrote one that sounded so frigid when she read it over that she tore it up. Better nothing than that! She began another on which, in spite of herself, tears fell, and she tore it up too. He should get no wifely weeping note from her. Better perhaps that he should hear the news from the family.

Piers had the car freshly washed for driving her to the station. He sent Wright to drive it and kept out of the way at the moment of goodbye. Pheasant had hovered about her all the afternoon. She had brought her two little embroidered handkerchiefs as a gift. She had led Mooey to her, and he had said, having evidently rehearsed the words—"I'm shorry I was a naughty boy, Auntie Alayne." And held up his face to be kissed.

Wakefield begged to be allowed to see her off. He had so little in the way of change that he was delighted when she

agreed. He and Wright carried her things into the Pullman
for her. It was the first time he had ever seen one. He
exclaimed:

"How jolly this is! I wonder if the day will ever come
when I'll be going somewhere. I've lived thirteen years and
I've never been anywhere. Isn't it terrible, Alayne?" Yet
there was a certain pride in his bearing, like the pride of the
oldest inhabitant. People about were casting admiring
glances at his dark eager face.

All night Alayne tossed in the grip of a nervous
headache. She was at the point of exhaustion when she
reached the pretty stucco house up the Hudson. Miss Helen
was just able to recognise her. In two days she died.

When all was over and order was restored in the house
she and Miss Harriet had long talks together. Alayne's heart
was wrung by her aunt's loneliness. She made up her mind
that she would remain with her for some time. She had written twice to Pheasant and had had two letters in reply.
Things were going on about the same as usual at Jalna. She
wrote—"R. was very much surprised when you did not
appear the next morning. He did not say much, but his look
was one of the completest astonishment."

There was not much time for thought in those first
weeks. Miss Archer had many friends eager to condole with
her and to see Alayne after her long absence. The friends
agreed that marriage had not improved Alayne's looks. She
had grown sallow and there were shadows under her eyes.
Rosamond Trent came out from New York exuberant, lavish
of her vitality. She had so much to tell that she took Alayne's
mind off her troubles. She spoke with admiration of Ernest
Whiteoak, but it was Nicholas who was her ideal of a country gentleman of the old school.

Miss Helen had left Alayne all her money, not a large sum, but one sufficient to make many things possible for her which had not been possible before. Miss Harriet expressed a desire to own a motor car. Her sister had been content to hire one and had been timid of the roads. Now one was purchased, and Alayne took pleasure in driving her over the smooth roads above the river. The autumn weather was delightful.

Alayne accompanied Miss Archer to a small club formed of ladies of the neighbourhood. At the meetings in drawing-rooms, where elegance and a certain austerity were combined, literature and questions of the day were discussed. Selected members brought intelligent articles in the best magazines, which they read aloud, enunciating so clearly that not a word was missed by their hearers. Alayne herself read an article of great interest, in which it was demonstrated, with quaint examples, that the rural people of the southwestern States retain in their dialect many words of Elizabethan English.

She liked the club. She was strangely exhilarated by the mental atmosphere of the place. She began to have the feeling of clear-headed alertness which she had known in the days before her marriage. She was like a plant returned to its native soil. Her complexion cleared, but the shadows beneath her eyes remained. These remained because of lack of sleep. No matter how well she slept during the night she woke at four o'clock, and there was no more sleep for her except a mere snatch, achieved between the time when the maid first stirred about the house and the time when she herself must rise. That snatch of sleep refreshed her. It took the edge off the sharp remembrance of the thoughts that had kept her awake. They were thoughts of how her life was ruined, of

how these cool and pleasant days were like a clean pinafore
that a child puts on to hide its torn and shabby clothes. They
were thoughts of how she had lain in the arms of Renny.

XXII

FREEDOM

WITH THE DEPARTURE of Alayne a change came over the family at Jalna. The spurious order that had afflicted them during the summer was thrown aside like hampering harness, and they ran free. In the basement, where her persistent weekly visits of inspection had been looked forward to with dread, it was as though the lid had been removed from a bubbling pot. The contents of the pot bubbled, boiled over, and the smell of its exuberance rose to the realms above.

"White wings, they never grow weary," sang Mrs. Wragge, in a rich contralto, as she threw the remains of a joint, of which she had no desire to make a mince, to the dogs. Her husband, with a cigarette in his lips and his sleeves uprolled, polished the best silver coffee pot, the inside of which had not been washed for many a day. Bessie was plucking a young goose, letting the feathers drift softly where they would.

"What was that the missus called them that first day she come rampagin' down here?" she called to Wragge.

"Plumage, that's wot. It's American for fevvers. She's got a rum way o' talkin'. She got on my nerves if ever a lidy did."

"It's not the way the boss talks," said Bessie. "He sort of shoots the talk at you. Makes you jump out of your skin sometimes."

"And serve you right," returned Wragge, blowing on the coffee pot. "You're the laziest young Canadjen I've ever seen, and I've seen a good many."

"Give me a Cockney for laziness!" jeered the girl. "What you do know is how to look busy! Why, you've been half an hour on that there coffee pot!"

Wragge set down the silver pot and advanced toward her. There was a scuffle in which the air was filled with feathers, as though the combatants were two birds. Mrs. Wragge stopped singing to stare at them with disapproval.

"Get on with yer work and stop yer foolin', Bessie," she ordered. "Alfred, don't you be makin' so free."

A baby voice sounded from the stairway. "Fight some more, p'ease! We're coming."

It was Mooey. He and his cousin Patience were descending the stairs, carrying their blue china plates in their hands.

Maurice Vaughan and his little daughter had come to stay at Jalna while Meg was at the hospital. The two children being hungry in the middle of the morning, Alma had set them down at their little table with bread and butter and brown sugar before them. They had soon devoured that and, Alma being engaged in trying to hide her freckles under some of Pheasant's face-powder, they had stolen from the room and laboriously descended two flights of stairs to the basement.

There they stood, three steps from the bottom, Patience in pink, Mooey in fawn, holding their plates before them like two small mendicants, and smiling ingratiatingly. Mrs. Wragge came to them beaming. She had the pneumatic bosom and fat red face that inspire confidence in children.

"Well, I'm blessed," she declared, "if I ever seen two lovelier kiddies!" Wragge and Bessie also gathered to inspect them.

"She's the spit of 'er mother," observed Rags. "Sime complexion. Sime smile."

"She 'as 'er daddy's grey eyes," said his wife.

"This one," continued her husband, placing the tips of his fingers on Mooey's head, "is the most beautiful blend of two parents I've hever seen. 'E's took the best points off both on 'em."

Mooey said—"I want gingerbed, p'ease."

"There is no gingerbread, dearie," answered Mrs. Wragge.

"Jam, then, and a piece of celery."

"Patty wants an egg!" said Patience.

"Listen to them! At this hour in the morning," cried Bessie.

"They're half-starved along o' that Alma," declared the cook. "Run you to the larder, Bessie, and fetch those two hard-boiled eggs. I cooked too many for the jellied veal."

While the eggs were being shelled the children ran round and round in a circle, holding their plates before them. They liked the feel of the brick floor under their feet. Presently Patience slipped and fell. The plate flew from her hands and was broken. Mooey tripped over her and fell too. They sat, shouting with laughter, among the fragments of china.

"That's nish," said Mooey, "now they'll not need to be washed!"

"Patty wants anozzer plate, p'ease," she said, holding up her hands.

"Give 'er that cracked one," said Wragge, "just to see w'at she'll do with it."

Finding it in her hand, Patty rose and, assuming the classic attitude of the disc thrower, she hurled it to the other end of the kitchen. At the crash she looked astonished for a moment, then said—

"Patty wants anozzer plate!"

Bessie brought a tin plate this time. Patience took it trustingly and, with a wide gesture, hurled it down the room. It fell with a thin clatter.

"Oh, hell," said Mooey, "that won't b'eak!"

"Chips of the old block," said Rags sententiously.

Bessie put the hard-boiled eggs into their hands. Patience tried to cram all hers in her mouth at once, but finding she could not do this she nibbled a little hole in the end.

"Dis is de little door," she said, "where de chookie comes out."

Mooey licked his all over. "Nish and slithery," he said. "I like chooky-eggs." But evidently the edge of his appetite was lost, for he seemed in no haste to eat it. Finally he held it toward the cook. "W'ap it up for me, p'ease, in a new shell. I'd like to keep it."

"Patty's is gone!" she shouted. "Dust my hands, p'ease." She held them out to the cook.

Mrs. Wragge wiped the small hands on her none too clean apron and admonished Mooey to eat his egg if he wanted to grow a big man. He got rid of it in four bites, then came and picked up the hem of Mrs. Wragge's long black skirt.

"You're a chooky-hen," he said, "and we're the little chookys. Come along and get under, Patty!"

With a squeal of delight Patty joined him, and they sought to take shelter under Mrs. Wragge.

"I'm a dog!" exclaimed Wragge. And he ran round and round the group, yelping.

"I'm a cat!" cried Bessie. And she ran after him, mewing.

It was good fun for all but Mrs. Wragge. She was too hefty for such artless gambolling. In trying to extricate herself from the game she stepped on a piece of china and fell in a sitting posture to the floor.

The children watched her with interest to see whether or no she would break. Patty fetched the tin plate and placed it on Mrs. Wragge's head. "You're Queen of the May," she said.

Mooey held a bit of the broken china to her lips. "You're my birdie," he said. "This is nish cuttlefish. Peck, little birdie."

At this moment, luckily for the cook, Alma came down the stairs in search of her charges. Alma was greatly disturbed. She had just discovered that Patience was Mooey's aunt as well as his cousin, and it made her head spin round and round. She explained how strange she felt, and Mrs. Wragge suggested that they had all better have a cup of tea. "For," she said, "I'm afraid my innards may go back on me along o' a jolt like that."

Maurice Vaughan had had an opportunity to let his house furnished for two months, and Renny had suggested that he take advantage of the offer, and make Jalna his home for the period. Meggie would be in the hospital for several weeks and, when she was convalescent, she would almost certainly recuperate more quickly in the atmosphere of her old home. Renny thought that Vaughanlands was unhealthy, situated as it was in a hollow and standing flat on the ground, with no basement. The presence of Maurice and Patience in the house would help to distract his mind from the awful fact that Meggie was obliged to undergo an operation. The very word hospital filled the Whiteoaks with loathing and fear. Not one of them had ever entered one as a patient. When their time came they simply took to their beds and died. That was all there was to it. No surgeon's knife had ever cut into their stubborn flesh.

Only once had Renny set his foot inside such a place. Then it had been to visit one of his men who had been injured by a kick from a horse. The smell, the sights, the crisp, hurrying nurses had inspired him with nervous dread... And now his Meggie was forced to enter one for an operation! It was useless for Maurice to tell him that he had got a quite nice private room for her, that the chance of her not pulling through was very remote. Nothing lightened his depression. He spoke in a subdued tone to Maurice, as though he were already a widower. He took Patty on his knee and questioned her sombrely as to her recollections of her mother.

Meggie had come to tell them goodbye, looking pale, but sweetly firm and reconciled. She had always had a sense of the dramatic, and it now helped her in this trying time. She embraced Mooey, exclaiming—"And you must always, always be a good boy!" She laid her two hands on Renny's chest and said, deeply—"You will always guard little Wake, won't you?" She visited her grandmother's room and stroked the silent Boney, murmuring—"Never more"—having evidently confused him in her mind with Poe's Raven.

The most heartrending thing was that she brought a little gift to each of them. As though they needed anything to remember her by! She brought a gift to even the least of the servants, which was Alma Patch, and adjured her to be kind to her baby. To Piers she brought a silk handkerchief-holder with a pink bow. To Wakefield, a little black lacquer writing-case given to her by her grandmother when she was a girl. To Renny, a diary. It had been given to her, she explained, the

Christmas before, but she had not had the strength to write in it.

Renny kept several account-books, but he had never owned a diary. He carried it darkly to his room that night, lighted his lamp and sat down at the table with the little book before him. He opened it and read on the flyleaf in a spidery hand—"To dear Meggie with love from Nellie Pink." This had been firmly crossed out, and underneath, in his sister's bold hand, was written—"For Renny with my abiding love, Meggie." Dubiously he fluttered the narrow pages under his thumb. Three-fourths of the year were almost gone, and it was difficult to know how to set about the enterprise. After giving his fountain pen the severe shake it always required before it would write, he pressed open the diary at January. The only event he could remember in that month (aside from events in the stable, of which a meticulous record was kept in his office) was the death of Lebraux. He wrote— "Tony Lebraux died. Age 45. Weather very rough."... In the space for the first day of March he wrote—"Finch of Age. Dinner party. Finch spoke." In May he wrote of the departure of Nicholas, Ernest, and Finch for England. In June he recorded Wakefield's birthday and his height and weight that day. In July he recorded his own birthday, adding the words—"Getting on." At the end of August he wrote— "Barney killed by four brutes with hay-forks."... His next entry was—"Alayne left to visit her aunt owing to illness (later death) of other aunt." He stared at this entry for quite a long while before he turned to the space for that day. Herein he wrote—"Meggie entered hospital today for serious operation. Gave me this book."... He heaved a deep sigh, leant back and filled his pipe... He never opened the little book again.

Like a sweet rain after a drought, word came that Meggie had not only survived the operation, but was progressing famously. Maurice went to see her and returned jubilant. She was weak, but she was out of all danger; her appetite was good, and she was cheerful as could be. Later, Piers and Pheasant went to see her and took her jelly and a cake. Wakefield was taken to see her, and visited several other patients besides. But Renny did not go. When Maurice suggested it, he ordered flowers to be sent her, but he could not go inside that place.

Now that she was safe, his spirits went up with a bound. Above stairs as well as below there was freedom and cheeriness in the house. Without the restraining presence of either Augusta or Alayne, dogs were allowed to make themselves at home in every room. Wragge dusted or not as he saw fit. Pheasant was ailing, and often did not come down to her meals. More and more frequently certain horsy friends of Renny's came to the house. One of these was a Mr. Crowdy, who had never until now got farther than the hall. Nicholas and Ernest were annoyed by the very sight of him, but now that they were not present to object he formed the habit of dropping in at mealtime. Renny liked him about. He was so burly that he filled the space ordinarily allotted to two people at table. His face was so rubicund and his eyes so twinkling that his mere presence lent an air of jollity to any scene. He bred racehorses, and he could watch one of his horses lose a race, even fall and throw its rider, with the same impenetrable beaming gaze with which he watched a success. He probably understood horses as well as is possible for any human being. Renny valued his opinions as jewels. He would stand gazing at a horse as though in a kind of trance, then, extending the palm of his left hand, he would, with the forefinger of his right, inscribe on it some hieroglyphic full of mystery to all but himself. After looking at this intently for a space he would utter his pronouncement in a thick wheezy voice that always had a squeak of merriment in it. You might take his advice or leave it. It was all the same to him. There was no hard feeling in him for any man. He admired fine things of many sorts. He would stand in the doorway of the drawing-room at Jalna and gaze meditatively at the Chippendale furniture, then, flattening his thick palm, he would inscribe some symbol on it with a massy forefinger, and remark: "Good stuff. Good stuff. Very nice and showy. Not things you'd ever want to part with, Mr. Whiteoak."

The other was a civil engineer named Chase. He was a man who had seen hard service in the War, and had experienced hard luck prospecting in the North. He made barely enough in his profession to keep him. He had no ambition now except to spend as much of his time as possible among horses and dogs. He looked on all time spent out of their company as lost time. He loved only two human beings—Crowdy and Renny Whiteoak. He disliked all women, from eighteen to eighty. He had a fund of droll, and sometimes bawdy, stories which he told without moving a muscle of his long swarthy face.

After supper these two, with Maurice and Renny, would play poker in the sitting-room until the early hours of the morning. Maurice and Chase both took a little too much to drink.

Once Crowdy said to Renny, while the cards were being dealt—"Mrs. Whiteoak is paying quite a long visit in the States, isn't she?"

"Yes," returned Renny, somewhat brusquely.

The horse-breeder laid his left hand on the table, palm upward, and made a minute memorandum on it with the forefinger of his right. Then he looked beamingly into the faces of the other three.

"A delightful lady," he said. "A very delightful lady. Not the kind you meet every day. No indeed."

Chase said—"Well, I've never married, and I thank God for that. I count it as the chief among my few blessings."

XXIII

The Young Poet

MEG could have given nothing to Wakefield that he would have liked so much as the little lacquer writing-case. It was so small, so pretty, with dim blue flowers on its satiny black surface. Inside it looked as though it had been the recipient of a thousand thoughts—some beautiful, some fierce, some sad. It had belonged to Grandmother when she was a girl in Ireland. It had travelled with her across the seas to India. All the way back to England it had accompanied her. Then came in the sailing vessel out to Quebec. Then up the St. Lawrence to Jalna. When Meggie was eighteen Gran had given it to her. Now, darling old Meggie had presented it to him.

Words had always fascinated him, but it was only of late that he had cared to write them down. In his early days he had delighted in repeating the stately words used by the elder members of the family. He had listened to himself saying them, his head on one side. He had rejoiced in the feeling of eloquence and dignity their utterance had created in the room. He had rejoiced in the expressions of wonder their coming from his childish lips had created on the faces of those who heard. He had marshalled the words like generals of noble lineage in the newly recruited army of his speech.

But now he had a fresh delight. This was to extract the sweetness from everyday words, to draw them together into rhymes. He beckoned to them, and they came to him like other children, now tractable and gay, now wayward and weeping.

This year he had hated his birthday. He was now in his teens, no longer a little boy. He dreaded the thought of grow-ing up. The day would come when Renny would no longer hold him on his knee, no longer give him those quick, tobacco-smelling kisses that somehow put strength into him. He wished Gran might have lived longer. It did not seem fair that the others should have had her strong arms to clasp them until they were great men, while he, who needed her most, must lean on weaker members of her sex.

He scarcely looked on Pheasant as a grown woman. If Mooey chose to regard her as such, there was no object in disillusioning him; but, as someone to lean on, she was not to be considered.

Of one thing he had come to be certain that summer. It was that Alayne did not love him. Once, a long time ago, he had thought she did, but that summer, he believed, she wished he were out of the way. She might even wish him dead, as Grandmother was dead. Out of the way for ever and ever. He pictured himself lying dead in the drawing-room as Gran had lain, with the silver candelabra lighted at his head and feet, and Uncle Ernest standing beside the coffin, telling of the noble and unselfish life he had led, of the pain hero-ically endured. He pictured his funeral winding up the slope to the graveyard, his grave, midway in size between those of the infants and the grown-ups, mounded with flowers. But there were no flowers from Alayne. He pictured how conscience-stricken she would come weeks later with a large nosegay and find Renny there, kneeling on the turf in his new green tweed suit, crying as though his heart would break. He usually ended these imaginings by shedding a few tears himself.

It seemed to him that Alayne was always watching him. Often when he raised his eyes to hers he would find her looking at him with what he felt was a forbidding look. He began to watch her closely. Scarcely a word spoken or a gesture made by her in his presence was lost on him. He knew she was immensely clever. Renny had told him that there were indeed few women that had an intellect equal to hers. Wakefield was greatly impressed by the parcels of books that came to her from New York. He would have very much liked to handle them, to dip into their pages. But once when she allowed him to look at one, of which she thought he might understand something, he had got a smudge on the clear green cover, and, though she uttered nothing more than an exclamation of annoyance, she did not allow him to handle her books again.

When she went to her room and shut herself in there to write, he formed the habit of going also to his room—his and Renny's—and sitting down at the table with a writing-pad before him. He thought that by emulating her habits he might, in some intangible way, absorb something of her intellect. He would mount the stairs with a calm detached expression, such as she wore, and close his door behind him with exactly the same note of precision. The trouble was that he had no new books to write about. However, there were plenty of old ones in the bookcase in the sitting-room, and he would carry, perhaps, one of Charles Lever's and one of the Waverley novels and lay them on the table beside him. He would earnestly read a page or so and then write—"This book is elegantly written. I would recommend it without hesitation to all my readers." Sentences of this sort stood out beautifully on the clean white paper.

Sometimes he would go into the passage and stand listening, with quickening pulses, for a sound from Alayne's room that might inspire him. Even though he heard nothing, he experienced the subtle thrill of intellectual contact and returned to his task with renewed spirit. Before long he abandoned the idea of writing the sort of thing Alayne did, and gave himself up to the pleasure of writing in his own way. Sometimes in prose, more often in rhyme, he wrote of the things he saw and felt that pleased or saddened him. One day Alayne went to town and left a new anthology of poetry in the drawing-room. He scarcely laid it down during her absence. He carried it to his room and copied out the verses he liked best. Soon he had them by heart. Afterwards, when he saw Alayne with the book in her hand, he thought—"I know as much of that book as you do. It's my book as much as yours." And, looking straight at her, he would silently repeat lines from one of the poems. And Alayne would think—"He is becoming more tiresome, more inquisitive every day."

He was so proud of the verses he himself wrote that he longed to read them to someone. A certain instinct told him not to read them to Renny. No—Renny would think he was being a sissy. And, if he read them to Rags, or Pheasant, or Meggy, they would be sure to tell Renny or Piers, and he would be laughed at. At last he thought of Alma Patch. There was something about her pale freckled face, her sandy head, that seemed ripe for listening. He carried his verses to her and sat down beside her on the lawn, where she minded Mooey. He commanded Mooey to be silent. If he moved or spoke, a tiger with eyes of fire would come up from the ravine and carry him off to feed her young. So the tiny boy, bare-legged and bare-armed, sat, scarcely breathing, staring fearfully into the shadows of the ravine, while Wakefield read his verses to Alma Patch. Alma was all receptivity. She listened, holding a blade of grass to her lips. When it was done she whispered—"My, how lovely!"

After that he read all his poetry to her, having first made her take a fearful oath of secrecy. At the end of each one she tickled her lips with a grass blade and whispered—"My, how lovely!" But, though her words and her look were always the same, her receptivity was so great that he was satisfied. He grew happier.

When Alayne was gone he was happier still. He hoped that her aunt would not get better too quickly. When he was told that she had died he thought it would be rather nice if the other aunt were to have a little illness—be just ill enough to want her dear niece at her side... He went boldly into Alayne's room and took the anthology of poetry from the bookshelves and laid it in the bottom of the chest of drawers where he kept his special things.

He did exactly as he liked in these days, and he noticed how well this agreed with his health. He had never felt better. Mr. Fennel was away on a holiday, so there were no lessons. The servants were jolly and devil-may-care. He could go to the kitchen whenever he liked and possess himself of tarts, cheese cakes, or currant scones. He washed or not, just as he felt inclined. He seldom combed his hair. Pheasant was too lackadaisical at present to notice his dishevelled look. Piers and Renny were in a relaxed mood, lenient toward everybody. They talked a good deal about their annual duck-shooting expedition, in which Crowdy and Chase were, for the first time, to be members of the party.

On this morning Wakefield had a most beautiful idea for a poem in his head. It was to be more ambitious than anything he had yet written—longer, more thoughtfully worked out, filled with smooth and singing words. He sat down to write it in his bedroom but somehow, for that poem, it would not do. For the first time he noticed the wallpaper, how ugly it was, with its green and yellow pattern of scrolls and bilious-looking birds. The shiny photographs of horses distracted his eyes. The calendar, tacked to the wall above the table, with its gaudy picture of a grinning girl, offended him; the smell of Renny's pipes... He looked about him disconsolately. What was he to do? Here he was, with a most glorious poem in his head—all atiptoe to be written—and suddenly he had turned against his own loved retreat... His eyes sought the window, rested on the treetops, gold and red against the hyacinthine sky. He gazed and gazed, forgetting himself and his poem, lost in contemplation of the brimming beauty of the day.

He knew what he would do. He would go out into the morning freshness and write his poem there. He would have lovely things about him while he wrote... He gathered up his paper, pencil, and the little lacquer writing-case, and glided down the stairs and through the hall.

He chose a yellow field from which the grain had been cut, and in which three old pear trees stood. He sat down on the warm sandy soil beneath one of these, his folio on his knees... He noticed his hands, how they were getting long, and the knuckles beginning to show, noticed that his wrists protruded from his sleeves. He bent his face to the shining lacquer of the folio, and caressed it with his cheek, his lips.

His face touched the flesh of his hand and he sniffed its warm sunburned sweetness. He loved himself passionately that day, as he loved the pear tree and the warm sandy soil. He pressed his body against the ground, feeling its warmth. He looked up into the innermost depths of the tree. The leaves were turning yellow, whispering together in the merest waft of air. Among them the fruit, beautifully shaped, golden green, hung ready to drop the very instant that its dried stem wavered in the support of its luscious weight.

He wrote and wrote. Frowning, he sought for words, found them, and, as a hound that has caught the scent, his spirit ran forward, panting after its quarry. To write a perfect poem! As lovely as one of Eden's. To write something that, in years and years to come, people would say over to themselves and feel happy... Who was the author? Why, the author was Wakefield Whiteoak, the brother of Eden Whiteoak... Poet brothers... the younger was thought by many to be the greater of the two.

Just as he finished, a pear fell, impaling itself on a spear of stubble. He reached out and curved his hand about it, held it to his nostrils, sniffing it. He was divinely happy.

He re-read the verses, polished them tenderly, copied them out again in his most careful handwriting. How quickly they had flowed out of his head! Only a short while ago the paper had been blank, and now a picture was drawn on it in lovely words that would last forever. Though the writing of it had not taken long, the thought of it had been haunting him for weeks; in fact, ever since he had watched the family of ducks with the new understanding that had come to him.

He had rushed to find Bessie when the thought of the poem had first come to him. "Look here, Bessie," he had said, "would you mind being called a farmer's wife in something

I am going to write?" Bessie had agreed with alacrity. Indeed she had simply thrown herself at the farmer's head.

To whom could he read the poem? He had read it to the pear tree, but her leaves had gone on whispering together as heedless of him as of the nuthatch that twittered among them.

He lay watching a flock of birds flying high on the journey southward. He saw how some of the birds would press forward in their haste, passing their fellows, and how the conformation of the flock was still unbroken. Passing and repassing each other, they were still contained in their formation like winging words in a poem.

The thought of Pauline Lebraux came to him. He remembered the way her lip curled when she smiled, giving her smile an odd shadow of pain. He felt that he would like to read the poem to her—for this one, Alma Patch's "My, how lovely!" would not suffice.

He would go to the fox farm and read the poem to Pauline...

He was panting when he reached the gate, for he had run all the way. He hesitated there to take breath. Standing behind the gatepost, he thought: "What if Mrs. Lebraux should come to the door? I cannot read my poetry to her. I must find Pauline and take her to some place where we can be all alone." He walked cautiously beside the fence, peering between the palings, hoping for a glimpse of her. But, before he saw her, he heard her laughing. She was squatting in the shade of a group of cedars playing with her pet fox.

It had been a puny cub, the smallest of the first litter of an immature vixen. It had promised to develop into a "Samson," of inferior woolly underfur and uneven rusty pelt. But Pauline had taken it under her protection. She had fed it with milk and stolen eggs for it. She had brushed it till it shone; had taught it to know its name. It was a secret name—formed of an English word spoken in a French way—and known only to the fox and herself. Now it was growing into a rugged animal of good girth, the glossy black of its pelt shading to blue-black, the silver bands on the guard hairs bright as polished metal.

Wakefield stood watching girl and fox romp gracefully together. A new shyness came over him. The thought of reading his poem to Pauline made him feel strangely timid. The very thought of speaking to her, of her speaking to him, made him shrink. Yet he liked to stand, hidden, watching her. He forgot all else in the pleasure of that till a voice calling from within the house caused her to spring up and, followed by the fox, disappear.

He turned back the way he had come and met Renny on the path through the birchwood.

"Hullo!" said Renny, "where have you been?"

"To the fox farm."

"Were you? I'm glad of that. I think you should go sometimes to see Pauline. She's a lonely girl."

"I just looked in... I wasn't speaking to anyone."

Renny stared. "But why did you go?"

Wake shook his head petulantly. "I don't know."

"Well, when you'd got there, why didn't you speak?"

"I don't think I like Pauline. She's so silly about her old fox."

"You wouldn't say that if you knew what she's made of him. He was such a poor specimen I was for stripping his pelt off him, but now he's to be saved for breeding."

"Well, well," said Wakefield judicially.

"It would be a good thing for you to have a companion of your own age. You'd better come back with me. I'm going there now." He noticed then the unkempt appearance of his young brother. "Look here. When have you had a bath?"

"I went to the lake with Piers yesterday. I took soap with me."

"But your clothes—" He touched the ragged jersey. "How long have you been going on like this?"

"Please, Renny, don't touch me! I hate to be pulled at... I like my rags."

"And your hair—Good Lord, I must take you to the barber. You look like the Minstrel Boy."

Wake's eyes blazed up into his. "I am! I've just been writing a beautiful poem!"

It seemed too bad to be true; but Renny controlled his lips, held back the expression of dismay that rose to them, forced them into a genial grin. "You have? Right now—out in the open? I see you have your writing-case that Meggie gave you. What do you say to reading the poem to me?"

"Oh, I'll like that! If you won't be contemptuous."

"Of course I shan't! We'll sit down here. Now, fire away!"

They sat down in the shadow of the silver birches—the little cold faces of the Michaelmas daisies were turned towards the young poet. Renny stared at him—his little boy, his darling—at that cursed rhyming already! Oh, that fanciful, second wife of his father's!

Wakefield opened the lacquer case and took out the verses. He read them in a small, carefully modulated voice, with an ecstatic singsong to it.

THE DRAKE

He has two wives, both plump and blonde,
    Complacent, roguish, kind.
I've never seen a family
    So sweetly of one mind.

In May beneath the hemlock's shade,
  Each duck arranged her nest,
And each upon a dozen eggs
  Composed her downy breast.

Each thrust her head beneath her wing
  And breathed the heady scent
Of feathers, warm straw, warmer eggs,
  While drake his ardour spent

In rocking round and round the coop
  To ward off stalking foe,
Or taking each in turn to swim
  In the cold stream below.

In dim green pools they floated, dived,
  Then up the slope he led,
Each in her turn, while wetly gleamed
  His jewel-bright, dark blue head.

Full twenty cowslip balls one morn
  Into the nests were spilled,
Drake, hearing those faint, infant pipes
  With pride of life was filled.

Down a green vista of rich shade
  The farmer's wife, their god,
Bore one warm duck, and the two broods
  To a run set on fine sod.

Nor anger, pain, nor jealousy
  Inflame the two outside,
Only between the bars they peer
  In love and simple pride.

Round and around the run they rock
  In ceaseless, sweet converse.
Each loves the other, each the brood
  For better and for worse.

But there's no worse, time sweetly flies.
  'Tis August now, the flock
Troop down the lawn to the cool stream
  And on its wavelets rock.

Wakefield's face was flushed, his lips trembled, as he waited for what Renny would say.

Renny said: "I think it's very good. I like it very much."

"Oh, Renny, do you really? I think it's by far the best thing I've done."

The best thing he'd done! So this wasn't the first time! He'd been at it for God knew how long. "You've written others, then?"

"Oh, yes, I've been working hard all summer. I've written any number of poems. I've read a whole book of poetry Alayne had. I've read Eden's two books, and I know some of his poems by heart. But this is the first thing I've done that I think is really beautiful." His eyes glowed happily into his brother's. "I'm so glad you think so too, Renny."

The master of Jalna achieved a wry smile. "Yes, it appears to me to be a perfectly good poem. The only question I should like to ask you is—why write it?"

"Why, that's the whole thing—writing it! You see something you like. Then you want to make others see it. Only you want to make them see it more clearly than they could ever have seen it for themselves."

"But why? Why not see it yourself and be satisfied?"

"Because"—he knitted his slender black brows—"you want to give them a picture to keep. You want them to see it the way you did."

"But you only give yourself a lot of trouble. People will read your poem and forget all about it in five minutes. I don't understand."

"But, Renny, when Cora had her last colt, and she was so proud about it, you came to the house and told us just how she'd whinnied to you, and how pleased she was with herself. You mimicked her till it was just as though we saw her."

"That wasn't writing a poem about her."

"It was your kind of poem, Renny."

"Now, look here! When Eden was a boy he was always writing rhymes. Now he's a man, he's still at it. It's never done him any good. It's mostly got him into trouble."

"Do you mean marrying Alayne?"

Renny's loud laugh shattered the quiet. "No, I don't mean that. The trouble there was all hers." He changed the subject. "Now, take young Finch. Music is his trouble. He's been strumming on the piano ever since he could toddle. He used to stand on tiptoe to reach the keyboard and got his hands smacked for it. I've spent a lot of money on him because I was made to believe that he was a genius. I never really believed it. He acknowledged himself that he had never played worse than at his recital last spring and yet he practised six hours a day for it. Music has brought him nothing but trouble. Poetry has brought Eden nothing but trouble. Neither of them is strong. Now, Wake, do you want to be like those two or like Piers and me? I know we're not artistic or anything of that sort. Intellectual ladies don't get hysterical over us. But we're normal chaps. We've good digestions, good nerves, and healthy appetites."

"But I'm sickly to begin with. What's the use in my trying to be like you and Piers?"

"You're not sickly!" retorted Renny angrily, "you have a weakness but you'll outgrow that. I want you to outgrow this other thing too. Why, I've never seen you look fitter than you do now. And, by George, how you're growing! Come and saddle your pony and we'll go for a ride... Poetry of motion, eh, what?"

XXIV

RETURN OF NICHOLAS AND ERNEST

IT WAS good to be at home again.

When Nicholas let himself down into the armchair in his own bedroom, with Nip quivering with delight on his knee, he felt that this was the return from his last trip abroad. Every few minutes Nip turned to give his face or his hand a quick lick of the tongue. The luggage had been carried upstairs and the box which contained the presents had been opened.

It was the rule that a returning Whiteoak should not fail to bring presents to the rest of the family. Especially was this the rule when the journey had been to the Old Country. Ernest had now unpacked and distributed the presents. He was beaming happily on his nieces with their scarves and strings of beads (Meg's a little the handsomer), on his nephews with their gloves and neckties. A flaxen-haired doll had been brought to Patience and a nigger doll in striped suit and red waistcoat to Mooey. Their eyes were sparkling with gratification. Ernest had enjoyed himself thoroughly, but he was now beginning to feel rather tired. He had arranged that the opening of the box should take place in Nick's room.

Now, at any moment, he might fade away to his own and relax. He had forgotten what splendid voices his nephews had. How their noise and laughter excited and fatigued one. Meg kept her arm about his shoulders. It was a lovely plump arm, but it weighed on him. In the midst of all the present-giving she was trying to tell him about her operation. Maurice was trying to explain something about having slept in his room which he simply could not take in because of the din. Patience and Mooey were running round and round him in circles, holding their dolls on high.

"Hold them nicely, children," he admonished. "Isn't yours a droll fellow, Mooey?"

Mooey halted in his gambols to examine the leering, black face. One of the eyes was tight shut while the other stared horribly.

"Isn't he nice?" urged Pheasant.

"He's only got one bad eye," returned Mooey.

Meg, too, urged her offspring to expressions of gratitude.

"Patience, tell Uncles how you love your beautiful dolly."

"Her's dot a daity face," answered Patience. She moistened a corner of her diminutive handkerchief on her tongue and began to rub the doll's cheeks. "I s'all wash her face," she said, "but not her breeches."

"Here!" cried Mooey, "you're not allowed to say breeches!"

"I am so!"

"You are not!"

"I am so!"

"Oh, hell, you're not!"

"Pig, pig, pig!"

"Nig, nig, nig!"

Ernest glided away to his own room...

Later, when all was quiet, he returned. He found his brother with a glass of whiskey and soda before him and Nip still on his knee.

"I had to have a peg," explained Nicholas to Ernest's disapproving look toward the glass, "to buck me up after all that row. What an exciting lot they are! Children getting badly spoiled too."

Ernest picked up one of the doll's shoes from the floor and put it on his finger. "Yes—but they're very sweet. I haven't seen two prettier children anywhere. It's very good to be home again."

"Yes. I've taken my last trip. Here I stick till they take me off to lie beside Mama. Sit down, Ernie, and rest yourself. You must be tired after all the to-do."

Ernest sat down near enough to stroke the little dog's head. He remembered Sasha and sighed. He asked:

"Did you notice anything about Pheasant?"

Nicholas grunted. "Strange we weren't told of it."

"We didn't get many letters. Meggie's operation was the subject of most of them. What do you think about it, Nick?"

"I think there are kids enough about the house, but I suppose she is going to have a regular Whiteoak family."

"Poor child! She looks pale. Much more ailing than Meggie." He tapped his teeth with the tips of his fingers and added, in a reflective tone—"Do you know, Nick, that the Vaughans are still staying here? I'd only been in my room a few moments when Maurice came to my door. He said he'd forgotten some of his things. There were his brushes on the dressing table and a coat on the back of the door. I naturally looked a little surprised and he explained, rather apologetically, that Meggie isn't fit yet for the responsibility of housekeeping. I remarked how well she is looking. Then he told me that their house has been let furnished and that the tenants were very keen to have it for another month."

"H'm. It is rather strange. But not half so strange as Alayne's not being home yet. Why, it must be two months since her aunt died. What did she say in her letter to you?"

"She said she was going to visit Miss Archer for a time, but I certainly expected to find her at Jalna when we returned. Meggie has her room."

"Well," growled Nicholas, "it was hers before it was Alayne's."

"Of course, of course, but if Alayne were suddenly to return it would be awkward."

"Where is Maurice going to hang out now?"

"In the attic, he said. In Finch's room." A yawn made his eyes water. He had slept little on the train. When, in a short while, the dinner gong sounded he was almost too tired to respond. Yet he still felt the exhilaration of the return and he was curious to press further enquiries about Alayne.

In the passage they passed Wragge carrying a tray, on which were arranged creamed sweetbreads on toast and a glass of sherry, to Meg. The two tall old gentlemen stood aside while the little Cockney, with an air mysterious and important, slid past them with the tray.

Nicholas chuckled as he heavily descended the stairs. "At her old tricks again, I see. I fancy this convalescence will extend through the rest of her life. She's always preferred her little lunches to proper meals and, at last, she has an authentic excuse."

Ernest, following, poked him warningly between the shoulders. Maurice was in the hall below. He was talking to Renny and two men who appeared at first to be strangers, but when they faced round turned out to be Renny's objectionable friends Crowdy and Chase.

Their presence in the hall came as a shock to the returned travellers. Renny was not quite comfortable about their advent either. He concealed his misgivings under a formal manner. He introduced his friends to his uncles as though unaware that they had met before.

Nicholas greeted them in a gruff tone, not claiming any former acquaintanceship. Ernest said—"I think we have met before," and went down the hall to look in his mother's room. He was astonished to find Mr. Crowdy at his side. He wondered what he could say to be rude to him but could think of nothing. It went against the grain to speak to him at all.

The door of the room stood open. It seemed that his mother had just left it. As the outline of her body was imprinted on the mattress of the old painted bedstead, so her spiritual shape had left its stamp on the atmosphere of the room. It would not be put aside. Though her fiery brown eyes had dried to dust in their sockets, they still kindled in this cherished retreat. The rubies and diamonds on her strong old hands still flashed. Her carven nose, her mobile mouth, around which a few stiff hairs had grown, were as existent in this room as the parrot that had fondly pecked at them.

He sat, humped on his perch, his pale eyelids updrawn. A piece of cardboard which had been given him to play with, lay torn in fragments beneath him. He stood on one scaly foot, while with the other he clutched a bar of the cage.

Mr. Crowdy stared at Boney over Ernest's shoulder, breathing portentously. When Ernest, with a deep sigh, turned away, Mr. Crowdy extended his left hand toward him, palm upward. With his right forefinger he traced mysterious marks on it. Then, with a piercing look into Ernest's eyes, he observed:

"Rare old bird."

"Yes," agreed Ernest, polite in spite of himself, "and he used to talk quite wonderfully."

"Hasn't spoken a word," Mr. Crowdy informed him, "for over two years. He'll never talk again."

"I suppose not."

They moved toward the dining room where the others were waiting. They gathered, six men and a boy, about the table. It was all so different from what Ernest and Nicholas had expected. It was their first homecoming without the extended welcome of their mother's arms. Instead, there were present these objectionable strangers. Yet, how delicious the roast beef was! They had tasted none like it—so juicy and so rare—since they had left Jalna. Renny drew them on to talk of their trip. There was a propitiatory air about him. Plainly he knew very well what they thought of such company. But nothing could have been more deferential than the manners of Messrs. Crowdy and Chase. After the elderly men had had their say, Mr. Crowdy told of his one and only trip to the Old Land in his young days, when he had gone—though he did not clearly explain in what capacity he had gone—with a rich American gentleman who had crossed to buy some thoroughbreds.

Chase had been born in Leicestershire but he had not a good word to say of his own country. He never wanted to set eyes on it again. However, at the close of the meal, he told several stories so amusing that Nicholas and Ernest forgot for the moment their dislike of him.

But when they had returned to their rooms it all came back. They drew each other's attention to a number of things that had jarred on their sensibilities. Had Nicholas noticed

Crowdy's nails? Had Ernest noticed the way Chase sat sideways in his chair with his legs crossed? And Renny's ill-
groomed appearance? And Wakefield's actual rags? And the
general air of rakishness about the whole establishment?
Where were Meggie's eyes? Even Pheasant, poor child,
should know better!

"Nicholas," said Ernest, in deep solemnity, "everything
in Mama's room was *grey with dust*."

They captured Piers who was passing the door, and brought
him into Nicholas's room. He came somewhat reluctantly.

"Are you," asked Nicholas petulantly, "in a very great
rush? We should like to have a word with you."

Piers seated himself on the piano stool and looked at
them questioningly out of his prominent blue eyes. He, at
any rate, they thought, looked just as he should.

"Now," growled his elder uncle, "what does it all mean?
How does it come about that those two ruffians are making
themselves at home in Jalna? Why are the Vaughans still
here? And why is Alayne not here?"

Piers blew out his cheeks and expelled his breath through
his lips. "Damned if I know," he said.

"Nonsense! Of course you know all about it," Nicholas
spoke sternly.

Ernest put in—"Don't bombard the boy with questions,
Nick! Ask him one thing at a time. I'll begin... Piers, can you
tell me why the care of my mother's room has been neglected during my absence? There is a film of dust over all the
furniture. In fact every room I have seen looks as though it
needed a thorough cleaning."

"I shouldn't think you'd need to ask that question,"
returned Piers. "You and Uncle Nick have been away. Renny
always spoils servants. If Mrs. Wragge cooks good meals and

Rags falls over himself serving them it's all that Renny asks. Renny doesn't mind disorder in the house. He rather likes it. Lots of food—plenty of company—and no one to criticise him or his dogs!"

"How long has this been going on?" asked Nicholas. "Didn't Alayne object?"

"Rather! Latterly, her life was just one long objection, I think. Once a week she stirred things up in the basement so that the Wragges were on the point of leaving. And she was after Wake, and after Mooey, and even after Renny and his dogs. Pheasant heard her tell Renny that he talked like a fool, and heard him tell her that she was the worst-tempered woman he'd ever met. I never expected that marriage to turn out well. Then there was the affair of that dog. I don't suppose anyone wrote to you about that. But, anyhow, Alayne and Pheasant and the house servants and Quinn, a man I took on since you left, all thought the dog was mad, and Alayne got Renny's gun and they stabbed him with pitchforks. Soon after that Alayne left."

During this quick recital Piers's full lips had scarcely moved. He sat regarding his uncles with an imperturbable expression while the tale of horrors that had wrecked the life of Jalna gushed from him as from a fountain. Ernest, who had been prepared to probe the matter with question after guarded question, felt slightly sick. Nicholas, with dropped jaw, sat dumbfounded. If the faded medallions of the carpet had parted, disclosing a chasm beneath, they could scarcely have been more aghast.

"But—but I thought Alayne's aunt had died!" stammered Ernest.

"So she did. Most opportunely. It gave Alayne an excuse for cutting out."

"Piers, I don't think you know what you are saying. If you are trying to—to pull our leg, I think you have chosen a very unfortunate time. As you have told it, the whole affair sounds a dreadful muddle to me. Can you understand it, Nick?"

"I only understand that if I had been here things would never have got into such a mess."

"Just what I was saying to Pheasant the other day," agreed Piers heartily. "We've never been without an old person in the house before. It was as though we'd thrown our ballast overboard."

Nicholas pulled at his grey moustache grimly. "I should have been something more than mere ballast if I had been here... Your explanation has been very incoherent, Piers. I wish you would tell me one thing clearly. What does Renny think about Alayne's leaving him?"

"I don't think he realises it."

"Doesn't realise—" Ernest spoke in a bass voice for the first time in his life... "Doesn't realise that his wife has left him?"

"No. I don't think he does. Pheasant and I both think that he believes she's just in a tantrum and that she'll get over it. But she won't. You can take it from me. She's found a second Whiteoak too much for her."

Nicholas and Ernest looked at each other. Ernest wiped the beads of sweat from his forehead and Nicholas reached for the soda-water siphon.

Piers rose from the piano stool. "Well," he said cheerfully, "I must be off!"

"Sit down!" ejaculated his uncles simultaneously.

Piers obeyed with a smile, sweet as Meggie's, curving his lips.

Ernest demanded—"When did the trouble begin? As soon as we had left?"

"I can't quite remember. Yes—I think it did."

"You say," put in Nicholas broodingly, "that Alayne got Renny's gun, in order to do away with some dog, and that they killed the dog with hayforks... I can't make it out."

"No wonder," answered Piers, "when the poor brute's head was examined not a trace of rabies was found."

"But what was the quarrel about?"

"Well, it began with Ben's getting on Alayne's nerves. Actually on her bedspread."

"Good heavens!" Nicholas turned red with anger. "They've killed poor old Ben, Ernie."

"Oh, no," Piers reassured them. "It was quite another dog. It's my opinion that he was inbred. But Renny won a flyer off me because he made friends inside of the month."

The uncles looked into his fresh-coloured face with positive distaste. He made them feel travel-worn and baffled. They wished he would take off that enigmatic smile.

"What I cannot get into my head," Ernest said wearily, "is why Mama's room should be neglected, and why Maurice should have been sleeping in my bed."

"Because Nip wouldn't let him sleep here," answered Piers.

"How long are the Vaughans staying on?" asked Nicholas, gratefully stroking Nip.

"Well, you know, Uncle Nick, that Maurice never minds taking favours. He'll never stop talking about the cost of Meg's operation. He has let his house and, if he can keep the tenants, I venture to say that he and his will settle down here for the rest of their days."

The brothers exchanged a look. They liked Maurice. They were deeply fond of Meg and her little one, but to have them always in the house! And with Pheasant obviously bent on increasing the tribe…

"It would be intolerable," said Ernest vehemently. "Alayne must be mad to have flown off like this. Her love for Renny is too strong, too fine, to be embittered by—by the events you've been telling us of… As a matter of truth, I haven't got it into my head yet. The cause of their quarrel, I mean."

Piers regarded him pityingly. "I suppose it is confusing for you, but you can take it from me that the real cause of the trouble is Clara Lebraux."

"Aha!" exclaimed Nicholas. "I remember very well that at Finch's birthday party Renny sat by Mrs. Lebraux most of the evening and that Alayne didn't trouble to hide her annoyance."

"And no wonder," said Ernest. "Mrs. Lebraux isn't at all the sort of woman we are accustomed to. She is one of these very modern women in my opinion."

"She would have suited Renny as a wife," returned Piers, "much better than the one he got. He spends half his time there now. He's looking to you, Uncle Ernest, to help him educate her youngster."

"I shall never," observed Ernest, "stay away from home so long again. Too many new situations develop in so long an absence."

"No more travelling for me," said Nicholas. "Here I stick till they carry me out."

There was a tap on the door and almost instantly it opened. Meg stood there in a becoming negligee.

"Come in, come in," said Nicholas. Perhaps Meg would be able to throw more light on the subject than it was possible to extract from Piers.

As she was passing him Piers stretched out his hand and drew her to his knee. She relaxed comfortably against him. The piano stool swayed and creaked.

She looked from one face to the other. "How troubled you all look! But really you must not worry so. It is all over, and I shall soon be strong again."

"Of course, dear, of course," agreed Nicholas.

"You are looking wonderfully well now, Meggie," said Ernest. "It is hard to believe that you have been ill for even a day."

"Yes, but all this flesh is so soft. Just feel my arm!" She extended her arm from which the lace sleeve of the negligee fell away, disclosing its rounded whiteness.

Ernest pressed his fingers against the smooth skin of her forearm. "It is a little soft. However, it will soon become firmer when you are able to take more exercise—when you are able to fly about your own house setting everything in order again."

She smiled rather pathetically. There was a hint of reproach in her voice as she answered:

"I'm afraid it will be some time before I am able to fly about. Maurice still helps me up the stairs, and I am not often able to go down to dinner."

"Yes, we missed you very much," said Nicholas. He gave her a penetrating look from under his shaggy brows. "Surely, Meggie, you do not agree to Renny's entertaining those disreputable fellows Crowdy and Chase. I must say that I felt very much put out at having them to dinner on our first day at home."

"It was a pity. But they really weren't invited. They just happened to come at the dinner hour. And Mr. Chase can be quite charming when he chooses."

"He hates women," said Piers, joggling her.

Ernest looked anxious. "I do not think that is good for her," he said.

"She takes no exercise," returned Piers. "She's far too fat."

Nicholas said—"I can tolerate Chase, but Crowdy is impossible. If he is to come to the house I shall stay in my room." He ran his hand through his thick grey hair, standing it on end.

With two fingers Meggie played a tiny tinkling tune on the extreme treble of the keyboard. To this accompaniment she said:

"In Renny's state of mind, I think that a wholesome, hearty man like Mr. Crowdy is very good for him. His company helps to keep Renny's mind off his own agonising thoughts." The candour of her blue eyes was sustained beneath the startled looks of her uncles.

"There seems to be a pretty state of affairs here," said Nicholas. "I only wish I could make head or tail of what you two tell me."

"It is all the fault of that American woman," explained Meg. "She is utterly selfish. She is ruining my brother's life with her lack of understanding."

"They are incompatible. That is all there is to it," added Piers.

"But," cried Ernest, "has Alayne definitely left him?"

"Quite," said Piers. "She'll never come back. He doesn't realise it yet. But give him time and he will."

Meg turned her head to look scornfully into the face of her brother. "What can you know," she asked him, "of the subtleties of a woman's mind?"

"Well, I've seen a good deal of them," he pouted.

"You've seen what they chose you should see. You have a wife who is as subtle as—as—" she searched her mind for a comparison that would not be too odious.

"Just leave my wife out of it, please," said Piers.

"Come back to the question of Alayne," begged Ernest.

"She is a very subtle woman," said Meg. "And a very determined one. She intends to stay away until Renny is thoroughly upset. She intends to frighten him. Then when his spirit is broken, she will come back to Jalna. She is determined to make an American husband of him."

Her uncles listened with troubled faces; Piers, with an expression of incredulity.

"Hers has always seemed a sweet and pliable nature to me," said Ernest. "I can never forget how she returned to nurse Eden—after the way he had treated her!"

This was more than Meg could bear. She rose from Piers's knee and began to pace the floor, clutching her negligee at the breast. "Oh, how credulous men are!" she exclaimed. "How tired I am of hearing of her self-sacrifice; even Patty would be sceptical of that, I think. No, Alayne did not come back for Eden's sake. She came back to capture Renny. And she captured him. Now she has set about making him over."

"I admire her courage," said Piers.

Nicholas asked—"What about Mrs. Lebraux, Meggie? What do you think of her?"

"She's a dear creature! What a life she has had! And how brave she is! There would have been a wife for Renny. And he adores little Pauline."

It was all very puzzling. When Meg and Piers were gone the brothers sat for a long while trying to piece together the various information they had gleaned, trying to discover what might be done.

In the evening Nicholas found himself alone with Renny. He said:

"I'm very much disappointed not to find Alayne here. I had no idea her visit would be such a long one."

He had a feeling that Renny stiffened, that a wary look had come into his eyes, as though he realised that his affairs were the subject of warm conjecture in the household.

"Miss Archer is Alayne's only relative," he said gravely. "She could not leave her until her affairs are in order and some sort of companion got for her." As though by an effort, he turned his gaze to Nicholas's face and looked steadily into his eyes.

"I have wondered sometimes," Nicholas went on, "if it would be better if you and Alayne had not quite so many of your family about you. It doesn't suit everyone, you know, to be mixed up together in the way we are accustomed to. Alayne's life must have been singularly quiet. I can't help wondering if the presence of all your people about her may not be rather overpowering."

"She's never hinted at anything of the sort."

"She's an unusual woman then. I don't want you to be afraid of hurting my feelings. Has she never said that she wished she could see more of you without so many of us about?"

"Never that I can remember. I think Alayne is happy. That is, as happy as it's possible for me to make a woman of her sort. I know there's a great lack in me. But she'll get used to me, I think."

"I think you should go down to see her. I'm sure Miss Archer would like to meet you."

"No! She disapproved of our marriage."

"I am sure she would be charming to you. I think you ought to fetch Alayne. A woman likes these attentions. I made a mess of my own marriage, Renny. I'm in a position to give advice."

"What have they been saying to you, Uncle Nick? There is nothing to worry about. When Alayne's visit is over she will come back."

Nicholas longed to continue his persuasions, but something in Renny's face forbade him. He looked on the point of leaping to his high horse. Either he had set his face against interference in his affairs or he was simply, as Piers had said, unaware of their precarious condition. Perhaps he was right and the others wrong! Perhaps there was nothing to worry about. Nicholas made up his mind to one thing however. He would write to Alayne and sound her on the subject of her return. He missed her presence in the house. She had brought something different into it to which he had become accustomed—her dignity, her interest in the affairs of the world, her half-sad gaiety.

XXV

ALAYNE AND LOVE

MISS ARCHER AND ALAYNE sat in the charming little living room of the house on the Hudson, surrounded by a bright coloured litter of folders advertising a world tour. Outside there was a raw wind, but in the room the gently sizzling radiator diffused a comforting warmth, and the vivid illustrations of the folders lent a touch of the exotic to the somewhat austere effect of the neutral tinted hangings and the black dresses of the women.

Alayne did not approve of the custom of wearing mourning, but Miss Archer was old-fashioned and insisted that she should. The black accentuated the pallor of her face, the fairness of her smooth hair. It intensified too the shadows under her eyes and the compressed line of her lips. She sat regarding her aunt with wonder.

For Miss Archer, after the first prostration of grief over the loss of her sister, had risen most astonishingly to the call of the world from which Miss Helen's delicacy had so long shut her off. First it had been the car. Then excursions in it, farther and farther afield. Visits to New York to view exhibitions of pictures by very modern young painters, over which she was unfailingly enthusiastic, for, though conventional in her life, she prided herself on being broad-minded, abreast of the times. No painter, no composer of modern music, scarcely a novelist, could shock her. But her conventional soul had received a shock by Alayne's marriage to Renny. She had taken to Eden at first sight. His air of deference to her, his poetry, the beauty of his person had charmed her. The breaking of that union had been a disaster. But she had heard nothing of Renny that had drawn her to him. His photograph had, in truth, repelled her. When by signs, rather than by words, she became cognisant of a breach between Alayne and him, she felt gratitude to the Good which she was convinced guided mortal affairs, and set about the planning of a world tour.

She had secured congenial companions in a professor of economics and his wife, old friends of hers and of Alayne's father. She sat now in the clear light from the electric lamp examining a fresh supply of "literature" concerning a tour which went round the other way from the last. She was now puzzled as to which one they should take. There remained in her mind only the question of whether they should turn to the right or to the left, both ways leading inevitably back to the house on the Hudson. Professor and Mrs. Card did not seem to care much which way they went so long as they went. Alayne too left the choice in Miss Archer's hands.

She sat there now in pleasurable indecision, her abundant white hair smoothly coiled, her large face, with its almost transparent pallor, alert and somewhat excited. Alayne sat watching her, comparing her in her mind to Augusta. Opposed to Miss Archer's indeterminate nose and gentle mouth she pictured Augusta's beak, the majestic curve of her nostril into her lip. Opposed to Miss Archer's white

hair and transparent pallor, Augusta's crown of magenta-
tinted black, her sallow, speckled skin. She recalled the complications of Augusta's dress, the beads, pins, brooches, and
bracelets. In Alayne's mind she compared unfavourably with
Miss Archer, and yet there was something about Augusta
one could never forget. She remembered how Augusta had
shed tears at her wedding in the church at Nymet Crews.
What would Augusta think if she knew the turn things had
taken? She thought of Professor Card and the intimate
information concerning all they saw on the trip that would
be diffused from him. She thought of the never-failing
curiosity with which he and Mrs. Card and Miss Archer
would view these strange lands, the pleasant curiosity they
would feel about all on board. She thought of Nicholas home
at Jalna again, his gouty leg propped on an ottoman while he
introduced, by sips, into his system, more of that which had
produced the gout. He and Ernest would have much to say of
their trip, but it would be familiar gossip of people and things
they knew. That was one of the striking things about the
Whiteoaks. They lacked curiosity about things that did not
concern themselves. Their own life, the life of the family,
that was the important thing and they would have carried it
with them round the world. If they could have been introduced into this room, she thought, with her aunt and
Professor and Mrs. Card, all the curiosity, the eagerness
would have been on one side. Augusta would have suggested
a game of whist. Renny would perhaps have tried to sell the
professor a horse... Oh, why had she thought of him! For
weeks she had scarcely allowed the thought of him to trouble her, now it came in a swift feverish rush making her feel
stifled in the little room, sickened by the sight of the gaily
coloured folders.

Miss Archer was saying—"Leaving the Red Sea we pass through the Strait of Babel-mandeb... Does not the very name thrill you? I can reach a peculiar state almost bordering on hallucination by the mere repetition of the name... And *Penang*... Doesn't it make you feel as though you were losing your very identity when you say *Penang*? I am so thankful that, even with age and all the ups and downs of life, I have never gotten over my enthusiasms." Her clear grey eyes beamed into Alayne's. She noticed the dark shadows under them, and took her hand and pressed it close.

"You have been so wonderfully good to me through all this time of trouble, dear Alayne. Now I must think of you, instead of myself. You are not looking as well as you should. But this trip will be highly beneficial, it will bring the colour to your cheeks... Just close your eyes and visualise you and me riding in a rickshaw... Or in the bazaars of Cairo... Watching the sunset at Penang... My mind will fly back to Penang!" The pressure on Alayne's hand became firmer. "You are happier, dear, aren't you? I love you too well not to have been aware of your unhappiness. But, day by day, I see a look of reassurance coming back into your eyes. Am I not right?"

Alayne nodded, clasping her fingers about those of Miss Archer, who continued:

"We all make mistakes in our lives. You have inherited your father's capacity for self-analysis. I am afraid that you are reproaching yourself for something."

"No, no... I am just drifting."

"Alayne, cannot you confide in me? I do not urge it, but it would make me so happy."

"There is nothing to confide. We cannot get on together. That is all."

"Must you see him—before we set out on our trip?"

"No. Not necessarily."

"But you write to him?" Miss Archer's clear mind could not reconcile itself to such a situation, but she clung with tenacity to the hope of a disclosure of feeling.

"Yes. Commonplace notes... To keep the family from guessing."

"And he replies?"

"Yes. In the same tone."

"Oh, he has failed you in your need for understanding: I feel that."

"Perhaps... We are just—not suited. He possibly thinks that I have failed him."

"But your love for him is—quite gone?"

Alayne withdrew her hand and rose with a gesture of irritation. She went to the window and looked out into the rain. "There is no use in my trying to explain my feelings for him. Or in trying to describe him to you. He is like no one you know. He is like no one else. I shall never be the same again after having lived with him. I couldn't make you understand... If I could think of a comparison well... this, we'll say... The ground that is torn open by an earthquake will close together again—but its formation will be different. It will not be as it was before."

"He must be a very peculiar man. From what I have heard of the family I feel that they are the victims of strange complexes and frustrations." Her ingenuous face was alight with the congenial task of psychological analysis.

Alayne looked blank. She scarcely seemed to hear Miss Archer. Then she said:

"The spiritual and the animal are so closely connected in him. They can't be separated. One would just have to take him as he is. Accommodate oneself... accommodate is a mild word for what I mean... But it's just that. The animal and spiritual in him..."

Miss Archer drew back. She made an almost repelling gesture toward Alayne. Little ripples of discomfort broke the tranquillity of her smooth face as the falling of a stone disturbs a placid pool.

"Don't, Alayne, please," she said. "It makes me shudder to think what you must have been through." Then she moved quickly to Alayne's side and put her arm about her. "It will all come right! I know it will. What we both need is to view our lives from a long way off. Utterly detached, in another hemisphere. Then we shall see the truth without morbidity or—dreadful remembrances."

Alayne embraced her, laying her cheek against the shining white hair, inhaling the delicate scent from her small fastidious person.

While they stood so linked, a sedan car stopped before the door. Rosamond Trent alighted from it and advanced energetically toward the porch. Inside she greeted them enthusiastically. Alayne thought for the hundredth time that no one she knew wore such becoming hats as Miss Trent.

She drew off her gloves and asked if she might smoke a cigarette. Miss Archer always kept a silver box filled with a good brand for visitors, though she inwardly deplored every puff of smoke in the air and crumb of ash on the rug. Rosamond Trent espied the SS folders.

"Heavens, how thrilling!" she exclaimed, picking one up and examining the picture of a group sporting in a swimming pool. "How these bring back my own trip round the world!" For it was she who had really put the idea into Miss Archer's head. "Hong-Kong—Honolulu—Colombo—Penang—"

Miss Archer caught her hand and held it. "I knew she'd say it!" she laughed. "Miss Trent, just before you came in, Alayne and I were saying how hallucinated the word Penang makes us feel. We actually see something that is not present."

Miss Trent glanced shrewdly at her friend. "Alayne looks it," she said.

They discussed the trip for a while, then Miss Archer said:

"I am just going to leave you two together while I run across to Professor Card's. I want to get a new book on the East that he has promised me."

They saw her briskly cross the lawns under an umbrella. They sank back in the relaxation of an old intimacy.

"Well," said Rosamond Trent, through the cloud of smoke she always achieved when smoking. "I'm back in the advertising business again. I enjoy it too, though it was hard to give up the antiques after such a marvellous start. If it hadn't been for the Wall Street crash I'd soon have had a grand business. I suppose you are still hanging on to your stock, Alayne?"

"Yes. I'm glad Aunt Harriet doesn't know how much of Aunt Helen's money I have had to pay out to hold on."

"Just be thankful you had it to fall back on! I haven't a doubt that it will all come right."

Alayne smiled faintly. She could not feel very cheerful over the affair, remembering that she had used her influence for rather than against Finch's investing, and that her friend had borrowed ten thousand dollars from him which he was not likely to see again.

In her dismay at the financial crash Rosamond Trent had told Alayne of the loan from Finch. Now, guessing Alayne's doubts, from the dubious droop of her mouth, she wished she had not been such a fool as to confess. She ejaculated with a sweep of the hand. "I will work these fingers to the bone to pay back every cent I owe!" She glared at her plump, manicured fingers as though she already saw them stripped of flesh.

At the extravagance of the word and the gesture that accompanied them Alayne felt an access of irritation. She had always thought of Rosamond as a creature of simple sincerity—a very real person. Now she seemed suddenly unreal—the reflection of an artificial life. Her air of knowingness, her obvious assurance that she was living in the very core of the world, were of the stuff of self-delusion. And she herself had brought Rosamond into touch with Finch. It was she who had been at the bottom of Finch's losses in the New York stock market—first by her example, then by her friend's borrowing from him. Whether or not Finch was holding his stock she did not know. She had written to him asking, but no answer had come. She had been deeply fond of Finch. Now she felt that she could not hold him, could not hold him any more than she could hold any Whiteoak. They could give one no comfort, they could not be held—but how real they were!

She felt stifled in the little room. Rosamond's voice came from a long way off. She was saying:

"You mustn't mind me speaking plainly, Alayne. But we have no secrets from each other, have we? You know positively all there is to know about my life. Now I can sense the fact that you are no more satisfied in this marriage than in your first. You need new scenes to take your mind off it. Many a time I've wondered how you endured life so far from all that makes it worthwhile."

Alayne did not answer. She let her friend talk on and on. Rosamond was thinking, she knew, that her poor heart was too full for words. Miss Archer came back, accompanied by Professor and Mrs. Card. The air bristled with information about the trip. Miss Archer had out her Trip Abroad book and wrote down numerous addresses and helpful hints.

When, at last, she was sitting alone in the living room, it was time for bed and her head ached dreadfully. She was enveloped in a cloak of depression beyond anything she had ever experienced... There was none of the active pain of grief. There was no anger to kindle it. There was only this choking sense of aloneness. She thought of the projected trip with shrinking. How could she ever, she asked herself, have thought of it otherwise? The company, in which she was preparing to cast herself for six months, now was presented to her as austere and even desiccated... And, at the end of the six months, what? She now had an income on which she could live. The world appeared to her as a pallid waste. What had happened to her? Only a week ago she had enjoyed a meeting of the women's club. But—had she enjoyed it? Could the paltry satisfaction of discussing world affairs with others, no wiser than herself, be called enjoyment? She remembered expressions of enjoyment she had caught on the faces of Piers, Pheasant, Renny, and even Finch. She thought of Eden's joy in certain things. She remembered the joy she had had in his poetry. She felt that she had had a wide emotional experience in her life. She felt, with a sudden pang, that her response to it, after the first rush of feeling, had been Puritanical and prudish!

For the first time in her life she directed sneering thoughts towards herself. In her life at Jalna she had always been considering whether or not things were congenial to her. When she had married Renny she had known exactly what life, there, was. At the time of her marriage the thought of changing that life or of altering Renny's habits had not even occurred to her. She had rushed into his arms her own outspread, but after the first embraces she had held him from her scrutinising him, being only too ready to see his faults… And Wakefield! From feeling tenderness toward him, she had come to feel resentment, and why? Because Renny had still continued to care for him as he had done before their marriage. And the servants! Why had she allowed their eccentricities to cloud her day? The leopard could no more change his spots than the Wragges their habits. All her life she had extolled the virtue of moderation, self-control. Yet she had plunged, with never a backward glance, into a family where there was little of either.

If he had not given her more of his time, why had she not gone in search of him as Pheasant went in search of Piers? Why had she not followed him to his stables and stood by his side dumb in admiration of the beauties of his beasts? If her clothes had smelled of the stables as well as his perhaps she would have become impervious to that odour. If she had tramped about with him in the mud she might not have counted his muddy footsteps on the rug. Good God, those same rugs had been lying on the floors of Jalna before she was born! Mrs. Wragge, or others of her sort, had cracked the glazing on the dishes years ago. Why try to remedy it? What matter if Renny threw burnt matches on the floor or old Ben napped on her silk bedspread or Mooey threw her talcum on his head? Surely she was not such a fool as to expect her life with Renny to pass in an unbroken rhythm of joy! She could not expect continued intimate contact with a soul so aloof and shy as his. "For he is of finer stuff than I," she thought in her heart.

If only she might live the past year over again! Her discipline of herself would have produced some richer fruit than a trip round the world with Miss Archer and the Cards. Why could not she and Renny give shapely expression to the best that was in them? What were his thoughts about it all? His brief letters told her nothing, but then she had heard him say that he had never written a letter of more than six lines in his life. And she had never told him that she considered a separation in so many words. It was possible that he thought that she had gone away in anger because of what he had said of her share in the killing of Barney. He had spoken bitterly, far too tragically, she had thought, for any man to speak of the death of a dog. But he was like that, and she had known he was like that and she should have comforted him. If one were to get on with him, one must bear with him and comfort him, for his blood was three-fourths Celtic. As against this, hers was Anglo-Saxon with a strong Teutonic strain.

In the midst of her regrets came the thought that perhaps it was well that she had cast loose from Jalna when she did and had come to the ordered domesticity of her aunt's house. From here she was able to look back on the Whiteoaks and see them as she never could in their midst. During all these weeks she had been dreaming, imagining that she could find tranquillity in sinking back into the subdued pattern of her old life. Now she was broad awake. That pattern appeared to her not only subdued but colourless, its background flimsy.

She went to the window and flung it open. The damp night air swept in. It was heavy with the smell of wet earth, dead leaves. It swept down from the north bearing the scent of the dead leaves of Jalna... Oh, if she might have a child of Renny's! If, when the new leaves thrust out, she too might quicken!

What had she been doing? Casting sweet love from her. Trying to create chill order in her life out of the entanglements of desire... Out of the darkness his face appeared before her and she felt faint with longing to see him in the flesh.

At breakfast she told Miss Archer that it was necessary for her to return to Jalna before she could make final arrangements for the trip. She had dreaded her aunt's questioning at this announcement, but she need not have dreaded it. Miss Archer was existing in such a daze of preparation, such an enchantment of anticipation, that nothing surprised her.

She saw Alayne depart that evening with confident cheerfulness.

Alayne had not sent word that she was coming. She did not quite know how she was to get to Jalna. She hoped that by now the Vaughans would have left the house. From Pheasant she had learned of their prolonged visit. But, even if they were not gone—well, she must see Renny—that was all there was to it.

She was, at times, conscious that her headache had not left her. For three days now it had been thudding against the back of her neck. Its thudding mingled with the throbbing of the train. Sometimes she quite forgot it in the feverish activity of her brain. She put up her blind and looked out into the new day. Noticed how white and graceful her hand and arm were. She had not considered her physical being for weeks. She was surprised to see snow lying in the furrows of the fields and feathering the shrubs alongside the track. She saw workmen's cottages with lighted windows and fowls emerging from their coops. An old grey horse stood in a snowy field, the wind tossing his long grey mane. Soon they passed through a manufacturing town and she saw a crowd of foreign-looking workmen going toward the factories. The train did not stop there but rushed through, giving her just a glimpse of its black sordidness and the brightness of the rising sun touching nothing but the gilt cross on the church.

While she was at breakfast they crossed the border and here there was more snow, but it was soft snow and was soon wet under the sun. The air was clear and bright, but quick-moving clouds cast their shadows on the fields. She sat in her seat with her things about her while the train sped past Weddell's, the station nearest Jalna. She saw Wright in the new car waiting for the barrier to be raised so that he might cross the track. The wholesome, kind look of him pleased her. Why, this little village looked like home!

She had secured a porter and was waiting for a taxi when her attention was caught by three men who were getting into a shabby car. Her heart missed a beat, seemed to turn in her breast when she saw that one of them was Renny. His companions were Crowdy and Chase. She took a few hurried steps toward him and called his name. In the chill light faces looked wan. All but Renny's. More than ever his looked fierce and highly coloured. He took off his hat and came toward her laughing in delighted surprise. She had forgotten how red his hair was, how red his face, how tall and thin and sharp and strong he was.

If he had been angry at her when she left, had brooded on what he thought her bad behaviour toward him, and kept his heart shut against her, he forgot all this when he saw her standing there in the wan light, her face pale with blue shadows beneath the eyes, her hair bright beneath her close-fitting black hat. He noticed at once that she had bought herself a new fur scarf. It set her off wonderfully, he thought.

They stood facing each other, she in tremulous wildness, he in amazed gratification.

"But why," he demanded, "didn't you write?"

"I only made up my mind at the last minute."

"But you could have telegraphed."

"I couldn't make up my mind to that."

"Oh, that mind of yours!" he laughed. "You're always making it up or not being able to make it up, aren't you?"

She drew close to him. She asked, in a choking voice— "Are you glad I've come?"

"What a question!"

"Oh, if only we could ever be alone! What are those dreadful men doing here with you?"

"We were shipping some horses. I've been in town overnight. I must get rid of that taxi for you. What luck that I should be here with the car! Crowdy and Chase must come with us, though. But they live just outside the city. I'll drop them there."

The two friends came forward looking rather crestfallen. Chase vouchsafed no more than a stiff bow, but Crowdy soon recovered himself and beamed at her. Somehow her luggage was stowed in the car. She was in the seat beside Renny. She was glad it was the old car—muddy, with ill-fitting curtains, rattling as though this must surely be its last trip. It had been just as it was now when she had first ridden in it, five years ago. In it Renny had first spoken of his passion for her. She recalled his words. They had been few and his tone almost matter-of-fact. It had been at night and it had rained. Neither had had any hope that they could come together. Now it was morning. Rain was beginning to fall. They were together, together, yes, together...

She could not understand herself, yet now she could understand him. She could not understand why it was that she did not mind the presence of Crowdy and Chase in the car. Yet she could sympathise with his feeling for them. They were real. That was it. They were as real as this raw wind that made the curtains flap. They were as real as Rosamond Trent and Professor and Mrs. Card had become unreal to her. She had changed. She was becoming a new person. It had been the birth pangs of this new self that had torn her.

Renny asked her questions about her life with Miss Archer. He seemed to think that it was the natural and proper thing that she should have made a long stay with her. He did not reproach her with the brusqueness of her letters, with her writing so seldom to him. Her heart turned with joy as she slid her eyes toward him… He reached for the cloth he kept for the purpose and wiped the windshield.

The lake was trembling in the wind. The waves were a light, translucent green. They buffeted each other like rowdies, knocking the caps of foam from each other's heads.

Gulls swooped and sank to the waves and rose again, whimpering. When the car was stopped for Crowdy and Chase to alight she heard the gulls' whimpering.

Chase bowed and backed away from the kerb, but Crowdy drew close to her. He extended his left hand and, on its palm, with the forefinger of the right, made cabalistic signs. His shrewd little eyes indicated Renny. He said:

"You have a fine husband, Mrs. Whiteoak. None better. Thoroughbred."

Alayne put out her hand to shake his. They gazed steadfastly into each other's eyes, she and the horse dealer. She could picture the hideous houses on hideous suburban streets into which he and Chase would disappear.

As they drove on again Renny's face wore a pleased smile at her magnanimity toward his friends. She found that her headache had quite gone, but it, combined with a sleepless night, had left her unutterably tired. She let her weight rest against Renny's shoulder and relaxed as she had not relaxed for months. Renny talked on and on about the horses they had been shipping that morning.

The heavy branches of the evergreens along the drive seemed to have extended since she had last seen them. They swept the windows of the car, drenching them. After the house on the Hudson this old red brick one looked long and rambling. There was a covering of wet snow on the steps of the porch and on the snow footprints of dogs. He carried her things on to the porch. She asked suddenly:

"Were you surprised?"

"A little. Not much. I was expecting you any day." But there was a shyness in his eyes. After a quick glance at her he opened the door and they went into the hall.

It was empty save for old Ben curled up before the stove. He rose, stretched, and came toward her wagging his bobbed tail. If they had had differences he had forgotten them. Now was her time to show that she too could be generous. As he raised himself, with his paws against her side, she put her arms about him as she had never done to a dog before.

Nicholas had been reading in the sitting-room. He came out, pulling off his spectacles as he came. He kissed her and exclaimed:

"My dear Alayne, how glad I am to see you! But you could not have got my letter. It was only posted yesterday. I had been intending to write you for a fortnight, but you know how bad I am at writing letters." He scrutinised her from under his shaggy brows, trying to pierce the wherefore of her coming. He had never untangled the wherefore of her going.

Ernest came, kissed her, and led her into the sitting-room. "But, dear Alayne, how pale and cold and tired you look! We must have some wine and a biscuit for you. I will get it myself." He hastened to the dining room.

"Thank God," rumbled Nicholas in an undertone, "that you're come! Otherwise, I don't know when we should have been rid of the Vaughans. Their tenants are gone but here they stick, just because it's so comfortable. And we have missed you dreadfully for yourself, my dear!"

As she was sipping her wine Meg came in leaning on Renny's arm. In the hall he had pressed her arm authoritatively: "Meggie, be nice to Alayne or I won't love you!"

She had delayed their entry long enough to say— "Nice to Alayne! As though I had ever been anything else! Surely Alayne will be nice to me when she sees my weak state."

Alayne rose and looked into Meg's flushed face. "Oh, Meggie," she said. "How nice that you are able to be about again! But I see that you are very weak."

Meg advanced and kissed her. "Yes, indeed I am! If only I had your strength! To be able to eat anything, at any time, as you do! I have no appetite. You have no idea what I've been through." Renny lowered her into a chair beside Alayne and stood looking down at them with old Adeline's very grin of delight in their reunion.

Meg laid her soft white hand on Alayne's knee. "When we are alone I must tell you all about it. But I am afraid you will be upset when you hear that I have your room."

"Not at all," Alayne assured her, though she would have given almost anything to have had her own bed to lie down in. "I will take Finch's room while you are here. You must not hurry away because of my coming."

Nicholas glared at her. "The ceiling in Finch's room leaks badly," he said. "It has been leaking for a long time. I'm afraid you won't be comfortable there." He added testily, turning toward Renny—"I don't like to see the place going to rack and ruin."

Renny went and began to poke the fire as he always did when repairs were mentioned.

Wragge appeared at Alayne's side, with the decanter on a tray. "May I give you some more of the sherry, ma'am?" he asked.

"Yes, a little." She watched him as he poured the wine with his air of mingled humility and impudence.

He said—"It's a great pleasure to see you 'ome again, ma'am. I hope you don't mind me saying so."

Wakefield was in the doorway. He did not come forward, but stood looking gravely at her. She held out her hand. She noticed that he had grown since she had last seen him.

"Wake, aren't you coming to kiss me?"

He advanced then and touched her cheek with his lips.

Renny said—"I haven't seen him as fit in a long while as he is just now."

Maurice, Pheasant, and Piers came in, followed by the two little ones, who clambered at once to Alayne's lap and the arm of her chair. There they were, all together in one room, as they liked to be, in the heat of intimacy, all barriers down. Once more in their midst, Alayne saw them as a crowded group in a picture, high-coloured, vigorous, resistant to change... On the centre table stood a vase filled with dahlias. There were as many as the vase could hold. Bronze, rust-coloured, orange, and scarlet; they were like the Whiteoaks, she thought, in their bold yet crowded commingling.

Meg saw her looking at the flowers. "Aren't they lovely?" she asked. "Do you know, I have never been without flowers since my illness." She drew Patience from Alayne's knee. "You must not stroke Auntie Alayne's fur, Baby. Stand up nicely and let her hear you say your pretty new piece. Stand beside her, Mooey."

She placed the infants side by side, facing Alayne.

Without hesitation Patience grasped Mooey's hand and recited:

> "Step out, baby cousin,
> Show your feet so small;
> Never fear
> While Patty's near,
> Lest you have a fall."

Mooey pulled away his hand. "Oh hell," he said, "I'm not f'ightened!"

At last she was up in Finch's room. She was back under the roof of Jalna. The roof leaked into the basin by the foot of the bed. There was a smell of wet plaster, Finch's things were about...

Renny came running up the stairs. He came in. He looked about. "You will be quite cosy here," he said.

She came to him. "Renny," she said with an effort, "I am so sorry about your dog. It was cruel that it should have been killed unnecessarily."

For a second there was a look of shrinking in his eyes. Then he exclaimed:

"You should see how Cora's colt is developing! It is growing into the most charming filly you ever saw."

"And Cora... Is she well?"

"Fit as can be! She has a heart of gold, that mare!"

XXVI

FINCH

FINCH was striding along a wet, winding road in the direction of his aunt's house. He had been walking all morning and he was tired, but he moved with the excited energy that possessed him when he walked, in opposition to the enervation he felt when indoors. He carried the stick to which he had become accustomed at the time of his strained ankle, swinging it and sometimes poking at things in the hedge with it. It had been a period of extraordinary gales and floods. Every now and again he came upon a fallen tree or a group of men removing one from the road across which it had been blown. A brimming stream hurried along the ditch, twisting and turning among the grasses and gurgling happily. Where the sky was not covered by smoke-coloured clouds, it showed a brilliant and tranquil blue as of springtime, though it was December. The hedges were a rich brown, against which the glossy clumps of holly stood out, with here and there a holly tree rising in berried brightness. Gusts of wind flapped against his face, wet and scentless, except when he passed a rick from which a man was cutting trusses of hay. Then the sweet smell of the hay came to him like an exhalation of summer. Above a ploughed field lapwings were flying in wide circles, uttering their cries that ranged from tender plaintiveness to a wild moaning.

He found one dead by the side of the road. It must have flown against the telegraph wires. He picked it up. It was still warm. The sheen on the dark green of its back was not dulled, but its long crest was moist and limp. He turned it over, letting it lie on his palms, showing its breast plump as a pigeon's, its white throat, and cinnamon under-tail feathers. Not again would it fly across the fields uttering that cry which moves the heart of the lonely walker. Its fellows cared nothing as they ran along the wind, now dark above the reddish loam, now, as they turned broadside, exposing their white underparts. If he had not come along, there would have been no one to notice its death.

He stood in the ditch, his stick hooked over his wrist, holding the bird. He would absorb the last of its warmth into his own body. Its vitality, its song, should pass into him, and he would hold it so while he lived. Its spark should not be lost.

"You shall not die, lapwing," he said. "You shall live in me. In the spring you shall cry to your mate through me in my music."

The eyes of the lapwing, which had been shut when he picked it up, now opened, and the glazed eyeballs stared up at him. Out of its long, sharp beak he fancied he heard these words

"Clodhopper! Do you think I can live in you? I who am a hen lapwing! Can you make the nest on the earth for me? Can you carry my eggs in your body until the shell is just the right shade of greenish brown, with just so many specks for concealment? Can you place them point to point? Can you warm them to life? Feed them?"

"They shall live in my music," answered Finch.

"The flight, the swooping, the crying of my younglets live in your music?"

"Yes."

"What of the tens of thousands of worms they and I should have devoured?"

"The worms shall die in my music."

"Birds fly and worms die in your music! Never can you compose three bars as beautiful as my tremulous and variable notes. Outcast of your own flock, do not imagine that you can steal virtue from me! My song turns to dust in my throat. My tongue cleaves to my beak. My eggs are silent notes that never can be touched to life."

He pressed her in his hands and she felt cold. A motor car passed, spattering him with mud.

He hastened along a lane between high banks towards a cottage where a thatcher lived. By the cottage there was a duck-pond, on the dark, ice-cold water of which several ducks and a drake were swimming. In the middle of the pond stood the thatcher's wife, red-cheeked, with a shock of coarse black hair. She wore high leather boots, from which she was scrubbing the mud with a corn broom.

Finch went to the edge of the pond and said:

"Good morning, Mrs. Rush. Will you please lend me your trowel? I want to bury this bird. I found it dead in a ditch by Ram's Close."

"Good morning, sir. What, a peewit? He'em dead sure enough! They pore creatures don't watch proper where they be flyin'. They'm half-mazed with their own hurry-scurry. Where be 'ee goin' to bury un, sir?"

Finch hesitated. "I scarcely know... Just here, by your pond, if you don't mind... But you mustn't hurry to fetch the trowel."

He stood watching her as she scrubbed her boots with the broom, noticing how the dark water crept in between the laces. When she had finished he followed her to the cottage, against one end of which bundles of faggots were piled to the thatch, and against the other was a shippen, from where came the lowing of a cow.

As he strode down the road, carrying the trowel and the lapwing, an idea came to him. He would bury the lapwing by the side of Ralph Hart... Why should not the dead bird bear the dead boy company? He gloated over the thought of their being buried side by side, as over a strain of music... Then a doubt of his own sanity assailed him for a moment, but he put it from him... He was sane enough, he was sure of that. But his mind was the playground of queer sensations. What in life would bring him peace?

As he descended the steep hill into the village he had a feeling of shame at what he was doing. He hid the lapwing under his coat and endeavoured to conceal the trowel.

The children were just let out of school. They passed him, running in laughing groups, their cheeks glowing, their stout legs purple from cold. He turned down the narrow street that led to the churchyard. He avoided the sexton, who was digging a grave, and slipped behind the gravestones to the distant corner where Ralph lay. From here was a noble view of the moors. The sun sent his spears of light through broken clouds, striking the humped shoulders of the tors. A sodden wreath of everlastings lay on Ralph's grave, but it was marked by no stone. Finch dug a hole close beside it and laid the lapwing there, smoothing its feathers before he replaced the turf. He straightened himself then, stared up into the sky and across the moor with a dazed look. He felt that life was as mysterious to him, as non-understandable, as when he had emerged from the shelter of his mother's womb.

Since the departure of his uncles, he and Augusta had seen less and less of the pair at the lodge. Eden had shown a desire to bring Minny to the Hall now that there was more room, but Augusta had had enough of company. Her manner became discouraging, even chilly. She felt herself tired out and she relaxed, finding the presence of Finch so congenial to her that she wished he might stay indefinitely. Finch, in truth, was leading a double life. In the presence of Augusta he was apparently cheerful, interested in all the small doings of neighbours and villagers that were the chief subject of her conversation at Nymet Crews. When a letter came from home he was almost painfully eager to hear news of the family. But no one wrote to him and he wrote to no one... When he was alone he relapsed into a state of deep melancholy, out of which he was only roused by some such incident as the finding of the lapwing. Then he was roused to a state bordering on exaltation.

The suicide of Ralph Hart, coming at a time when his nerves were swept by the storm of his hopeless love for Sarah, was a shock from which they were in no haste to readjust themselves.

He could not play the piano in the evening to Augusta without becoming unstrung. He would be forced to stop in order to wipe away the sweat that trickled down his forehead and sprang out on his palms. He would offer a stammered apology, avoiding Augusta's calm gaze. She would say then—"I think we have had enough music for tonight, dear. I am rather tired, and I can see that you are."

She saw more than he imagined she did. She thought that, in his present state, he was better off with her than in his own home. He was a fanciful boy and, she guessed, had had some sort of spiritual upset in connection with his cousin. She could not fail to notice Finch's repulsion from her, his tendency to sneer at her. Arthur had sent photographs of himself and Sarah taken in Paris. Augusta was for having them framed at once, but Finch exclaimed—"For heaven's sake, Aunt, don't force me to see that smug-looking pair every time I raise my eyes! Please wait till I am gone!"

Ellen told her mistress that she had found rosemary strewn over the floor of Finch's room and that sometimes he stole out of the house at daybreak. Augusta stared at her. "We will not worry about that, Ellen," she said. "Rosemary is quite clean and easily swept up. And, so long as Mr. Finch is stealing out at that hour and not stealing in, I have no cause for anxiety." But she was anxious. She suggested that he go to London or Leipzig to continue the study of music.

"Like this?" he exclaimed. And, as though at his bidding, his nerves had begun to quiver, and she had been made still more anxious by the sight of him standing trembling before her, with nothing whatever to tremble at.

His appetite reassured her. He was always hungry, as he had ever been. Mutton, winter greens, suet pudding were swept clean from his plate and, if a dish of nuts and raisins were carried to the drawing-room he was sure to finish them. Yet he grew thinner.

He disliked meeting people and would skulk out of reach when there were callers. He had avoided Eden and Minny for weeks. When he saw them in the distance on his walks he turned down a lane or climbed a stile to escape. He went to and from the house by the back entrance to avoid passing the lodge.

Today, however, the clock in the church tower struck the three-quarter hour as he left the village. He would be late for lunch unless he went by the drive. Augusta could forgive anything but unpunctuality at meals. It had never been a failing of the Whiteoaks. He made up his mind, after several hesitations and turnings away, that he must pass the lodge. He remembered with relief that Eden and Minny were usually at table by this hour.

As he was closing the gate cautiously so that it might not clank, Minny's voice called to him from the porch. She came hurrying down the flagged walk to intercept him. The wind blew the hair back from her very white forehead which she had drawn into a pucker of anxiety. It also blew her thin dress against her body, exposing the modulating conformations of breast and hip and thigh.

"Oh, Finch," she called, "we're having the most awful time with our chimneys! They smoke and smoke! I do wish you would come in and see what a state we're in. It's a perfect shame that Eden should be so uncomfortable."

Finch saw that she was blue with cold, yet she did not give a thought to herself. He made as if to walk on. He said hurriedly:

"Sorry. I'm late for lunch already. Aunt Augusta is a regular martinet about meals."

"Whatever have we done?" cried Minny angrily. "You haven't been near us for a month! You go the other way when you see us coming!" She ran through her little gate and caught him by the arm. In her thin-soled high-heeled slippers she splashed through a small puddle.

He looked down into her face. "Minny, don't mind what I do! I'm a beast. I don't know what's wrong with me but—just now—I'm not fit company for anyone."

She patted his arm. "Poor old boy! Eden has the blue devils sometimes, too. Thank goodness, I don't! If I did, what would become of us?"

Eden appeared in the doorway. He said loudly:

"Don't ask that fellow to come in, Minny! He thinks of no one but himself. Let him go!"

"He's just been explaining. He is not feeling quite himself. But he wants to come in, don't you, Finch?"

Finch turned back with her. He was surprised to see how pale Eden was. He had dark shadows under his eyes and, as he turned petulantly away at their approach, his shoulders were shaken by a harsh cough.

Both back and front doors of the lodge stood open. The interior was dense with smoke that was blown down the chimney and out of the great fireplace with each blast. Not only was the table not yet laid for lunch but the remains of breakfast still stood on it. In here was a chill more damp and penetrating than that outdoors.

Eden kept his back to Finch. He stood talking in a high irritable tone to a loutish boy with sooty face and hands.

"Can you tell me what your master's going to do when he does come back?"

Minny added—"Yes, I wish I knew how soon he can put it in order. Just look, Finch. They've swept out all that soot!" She pointed to a bucketful that stood on the hearth. "After he'd got that out we thought surely the chimney would draw and Eden built up a huge fire. He was so cold. But it was worse than ever and we can't get the fire to go out."

Eden began to put ashes on it. A descending gust sent a puff of black smoke and a swirl of ashes over him. He backed away swearing under his breath.

The boy stood regarding his efforts with dull interest. He kept rubbing his ear against the corner of the mantelshelf as a pig might scratch itself against a gatepost. "Master'll put un in order," he observed.

"But what will he do?" asked Minny desperately.

"Put un in order."

"He's going to have a damper made," said Eden.

"Will that take long?" asked Finch.

The boy rubbed his ear with a circular movement on a corner of the shelf. "A proper long time it'll take."

"If only the wind would fall!" cried Minny.

The youth turned his eyes heavily toward the open door. "He won't fall. He's a master gale, he is."

Eden asked—"Do you know anything about this chimney? Has it ever done this before?"

The youth had ceased rubbing his ear in order to comprehend a question requiring so sharp a mental effort to answer. After weighing it conscientiously he began again the circular movement against the shelf. He then replied:

"He'em allus smokin' in November gales. Widow used to send for we."

"And what did you do?"

"Swept un."

A fresh cloud of smoke enveloped them.

"Look here!" cried Finch. "This will never do! You mustn't stay here. Why, it will be the end of Eden! You'd be better out of doors."

"And it's been so damp too the last month," said Minny. She led him to the kitchen and showed how the moisture on the wall collected into a little runnel that trickled across the floor. Finch asked in a low voice—"How long has he had that cough?"

"About a week."

"But you should have told me! He must get away at once."

Minny's expression became pathetic. "But how can we, Finch? It's all we can do to make ends meet here."

"I'll attend to that."

They returned to the other room. The fire had died down. Heavy raindrops were spattering into it. The wind too was dying. The youth had gone off for his dinner. Eden went to the mantelshelf and began to rub his ear against it, looking mischievously out of the sides of his eyes at Finch and Minny.

"Us had better pip out," he said, in a singsong. "There seems to be nothing else left for we! 'Tis a proper failure us have made of our life, Min."

Finch was filled with compunction because of his forgetfulness of them. Minny was one of the bravest, sweetest girls he had ever known. Now she was kneeling on the cold hearth, the bellows in her hands, fanning the struggling flames. The wind had fallen.

He hurried to the house and told his aunt of the condition in the lodge. Augusta did not, as he had expected, declare that Eden and Minny must come to her at once. If the chimney began to smoke again there would be time enough. But she had a hamper packed with a hot lunch and Finch carried it excitedly to the lodge. She had put in a bottle of sherry, too. When he arrived a fresh fire was blazing and Minny had washed up the breakfast things. Eden was writing at one end of the long table. He looked up eagerly at Finch.

"Here's one of the best things I've done," he exclaimed. And he read aloud a charming lyric.

"Did you just write that this morning?" asked Finch.

"I've been working on it a week!"

Eden made no further reference to Finch's neglect of them. He allowed his own instincts to govern his life and, except for an occasional flash of temper, he was willing that others should do the same. If Finch wanted to keep to himself, well—he probably needed the solitude.

Minny spread out the lamb chops and mashed potatoes, the hot apple tart which Augusta had refused to cut into herself so that it might be unbroken for them. The room felt hot and steamy.

After lunch they sat talking and smoking. It was arranged that they leave for the South of France in two days. Finch would write a cheque for Eden at once.

Now that he had been with them again he had a moment's regret that they would be leaving. In the back of his brain, however, was a feeling of relief that the lodge would be empty, that he could come and go as he liked without fear of meeting them.

When they parted, Minny flung her arms about his neck and kissed him gratefully. "What should we do without you, Finch!" she said. "You are our guardian angel!"

XXVII

CHRISTMAS—AND AFTER

WHEN the lodge was shut up and Eden and Minny had left for France, Finch resigned himself with morose satisfaction to an increasing melancholy. The gales from the moor, the vaporous sunshine that wavered across the tors, the deep, spongy, relaxed quiet of the intervals between gales, combined to dissolve his resistance.

He was woken in the morning by Ellen coming into his room with a can of hot water. She drew apart the window curtains and closed the window. She carried a candle, and her shadow, grotesque and ponderous, leant across the ceiling above him. It was strange to think that this sinister, pendulous shadow belonged to the spare, upright, deprecating woman. He watched woman and shadow over the edge of his blanket, usually pretending to be asleep.

But sometimes he asked—"Is it a fine morning, Ellen?"

She would answer—"Oh, no, sir! It is frosty."

When he got up, he would see the sun rising, a round, red ball, and the grass of the meadow would be white and shaggy, like an old man's beard. The fleece of the ewes would look rosy in the thick sunlight as they nibbled the frosty grass or raised their heads and gazed toward the gate where the shepherd would enter. He would come at last, bending under a truss of hay, and the ewes would lumber heavily down the sloping field to meet him. Every week Finch could see how their girth was increasing. He longed to see the young lambs with the sick longing of one who expects to be underground by the next lambing season.

His body steamed as he washed himself in the cold room. Through the window he could see the winter spinach that Ralph Hart had planted, lusty and dark green... Even at that early hour he would ponder on the decay of Ralph's strong young body. He would think of the lapwing buried beside him, think of it as uttering faint yet beautiful cries that stole through the sodden earth, crept up through Ralph's ribs, and echoed in his empty skull.

He thought of a process of disintegration going on in himself. He pictured himself as, by degrees, being reduced to a vegetable growth, unable to move from the one spot... his legs resolving themselves into twining roots, his arms spread into great flabby leaves outstretched on the wet earth... his head a huge cluster of sickly buds that would burst, at last, into pallid nightmarish flowers.

He would sit before the piano trying to wrench from it some magic essence that would restore him, but the piano no longer was his friend. When he opened it the keyboard grinned up at him—the keys like white cruel teeth. Sometimes when he was sure that he was alone the power of playing would return to him. He would release his spirit in strong, full-sounding harmonies. He would compose, groping his way from rhythm to rhythm, but he could not tell whether or not what he composed were good.

Sometimes he would sit with his arms folded on the rack dreaming of the times when he and Sarah had played together. He would see her standing, tall and graceful, her cheek laid against her violin. He would see the curve of her wrist as she raised the bow. He would try to recall minutely all their meetings, the words they had spoken. He would begin with the first meeting, when she had come in late for tea, and proceed with them, omitting no gesture that he could recall, to the day of her marriage with Arthur. He would live again through the weeks by the sea, be racked again by the increasing hunger for her, the hopelessness of it. He would relive the scene on the cliff, when he had clasped her to him—taken and received one passion-breeding kiss. He would set his mouth in the form of a kiss and his lips would burn and his eyes grow feverish. He would spring up from the piano and walk the floor. Once he shouted—"I will have her! By God—I will!"

He pictured himself as following her to France, meeting her on the street with Arthur, and going straight up to her with the words—"You belong to me and you cannot deny it!" He saw himself kissing her in front of a street full of people.

He would crouch so long before the piano indulging in these imaginings that, when he rose, he would find himself rigid and cramped. If Augusta looked into the room at him he would cover his face with his hands until she had retreated. "The boy really must be a genius," she thought, "or he would not act so queerly."

Once that he was settled in a certain position, his imagination rushing over its usual course, overflowing like a river in spate, no part of him must move a hair's breadth or the spell would be broken. A pain came in his head and he took his hand from where it was in order to press it against the spot. But when he would replace his hand he could not remember where it had been. He tried it here, there, about his person and the keyboard, but he could not find the right place. His hand became enormous, a gigantic antenna waving in space, impossible to control. He wished that he might cut it off rather than have it plague him so.

To go on dreaming of Sarah, alternately loving and hating her—he felt that he could do this forever.

A concert for a charitable purpose was to be given in the schoolhouse. Augusta begged Finch to play at this concert— "just some simple little piece," for it was not a musical neighbourhood. Yet everyone would appreciate it so much and she was so proud of her brilliant nephew.

He could not refuse. He would play something—perhaps *Tales of Hoffman*—which he knew so well that it would be impossible for him to break down. Augusta's gentleness with him, her gratitude for his agreeing to do this, made him ashamed. He prepared himself for the concert by trying to live a more normal life in the week preceding it. He did not wander about the lanes so much. He sat with Augusta and even read aloud to her. Eden had left a number of books at the lodge. One of these was a novel of student life in Munich. When Finch read the intimate descriptions of the life toward which he had strained, of the gathering together for the study of music of all these young people, his heart ached with longing and despair. If only he could throw off these shackles that held him and join his life to theirs, discover of what stuff he was made!

Augusta could see that the book disturbed him. She said that she did not care for it and asked him to read another. He sat up late that night and finished it.

Every day, as the time of the concert drew nearer, the thought of playing at it became more horrible to him. He could not sleep for thinking of it. His nerves became so unstrung that he could not hand Augusta a cup of tea without slopping it. At last he got out, in a hoarse voice:

"There's no use in my trying, Auntie! If I play at that concert I shall make an ass of myself. You'll be ashamed of me."

She gave him a penetrating glance. "Whatever am I to do with you?" she exclaimed in despair.

"I'm sorry," he muttered, and went into the hall for his cap and coat.

She thought—"I wish Renny were here. Surely he could do something with the boy!"

Christmas came. A time of gales and floods. Cards and presents came from home, and a long letter from Alayne, urging him to write and tell her all about himself. She seemed to be very happy to be back at Jalna. It all seemed very far away to him, like a half-forgotten dream. Augusta had bought Christmas cards for him to send, and he had mechanically inscribed one for each member of the family.

On Christmas Eve Augusta doubted that the waits would face the gale. She hoped very much that they would come, for Finch's sake. It would be something quite new to him. It was a good season for holly. Thick clusters of brilliant berries shone against the glossy branches that Augusta and Finch had placed in vases and above pictures. They had trimmed the windows and the mantelpieces with ivy, and lighted candles in all the candelabra.

Finch thought of the soaking land, the drenched moor, the streaming sky, black as a hole… the rain flowing in rivers down the pane… the gale crying out in its passion… He walked from one room to another watching the reflections of the dancing candlelight... He touched the holly berries and the cold fresh ivy with his fingers... He saw the images of himself and his aunt in a mirror... a woman of nearly eighty, and a boy of twenty-one... Both were equally unreal to him.

He went to a window and he could hear the water gurgling from the eave. He saw a glimmer of light moving along the drive. It was possible to make out a little group of figures struggling against the gale. They stopped before the door.

He called to Augusta and they stood together at the window. The blurred gleam from an electric torch was directed at a piece of music held by one of the waits. The others clustered close, their streaming faces peering at the music. In the feeble light their faces were without bodies. They clustered together like wet berries on a single stem. But why did they not sing, Finch asked himself. Then he saw that their mouths were stretched wide but that the force of the gale tore the sound away. Only once a faint howl penetrated the room. They heard the sacred Name uttered as in an appeal for succour. Then one of the giant firs at the edge of the lawn fell like a shadow, almost obliterating the singers.

"Take them money," cried Augusta, "and tell them to go home!" She took a florin from her desk.

Finch found another in his pocket.

The waits touched their caps and staggered back along the drive out of sight. Finch raised his face and let the rain dash against it.

In the morning when Ellen brought his hot water, he asked—"Is it a fine morning, Ellen?"

"Yes, indeed, sir. And the bells are chiming luvely."

The chimes came swinging through the mist and in at the open window. The bells clamoured in ecstatic confusion.

He sat up in bed and looked out. There were rose-coloured streaks in the sky. Beneath the thin crescent of the old moon a rook was flying. He saw an owl skim past.

While he dressed he watched the sheep in the meadow. Some of them, he was sure, must soon drop their lambs. They were enormous and stood motionless as though listening to the chimes. He had got very fond of the ewes. He watched them in the evening when their fleece was reddened by the sunset, and in the morning when they looked so white against the green of the grass that one would have thought they had just been washed. He watched them on foggy days when they looked like fragments of the fog made solid.

He had become acquainted with the shepherd and, as January advanced, he had frequent talks with him. He stood by while the shepherd and his boy built a shelter of bundles of faggots and covered it with thatch, where lambing ewes and ailing young ones might be kept warm.

One morning in late January he discovered twin lambs standing beside one of the ewes. The other ewes stood about her staring as though envious. She bleated loudly to her lambs and they sent up weak, nasal baas in reply. They staggered on their thick woolly legs.

Finch gave a sudden laugh of delight, then started at the sound of his own laughter. It was so long since he had laughed. The muscles of his face felt stiff and unaccustomed to it. He stood grinning as the lambs began to suck, almost shaken off their feet by their efforts. He could scarcely wait to get down to breakfast that he might tell Augusta about them.

Every morning he hurried to the window to see if there were new lambs. Every few days a new one would appear, and one morning there were four. The first pair had become hardy and strong on their legs. They bunted their mother's udder while they nursed, their tails excitedly shaking.

One evening he heard plaintive cries in the meadow. He went through the gate and discovered a lamb lost. Its mother was lying among the other ewes chewing her cud, quite satisfied with the twin of the lost one. Finch picked it up in his arms. Its legs dangled, its dense wool was tightly curled, it raised its face, full of entreaty, to Finch's. He hugged it to him, his bones seeming to melt with tenderness. This was how he used to feel when he had held the infant Mooey in his arms. He carried the lamb from ewe to ewe, seeking the mother. His long face bent above it with an expression of great tenderness. He patted it comfortingly with his large, finely articulated hand. At last its cries attracted the ewe from whose body it had come. She stopped chewing the cud and turned her pale eyes, with a look of cynical benignity, toward the lamb. Finch laid it by her side.

He stood gazing at the sheep that were becoming pale blurs in the twilight and a feeling of peace rose into him as though from the earth itself. He remembered how often he had seen the shepherd standing there at night with his lanthorn, watchful of the ewes that they might not lamb uncared for in the night.

He returned to the house hugging this new-found peace to him as he had hugged the lost lamb. He was afraid to speak, afraid to be spoken to, lest it should leave him. He went and sat by Augusta and stroked her sallow, blue-veined hand with his. She blinked and drew back her chin, feeling something magnetic in his touch.

"You're feeling better, aren't you, my dear?" she said.

He did not answer but went on stroking her hand. He would have liked to talk to her about himself but she could not have understood.

A few days later she drew his attention to the steadiness of his hand. He had not known that she had noticed how it shook.

She ordered that a bright fire should be kept in the drawing-room, and herself opened the piano and laid music on the rack. She stood holding the pieces a long way off so that she might make out the notes and discover whether or not the music were lively.

He saw through her, and he was touched and ashamed. He realised that he must have been an uncomfortable visitor of late. Yet she had never once been sharp with him. Then, as he felt compassion for Augusta he thought less about his own plight, but days passed before he could make up his mind to walk into the trap.

At last he did, and found that his nerves, instead of reacting painfully, were quite tranquil. He felt firmer in his mind than he had for months.

Now he played each evening to Augusta, bending above the keyboard with flying hands, his forelock dangling. He played his favourite Chopin, finding in his masculinity assuagement for his own futile passion. He realised that the architecture of his existence was being built up and that he himself had little to do with the founding of it.

XXVIII

The Hunt

ON A MORNING in early February, when Finch had gone to
the village to post a letter for Augusta, he was surprised to
see, scattered over the green, a number of horsemen, some
wearing red coats. He remembered then having heard the
gardener say that the Hunt was to meet that day in Nymet
Crews. Just as he dropped the letter in the box and turned
away, the huntsman rode up, followed by the pack of hounds.
He stopped outside The White Swan and, a moment later, the
publican himself came out, carrying a glass on a small tray.
The huntsman bent forward, took the glass, and emptied it in
one gulp. He shouted good morning to another man in a red
coat who was riding a tall bright chestnut with white eyelashes on one eye. Several others came cantering up, among
them half a dozen ladies and young girls, some riding astride
and some side-saddle. There was a charming little girl of
twelve on a black pony. She sat very upright and had a flaxen
pigtail on each shoulder.

Finch strolled about examining the horses. He realised that
he knew much more about them than he had thought. When
he was at home he was always made conscious of his own

ignorance. Groups of people had gathered on the pavement to watch the assembly. The idiot wheeled his little cart excitedly up and down, his moon face raised to each horseman in turn. The schoolchildren had been let out and stood stolidly gazing, kept in order by their mistress. There were quite a number of farmers and their sons riding, to judge by the grey and brown coats. One old mare, ridden by a pink-cheeked youth, came lolloping up, her rough woolly legs caked with mud. Finch judged that the white-moustached old gentleman with the eyeglass and the top hat well back on his head was riding an Irish horse. He wished, with a sudden pang of homesickness, that Renny were there. How he would have enjoyed all this!

They hung about waiting for latecomers, talking in small groups. The village green lay in bright sunshine. The ducks on the pond quacked without intermission. The hounds relaxed against the sunny wall of the inn garden. One of the riders was having trouble with his horse. It wheeled and backed continually. He dismounted and examined the bit and saddle. He took off his hat and wiped his forehead, the sun shining on his yellow hair and florid face. Again he mounted and, at the same moment, the stragglers trotted up, and all fell into procession.

As the hounds, trotting close together with waving tails, disappeared along the cobbled village street, followed by the hunters, their scarlet coats and the gleaming flanks of their mounts bright in the morning sun, Finch wished he might have been one of the group of cyclists who followed after.

As he climbed the long hill to Lyming a mist advanced from the moor, blurring the landscape and reducing the sun to a pallid metal disc. The sun seemed lost to the world until, suddenly, its reflection glared up at Finch from a puddle. Far away he thought he heard the sound of a horn. The song of the missel thrushes, that had but lately arrived, came muted through the mist. As he walked along the drive he saw that the preceding night had been cold enough to form thin ice. It lay like a skein of silver thread along the edge of a rivulet left by the recent floods. In its bitter kiss the pointed tongues of the ferns were caught.

He went into the house and gave Augusta the newspaper he had brought. He was telling her about having seen the huntsmen when, quite near, as it seemed, they heard the mournful, musical baying of the hounds. Augusta threw a shawl about her and they hastened out to the drive. Along the slope beyond the orchard they saw a blot of red against the fog. Another and another appeared, and the baying of the hounds did not cease.

"The fox has likely run through Ram's Close and is going toward the Millford covers," said Augusta. "If you will run to the bottom of the orchard, Finch, you will quite likely see them cross the stream, unless they go round by the lane. If you were going to stay here with me, you should certainly buy a horse and join the Hunt. What a pity a fog has risen!"

Finch left her side and ran through the long grass of the orchard, where every blade, from tip to root, was hung with beads of moisture. He went in leaps till he reached the wall at the foot. From the top he looked down on the eight or ten riders who were crossing the stream. Others who had already crossed were galloping up the steep of Ram's Close in the direction of the hounds.

The opening in the bank through which the riders passed, in order to cross the stream, was narrow. A rider would dismount, drive his horse before him with a slap on the flank, himself cross the stream on the stepping-stones, capturing the horse on the other side and remounting. In some cases this answered very well, but in others the horses were averse from entering the stream and, once they were loosed, meandered about in the mud, tried to return the way they had come, or, having got into the stream, floundered with as much apparent alarm as if it had been a river.

Finch, perched on his ivy-covered wall, chuckled at the antics of the perspiring horses and riders. He would have liked to shout his approval when the little pigtailed girl, having got her pony across in good order, mounted him and galloped up the field, showing a back plastered with mud from a fall.

One rider, a man in a grey coat, was in difficulty. His horse, tall and raw-boned, could not be persuaded to cross the stream. Time and again he drove it before him with shouts and cuts, but, just as it had floundered over mud and stones to the opposite bank, it invariably wheeled about, facing its master with ears laid back and plunged back to its starting-point. When it reached there it turned its face toward home, and its rider was forced to chase it halfway across a ploughed field before it could be captured.

One by one the others disappeared up the grassy slope of Ram's Close. With a furious shout the grey-coated man made a final attempt to force his beast across the stream. This time he succeeded. The horse mounted the opposite bank with a natural, unflurried air and broke at once into a sprightly canter. The man slithered across the stepping-stones and began, with blood-lustful imprecations, to run after him up the slope. It was steep. Sweat poured down his face. He was mud to the thighs.

Finch squatted on his wall, his mouth stretched in a hilarious grin. The horse hesitated and looked over his shoulder at the man.

He shouted: "Stop! You…! Stop!"

With a toss of its mane the horse cantered on. Finch saw then that some of the preceding riders had opened the gate at the crest of the rise and had neglected to shut it. The man saw it too.

"The gate!" he bawled to Finch. "Shut it!"

Finch bounded along his wall. He leaped from it and sped toward the gate. His sudden appearance startled the horse and it broke into a gallop, passed through the gate, and disappeared over the crest of the hill.

The man, without another glance at Finch, laboured on. As he went through the gate which Finch held open for him, he panted:

"If ever I lay hands on un—God help un!"

Finch saw that he was a neighbouring farmer. He disappeared after his horse, calling on the Almighty to witness what he would do to him when captured.

If only young Wake were here, how he would have enjoyed the spectacle! For the second time that morning Finch found himself thinking of those at home with longing.

He trotted across Ram's Close to the far end, where another steep slope disclosed a rich panorama of red ploughed fields, green meadows and dense copses, and an encroaching arm of moorland. From afar came the silver call of the huntsman's horn and the confused, musical whimpering of the hounds, but nothing was to be seen. The countryside lay in apparent unbroken peace.

In the next field a man was ploughing, followed by a flock of rooks, walking sedately, peering into the freshly turned furrows. As the horn sounded anew he dropped his plough and ran toward the bank which separated the field from Ram's Close. He scrambled through the holly bushes that topped it. As he drew near Finch, he called:

"Be goin' to see Hunt, zur? They'll kill, I'll warrant, down in Childerditch Wood."

Finch ran by his side. They crossed the field and entered a lane. A little later they were joined by two men who had been cutting trusses of hay from a rick. The fog had passed, leaving the air of a surpassing clearness.

One of the men, an old one with a white beard who jogged along easily without once falling behind, seemed to know by instinct just where they would have the best chance of a sight of the Hunt. He spoke in such broad Devon that Finch could barely make out what he said.

From the lane they turned into a road and saw a score of people on foot, on bicycles, and in motors hurrying along it.

They entered a gate through mud ankle-deep and found themselves on a ridge overlooking the covert, from where came the clamour of the hounds. There was silence in the group as all eyes were fixed intently on the unruffled scene below. Finch was delighted to see the man in the grey coat mounted on his horse galloping across the adjoining field. He headed the horse at a bank, over which it literally climbed, sending down clods of earth and stones, while the rider, purple-faced, held up his feet out of the way. He then galloped across the next field and disappeared into the wood.

Finch's eyes wandered to the faces of those about him. Wholesome ruddy faces, turned in intense concentration on the one spot. How many generations of outdoor-living, sport-loving ancestors lay behind them! Two young girls stood near him. They had come in a motor car and were apparently prevented from hunting by accidents they had sustained at the last meet.

"They might as well hunt for a needle in a haystack," said one. "We lost the last one there."

An elderly man said—"Ay, the Hunt dance were a proper long one. They kept it up till red sky showed." But not an eye wavered in the combined gaze bent on the wood.

Suddenly the old man nudged Finch. "Look 'ee," he said. He pointed to a long open field that lay between the wood and a hillside covered with gorse.

Finch, following with his eyes the direction indicated, saw a small tawny body running across the field. Half a dozen voices babbled, "Look—Look!" But all looked in the wrong direction save him and the old man. Finch's heart began to beat in heavy, precise thumps. He stared so hard at the fox that his eyes ached. He longed to help it. He longed for it to escape. Not one of these others was on the side of the fox. Yet in some mysterious way his heart was also with the Hunt. Those about broke suddenly into an excited shout of "Hoick—Hoick!" He kept his eyes riveted on that tawny streak, so isolated, flying across the field. It disappeared into the bushes. But, louder than any, he shouted—"Hoick—Hoick!"

At the same instant there came a screech from the Whip, who had suddenly viewed the fox. In an instant the huntsmen were out of the woods. The hounds crossed the field in a long dappled stream. The riders, in scarlet coats and white breeches, in grey, in brown, in long black habits, followed after.

Finch was proud to find that he and the old man were the only ones who had seen the fox. The onlookers talked together like one family. The opinion was that the fox had had too good a start. They would never get him. He had likely crossed the road and sought familiar burrows near Charity Wood. With one accord they shouldered their way through the gate and into the road. Those who had motor cars scrambled into them. Those who had bicycles hopped on to them. Those on foot jogged doggedly through the mud.

About a quarter of a mile farther on they went into another field and ran across a furze-covered down toward another wood, into which they could now see the Hunt disappearing. But the wary old fox had escaped them. Scarcely a sound issued from the wood. A missel thrush sent up a sweet fluting from the tall bough of an alder. An affrighted rabbit bounded by, showing a flash of white scut.

When hounds and horses reappeared, jogging toward a fresh covert, Finch turned homeward. He had seen enough. Now he knew what the Hunt was. Had been exalted by it. He wished he had hired a horse and joined it that winter. He was surprised at himself. He must be something of a Court after all. But how glad he was that the fox had escaped. The old man had told him that he had been hunted time and again— enjoyed it. And certainly there had been no appearance of terror in his flight. He had sped down the field with an air of wary assurance.

How Piers would take to fox-hunting! Like a duck to water. Finch wondered how it was that the thought of his brothers kept recurring that day. One after another their faces had risen before him—Renny, Wakefield, Piers. He had thought of Meggie too, and Pheasant, and the little ones. Was it the thought of them that had made him happier? Or was it the forgetting of himself that morning? Whatever it was, he found himself tingling with a new vivid pleasure in life. Then he realised that for weeks he had been less unhappy. At that realisation his spirits shot up in renewed hope. He had freed himself without knowing it from the chains that had bound him. He had been free and had not known it...

In the orchard he found a clump of snowdrops in blow. They were clustered on a knoll beneath a lichen-covered apple tree, their pure bells shaking out faint fragrance above grey-green leaves. As he knelt, bending his face to them, he saw that all through the grass a thousand spears of daffodils were thrusting up, holding tight their gold till the moment came for flinging it across the grass. How lovely this orchard would be in another month! And he not here! No, he would not be here—he would be in the snow at Jalna. He was going home.

That afternoon he passed the little girl with the flaxen pigtails, jogging back from the Hunt on her stout pony. She leaned from the saddle toward him displaying a smear of red across her face.

"I've been blooded!" she cried triumphantly.

"And so have I," he returned.

XXIX

His Own Place

He was in his own room. It was unbelievable. He had passed through terrific things and was home again. Back in the very room where he had dressed for his birthday party a year ago. He had landed at St. John from a steamer armoured in ice, he had rumbled through days and nights on the train, Piers had met him at the station in style, driving the new car. When they had turned into the side road at Weddles, what drifts, what ruts of snow there had been. All the trees along the drive drooped their branches under the weight of snow. On each side of the porch rough mounds of it had been shovelled from the steps but on the lawn it lay virgin white and unbroken.

The first greetings were over and he had run up to see his room before dinner. It was all ready for him, clean counterpane and pillowcases—why, the curtains were freshly laundered and a new rug had been laid on the worn spot before the chest of drawers! He could scarcely believe in his room or in himself. The room seemed to turn about—and he turn in it—as the snowflakes floated and turned outside the window. There was the very chair he had sat in, wrapped in his quilt, waiting for the moment of his birthday dinner! There

was the table, ink-stained and shabby, at which he had swot-
ted for his exams! There were the shelves with his books!
Lord, there was the stain on the ceiling where the roof
leaked, and there was the basin on the floor waiting for the
next drops!

He opened the door of the clothes cupboard and looked
in. There were the clothes that had been too old to take away
with him! They would come in very well now that he was
home again. Why, there was the brand new sweater that
Uncle Ernest had not allowed him to take because it was too
loud for England! He had forgotten all about it. How he
wished that he had bought a new supply of clothes in
London! What a dud he was! The fellows would be sure to
ask him what new clothes he had got.

He pictured himself going in to dinner, just a little late,
wearing a new suit, perfectly tailored by one of the best tai-
lors in the West End, imparting to him an air of negligent
elegance. And above the suit his face rising, world-worn and
disillusioned, showing new lines of suffering. He went to the
mirror and examined his face to see whether or not there
were any lines on it. He could discover neither new lines nor
old. It was hollow-cheeked, to be sure, but looked as fresh
and youthful as it had when last reflected in that mirror. He
drew a deep sigh. Strange that one should go through hell, as
he had done, and show no sign of it…

The gong sounded for dinner. He felt so natural descending the attic stairs that all the past year seemed suddenly a
dream. Yet he realised that it was no dream when Mooey
appeared outside his mother's door grown almost half a head
taller. And there was Pheasant—he had only seen her for a
moment—how terribly different she looked! Her little face
had looked tired and white and her body so heavy that

movement seemed painful. Poor young Pheasant! She had looked like a boy in her tweed coat and cropped head the day she had come to see him off.

"Hello," he said to Mooey, "do you remember me? I'm Uncle Finch."

"What did you b'ing me? Mummy says Unca Finch will b'ing p'esents."

Finch almost staggered in his dismay. He had been in such a hurry to get home that the thought of presents had never once crossed his mind. What a blasted fool he was! The first day he had been in London he had stared in shop windows choosing imaginary presents for each one, and then, when the time came for buying them, he had forgot! He gave a sickly smile at Mooey.

Mooey took a threatening step forward. "I want my p'esent," he demanded.

"Why, look here," stuttered Finch, "look here, the presents aren't unpacked yet."

"Unpack them, then," commanded Mooey.

"Mooey," called Pheasant's voice from within the room. "You must not ask for your present till after dinner!"

Finch skulked down the next flight of stairs to the hall. The family were already in the dining room. He stood hesitating, knitting his brow, as he tried to think what to do about presents... He would just have to say that the bag they were packed in had gone astray. At the first opportunity he would go into town, ostensibly to inquire about it, and buy presents all round. He must make sure that each was marked with the name of an English firm. It would be terrible to be caught in so callous a deception.

He stood for a moment in the hall, absorbing the feeling of home. Old Benny and the two spaniels lay beside the round stove which glowed, almost red hot. He thought of the cellar-like atmosphere of the hall at Lyming. And not a dog in the house—not even a cat! He remembered the dining room—he and his aunt facing each other across the not too well-laden board. It needed long absence and experience abroad to make one appreciate home.

The Vaughans had come to dinner. Ten people were ranged about the table. Pheasant was having hers in her room. Finch sat between Piers and Wakefield. On his left, Wake's narrow, olive-tinted hands. On his right, those of Piers, whitened by the long winter, broad, strong, the sight of them bringing recollections of rough handling, of hearty thumps. How often he had felt helpless in the grasp of those hands!

Across the table was Meggie smiling at him, looking even plumper than before but rather pale.

"Just the tiniest bit of beef, Renny! No—not a scrap of the fat! Perhaps—when spring comes—I shall get my appetite back!"

Renny scowled as he watched her help herself to a morsel of cauliflower from the dish Wragge held. He said:

"You are not eating enough for a baby. You will never get your strength back at this rate. Does she go on like this at home, Maurice?"

"Just the same," returned Maurice stolidly.

"Well, you should force her to eat."

Alayne gave an impatient movement and began to talk to Ernest on her left.

Meg said—"The doctor insists that what I need is a change. He suggests a month in Florida. Fancy suggesting Florida to me, when he knows it has almost ruined us to pay for my operation."

"Oh, no! Not quite," objected Maurice, somewhat embarrassed. "But certainly a trip to Florida is out of the question."

Wragge ostentatiously proffered a dish of buttered turnips to the convalescent.

"No, no, Rags! But how nice they look! I only wish I could!"

Renny asked Maurice in an undertone:

"Does she have many little lunches at home?"

But Meg overheard. She replied for her husband.

"I have nothing else. I have never had a real meal since…" She did not need to finish the sentence. She put her elbow on the table and rested her head in her hand. She smiled, but her smile was pensive.

Alayne asked crisply—"Have you tried a good tonic?"

Instinct told Maurice that he was expected to answer Alayne's question. He said:

"She has taken five bottles of the tonic her own doctor gave her, and two from a prescription that Mrs. Lebraux let her have."

"But—do you think it is sensible to take other people's prescriptions?"

This time Meg answered. "Not anyone's, of course. But Clara Lebraux is such a darling! And she told me that Renny asked her to let me have it."

Renny shot a glance of annoyance at his sister. "It was a tonic that was given her after Tony's death. She was badly run down. It helped her." Why should Meggie have dragged in Clara's name?

Finch observed—"Mrs. Court had a great opinion of cod liver oil. She insisted on dosing Leigh with it."

Meg leaned toward him. "Do tell us about Mrs. Court and Sarah! What did you think of the girl?"

The sudden introduction of Sarah into the conversation startled Finch. For a second the faces about him were blotted out by a vision of her, standing on a Cornish cliff, facing the wind. "Over there is Ireland." Her beautiful pale face alight with a sudden wild joy.

Ernest put in—"I don't think Finch was attracted by her. She is a strange, uncomfortable girl. Not a girl to please the modern young man."

"Let him speak for himself," said Nicholas, remembering the day he had come upon them making music when they had believed the others to be out.

Finch tried to speak nonchalantly. "Well, she is a curious sort of girl. Awfully self-centred. Not at all sympathetic." He felt the peculiar weight on the chest that the thought of Sarah always brought. "As a matter of fact, I feel rather sorry for Leigh."

"What a pity!" exclaimed Meg. "Arthur Leigh is such a sweet young man. It is too bad that he should have a hard, unsympathetic wife. Still, it is rather nice to have our cousin married to him. It will make an interesting connection. Is she pretty, Finch?"

"Not at all. She's a rigid pale creature with something witchlike about her."

"Heavens! Whatever did young Leigh see in her?"

"I can't imagine." What lies he was telling. He wished that the conversation might change to another subject… He remembered a letter in his pocket, and said—"Oh, Meggie, I have a letter for you from Aunt Augusta!" He pushed it across the table to her.

It had the desired effect. Meg must peep into the letter to see what Augusta had written.

Finch said—"Look here, I've just discovered that a suitcase is missing. The worst of it is, that it was the one that had the presents in it. I must go to town and see about it."

"Are you sure you're not bluffing?" asked Piers.

Finch flushed angrily. "Of course I'm not!"

"What did you bring me?" demanded Wakefield.

"Wait and see."

"May I guess?

"Why not?"

"I see that you're as great a nuisance as ever."

"Tell him what you have brought him," said Renny. "He'll like to be thinking about it."

"Very well... I brought you a camera!"

Wake shouted—"One of the sort you can take moving pictures with?"

"Yes."

"Good! Good! Oh, splendid! Oh, thank you, Finch!"

The family was genuinely impressed. Each speculated pleasurably on what Finch had brought him.

Finch was the last to leave the dining room. Wragge said, with an ingratiating smile, as he passed him:

"I do 'ope as 'ow the little purse you were kind enough to accept on your birthday 'as been of use, sir."

Finch muttered that he did not know how he should have got along without the purse. Outside he thought—"Lord, he expects something, too!"

Renny and Piers were standing by the stove in the hall. They were smoking, and Renny was pulling the ears of his spaniels, which had reared themselves against him. His brothers turned toward him, their faces expressing amused friendliness. Here he was, young Finch, back in their midst with the varied experiences of a year behind him. They wondered what he had been up to during that year. At that moment he felt very much the man of the world, almost patronising toward these stay-at-home brothers. Piers offered him a cigarette and looked him over.

"I can't say that you've improved," he said. "You look half starved as always. Haven't you any new clothes? That's the suit you went away in."

"I bought a few things. But I haven't unpacked them yet."

"Perhaps they're in the suitcase with the presents."

Finch coloured. What a shrewd devil Piers was! It was plain that he suspected something.

"Just what did you buy in the way of clothes?" asked Renny. "They're so much cheaper over there that I hope you got a good supply."

"Not as many as I should, I'm afraid. You see, I was in the country almost all the time."

His brothers stared.

"How long were you in London?"

"A fortnight," he answered heavily.

They could scarcely believe him.

"And Paris. How long were you there?"

"I didn't get across to Paris."

Good God! He hadn't got across to Paris!

Had he seen the Derby? Had he been to Newmarket? Any boat races? Polo? What shows had he seen?

As they questioned and he answered, he felt that his stock had irrevocably gone down, so far as they were concerned. He thought what either of them would have done with a year in England. He could not tell them all his real experiences. He mumbled his negations, avoiding their eyes.

"By Judas!" exclaimed Renny. "You are the limit! I send you off when you are twenty-one to see the world. You take two aged uncles with you and spend ten months in the house with an aged aunt! You've seen nothing—done nothing so far as I can see but mope about a village green, passing the time of day with the village idiot. Did you keep up your music?"

A shiver ran across Finch's nerves. He began to feel that this questioning was too much for him. He was relieved to see Maurice emerge at that moment from the coat room behind the stairs where he had been in search of his pipe. He came up to them, filling it from the pouch which he held in his disabled hand.

"Come and join the wonder-struck circle," said Piers. "Hear what this bright young man is telling us poor yokels about his trip abroad."

Maurice grinned expectantly. "Well, the girls are out of the way. Let's have the dregs! I haven't been shocked for a dog's age."

"Well, I am shocked," said Renny. "What do you suppose Finch has just told us? He spent a fortnight in London—that was with the uncles when he first arrived—and the rest of the year he never left his auntie's side! What do you make of it, Maurice?"

"He's telling you just what is good for you to know, aren't you, Finch? Meg and I have said all along that you must be having a devil of a time since you never put pen to paper." He lighted his pipe, with a sly look at Finch.

Renny said—"No, Maurice. You're wrong. He hasn't been having a devil of a time. I've never known anyone so absolutely incapable of enjoying himself. Set him down in the middle of a harem, and he'd have all the houris and himself in tears inside of the hour."

"The point is," returned Maurice, "that he's too subtle for you. He has ways of enjoying himself that you know nothing of."

"You've hit it!" ejaculated Piers. "Why didn't we think of that? He has spent the whole year in sucking up to Aunt Augusta. He's after her money! Gran's wasn't enough. He wants to be lord of the manor at Lyming!"

Although Piers was laughing as he talked, it was clear that he was half convinced of what he said. The other two looked suddenly serious. Through the tobacco smoke that enveloped them, they stared at Finch with misgiving.

"Lord, I hadn't thought of that!" said Renny.

"You'll think of it," said Piers, "when Auntie's will is read and you find yourself, with all your charms, left out in the cold."

"Don't be an ass!" growled Finch. "If you think I want another legacy, you're mistaken. I went through too much with the last one." He searched his mind for something to say that would astonish them. Something that would show himself in a quite different light from their stupid imaginings.

He burst out—"Well, I'll tell you one thing I did. I went on a honeymoon—not my own either—a whole month by the sea."

"Whose honeymoon?" asked Piers, unbelievingly.

"Arthur's and—Sarah's."

He cursed himself instantly for having told of it. There was a roar of laughter.

Piers said—"Well, you certainly must have been a death's head at the feast! However, I can believe anything of that sissy Leigh."

Renny made a ribald remark in the vein of his grandmother, and Finch, furious with himself, as with them, turned away and went into the drawing-room.

He stood in the doorway a moment quieting his nerves with the peaceful, reassuring scene.

Ernest had got his magnifying glass and was showing Wakefield, who perched on the arm of his chair, the texture of the skin on the back of his hand. "Oh, Uncle Ernest, you're just like a lovely pink hippopotamus!" Nicholas, his gouty leg stuck out stiffly, was on the piano seat, thoughtfully strumming one of the frothy melodies of his youth. Alayne sat nearby on the sofa. She held a book, but was gazing appreciatively at Nicholas's massive grey head silhouetted against a window. Meg had unearthed an old photograph album, and sat by the fire, in a low, comfortable chair, turning its pages with an expression of pensive sweetness.

Large snowflakes drifted against the windows, clinging an instant before being dissolved by the inner warmth. The fire was of pine wood crackling noisily, filling the room with a resinous smell. Though his sister gave him an inviting look, Finch went and sat down by Alayne. He was impressed by a change in her. He could not have told what it was, but she had the appearance of belonging in the room as she had never belonged before.

She welcomed him to her side with a smile. "How nice of you to come and sit by me! You have no idea how I have missed you. You know, you were my first friend here, Finch."

"Even then," he said, "I was whining to you about my troubles. I was wanting music lessons!"

"What is it now? I had a feeling—from the sound of the laughter out there—that Piers was tormenting you."

"Well, not exactly. But ragging me. And the others, too. I'm an easy mark. I take all they say so seriously, and I don't seem able to help it."

"I know. I've learned things since you went away, Finch."

"Then I didn't imagine the change in you."

"Is there a change in me?"

"Yes." He hesitated and then added—"You look more like the women of our family."

She laughed, half pleased, half rueful. "Is it an improvement?"

"I think you're happier."

She looked at him, startled. "Did I strike you as being unhappy?"

"No—but I thought you would never be one of us. Now, I think, you are."

"You say 'one of us' and yet you are not like the others."

"Eden says I am a Whiteoak—as much as any."

She considered this. "Perhaps he is right. He and you both see life in a peculiar distortion of your own. You are both artists. Yet your ultimate vision is that of the Whiteoaks."

"Perhaps." He spoke vaguely. He was looking about the room, feeling in it an embrace of the spirit. "I like that thing Uncle Nick is playing, don't you?"

"I haven't been listening. I've been watching him. It's the first time he has sat down at the piano this winter. I think you have brought the feeling of music with you."

"I don't know why I should. I've scarcely played for months. Renny was just asking me if I had kept my music up. Thank goodness Maurice came along just then and nothing more was said."

"Was there something that troubled you—kept you from playing?"

His mind closed against hers. "Oh, I had a kind of nervous breakdown, I think."

"Can't you tell me about it?"

That was the worst of her, he thought. She was too persistent, too keen to know the why and wherefore of things.

Now he felt uneasy, and, seeing his sister's eyes on him—
"Meggie has something she wants to show me," he said, and
went across to her.

He sat down by her on an ottoman embroidered in bead-
work in a design of an angel carrying a sheaf of lilies. She
said:

"It's time you came and sat by me. I was feeling jealous.
I have been looking at old photographs. Isn't this an adorable
one of the uncles and our father in braided velvet dresses?
Do you think Patty is like Papa?"

"A bit. But she is like Maurice, too." He lifted her hand
from the album and raised it to his cheek. "Meggie," he
whispered, "I can't bear to see you ill. You must go to Florida.
I'll foot the bill."

She beamed at him. "That would be lovely! And I could
take Wake with me. The change would do him so much good.
And, as he often says, the child has been nowhere."

"Right you are. I'd intended doing something for each
one of you, and this will be your treat and Wake's."

The three men entered from the hall. Renny went
straight to Alayne and sat down by her side. He picked up the
book she was reading, looked at the title and laid it down
with a grimace. Maurice turned toward Ernest and
Wakefield, putting his fingers inside the boy's collar. Piers
joined Meg and Finch. He regarded Finch with animated
interest. He had convinced himself that Finch was a subtle
devil well worth watching.

Nicholas continued to play half-forgotten fragments. The
dogs also had come in and stretched themselves, with intermingled bodies, on the hearth rug.

Rags entered carrying the coffee which was taken in the
drawing-room on festive occasions such as this.

From above, the laughter and pattering feet of the children could be heard.

Meg raised her voice. "What do you suppose Finch has done?"

"Seduced Alma Patch?" offered Piers.

"Piers! How can you! No... something much more thrilling. He has promised to send me South for my health. And I'm to take Wake with me."

"By George, that's good of you, Finch!" said Maurice warmly. He was glad he had not joined in ragging Finch in the hall.

Wake uttered three staccato yells of triumph.

Nicholas stopped playing to demand:

"What's the to-do?"

"It's Finch," answered Meg. "He's going to send Wake and me South for our health."

"Well, I call that handsome of him. If you two enjoy your trip as much as Ernest and I enjoyed ours it will certainly be a success."

Renny said, looking at his boots—"I can't let you take the kid away on a long trip like that without me."

"Not let me take him! You must be crazy, Renny! Do you think I can't look after him properly?"

"You'd let him over-exert and eat too many sweets. The last time he visited you he came home and had a bilious bout."

"Rubbish! As though you watched him all the time!"

"I do."

"Then a change from so much coddling would be good for him. I hope I can look after my own little brother!"

Wakefield sat, his bright eyes flashing from one face to another, while his fate was being discussed. Even while he had shouted in triumph he had not really believed that the adventure would come to pass. It was too stupendous. Such things were not for him.

Everyone was against Renny in the matter, with the exception of Alayne who had not spoken. Meg turned to her and said:

"Surely you agree that Renny is being very perverse, Alayne!"

Alayne thought he was, but she said—"I think Renny understands Wake as no one else does."

"Well, I suppose he must decide, but it seems rather hard that the child should be deprived of such a change."

Nicholas rose from the piano seat. He said—"Give me an arm, Piers. My gout is very bad today."

Piers went to him and assisted him to an easy chair. He sat down beside him.

"I suppose," he said, with his prominent eyes on Finch — "that you have all heard of Finch's honeymoon."

"I have not heard of Finch's honeymoon," returned Meg with solemnity. "But I have heard other things about Finch that have upset me terribly." She drew a deep breath, drew in her chin and looked accusingly at Renny. He had offended her.

Finch gave her an agonised look. What was she going to say? To what new torture was he to be subjected? Involuntarily he drew away from her, but she laid her arm about his shoulders, her hand with fingers outspread, in a gesture at once pliant and commanding, such a gesture as that with which a cat draws her kitten to her.

Renny did not like the look nor the gesture. He stared aggressively at her.

"Finch has brought me," she proceeded, "a letter from Aunt Augusta. I have managed to keep what she says to myself until dinner was over." Finch writhed under her arm.

"What the devil does she say?" asked Renny.

Meg answered—"I need not read you all her letter. Just the bits of it that I think you should hear." She had it ready in her free hand and held it close to her eyes, for she was short-sighted. She read:

"'I have been observing Finch closely.'" Meg turned from the letter to observe him herself closely. All the family observed him closely. Then she went on:

"'He has been in a state of melancholy brooding.'"

"Brooding on his honeymoon, I suppose," said Piers.

"Shh," exclaimed his sister, furiously. "This is not a matter for joking."

"Look here," exclaimed Finch," I don't know what this is all about, but you're not to read that letter!"

"I must read it!" she continued—"'No wonder he broods, poor boy. It is terrible for him to think that he has been the *victim of mercenary* relatives. I feel that I must speak out to you, Meggie, so that you may use your influence to prevent my mother's money from being scattered to the four winds. I should write this to his guardian Renny, but I find, from careful questioning of Finch, that Renny has *utterly failed* in his duties as a *guardian*. He has given him not *one word* of advice regarding investments. He has allowed this inexperienced boy to lend his money (to *give* it, one might better say) to *any* and *every* one who importuned him. I shrink from the disclosure I am about to make, but I feel it is my *duty*. I have discovered that a certain Rosamond Trent of New York—'"

Ernest interrupted in a shaking voice:

"I will not have Miss Trent brought into this!"

Nicholas gave vent to subterranean chuckles.

Ernest turned on him with an air of outrage. "Nick, this is your doing!"

"I never mentioned Miss Trent's name to Gussie," answered his brother.

"Finch, then, it was you!"

Finch answered heavily—"I only told Auntie that I had lent money to Miss Trent and that she had lost everything in the Wall Street crash. I didn't mind a bit lending it. You must know that, Uncle Ernest."

Nicholas exclaimed—"You lent her money! This is the first I've heard of that. Ha, the hussy! So she was just making a dupe of you, Ernie! She got at Finch's money through you, eh?"

Ernest was too affronted for speech. He sat making faces, his fingers twisted together.

Meg could be almost heard to purr. She never released her protective hold on Finch. She said:

"I think Miss Trent's your friend, isn't she, Alayne?"

Alayne answered in a controlled voice—"Yes. She met Finch through me. No one can regret more than I do that Finch lent her money. I honestly believe that she will try to pay it back."

Renny, with hands deep in his pockets, continued to stare at his boots.

"What's this," asked Piers, "about Uncle Ernest and Miss Trent?"

Nicholas answered, his voice indistinct with mirth— "Why, Finch and I were almost frightened to death on shipboard! We thought he was going to propose to her. You should have seen them clutched at the fancy-dress ball—she in a pink domino, he in a mauve."

Ernest's face went a violent pink. "I'll not forgive you this in a hurry!" he snarled.

Nicholas ignored him—"Why, he toddled all over England after her, ransacking the country for antiques for her shop!"

The colour in Ernest's face subsided as quickly as it had risen. He said—"Miss Trent is a charming woman. It was a pleasure to me to have her company on shipboard. I enjoyed going about with her a little in England. I did not know that I was making myself ridiculous. The thought of marrying her never entered my head. If you want to amuse the family, Nick, just tell them how you made assignations with the wife who divorced you thirty years ago."

Nicholas thrust his hands through his grey hair, making it rise into two antlers. He looked like an old stag at bay. "By God, you are a sneak. How did you know I met Millicent? It was by the merest chance. And what were you doing at the time? You were in the kitchen with that Trent woman buying the very pots and pans!"

"And you in a bedroom with the door shut, with a woman of whom you have declared you couldn't endure the sight!"

"I'd never have married Millicent if you hadn't put me off Ruby Fortesque!"

"Put you off Ruby Fortesque! How the devil did I do that?"

"You whined to me about how you were gone on her yourself. And then—when I left her to you—you hadn't the guts to marry her!"

"I would have married her but that I had lost so much money through backing that disreputable friend of yours—I forget his name!"

They glared at each other. There was an interval of silence while the younger members of the family absorbed what they could of these ancient revelations. One of the pine sticks on the fire gave forth an angry crack. The three dogs leaped from the hearth rug and stood in cowed attitudes gazing at the fire. Then slowly they returned to the rug and once more disposed themselves on it.

Piers said—"Well, Miss Trent evidently has a gathering eye. How much did you lend her, Finch?"

"Ten thousand."

"It's perfidious," said Nicholas, "that my mother's money should be thrown about like this."

"Miss Trent will pay it back, never fear!" exclaimed Ernest.

Meg said—"Now I will read a little more of the letter— 'I do not know whether you are aware of it, but Finch borrowed money before he attained his majority in order to maintain Eden in France while he worked on his new book. Arthur Leigh, from whom he borrowed it, told me this as an evidence of Finch's magnanimity. Finch himself told me that he gave (why should I trouble to say *lend*!) another thousand to Eden before his return to France in December. Eden *must* be looked after until his health is regained or he has become famous, but why should Renny shift the responsibility of this to Finch's young shoulders?'"

"I sent him a thousand in the summer!" put in Renny, hotly.

To two of those present the bringing in of Eden's name was almost unbearable. The others were conscious of this, so the loan to him was allowed to pass with no more than a faint sputter of exclamation.

Meg was obliged to remove her arm from Finch's shoulder in order to find the next part of the closely written letter.

He straightened himself and a certain mordant pleasure in the scene took possession of him. Well, let her go through with it, let them see what he had done with the money they had made such a howl about his inheriting!

"Here endeth the first lesson," said Vaughan, jocularly. "Now for the second..."

"The second," said his wife with her eye on Piers, "is the piggery."

"I'd like to know what anyone has to say against the piggery!" exclaimed Piers.

Meg replied by reading from the letter. "'If Mamma had wished to build an expensive piggery, she would have built one long ago...'"

"Yes, indeed," agreed Ernest, glad of the introduction of a subject so far removed from himself. "She detested piggeries."

Meg read on—"'If Mamma had wished her money to be spent on an expensive motor car she would have bought one long ago. The one motor ride she had was the one which conveyed her to her grave. She would turn over in that grave, I am sure, if she knew of all that has been going on.'" And Meg added briskly—"I quite agree."

Piers eyed her truculently. "I suppose you do. But what about the mortgage?"

"What mortgage?" she asked, in a shocked tone.

"Why, your own mortgage. The one you chivvied young Finch into taking over. I'll wager that you've never paid the interest on that yet!"

Meg's glance was benign as she turned to Finch. "Tell him, Finch."

"She paid me this morning. As soon as she came over."

"Before she'd read that letter?"

"Yes."

Piers shouted with laughter. "You've managed to save your face, Meggie!"

"Nothing but extreme necessity because of my operation delayed the payment," she returned.

"I like the new motor car," said Wakefield.

"Of course you do," Piers answered. "And you're not the only one that likes it. Everyone here seems willing to make use of it. You jumped at the chance of being driven to the hospital in it, Meg."

Meg folded her short, plump arms and surveyed Piers with sisterly disapproval. "You are far too critical, Piers, for a young man who has had no more experience of life than you have. Where have you been? As far west as Niagara Falls. As far east as Montreal. Think of it! Yet no one in the family is so aggressive as you!"

"Where have you been yourself?" he flared.

"I leave shortly for Florida."

"That's still in the future. In the past, all you've done is to move across the ravine just in the nick of time to have a baby!"

"Maurice!" shouted Meg. "Are you going to let him insult me?"

Maurice made himself heard above the general laughter.

"You let my wife alone!" he scowled, as he knew Meggie expected him to scowl, at the brother-in-law who was also his son-in-law.

Piers, unabashed, continued—"As for the piggery, it's not mine at all. It simply adds to the value of Jalna. It belongs to Renny."

"The hell it does!" said Renny. "I won't have it!"

Piers turned to Finch. "Whom does the piggery belong to?"

"Jalna," answered Finch. Gradually, from being most unhappy, he had become rather pleased with himself. Here he was, the centre of a row, yet no one was blaming him. He took Meggie's hand and replaced it on his shoulder. She gave him a tender smile. "What this poor boy has suffered!" she exclaimed.

Nicholas said—"The great mistake was to allow him absolute control of the money at twenty-one. I should have been made his trustee."

Renny shot him a look. "You! I was his guardian."

"A lot you've guarded him," retorted Nicholas. "You've allowed him to follow every whim."

"I wanted to keep out of the affair."

"But why? It was your business more than anyone's, as you say."

"It would have been very different," said Ernest, "if Mamma had given me control over the money."

"Hmph!" growled his brother. "Out of the frying pan into the fire, I should say."

"What I have never been able to understand," said Meg, "is this—Why did Granny leave me nothing but her watch and chain and that old Indian shawl. No one carries such a watch now. And she thought so little of the shawl that she used to let Boney make a nest in it. And then to give Pheasant that gorgeous ruby ring!"

"For God's sake, forget about that ring!" ejaculated Piers. "When Gran's things were divided you got two rings."

"Neither of them could compare with the ruby! And how can I forget it when Pheasant is so ostentatious with it. Why, she's taken to wearing it on her forefinger!"

"She'll wear it on her nose if she chooses!"

Maurice scowled without any urging from Meg. He refilled his pipe and lighted it with a coal from the fire.

"All I got was her bed," said Renny.

Meg curled her short upper lip in a sneer. "A pity about you, truly! When you have the whole estate!"

"Yes," grunted Nicholas. "Jalna thrown in!"

Ernest added: "He did not think Jalna worth considering!"

The face of the master of Jalna became as red as his hair. "Gran had nothing to do with my getting Jalna! I got it through my father."

Another silence ensued in which each seemed to be searching his own mind for a weapon to turn against the others. Alayne refilled the coffee cups. The pot was emptied. She thought—"I cannot endure to stay here. I must leave them to have their row out in their own way." But she did not go. Since her return the life at Jalna had become her life, as never before. If she left the room she would be tacitly acknowledging that she was of weaker fibre than they. She would stay, no matter how her head ached, no matter how she inwardly shrank from the things they said.

Wakefield's clear voice was heard. "Was there anything more in the letter, Meggie?"

"Yes. There is more in the letter." There was an increased tension as she read—"'Are you aware that Finch invested thirty thousand dollars in New York stocks and lost it? He informed me of this without *visible* emotion. But he was never the same again. He seemed *sunk* in apathy. As for me, no words can express my pain at seeing the fortune, so many years *hoarded* by my mother, come to such a queer *unnatural* end. Writing without violence I may say that I consider Renny's *callous* neglect to be at the bottom of the disaster.'"

A smile flickered across Finch's pale face. Now what would they make of this? He clasped his knee in his hands, and his eyes, in which the large pupils were unusually bright, took in the scene before him without moving.

Nicholas's voice came from a long way off. "You have lost thirty thousand dollars in stocks... what stocks?"

He answered, in a low hurried voice—"I bought on margin. Fifty thousand each in Universal Autos—Upstate Utility Corporation—and Cereal Foods... I put up a twenty per cent margin. My broker cabled me—when the crash came—that I must put up the eighty per cent balance if possible—if I was to save my holdings. I refused."

"You refused!" shouted Piers. "You blithering young ass!"

"You let the money go!" said Maurice. "My God! But why?"

"I was sick of the business. I wasn't going to throw good money after bad."

Alayne cried—"Oh, Finch, and I cabled you, too! Oh, why didn't you hold on? I never dreamed that you would let it go!"

Ernest turned on her. "So, you were into it, too, Alayne! I'm astonished at you. This is terrible." He took out his handkerchief and mopped his brow.

Piers asked of her—"Did you hold on? Finch told me that you had invested."

"Yes, I am holding on."

"You're lucky. They'll be rising again."

Meggie spoke. "Alayne Archer, it is your fault that my brother has lost all this money. You excited him by your own speculations. The decent thing for you to do is to make up his loss to him out of what your aunt left you. He is only a poor, misguided boy!"

"She'll do nothing of the sort," said Renny emphatically.

Nicholas said—"You evidently knew of the investment, Piers, and you told us nothing. It's a damnable shame!"

"He told me, in confidence."

"It was your duty to speak. You were the only one who knew."

"You are greatly to blame, Piers," said Ernest.

Maurice and Meg, who had both approved the investment, kept silent.

"Let us calculate," said Nicholas. "There is this absolute loss of thirty thousand. There is the ten thousand to the Trent woman..."

"He will get that back," interjected Ernest.

"Don't be a fool," rejoined his brother, and continued—"That's forty thousand. Then, we'll say five thousand for Eden. Another five for the motor car and that accursed piggery—"

Piers put in—"Don't forget your trip abroad, Uncle Nick!"

Nicholas went on imperturbably. "Well, add another five thousand for that. Then, there's the fifteen thousand mortgage for the Vaughans..."

"Merciful Heaven!" cried Meggie. "You're not counting that as a loss, are you?"

Nicholas regarded her, sceptically. "That remains to be seen. Now, my friends, this lad has about forty thousand dollars left of Mamma's bequest to him. And, by the time he has paid for this visit to Florida he will have still less. Interesting, isn't it, to see how rapidly money can be dispersed?" He tugged his grey moustache and smiled bitterly at his kinsmen.

"Renny, Renny," said Ernest, "you are greatly to blame for this! You treated Finch as a child till he was twenty-one and then you threw him out from the nest to do what he willed."

"It's true enough," said Piers. "Several times, in my hearing, Finch asked his advice about his affairs and Renny simply turned away and left him."

"His pigeons will come home to roost," said Meggie.

"A fat lot they will," said Piers. "Here's his wife with a fresh fortune left her."

They all looked at Alayne. She had probably never felt quite so embarrassed in her life. To add to her embarrassment Renny began sulkily to play with her fingers. For the first time in her life she could think of nothing to say. She opened her mouth and shut it. Her mind floundered among the wreckage of argument and complaint that had been cast upon this sea of dissension. They did not wait long for her to speak. They were all talking at once. The talk surged about her and Renny, who also was silent. Finch, hedged round with Meggie's solicitude, sat clasping his knee, an enigmatic smile on his face, now and then replying to a question in the same untroubled tone.

At last Piers rose, stretched himself, and went to the dining room. He returned with a decanter of whiskey, a siphon, and some glasses.

"How about something to light up the old innards, Uncle Nick?" he said. "Have a spot, medicinally, Uncle Ernie?"

Finch drifted to the piano. He could not understand why it was, but he wanted to play to the family. All the tremors of the past months had left his nerves. He felt strong and free and, for some subtle reason, rather proud. They had been waiting for, watching Gran's money since before he was born. He had suffered obloquy because it had been left to him. Now two-thirds of it had melted and they were still talking, but blaming each other now rather than him. His music was come back to him, flowing through his veins like wine. The past year was not wasted. He had loved and he had suffered. He was home again in his own place. He would work hard and become a great musician yet. He would spend every cent of what he had left on his music. He felt his heart go out with longing toward Renny.

He played Chopin to them. He pictured himself as sweeping them along with him on those deep masculine waves of melody. Through Brahms and the faint sounds of Debussy he led them to the tolerance and tranquillity of Mozart. He played for an hour. Then he looked round with an almost mystic curiosity to see the effect of his spell.

Nicholas, Maurice, and Piers formed a group around the siphon. From them came a rumble of talk that was apparently agreeable, for it was broken by low laughter. Wakefield now sat on the ottoman beside Meggie. Finch could hear them discussing means of transportation to Florida and whether or not, in the event of his going, Wake should take his fishing tackle. Ernest was on the sofa beside Alayne. They were apparently discussing him. They smiled at him and Ernest said—"Splendid, Finch! I've never heard you play so well!" Alayne said nothing, but there was a glowing look in her eyes that meant more than words.

Rags brought in the tea. There was a fruitcake which Finch particularly liked and small cakes filled with custard and covered with cocoanut icing. He was ravenous. Alayne asked Meg to pour the tea.

She said—"Run and find Renny, Wake, please! I do hope he has not gone to the stables." She wondered if he had been very angry when he had left the room. His expression had been gloomy, and no wonder, after so much combined criticism. She herself felt tired out. There had been a time when she would not have been able to eat a morsel after such a wrangle, but now she found herself eagerly devouring bread and jam like the rest of them. A lock of fair hair had loosened and hung into her eyes. She looked pale and wan.

Meg began talking to her in the most friendly way, asking her advice about clothes for the South. She waited impatiently for Wakefield's return.

He came running in and instantly snatched up a piece of bread. "I can't find him anywhere," he said, with his mouth full. "I've been up to his room and down to the kitchen. Wright had just come in and he said Renny wasn't at the stable. His hat is hanging on the rack and his dogs are lying in the hall."

"I should think he would hide his head," observed his sister. "I think he has taken Aunt Augusta's letter very much to heart. He realises, too, that we all blame him in this matter."

"He'd be deaf as a post if he didn't," said Piers.

"He has found," said Ernest, "that such high-handedness only reacts against himself."

Nicholas growled. "Renny has inherited all the worst traits of the Courts and the Whiteoaks combined."

"And yet," cried Meg, "I have heard him boast that he had inherited the best from each family. What was that he said to us, Maurice, just the other day?"

"He said—'From my English forebears, I got my love of horses. From my Irish, the instinct for selling horses. And from my Scotch my horse sense.'"

"That was it!" cried Meg delightedly. "Did you ever hear of such conceit?"

Piers said—"I'd forgotten that Renny's mother was Scotch."

"She was Scotch," affirmed Meg. "And of an excellent family. Very different from—" She did not finish the sentence.

"Just the same," said Piers, "I think the poor old chap should have his tea. I'll have a look for him myself."

"Oh, I wish you would!" breathed Alayne.

Piers left the room and before long returned with a puzzled expression on his candid face.

"He's gone to bed."

"To bed!" they echoed, in one voice.

"But I was in his room," said Wakefield. "He wasn't in bed then."

Piers answered—"He's not in his own bed."

Once more the family turned and looked at Alayne. She felt her face tingling with the blood that had rushed to it. Like Ernest, earlier in the afternoon, she could utter no sound, only make grimaces.

Ernest laid his hand on hers. "Never mind, dear girl," he said soothingly. "It's only natural."

Finch gave a loud guffaw, and his eyes sought those of Piers, which beamed back full of laughter.

Piers said—"He's not where you think he is. He's in Gran's bed. The old painted bed he inherited from her."

Food which was being masticated lay undisturbed in the mouths of the Whiteoaks or was hastily bolted. It was as though old Adeline herself had walked into their midst, her velvet tea gown trailing, her cap with the purple ribbons set for their subjection, her rings which had been divided among them, again flashing on her long fingers. "Renny in my bed? Well, why not? I left it to him! I bore his father there. Renny is bone of my bone… Let him rest his red head on my pillow and cool his hot temper in my bed. It's his own place."

Nicholas got himself with difficulty out of his chair. He hobbled towards the door and, after a moment's wavering, all the others rose and followed him. They went down the hall where the late sunlight, diffused through the stained glass window, cast bright splotches of colour upon them. Wragge had built a great fire in the stove. Its sides were red and the smell of overheated pipes made the air heavy.

Nicholas opens the door of his mother's room and looks in. There, propped on two pillows, lies the master of Jalna. His eyes closed, his thin muscular hands clasped on the coverlet, he appears to be lying in state. Boney, on his perch by the head of the bed, his plumage less bright than the plumage of the painted birds on the headboard, lifts his wings in a rage at the intrusion. He is moulting and, with the flapping of his wings, bright feathers are thrown from him and drift on to the bed.

"Shaitan! Shaitan Kabatka! Iflatoon! Chore! Chore!" He pours forth a volley of horrible Hindoo oaths. All the curses that have lain simmering in his drowsy brain, without utterance for the past three years, now come hurtling through his beak. His eyes revolve like the lamps in a lighthouse. At one moment he turns them full of ire on the family collected about the bed. At the next they beam, full of possessive affection, on the occupant of the bed.

"Is he ill, do you think?" whispers Ernest.

"I don't like it at all. He has gone too far," growls Nicholas.

"To think that Boney should talk again—after all these years!" says Meg. She goes to the bed and lays her hand on her brother's forehead. "Speak, Renny. Are you ill? Or is it just that your feelings are hurt?"

Oh, their glorious lack of self-consciousness! thinks Alayne. Oh, that I could so grandly let myself go! That I could be so magnificently a fool!

"Bring Wakefield! He will notice the child," says Meg.

Piers, his teeth gleaming, pushes the boy forward.

Wakefield has been sadly overwrought. He bursts into tears and wrings his slender hands. "Renny, you're not dying, are you?"

Renny opens his eyes. They look black in the dim light. "Somebody..."

Nicholas interrupts him. "You are not to say that! That's carrying things too far!"

"Somebody fetch me a cup of tea."

"Go and fetch him tea, Piers!" cries Meg. "Oh, Renny dear, whatever is the matter?"

He turns and hides his face in the crook of his arm. "Everyone is against me... no one has ever understood me but Gran..."

XXX

WHAT OF PAULINE?

WAS he hers, Alayne questioned, or did he belong to the family? She had been ashamed for him. She had felt chagrin that he had so played up to the family's attitude toward him. Yet she felt a certain elation, for, without doubt, she had solidified her own position in that flamboyant circle.

The next day was Sunday and they had all gone to church. No disruption could prevent their going to church. Sometimes she thought that they had the unquestioning faith of the Children's Crusade, as they braved all kinds of weather, and sometimes she thought of them as pagans with a savage tenacity for the rites handed down to them by tradition. Once, just to test them on the subject, she had read aloud an illuminating chapter from a book by an eminent scientist on religion. The only one who had shown any interest in it had been Pheasant, and the opinion she had offered had been that the writer was talking about things he did not understand.

Alayne sat in the Whiteoaks' pew, her feet on the hassock on which for so many years old Adeline's large shapely feet had rested. On her left sat Piers and Finch, on her right Nicholas, Ernest, and Wake. Across the aisle, in the Vaughan

pew, sat Meg, Maurice, and Patience. The little girl peeped
between her fingers across at her uncles. Wake shut one eye
and glared at her with the other. She giggled and was repri-
manded in a stage whisper by her mother. Meg was looking
handsome, with black fur about her neck. Maurice's face
wore the expression of callous reverence attained by forty
years of church-going. He had begun when he was four. The
backbone of the responses and the hymns was supplied by
these two pews. They never failed or faltered. Their fervour
was not controlled by any graduations of volume suggested
by the letters *p* or *dim* at the beginning of hymn lines.

Renny had been the lay reader since his return from the
War. Now he mounted the steps behind the brass eagle that
was a memorial to Captain Philip Whiteoak. Alayne had a
glimpse of his thick-soled boots beneath his surplice. She
thought of him as he had lain in his grandmother's bed, from
which he had only risen to come to church that morning.
Would he return to it that night? Or would he, perhaps, just
take to it when things upset him? No one could tell and no
one had dared question him. By his act he had re-established
himself as chieftain of the clan. His grandmother's mantle
hung about him. Because of it Boney had found his voice and
had since raised it repeatedly, dragging from the feathered
limbo of his brain every Hindoo word taught him by old
Adeline in the thirty years of his life in her company.

Renny read the lessons in a loud voice with a modicum
of respect for punctuation. But when he said—"Here endeth
the Lesson—" he did so in an abrupt, hurried mumble. The
family did not take their eyes off him. Patience covered hers
with her fingers and peeped at him. When he had finished he
returned to his seat and sat with bent head, his handsome
nose outlined against dark oak carvings.

Piers and an old man with a beard took up the collection. Piers stood, stalwart and impassive, at the end of the pew while his family fished for their contributions. He and the old man marched up the aisle together and stood at the chancel steps facing Mr. Fennel, the old man's bald head and bent back, Piers's blond head and flat back toward the congregation.

It was Finch's first Sunday at home. He thought of all that had happened to him since he last sat in that seat, and it seemed unbelievable. His brothers had jeered at him for sticking in one spot while away, but he wondered whether, if he had toured the whole of Europe, he could have had deeper and more varied experience. He had left a part of himself, that could never be regained, in Nymet Crews. He had brought away something within himself that would not die. The mood of hope and purpose that had risen in him the day before had not failed. He still felt that he would do great things with his life.

He left the church with Renny and Wakefield in the old car.

"I'm driving round by the fox farm," observed Renny. "I must see Mrs. Lebraux for a moment on business."

The roads were deep with snow. Finch remembered how spring had been coming in Devon even when he had left. How delicately, with what shy misgivings spring would come there! She would push one white foot, the toes as white as snowdrops, from under the coverlet of winter. She would let loose her hair, in a coil of golden daffodils, across its darkness. She would open her violet eyes, expose one bare shoulder. But these movements would be tentative. She would withdraw and weep softly to herself... And though spring still slept profoundly here, how she would leap up when, at last, she was roused! She would bound from under her coverings stark naked, her breast thrust forward to meet the sun's kiss. She would be brown as a berry almost before her whiteness had been acclaimed...

As the car stopped before the fox farm Wakefield asked— "Are you going to let me go to Florida, Renny?"

Renny gave him a rough caress in passing. "You will stay with me," he said.

When he had gone Wake threw himself back in the car exclaiming—"I might have known! It was too good to be true! Yet—I shall always look on you as my benefactor, Finch, even though I don't go!"

"Don't be a young ass," admonished Finch. He added: "Tell me about Mrs. Lebraux and Pauline. How have they been getting on?"

"Not very well. You see, they have no man about the place."

"I can't see what good Lebraux was to them."

"Well, he made them a widow and an orphan. Women cannot be even those without a man having been about."

Finch laughed and looked curiously at his young brother. He noticed his growing length of limb, the new curves of mouth and nostril. Whom was he going to be like? There was something of Eden about the lips, something of Gran in the eyes. A strange combination. One for poetry, passion, and pride.

"Finch, will you be my friend?"

"Of course, I will."

"Will you shake hands on it?"

"Rather."

Finch grasped the slender hand in his and they smiled into each other's eyes.

"Do you often see Pauline?" Finch asked.

"Scarcely ever. I brought a poem I had written to read to her. It was in the autumn. But she was playing with her pet fox and I changed my mind... I'll read it to you, if you like, Finch."

"I didn't know you wrote poetry."

"I have been writing it for almost a year. I sent this one to Eden. And what do you suppose he wrote back to me? He wrote—"'You are not *going* to be a poet. You *are* one!'"

"Don't believe everything Eden says."

"Wait till you hear the poem! Now that you're going to be my friend, I'll read it to you. I have read it to Renny."

"What did he say?"

"He said it was good," said Wake, triumphantly.

"I think you should read the poem to Pauline. I might be there too. I should like that."

"Should you? I will, then. Here she comes! She has been to Mass."

They saw Pauline Lebraux approaching along the empty white road. Her movements were uneven as she walked over the deep ruts in the snow. The sun had the warmth of approaching spring in it and the snow was becoming soft and wet. As she drew near Finch saw that she still wore no touch of colour, but that her face, under the black beret, was flushed delicately pink by the exertion. She wore goloshes, above which her black-stockinged legs showed long and thin.

He opened the door of the car and sprang out, but, when he was face to face with her, he did not know what to say. He just stood smiling inanely, noticing the worn little prayer-book and rosary she held in her hand.

Wakefield was out beside him. He said, in the patronising tone Finch found so irritating:

"Pauline, do you remember my brother Finch?"

She smiled and gave Finch her hand. Again he saw that shadow of pain in her smile. It was purely physical—the sensitive curling of the lip—but it moved him to a strange compassion toward her. In spite of the hardships which he knew she must undergo in her life, he thought of it as an idyllic one. He thought of her as a young wilding, untouched by common things.

"I am glad you are back," she said.

Did she really mean that or was it just politeness?

Wakefield said—"Pauline, I am going to read my poetry to you and Finch. Shall you like that?"

"Oh, yes! I shall love to hear it. Is Mr. Whiteoak in the house?"

Wakefield answered—"I think I see him by the fox pens with your mother."

"Won't you come and see our foxes?" she asked Finch.

She led the way, and, as the boys followed her, Wakefield whispered—"Her education is being neglected. She knows almost nothing—except French. Renny tried to make Alayne read French with her but Alayne refused. We had a terrible time."

"I feel very sorry for her. Think of her walking almost four miles to Mass! I think we ought to send a car for her."

"I might go with her. I think it would suit me very well to be a Catholic."

They found Mrs. Lebraux and Renny standing in deep snow by the enclosures. She wore a heavy jersey that had been her husband's, breeches tucked into grey woollen stockings and moccasins. She stood leaning on a snow shovel and smoking a cigarette. She was bare-headed, and her hair, with its unusual shadings of brown and tow-colour, stood out about her face in short, thick locks. Finch's eyes moved from mother to daughter. He was disturbed by the sharp contrast between them.

Renny put his arm about Pauline and drew her to his side. "Are you feeling better?" he asked. "Have you got over the tragedy?"

Mrs. Lebraux explained to Finch—"Pauline has been inconsolable. One of the vixens got out of her own pen into the next one and the foxes there attacked her. They tore off a leg and she had to be killed."

"It was not the pet fox, I hope."

"No, but one of her favourites. She is far too tender-hearted. Life is going to be hard for her."

Finch felt angry with Mrs. Lebraux. Why should she be dressed as a man, shovelling snow, sending her child to church alone? Yet, though he felt angry, he could not help liking her.

The snow in the pens was indented by many little foot-prints, but most of the foxes had hidden themselves in their kennels at the approach of strangers. However, the old dog-fox stood at a distance surveying them, his clear-cut shadow bluish on the snow. Pauline had run into an outhouse to bring fox biscuits to tempt them from their dens. She had put her prayerbook and rosary into Finch's hand to hold for her. Clara Lebraux glanced at them, then into his eyes, and said—"Poor child!"

What did she mean by that, he wondered. There was something mysterious about her. He felt a troubling, exqui-site intimacy in holding these things belonging to Pauline.

She came back running, and threw biscuits into one pen after another. The foxes, surprised at being fed at this unusual hour, crept out timorously, snatched the biscuits, and fled with them to their kennels. But her pet fox ran to her, bounding about her like a dog. She went into the run and brought him out in her arms, displaying him proudly to Finch and Wakefield. Her face showed lively above his long fur that was electric with health and the keen air.

On the way home Finch said—"Wake tells me that they are having rather a hard time of it."

Renny sent the car over a drift that almost threw the boys from their seats. "Yes. Things are rough for them. But they will make a success of it yet. Clara Lebraux is one woman in a thousand, and that little Pauline is wonderful with the foxes. She has a stove in the outhouse. Cooks meat for them. Makes all their mashes herself. The worst is that they must sell some of their best stock this spring just for lack of capital."

Finch asked hesitatingly—"How much would it take to tide them over?"

"A few thousand would do wonders for them. Practically save the situation." Finch was sitting in the front seat with him, and Renny had lowered his voice so that Wakefield might not hear. "I let them have a thousand myself—last year. But this spring—I simply hadn't got it. They'll have to get along as best they can." He sighed.

"I'd love to help them—if you think they wouldn't mind," said Finch in a low tone.

Renny shot him a quick, grateful look. "Oh, would you? That would be splendid. There would be no risk, but she could not pay a high interest."

As they turned into the drive he muttered—"Don't say anything of this to the family. They are down on Mrs. Lebraux."

Finch walked on air. He was hand in glove with Renny. Between them they were going to look after Pauline...

What of Pauline? He could not put the thought of her out of his head. That sweet face, delicately flushed by the long walk through the snow, was between him and all he saw. A bright stream flowed between Jalna and the fox farm. Along it his spirit moved in exaltation, like a ship with all sails spread in full moonlight. That other face, pale, remote, with its close-set mouth, was as a distant promontory veiled by clouds.

XXXI

Birthday Greetings

Pheasant had her mind set on one thing. That was that her baby should be born on Finch's birthday.

In the first place it would be a remarkable coincidence. A double birthday in the family would be an event of great importance. In the second place she thought the date a lucky one. Finch was talented, and he had inherited a fortune. In the third place, if the baby were born on Finch's birthday, Finch would, in all probability, take a keen interest in it, feel a personal pride in its advancement.

Now, here it was five o'clock in the afternoon on the first day of March and no baby! The doctor had been to see her and was coming back in a few hours. Her time was drawing near. Yet so was midnight and the second day of March. She had had a cup of tea, but she could not eat anything. She sat by the window in her dressing gown, her face flushed, her eyes feverish, her short brown hair in damp tags on her forehead. Piers was walking about the room. He fidgeted with things on the dressing table, played with the tassel on the blind. He had a reassuring smile ready for her when their eyes met, but when he looked at her unobserved his face wore an expression of acute anxiety.

Above the treetops, in the translucent green sky, he saw the pale curve of the new moon. He said:

"There's the new moon, little one! It's a good omen!"

"Oh, oh," she said. "I must wish on it! But don't let me see it through glass! Open the window."

He opened it and the cold air came in on her. There had been a fresh fall of snow. Every twig bore its fragile burden of whiteness. She placed herself sideways in the window. "I must see it over my right shoulder!" He took her head in his hands and turned it so that she faced the new moon across her shoulder. He pressed his fingers against her head, and a well of tenderness rising in him constricted his throat, blinded his eyes with tears. She opened hers.

"Now," he urged, "wish quickly! I must not let you take cold."

She fixed her eyes on the moon that looked no more than the paring from a silver apple, and murmured to herself— "Oh, let it come soon... More midnight, please, moon!"

Piers put down the sash.

"There," she sighed. "Perhaps that will help! But I don't feel as much like it as I did two hours ago."

"I wish you hadn't set your mind on such an idiotic thing," he said. But, in spite of himself, he was influenced by her. Then, there was the anxiety to have it all over. He counted the hours till midnight. "Try to eat something, to please me!" He brought a plate on which was a thin piece of bread and butter. He cut it into small bits and fed them to her. She held up her mouth like a young bird for the morsels. As he put the bits of bread into her mouth and saw the confiding look in her eyes he thought—"I didn't feel like this when Mooey was born... She must be going to die."

They could hear Mooey and Patience laughing and running in the passage. She had been brought to spend the day with him.

"Do those kids annoy you?" asked Piers. "Where the dickens is that Alma Patch? She ought to be minding them."

"Bring them in here for a moment. I'd love to see them."

He opened the door of the bedroom and the two came running in side by side with the air of having intended to do this particular thing at this particular moment. They had been having their tea in the kitchen. They wore their bibs, on which were buttery crumbs of toast. Patience carried a toasting fork.

"I made toas'," she cried. "I made my own toas'. And Mooey's."

Mooey went to his mother and stood gravely by her knee. She laid her fingers among the soft rings of his hair. "Darling, would you like a baby sister?"

"Yes." He spoke emphatically, softly thumping on her knee with his shut fist. "She could fall downstairs."

"Oh, but she wouldn't! You'd take care of her, wouldn't you?"

"Yes. I'd pick her up and put her in a bastick."

"Patty, would you like a baby cousin, this very night?"

Patience made her eyes enormous. "Oh, the darling! I'll wide her on my pony!" She looked about the room. "Where is she? Patty wants to see her!"

Pheasant said—"Open the window, Piers, and let the children wish on the new moon."

"Don't be silly!" He patted her back. "It will only let in the cold and it will do no good—if that's what you're thinking of."

"One can never tell... Why, I've heard tell how, in the war, Kitchener or some other great general said—when he heard a battle had been won—'Somebody must have been praying!' Just think of that! A great general and a battle! And this just the matter of a different birthday for my baby! Surely it might help!"

To please her he opened the window. She turned the two little faces up toward the moon. "Now say after me—'I wish that the new baby may come before tomorrow...'" Obediently they lisped the words after her.

"I don't see anything religious in that," observed Piers. "It's purely pagan."

"I am tolerant," she said sagely, "of all religions."

"Not only tolerant. You believe in them all."

Patience stabbed her toasting fork in the direction of the moon. "Patty wants the moon!" she cried. "Come down, moon, and be toasted!"

"I'm not f'ightened," said Mooey.

Piers shut the window. Already the lower point of the moon had touched the treetops. She was fast sinking. Pheasant looked at Piers with a strange stare in her eyes. Then she uttered a cry.

"Take them away! Oh, take them away from here!"

Piers caught a child in each hand and hurried them from the room.

But, five hours later, when he and his brothers and uncles were waiting below, the birth had not taken place. Pheasant had asked for an egg and was eating it...

Finch stood by the window looking into the starless night while the others played a half-hearted game of bridge. How could Piers play cards when his girl lay in dreadful anticipation in a room above! He pictured himself in Piers's position.

He pictured a girl whose tender flesh was soon to be torn to produce his flesh conceived in a moment of uncalculating passion... He should not be able to endure it. His spirit would bear every pang... He shrank from the thought that any woman should go through that because of him... No, let him go childless to his grave rather than that... Even though it were possible to bring his child into the world without pain, better far that no child should inherit the torment of his nerves. Had he ever been really happy? He could not remember it, even in childhood. There had always been that haunting of fear, that moving shadow of the unknown.

He could discover just one pale star. The soul perhaps of this new Whiteoak waiting to descend, when the moment came, into the troubled body.

Nicholas was dealing and he said:

"I remember well twenty-two years ago tonight. We sat at this very table playing cribbage—Ernest and I—your father walking the floor. We were waiting for young Finch to arrive. And he was tardy enough about it."

"Philip was very nervous," said Ernest. "I remember that when we gave him a glass of rum and water, to quiet him, the glass rattled in a quite alarming manner against his teeth... Poor Mary was suffering greatly."

Piers held his hand above the table. "Look at that. Steady enough, eh?"

"Yes," agreed Ernest, "but all is not over upstairs."

"Pheasant will be all right," said Renny. "The doctor is with her. And Mrs. Patch. Meg and Alayne in the next room."

Piers was examining his cards. "Alayne ought to be having this baby. It's her turn," he muttered.

"We don't all of us have families," replied Renny. "I've responsibility enough as it is."

They played out the hand.

Piers looked at his watch. Half past ten.

"A year ago tonight," observed Ernest, as he dealt, "we were in the midst of your birthday party, Finch."

Finch turned from the window. "It was a very different birthday from this. It seems years ago."

"You made a good speech that night," said Renny. "You had everybody laughing."

Finch looked pleased. "I forget what I said. It was awful rot, I guess."

"No. It was very good. By the way, I met Mrs. Leigh and Ada in town today. They're expecting Leigh and his wife next month. But you didn't like her, did you?"

"No, I didn't like her." He turned again to the window.

"Play!" said Nicholas. His tone was testy because of the delay.

Why had that name been spoken tonight? Why had that pale face, with its indrawn mouth, been introduced into his thoughts? It was there, outside the pane, looking in at him mocking, beseeching, by turn. It was of the figment of night. Of pale starlight. Of shadow darker than darkness. And from it issued that voice which would always trouble his soul, that voice sweeter than the sweetness of her violin.

From above came a piercing cry. Piers threw down his cards and ran up the stairs.

At twenty minutes to twelve the new Whiteoak came weeping into the world. Meg brought the news down to them.

She put her arms about Piers and kissed him. "A little son, Piers! Quite strong and well... And on your birthday, Finch!" She kissed him, too. "Many happy returns to you both, darling boys!"

Piers said—"He did it, by the skin of his gums!"

"Did what?"

"Arrived on Finch's birthday. Pheasant had her heart set on that." His face was contorted. He was between laughter and tears.

Nicholas hobbled up and down the room. "Well, well, this is good news! Another boy, eh? And on your birthday, Finch! A new Whiteoak. I remember how a year ago tonight we sat up till dawn in this room celebrating..." And he began singing in an undertone,

> "Zummer is icumen in.
> Sweetly sings cuckoo!"

Piers's head was hidden in the long maroon window curtain. His shoulders were shaken by sobs.

The next day was Sunday. Just as breakfast was over, Wright brought a package addressed to Finch which he had got from the post office the night before. Wakefield carried it, with an important air, to Finch. "Wright is awfully sorry, Finch, that he forgot this last night. Whatever do you suppose it is?"

He stood by expectantly while Finch undid it. It was a book, fresh from the press. Poetry by the look of it. Wake read the title—"*New France*, by Eden Whiteoak." He wanted to take it in his hands, but Finch held him off. "No—let me see it first..."

He took off the jacket. The cover was green with gold lettering, and there was a design of lilies. How well Eden's name looked in the gilt letters. How jolly nice of him to have sent him this for his birthday! Finch had not known it was published yet. He raised the cover and looked inside. On the dedication page, he read—*For Brother Finch.*

Wakefield read it, too. They looked at each other, stunned by the magnificence of it. Eden had dedicated his new long poem, which had taken him a year to write, to Finch! He was overcome. What had he done to deserve being singled out for such an honour. Eden... *New France*... For Brother Finch. God, life was terrific!

He carried it to the dining room to show it to his uncles and Renny, who were still at the breakfast table. They were duly impressed. Rags, with a tray in his hands, bent his inquisitive gaze upon it.

"I'm sure we're all proud of both you and Mr. Eden, sir," he said. "You've both of you turned out better than we could 'ave 'oped."

Wakefield had rushed back to the sitting-room at the sound of a plaintive cry there. Now he hastened back to the dining room, exclaiming:

"Come quick, Piers has something to show you!"

Nicholas made his table napkin into a ball. Renny heaved him to his feet. Nip, who had been on his knee, circled about the table yapping joyously. One of Renny's spaniels reared itself beside the table and licked the toast crumbs from his plate. Ernest surreptitiously took an indigestion tablet. All these excitements tended to discourage the gastric juices.

In the wintry sunlight Piers was holding something on a pillow. In his eyes was pride and on his lips a deprecating tenderness.

They gathered about the newcomer, staring at him ruthlessly, while his weak eyes shrank from the light and he made a shamefaced grimace as though he would ask nothing better than the opportunity to obliterate himself. Young as he was, he had been put into clothes. Bands, napkins, safety pins, hampered him. His tender arms had been thrust into sleeves by Mrs. Patch. He had been washed, the faint down on his head had been brushed. His nose had been wiped. He was ready for life.

Renny caught sight of Mooey in the hall. From a disorganised household the tiny boy had escaped to the coal cellar and was smudged from head to foot. With a stride Renny was on him. He snatched him up and carried him to join the circle.

"Mooey, you sweep!" he shouted. "Mooey, you miserable tripe, come and see your baby brother!"

Mooey, with a sooty forefinger in his pink mouth, stared long and dubiously at the newcomer. Then—"Oh hell, I'm not f'ightened!" he said.

His uncles and great-uncles agreed that, while not handsome, the infant showed unmistakable signs of having the Court nose.

Piers fixed his prominent blue eyes on Finch's face. He had got an idea. "Why, look here," he said. "This kid's got a long nose, a long, melancholy face, he's a depressed-looking cuss! By George, we'll call him Finch!"

"Not after me?" cried Finch, incredulously.

"Yes, why not? Pheasant was awfully keen to have him born on your birthday. Thought he might shine in your reflected rays. I believe he's going to take after you. I'd like damned well to call him Finch—if you don't mind!"

"Good idea!" said Nicholas.

"Splendid!" said Ernest.

"He might do worse than take after his Uncle Finch," said Renny.

"Do you mind?" reiterated Piers.

"Mind!" Finch was touched to the heart. His features broke into a tender smile. He took the tiny pink hand in his large bony one. "Mind! Why, it's the most beautiful thing I've ever had done for me in all my life!" His voice trembled with emotion.